Neither King Nor Country

Neither King Nor Country

By

Alan N. Kay

This is a work of fiction.

Any resemblance to any person or place is purely coincidental.

About the Author: Alan N. Kay

Alan N. Kay is an award-winning teacher and author with more than 25 years of experience bringing stories to life. Known for creative teaching as well as creative writing, Kay has won multiple awards. They include: the 2002 Daughters of the American Revolution Nation-wide Outstanding American History Teacher of the Year, the state of Florida 2002 Outstanding American History Teacher of the Year, the Gilder Lehrman 2006 American History Teacher for the state of Florida , the 2004 Outstanding Educator of the Year in Pinellas County (a county of over 8,000 teachers), the 2001 Florida History Fair Teacher of the Year, and a Finalist for the 2001 National History Day Teacher of the Year. He was recently presented with a lifetime achievement award on the 20th anniversary of Pinellas County History Day; a competition that he started in 1999.

Alan N. Kay is also the author of the *Young Heroes of History* set of novels: a historical fiction series for children. In addition he has also written a non-fiction book titled "I Love History but I Hated it in School" as well as numerous articles for various publications over the years. He will always be the most proud however, of his three beautiful adult children who are all finding their own paths to success.

A transplanted Yankee, Kay completed his Master's in Education at the University of Massachusetts in Boston and received his Bachelor's in history Cum Laude from Brandeis University in Waltham, Mass. He currently teaches History at East Lake High School in Tarpon Springs, Florida.

To my beloved Nana: your sweetness and love for family will never be forgotten. Thank you for sparking my passion to begin this incredible journey. I hope I have made you proud.

Acknowledgements:

There is no way this journey I have been on for over a decade could even begin without the support and love of my incredible wife and soul mate Heidi. She has not only been there every moment of every day to encourage me and join my crazy passion for history and family, she has been my editor, my chief marketer, my consultant, and the only one brave enough to tell me when I was doing something wrong. Without her this book would not even be a gleam in my eye. I will love you forever.

On a less sappy note, and in no particular order: Thank you to Cameron McLeod, AP student extraordinaire for typing the bibliography; Aliyah Cruz, East Lake High Alum for designing the awesome cover. (There are so many well placed messages in this cover, when you are done reading, take another look at it and see all the things Aliyah placed so perfectly. Hope you love it as much as I do!) Thank you to Dee Beardsley, PP, PLS, CZT for a painstakingly thorough and well-advised editorial process. Thank you to the many librarians and national park guides who helped me in all of my research and who set me on the right path. From local libraries like Largo, Clearwater and Eastlake, to the National Archives itself, I have truly utilized the wonderful free information available in this great nation. I have toured the National Parks of Philadelphia and Boston. I have journeyed to New Brunswick, Halifax and even to Dublin in my search for this story. In every location, guides and curators were enthusiastic, friendly and encouraging. To anyone living in the towns of Fairfield Ct., Milford Ct., Deer Island New Brunswick or even Campobello Island; I apologize if some stranger taking pictures in your neighborhood freaked you out. It was all part of the research. Perhaps no one was more confused than the desk clerk at the hockey rink in southwestern Connecticut who could not understand why this man was taking pictures of dingy locker rooms! It has been quite a journey and there is no way this book would be anywhere near as good without all of these people's help whether knowingly or not.

Further back in time is Harold Collier and White Mane publishing who gave me one of my first starts as a writer. My *Young Heroes of History Series* for children allowed me to grow as a writer and as an educator and gave me the confidence to make the jump to adult historical fiction. To the women of the D.A.R. who were the first to notice my writing and my teaching, your award became a vantage point for so many more awards. The recognition I received over these years gave me the confidence to keep fighting my fight to make history alive and exciting. And finally to Carmela Haley, Kyle Johnson and all the people at Dunedin and East Lake High who nominated me for those awards and supported me in all of my years of creative teaching, History Day exploits and just being there when I needed them.

Thank you!

Alan N. Kay

Map Courtesy of Curtis Rindlaub and *A Cruising Guide to the Maine Coast*

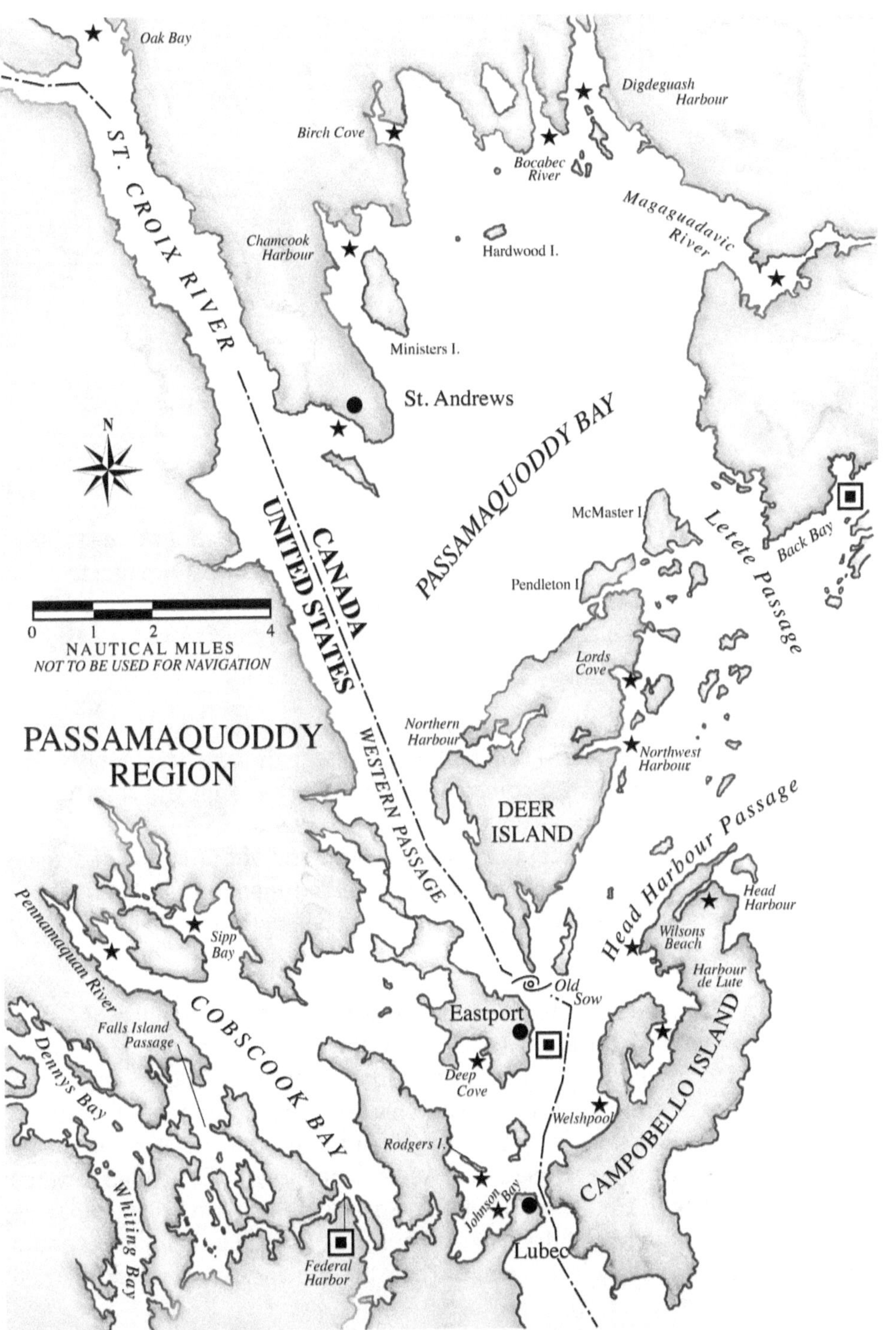

Prologue

July 12, 1776

New York City

Twenty One year old Captain Alexander Hamilton wasn't about to waste this opportunity. Ever since he had been a little boy, he had been determined to work hard and earn his way despite the "stain" of being born a bastard. His artillery company would be the best in New York, and if he got the chance, the best in George Washington's army.

Hamilton took out his spyglasses and scanned the mouth of the Hudson River. The smoke from the haphazard cannon fire had already started to blur his vision but the strong summer breeze coming in from the ocean kept the smoke from getting too thick. It would have been a beautiful day if not for the menacing British ships. The sky was blue, the sun was warm and after months of digging and scraping and drilling, Hamilton's smartly dressed men in their hand-picked blue coats with white diagonal sashes were finally beginning to feel like they had secured their position.

Their battery armed with four cannon, Grand Battery it was named, was one of many batteries set up according to General Washington's defense plans. Hamilton was proud that he and his sixty or so men had been given such a prominent position and not far from Wall Street. From his vantage point in south York Island (Manhattan) he could see the entire harbor and mouth of the Hudson but he barely needed to focus his spyglasses to see the ominous sight headed towards them. His two targets, the *Phoenix* and the *Rose*, were massive British gunboats carrying 60 cannon between the two of them. They occupied Hamilton's entire sight, floating menacingly in full view. Their tall brown wooden masts carried several large white rectangular sails each and they billowed out in the wind with pride and power as if the Naval Commander, Admiral Howe himself were puffing up his chest in challenge. It was so British, so pretentious of them to openly confront the American colonists with their might. Hamilton could not help but feel a mix of respect, awe and dread.

"Fire damn you!" he repeated. "We can't let those ships make it up river!"

The guns roared in response. Hamilton's company was not the only ones stationed at this New York City battery. There were at least three other companies with them and a total of over 20 artillery pieces roaring out at the British ships. The sound was deafening and Hamilton's entire body vibrated from the concussive force of the cannons. Unfortunately, not all of them were being used and not all of the men were at their posts. It didn't matter. The British ships moved straight on as if the colonists weren't even there.

Hamilton would have been impressed if he wasn't so angry at his own men. He looked to his left and glared at two soldiers who were merely standing on the edge of the earthworks, staring at the British ships. "You!" He shouted.

A concussive blast sent Hamilton spinning. His body landed hard against the earth and his eardrums felt as if they had shattered from the blast. Immediately he realized that the explosion which sent him to his knees could not have come from a British gun. With horror he searched through the smoke for what he knew must have happened; one of his own guns must have exploded. How many of his men had died with it?

General George Washington could not believe his eyes. Everywhere he looked, men were staring at the British ships instead of manning their posts. It was if the majesty and power of the British Navy had so taken them by surprise that they were hypnotized beyond reason. His heart filled with rage at his men but also at the British. How could they hope to defeat an enemy that inspired such fear and awe in its subjects? The sight of a British warship or Redcoat seemed to turn the colonists into children.

Yet they were children. In so many ways, the men under his command were infants in comparison with the well trained fighting force on board those ships. All around Washington were shopkeepers, farmers, merchants, men without any uniforms, without any training. His own Colonel Knox, the savior of Boston and Washington's trusted friend, had been a bookseller before the battle of Lexington.

To even call it an army was an exaggeration. Colonists from New England, Pennsylvania, Maryland and as far south as Virginia had cultures as different from each other as the clothes they wore. New Englanders wore almost no uniforms except for the few who had sewn together pieces from old colonial wars they or their father had fought in. Virginians had full-fledged British style blue uniforms and looked down in shock as even free black men from New England joined the ranks. They were more like separate countries than a united army.

Washington could barely hold them together. For months he had been dealing with desertions and debate, begging Congress for money and men. Devoid of any reason to stay other than what was in their hearts, the volunteer army was finding little reason to go on against the world power in front of them. Thank Providence that just last week, after months of wrangling Congress had finally done what Washington had been begging them to do for so long. They had given the men a cause to fight for.

"We hold these truths to be self-evident, that all men are created equal." Jefferson's Declaration of Independence was a masterpiece. It stirred the passions and reminded him of what they were fighting for. Washington could not help but be brought to tears the first time he heard it. So moved by Jefferson's eloquent and powerful words, he ordered it read to all of the men as soon as possible. And it had the desired effect. The men cheered. They cried out as one fighting force. They celebrated. They cursed the British. And while Washington publicly did not approve, he could not help but be heartened with the news of the Patriots tearing down the obnoxious white marble, gold laded statue of King George the III in the heart of New York City itself.

They would prevail, Washington reminded himself. The victory in Boston would be followed by a victory in New York. Their cause was just and the time was now. After all, just 10 days ago he had stubbornly written in his General Orders to his men:

"The time is now near at hand which must probably determine whether Americans are to be Freemen or Slaves... the fate of unborn Millions will now depend under God, on the Courage and Conduct of this army–Our cruel and unrelenting Enemy leaves us no choice ...We have therefore to resolve to conquer or die."

But as Washington watched the skies fill with smoke, as he felt the gunpowder in the air sting his lungs and listened to the screams and cries coming from the citizens of New York city who were being bombarded by the British gunships, the doubts started to take hold.

Boston had been a simpler story. The British were surrounded there. Washington's men could park their stolen cannon on Dorchester heights and bombard not only the British army in the city but the British ships in the harbor as well.

New York was an entirely different situation. Where Boston had been a smaller city, like an island stuck in the middle of a harbor, New York was already one of the largest cities in North America, second only to Philadelphia. Two rivers, a bay, the Jersey shore, Staten Island, Long Island, Brooklyn and even the heights of Harlem would all have to be fortified and protected. The British Navy, with their command of the sea, could land their forces wherever they wanted and attack at will. Washington's small army of 15,000 men, already decimated by small pox was split up all over the area.

At least Washington had been given some time. After their evacuation of Boston, the British became busy with their fleet bringing Loyalist refugees to Canada while Washington headed south to New York and began fortifying the city. For two months, the Continental Army and New York militia built forts, dug earthworks, cut down trees, put barricades in the streets and guns all along the Hudson and East Rivers. They drafted freeman and slave alike and ran the Loyalists out of town. Washington even had a signal corps set up to warn them of when the British were coming.

On June 29, 1776 the first British ships began to arrive. A once empty harbor suddenly filled with ship after ship after ship. Within hours there were more than 30 ships and within days over 100. And with every ship having two to four wooden masts sticking up high into the air, it seemed as if an entire forest had been planted in the waters surrounding New York. Washington had heard one of his men describe it as if all of London was afloat in the harbor.

It was the greatest spectacle of power any of them had ever seen. From his relative safety on the shores of the Hudson River, looking south to the bay, Washington was overcome with dread as he saw what the victory at Boston had truly accomplished. All he had managed to do was arouse the sleeping giant. No British ships had been destroyed in Boston. No British army had surrendered. The British may have left Boston with their tails between their legs, but they were returning with a vengeful desire to put the unruly colonists in their place and they had the power to do it.

The British Navy was the largest navy in the world. The British army was the best trained fighting force in the Americas. The British King, George III, had more than enough money to hire more men and material than Washington could ever hope to match. It was the largest fighting force ever assembled in North America and it looked like all of it would be used against Washington and his army of shopkeepers and farmers.

More than a week had gone by and still the ships did not approach Washington's position despite their overwhelming superior numbers. Instead they just continued, day after day, to ominously add to their forces and land their troops safely on the shores of Staten Island. Yet another Loyalist stronghold, the island welcomed the troops with cheers, looking forward to the day when the

Patriot rabble and their rebel mobs would disappear and order would be brought back to New York.

These Loyalists, Washington had come to realize, were a real threat. Only days ago, a conspiracy to assassinate the General himself was uncovered. Not only were soldiers in his own service involved, but the Mayor of New York city was suspect. It was getting to the point where Washington could not trust anything or anyone.

And so finally today, two weeks after the first British ships had appeared in the harbor, they made their first move. Despite their power, the British still moved slowly. The enormous gunships Phoenix and the Rose accompanied by only three support vessels sailed effortlessly up the river past Hamilton's position and towards Washington. The rest of the fleet remained behind. Even with this small force, Washington realized in anger, the British treated his army like gnats to be ignored or swatted away, boldly daring him to stop them. After hours of bombardment by all of the guns at Washington's command, the ships calmly, obnoxiously, moved on past the General and further up the river to begin Washington knew not what. And he was helpless to stop them.

Perhaps, Washington wondered, they will take the forts Montgomery and Washington. Those were not even finished being built yet. If the British could cut off the Hudson River, they could cut off New England and continue cutting the colonies in half until they were no more. Perhaps they would land a force and unite with the many loyalists in the Hudson River valley. Loyalists owned more than 2/3 of the property in New York, were represented at all levels of society and in many places in the colony were even the majority. Perhaps, he realized with more dread, they were bringing arms to those same Loyalists and creating another home grown army even more powerful than his own.

As Washington quickly called for a messenger he thought to himself, *"How could they ever win this war if they were not only fighting the mightiest empire on earth, they were also fighting each other?"*

Part One

*"These are the times
that try men's souls."*
Thomas Paine, 1776

L1

December 1776

The woods of southwestern Connecticut

Samuel could feel his heart racing in his chest and pounding in his ears. As a 17 year old teen, he was in the best shape of his life. Working on a farm, doing chores with his father from sunrise to sunset had given him more of a man's body than a boy's. He was strong and he was fast. It was panic that was making his heart race more than his burning lungs. What was he going to do?

He looked down at his black leather boots and cursed the footprints they were making in the snow. He cocked his head back and listened to the sounds of the dogs barking in the distance. He didn't have much time.

Covering up the tracks, trying to fool the dogs, was useless. They knew where he was going. Samuel just had to make sure he got there first.

What was he going to do? He panicked again. What would he tell his father? How could he stop them from hurting him, or burning the farm or worse?

Samuel ran even faster. He unbuttoned his burlap jacket. Even though it was around 40 degrees and snowing lightly, he was burning up from running so fast. He ducked suddenly to avoid a low hanging branch. The full moon, reflecting off the snow covered ground illuminated the night sky fairly well, but he still had to be careful with all the oak and pine trees everywhere. Their leafless limbs stuck out into the path like the fingers of the dead grasping for one last piece of Thomas' skin. He shuddered at that thought and decided to keep his head bent.

He stopped suddenly as he entered the clearing where his home lay and stared for a minute. It was a well built, colonial two story house that he and his father had built themselves three years ago. Even though Samuel was only fourteen at the time, he was quite large for his age and was able to help his father in every way that a full grown man could. It still filled Samuel with pride every time he looked at the home. It had a red brick chimney on the center of the roof, five second story windows, four first story windows and a simple oak wooden door in the center. Even the warp in the wood near the front door made him smile. It was there from when he left the wood out in the rain. His father had insisted they still use it to remind Sam of how important every last detail was.

He shook the small amount of snow flurries from his black hair and smiled a little remembering his father's obsession with details and rules. It could drive Samuel crazy at times; like now.

"Damn it father," he cursed, sprinting across the front lawn and through the front door. He jumped up the wooden stairs two by two and burst into his father's bedroom. He didn't care if he woke up his sister and brother down the hall.

"Father, Father, wake up!" Samuel crossed the plain wooden planks of the small bare room in seconds. The old floorboards creaked and groaned under his weight and his black leather boots clopped like a horse but still his father Thomas didn't budge.

Samuel paused suddenly at the edge of his father's bed and stood over his father's sleeping form. The moonlight was just enough to illuminate his worn face. *"He's so exhausted,"* Samuel thought sadly.

The urge to leave him alone, to protect him from the new and violent world around them, halted Samuel. In the eerie quiet of the moon lit night Samuel could almost believe that peace was something they could still hope for; that his father and sister and brother could still wake up in the morning, toil and sweat on the farm and enjoy the rewards of a hard day's work.

Samuel yearned for those days. His heart ached and a tear formed in his eyes as he recalled all the laughing and crying amidst the hard work that defined his childhood. He remembered fondly looking up to his father as if he was some kind of folk hero, resisting the world and protecting his family.

Samuel's father, Thomas Appleby was a strong man, both of conviction and stature. It was not so much choice as circumstance that made him this way. Ten years ago everything was going right for him and his family. His beautiful wife Sarah had just given birth to their second son, their farm was running independently and his new blacksmith shed was beginning to attract customers. Life for a British subject in America held nothing but promise and opportunity.

Then his wife died of smallpox. It devastated Thomas. With Sarah gone, there was no one to share his joys with, no one to plan for the future with and no one to help him raise their daughter and two sons. Only the work, his faith and his dedication to his family kept him going.

To make matters worse, a civil war was brewing in the country. Stamp Acts, Tea Parties, mob rule, tarring and feathering; his world was being torn apart as neighbor fought neighbor over taxes, Kings and self government. Old friends, even family members turned on one another. Samuel grew angry thinking of how his father's stubbornness had led their own family to fight.

It had started with Samuel's uncle, his father's younger brother David joining the local Sons of Liberty. At first, there were discussions and heated family dinners. Then there were arguments and cursing. Uncle David was not only taking an active role in the uprising, he was pressuring his brother Thomas and even Samuel to get involved as well.

Uncle David was passionate, energetic and strong. Samuel admired him immensely. He could listen to him talk for hours about rights and justice and taxes. If his father had not strictly forbid it, Samuel would have become a courier for the Sons years ago. Perhaps, Samuel had thought back then, father just needed some time.

Everything changed after the tarring and feathering. At first, Samuel could not stop laughing, listening to his Uncle describe how, Joseph Seabury, the local tax collector, was running all over the town square like a big chicken. Feathers from ten different farms had been used and hot tar collected from the docks. Held in place by six members of the Sons, the tax collector could only stand helplessly as boiling hot tar poured over his skin and feathers were immediately dumped as well. He truly looked more like a giant chicken man, squawking and screaming as he ran from the square in search of a pond or stream to save his burning skin.

Samuel's laughter turned to anger however, when his father not only scolded him, he scolded Uncle David as well. How could he use such cruelty? His father had shouted. Where Uncle David and Samuel saw an annoying servant of the King running around like a chicken, Thomas saw the pain and suffering. He described in detail how the man's skin was burning under the tar, how he was literally being cooked alive. He told of other victims who had died from their wounds and then asked David if he checked on the man to see if he was alright. When David laughed and said no, Thomas kicked his brother out of the house. Then he sent Samuel to his room and went off to the gravesite at the edge of the farm.

Ever since that moment, the lines had been drawn. The fighting and the arguments continued, but no one, not Samuel, not Uncle David and certainly no Son of Liberty could make Thomas change his mind.

"Wake up father!" Samuel angrily reached across the half empty large bed his father had made and shook him by the shoulders. The bed had been made for two, and Thomas could never bring himself to change it.

"What is it?" Thomas burst awake, grabbing the rifle that lay where his wife once slept. He snapped his head towards his son.

"The Committee!" Samuel stepped back a little to let his father rise. "They are on their way!"

"At this hour?" Thomas cried as he jumped out of bed and began to throw on his own black leather boots and heavy jacket. The wooden walls of his house stopped some of the cold winter air, but they could never match up tight enough to make a perfect seal. As soon as he was out of the covers, he could feel the chill right through his nightshirt. He looked around the room trying to orient himself and could see moonlight through his window and the snow falling lightly. It had to be past midnight.

"They come with pitchforks and torch," his son said anxiously. "They mean to have you sign the oath."

"The oath?" That woke up him up. He knew what that meant. For months now he had resisted signing the oath of allegiance.

"You know I won't sign." He was standing tall now, facing his son directly. He could see the worry on his face.

"But father, we are a new nation now! We have a Declaration of Independence. If you do not sign the oath, they could imprison you or take our land or both!"

"Samuel," his father interrupted. He turned his back to Samuel and headed towards the hall. "Must we have this discussion again?"

Samuel's worry turned back to anger. He hated how stubborn his father could be, and on this issue he would not budge. Even with Uncle David joining the Patriots at Bunker Hill his father refused to take sides.

"Wait," Thomas stopped suddenly before leaving the room and turned back towards his son. "How did you know they were coming?"

"I-I just do," Samuel took a step back.

"Samuel!" His father bellowed. It was an explosion of anger, grief and frustration. His eyes bore into his son as he waved his index finger menacingly. "What have you done?"

"Nothing," Sam said defensively. Then he stood a little straighter. He grew a little angry at having to defend himself. What he did was right. "Nothing," He repeated firmly.

"You've taken sides haven't you?"

"Yes father, I have."

"After everything we've talked about?" Thomas stepped even closer to his son. His warm breath blew the thin black hairs on Samuel's head.

"You mean after everything you've talked about," Samuel stepped back. "You never let me give my opinion at all."

"Father what is it?" Anne suddenly appeared at the door. At fifteen years old, she almost completely filled out her mother's old white nightgown and in the eerie moonlight it seemed as if the ghost of Thomas' wife was standing before him. Thomas froze.

"It's the Committee," Samuel answered quickly before his father could renew the argument. "They are here for father."

"What do they want with father?" Isaac, the youngest boy appeared at the door as well. His bright blonde hair was still a mess and he instinctively reached for Anne's hand. At eleven years old, he had barely had time to know his mother. Anne filled that role for him now.

"Don't you worry," Thomas laid the rifle next to the bed and gently bent down to look into his son's innocent blue eyes. He rubbed the blonde hair gently and straightened some of it so the boy could see. "Nothing will come of this."

"It's not nothing father," Samuel reminded him. "You have got to leave."

"Leave?" Anne repeated.

"No one is leaving," Thomas picked up the rifle again.

The harsh, high pitched sound of dogs barking suddenly split the air. They all froze. One bark was their own dog, Scout, but the other barks were strangers.

"They're here," Samuel said. "Please father, you have to leave."

Thomas said nothing. Instead he gave his oldest son a stern stare and a frown, pushed him gently to the side with the back of his hand and headed down the stairs. "Please father," Samuel called after him.

Thomas could hear the angry voices and the dogs barking as he headed towards the front door. He looked out his front window and could see the lights of their torches.

"Get behind me children," he held out both his arms wide and gently pushed Samuel, Anne and Isaac back into the house. "And do not say a word."

Thomas opened the door just as five dogs and their men were emerging from the woods and into the clearing in front of his home.

"Scout!" Thomas commanded his dog to back off. He had been barking viscously at the invaders and bearing his teeth. Scout may have been a large, loyal golden retriever but he could not take on five dogs all on his own. Thomas did not even want to see him try.

Thomas looked beyond the dogs at the men. There were fifteen of them dressed in various shades of black and one man was even in a blue militia uniform. Each one had a torch, some had pitchforks and a few had rifles. He could not see their faces yet but he could hear angry shouts already of "Tory, traitor, King friend," and even "coward".

Thomas turned and looked back at his children. He eyed the rifle he was holding firmly in his hands. He looked at his oldest son. Samuel was such a wonderful, stubborn, impressionable, idealistic young man. How had he grown so fast? It seemed like just yesterday when little Samuel had run into the house in dread thinking a bear was chasing him. It took three days before the boy was able to leave the house again. Thomas smiled at the memory and realized he had to be strong for his son. He shook his head. "No guns," he held Samuel's stare and placed the rifle down next to the wall.

"Tory!" the accusation split the air.

Thomas turned towards the men again and took a step out into the yard. He could see their faces now and he recognized almost everyone. Most of them were members of the Committee of Inspection; self-appointed men whose job it was to make sure no one sold to or dealt with the King and his men. The rest were neighbors or militia men. Even Captain Coley was there in full Colonial Uniform. He had been the one who led the charge storming out of the Episcopal Church. Reverend Mark had tried to keep his parish out of the war and his sermons often talked of Loyalty to the King.

"Thomas Appleby!" the lead man said. It was Paul Knox, the leader of the Committee of Inspection. Dressed in his formal gray coat and breeches, with knotted white cravat tightly woven around his neck and even wearing the official white wig topped by his brown Colonial Triangle hat, Paul looked every bit the official and nothing like the neighbor Thomas had known for years. Thomas had even helped him build his house and their wives spent many hours together sharing stories and tears. Indeed the same pox that took Thomas' wife Sarah almost took Paul's wife as well. It had given the men a bond that Thomas thought was unbreakable.

Paul put up his bare hand and the men behind him stopped about 30 feet from the house. The dogs continued to snarl but the barking had ceased. Paul and Thomas locked eyes for a moment. They both were sad that it had come to this and Thomas could see the unspoken pain in Paul's wrinkled face and dark brown eyes.

"You know it's me Paul," Thomas stepped further away from his children. His eyes remained locked with Paul. Anger, sadness, confusion and resolve; they all whirled back and forth between the two men. "What's all this about?"

"You know what it's about." Paul replied.

"Didn't your boy tell you?" someone else in the mob shouted out. Thomas turned back to his son for an instant. Samuel said nothing.

"Sign the oath Thomas!" Paul commanded. He had prayed it would never come to this but now his patience was near an end. He had held out so long for Thomas. He had convinced his friends in the committee to leave Thomas alone for months. He had argued on his behalf. He had pointed out Thomas' standing in the community and his dedication to neighbor and God. He wondered if Thomas had any idea how long Paul had protected him and he grew angry at Thomas for forcing his hand. Why was the man so stubborn?

"Sign the oath!" a man Thomas did not recognize shouted angrily. Unlike most of the others, his gun was cocked and he held it high in the air. "Sign the oath or we will burn your Tory house and take you back in chains."

Thomas turned back and looked at Samuel.

"Please father," Samuel begged.

"Sign the oath!" the shouts grew even louder.

"Please father," Samuel repeated.

Thomas looked at his younger children. Their eyes were wide and they shook as they stood but not from the cold. Their fear tore at his chest. But what could he do? To sign the oath would go against everything he ever believed in. He was not a man who could be bullied. How ironic that these men talk of freedom yet try to take his own away. He did not believe in either side. He did not believe in war, at least this war. Thomas was no coward. He would fight and die to protect what he believed in and right now, with his wife long gone, there was only one thing he believed in; his family.

"Father?" Anne said softly.

One

Today

Rob closed his eyes and let out a small sigh.

"That feels nice." It was childish, immature even for Rob to be feeling this way, especially considering the circumstances, but he couldn't help himself. He hadn't been touched by a woman in months. Something about, young, athletic, untouchable women, always excited him.

And Lindsey certainly was all those things and more. A member of Rob's adult hockey team for over two years now, Lindsey Craig was adored by everyone on the team. She had an athlete's body, a model's blond hair and blue eyes and a hockey player's personality. Her skill on the ice, her presence in the locker room and her familiarity with the guys made her the perfect teammate. Of course Rob had the hots for her; everyone on the team did. But that just made her all the more untouchable. She was both everyone's and no-ones at the same time. They protected her as a wolf pack protects their most promising new cub.

So to have Lindsey touching Rob on the arm like that just sent his whole body into a whirlwind. His pulse raced, the hair on the back of his neck stiffened, he was even beginning to sweat.

"All she did was hold your arm you dumb shit," Rob tried to mask his feelings. He was losing control and he hated that. *"It's a fucking funeral, act like it!"*

There were close to one hundred people all dressed in various styles of funeral black packed into his Fairfield, Connecticut home. It was a huge, two-story ranch house with a converted basement and three car garage. It had been their home for almost 10 years and Rob was determined to make it another 10 or at least until the boys were off at college. Its back yard allowed for plenty of space for playing football with the neighborhood kids and the third car of the garage had been converted into a hockey workout room so he and the boys could work on their slap and wrist shots as much as they wanted without getting puck marks all over the house. He had even found a used goal on-line to put in there.

The boys each had their own rooms, both upstairs just down the hall from his room. Now that his wife had left, Rob found not only the room, but the house, much bigger than it had been before the separation. Still, despite the converted basement/den, living room, dining room, kitchen, family room and even the outdoor porch, the house was still crowded with guests. It was almost wall to wall.

Many of them were in the kitchen, chit chatting and hovering over the various finger foods and party trays. Others were lounging downstairs in the pool room, or on the living room couches and of course at the bar. Friends, relatives, acquaintances, people Rob did not even know had come to pay their respects to his mother. It was a testament to how well regarded she and Rob were in the community. It made his heart swell. Some of these guests were people he had not seen in years.

"That didn't take long," Rob's estranged wife Deborah burst from the crowd of mourners and hissed at her husband. Her arms were crossed in judgment and her piercing green eyes held daggers. Rob stopped in mid stride almost tripping Lindsey in the process. Despite his grace on the ice, Rob was not the smoothest walker. He tripped occasionally, bumped into walls and stumbled around like some kind of a Clark Kent. He even had the dark glasses, although those were just for reading.

Perhaps it was Rob's boxy frame that made him appear clumsy at times. He was tall and well built. Everyone would give him that. His broad shoulders and muscular chest had been sculpted from decades of ice hockey. While the tightly forming black suit Rob wore elevated his shoulders and chest even more, it constricted his biceps and leg calves so much that Rob was always stretching and fidgeting trying to get comfortable. He looked like a boy forced to wear the suit grandma picked out that never fit right.

"What didn't take long?" Rob was taken aback by his wife's sudden appearance especially with his head still swirling around Lindsey. He had been trying to avoid his wife all day, but he knew a moment like this would come. He hoped it would at least be cordial.

"To find someone else," his wife Deborah accused with a dismissive nod towards Lindsey. In a moment she had sized up the competition. Lindsey was smaller than either Rob or his wife but she was clearly athletic. Her shoulders were square, her jaw was tight, yet she still held that softness in her face and cheeks. Despite herself, Deborah had to admit she was pretty. She hated her immediately. "You could have at least waited until I finished moving out."

"Her?" Rob's face contorted as he thought for a moment. Had Deborah read his mind? It wouldn't have been the first time. After 16 years of marriage, they knew each other sometimes better than they knew themselves. He glanced at his companion and back at his wife. "Lindsey?"

"Yes!" Deborah snapped and repeated sarcastically, "Lindsey. She's been all over you the last two days."

"Hey," Lindsey jumped in, "I was just-"

"Lindsey is a member of the team," Rob placed himself in between the two women. His embarrassment was turning to anger. Lindsey had only been trying to help him through this, "and she was only trying to help."

Deborah took a step back and bumped into one of Rob's teammates. They had formed a circle around her; Billy, Stevie, Al, Lou, Marty, Timmy, Tony, Rick, Craig, Tom and a few she still could not name. Never far from each other, these guys on Rob's hockey team acted more like an army unit than a beer league group of men who shared the ice once a week. They had some kind of bond that Deborah had never been able to understand or to influence. Even though she herself was an athlete, this hockey bond seemed different. The guys stood up for one another, looked out for one another, on and off the ice. They had the same old jokes and the same bad habits. Perhaps it was the nature of the sport. Deborah didn't know and at this moment, she didn't care.

"And who do you think you are?" Rob's temper began to flare. "Showing up after the funeral is over, the funeral for your kid's grandmother I might add, and throwing this in my face the first chance you get?"

"I was at the funeral!" Deborah took a step forward again. Rob might be a tall, well-built hockey player, but she was no slouch herself. It had been a long time since she played basketball in high school but she could easily meet Rob's height and his gaze. Yet where Rob was sometimes boxy and clumsy, Deborah was smooth and elegant. She moved with grace and style not only on the basketball court, but wherever she was. It was almost intimidating to Rob just how strikingly beautiful his wife was. Her flowing black hair, high cheekbones, long legs and athletic build made her look more like a model than a doctor. In some ways it helped lead to all the problems they were going through now. "But I kept in the background for your sake because I didn't want to be a distraction." Deborah waved her hands in dismay.

"A distraction?" Rob repeated incredulously. "Then what the hell is this?"

"I just can't believe," Deborah's demeanor suddenly changed as tears began to swell up and her voice began to catch, "that you could dismiss me this quickly."

"I didn't dismiss you," Rob was still angry. Once his temper peaked it did not retreat so easily, even at the sight of his wife almost in tears. His short fuse was one of his biggest problems and he still did not know how to control it. "I didn't even think about you! All I could think about was the kids and mom and how you weren't there!"

"I was there I said!"

"Lindsey is a teammate, a friend," Rob ignored his wife's anger. She was in the wrong, not him. All Lindsey had done was put a comforting hand on Rob in a time of stress. His silly reaction to it was unspoken and meaningless. "She's here with the rest of the guys. I would think after all these years with me; you would know how beer league hockey works."

"I know how your stupid beer league works!" Some of the heads from nearby guests turned in surprise. "I know all about your drinking and your fighting and 'being one of the guys' and how much it means to you. I just don't know what she is doing in your locker room."

"Hey you two," Lou, the captain of Rob's team interrupted. He was almost as big as Rob, yet he somehow managed to gently place himself between them. "You both know this is neither the time nor the place for this."

"You're right Lou," Deborah quickly agreed as she turned to their old friend. Only a few of Rob's hockey buddies made the crossover into the family circle and Lou was one of those. His wife Michelle was a good friend to Deborah as well and their kids pretty much grew up together. As families or as couples they often went out to dinner or the movies and every once in a while made the trip into New York for a Rangers game. Lou was just a little older than Rob and was a Captain in ways that went far beyond hockey. Deborah often turned to him for words of wisdom and advice. Today especially, with everything that was going on, Deborah was warmed by his words and the sincerity on his face.

A flash of shame and frustration hit her hard. She didn't even know why she started this in the first place. She really had come to show her husband that she still cared for him and maybe even still loved him. She never meant it to go like this. It was just that seeing him with that woman on his arm just set her off. "I am going to find the kids," she said, placing a warm hand on Lou's shoulder as she turned away.

"Hey!" Rob called after her as she quickly headed into the crowd. He wasn't done yet.

"Rob," Lou placed his hand on the big guy's shoulder. "Let it go. Let her go. Lindsey can take a hit or two." He smiled at her.

Lindsey smiled back, glad it was all over. She hadn't given a thought to holding Rob's hand. He seemed to need it. Sure, Lindsey admitted to herself, she was attracted to Rob. Who wouldn't be? He was smart: graduate of Tufts University.

He was good looking: face was a cross between Brad Pitt and Brett Favre. He was tough: how many hockey fights had he been in? And best of all, he was honorable. Rob stuck to his word. He defended his teammates and his family. He had integrity both on and off the ice. But first and foremost, Lindsey reminded herself, they were teammates. She wouldn't allow herself to think that way. She had worked too hard to earn their respect and be treated like one of the guys. Plus, she added to herself, he's technically still married.

"She can give a few hits too," Rick broke the tension. You could always count on old man Rick for a quick joke or jab. His wit was quick, probably from all the decades he spent in the locker room. He had to be the oldest guy on the team if not the rink.

"She's a thug," Billy chuckled.

"Coming from the master himself," Tony elbowed Billy.

The team burst into laughter with the return of their locker room banter. Rob joined in, took one last glance towards where his wife had disappeared and motioned them all over towards the bar downstairs.

"C'mon guys," he led, "I need a good belt."

"Took long enough," Lindsey followed.

"Wouldn't be an Irish funeral without it," Rick said.

Meanwhile Deborah had made her way back into the crowd. Thoughts of Rob, his team and that woman quickly faded as she encountered more and more of her friends. She and Rob had been married for sixteen years, most of them inseparably. Rob's friends were her friends (except in hockey of course). She knew almost everyone there.

"Hey," their neighbor Maggie interrupted. (Or was it Fran? It was so hard to get to know the neighbors these days. Between work schedules, taking the kids to the rink and the endless errands, everyone in the neighborhood always seemed to be going their own way. Add in the tinted car windows and garage door openers and you could live next to someone for five years and not know what they looked like.) "So sorry to hear about your mother in law," she placed a hand on Deborah's forearm. "How are the kids?"

"They're doing ok," Deborah lied as her eyes scanned the kitchen for her sons again. As two growing teenage boys, they were never too far from the food.

"If there is anything I can do to help out with the kids or the house-"

"Rob takes care of all that now,"

"Oh, of course," the neighbor's eyes looked down at the food, hoping to find an out. "Sorry," she continued as she reached for the meatball tray.

"No need to apologize," Deborah reached for a deviled egg, also trying to escape the awkward interchange. "I am still trying to get used to the new dynamic myself. Excuse me," she turned away, "I think I see my son over there."

Deborah nudged her way through the kitchen between another neighbor she recognized who was holding a glass of wine and talking too loudly with another person she didn't. "Excuse me," she said forcefully, keeping her head down to avoid any more conversations and deftly weaving her way through the living room crowd and towards the staircase beyond.

She turned lithely around the banister and made her way up the stairs. The door to her younger son Adam's room was slightly ajar and the light was on. "Adam?" she tapped lightly on the door as she nudged it open and peered in. The room was not as messy as she expected. Of course clothes were on the floor, comic books were on the bed and posters of hockey and football players covered every wall, but it was neat compared to her older son Bobby's room. Probably because Adam was still not quite a teenager at age eleven. "Can I come in?" she asked gently.

"Whatever," Adam replied without turning around. All Deborah could see was his bright blond hair that she loved to mess with every chance she got. As a baby, Adam looked practically bald with his fine white hair but as he got older and the blond filled out, Deborah would show her affection by rubbing the top of his head vigorously and obnoxiously telling him how much she loved him. Adam hated it. She wondered if she could get away with it now.

"How are you doing son?" Adam's back was facing her and his eyes were focused on his computer screen. His hands held a video game console in between them. He was playing NHL 2019 again.

"Fine," Adam replied in a monotone voice. His fingers pounded on the remote control and his body jolted to the right as if he was trying to avoid the players on the screen.

Deborah stepped carefully around the various piles of clothes on the floor. She laid her hand on her son's right shoulder and repressed her natural need to comment on how much he played video games. She had no desire to play the role of nagging mother to pre-teen boy. She just wanted to feel his love.

"Are you sure you're ok?" She prompted.

"Of course I'm sure." Adam snapped, "Why wouldn't I be?"

Deborah stood silently for a moment trying to decide what to say next. She knew many things were wrong and wanted to avoid an explosion. "Your Nana-"

"Damn," he shouted as he threw the remote. The loud deep blare of the arena siren rang out from the speakers ending the hockey game. "See what you made me do?"

"I didn't mean to," she said softly, pushing a comic book to the side and sitting on Adam's bed. "I just wanted to see how you're doing."

"I'm doing fine," Adam repeated, turning away from his screen to finally look at his mother. He stared innocently at her, not sure what to think or say.

Deborah looked back at her son. He still had a baby face despite his size. Over five feet tall, he towered over his fellow fifth graders. His shoulders were broad like his father's and he had his mother's long legs. He was still a work in progress. Deborah couldn't help but smile.

"What?" Adam reacted to the sudden smile on his mother's face. He saw nothing to smile about.

"Nothing, sorry," his mother quickly pulled back the smile. "I was just noticing how much you've grown."

Adam groaned and rolled his eyes, although he couldn't help but smile. He was pretty proud of his size.

Deborah laughed at his reaction. "I've missed you," she smiled.

Adam sat, silently waiting. The lack of an "I missed you too," stung his mother. "How are your last few weeks of elementary school going?" She continued after the painful silence.

"Fine," he continued with the one word answers. Those would have to stop.

"You're going on to middle school soon. Are you nervous?"

"No,"

"Adam!" Deborah exploded slapping both her knees at the same time. "I am trying here! Do you have any idea how hard this is?" her voice started to crack again. "Do you have any idea how difficult it is to not see you every day, to not be able to kiss you goodbye in the morning?"

"Well maybe you shouldn't have left then."

"I had no choice!" she screamed at him, standing up and towering over him. Adam pushed back in his chair. He had never seen his mother so angry. "Your father-" she yelled and then stopped abruptly.

"What was she doing?" She saw the fear in her son's eyes. *"This is not who she was. She was not a mother who screamed at her children. They did not need to hear the dirt of her marriage. How did this happen to her?"*

"Mom?" The door opened and her older son Bobby walked in. Thick black hair, dark brown eyes, square chin and a muscular build, Bobby was also ahead of his peers in size but as a rising ninth grader he was already beginning to be a knock out. "I thought I heard you in here."

"Bobby!" Deborah cried in relief and joy. Her oldest son always brightened her day; so much like his father in all the good ways and so unlike him in all the bad. She opened her arms wide.

"I've missed you," he said as opened his arms wide and hugged her tight. Deborah's heart melted as much from the hug as from those words that she so needed to hear.

After several seconds of that wonderful warm hug, Deborah pushed back, wiped the tears from her eyes and stared at her son. "How are you?"

"Confused," Bobby admitted. "I have no idea what to do or who to talk to. Everyone just says the same thing, asks me how I am doing and then quickly changes the subject. I feel like I have the plague or something."

"I'm sorry."

"Your timing sucks," Bobby blurted out with a half-smile.

"I know."

Silence overtook the room. No one wanted to talk about the separation or the funeral yet they all knew they had too. Adam turned around and started his game up again.

"Hey loser," Bobby smacked him on the head. "Mom is here."

"So?"

"So get off the game."

"It's okay," their mother interrupted. She knew what was going on. Adam was still angry at her. Bobby, four years older and going into high school, had begun to understand the complexities of the adult world. "Leave him alone. It's how he's coping."

Again silence. Adam stayed focused while Bobby and his mother watched over his shoulder. "Score!" Doc Emerick, the Emmy winning NHL announcer shouted. Adam pumped his fist. Bobby and his mother smiled a little. The game was so much like the real thing.

"Are you coming to Nana's tomorrow?" Bobby asked.

"What's at Nana's?"

"Dad wants to go through all her stuff. You know, all those old letters and pictures and family tree junk she's kept over the years."

"Oh," The pains of being outside the family hit hard. "I wasn't invited."

"I'm not surprised," Bobby's face turned angry. "I think Dad invited that Lindsey girl from his team to join us."

"What?" Pain quickly turned back to anger. "Why?"

"Dad says she knows all about genealogy," Bobby explained. He could see the anger on his mother's face as he tried to make sense of his father's actions. "Guess she has traced her own family back a couple hundred years to the Revolution or something and she is some kind of expert."

"Expert," Deborah repeated in disgust. A theory began to form in her mind. Maybe their separation was not as innocent as she thought. Maybe it wasn't Deborah's fault at all. "We'll just see about that."

"Sign the oath Thomas!" Paul Knox warned one last time. His face contorted in anger as he gritted his rotting teeth. In the cold night air, his breath came out in a fog and despite his anger he shivered through the thick blue overcoat he wore. He raised his hand high in the frigid air for all to see. In it was a long piece of parchment paper. "It's your duty!"

"My duty is my own business!" Neither King nor country would tell him what to do. Both sides had made mistakes in this war. Both sides had committed acts of selfishness and violence. Both sides were right but neither side was willing to budge. Well he was a free man. His duty was to God and to his conscious. No matter how he felt about the war, he had a family to protect.

"Traitor!"

"Tory bastard!"

Some of the men started to rush the house.

"Wait!" Paul commanded them with another outstretched hand. The men stopped momentarily but they would not be held back long. Their dogs had joined them and were snarling fiercely. Scout stood ready to protect his master, his golden fur had become damp with snow flurries. Paul turned back towards Thomas , "We are no mob my friend," his voice grew soft as he took a glance at the children still shivering and standing by the front door. "Please, we know you are a good man."

Thomas looked out at the crowd of men and dogs again. To him they looked like a mob. Their many breaths created a cloudy shroud in the frostbitten air around them. The lights from their torches illuminated their angry faces and the pitchforks and rifles held high. The reflection of the moon light in the snow showed their booted feet and the many nervous footprints they had made. Still, they were his friends and neighbors. Thomas took a step towards them.

"We're all good men," He reminded them. "We've all worked together and celebrated together and drunk together."

"And fought together," George reminded him of the war they both had served in as lads. Twenty years ago the two of them, eager and naïve, had answered the call to arms against the Indians and the French. Thomas had served bravely; George even more so. And when a bullet tore through George's right bicep in the midst of a battle, it was Thomas by his side who applied the tourniquet and saved his friend from bleeding to death. Today it seemed that not a month went by without George knocking on the door of his old friend's shop for a repair or to share a story. The neighbors assumed it was because George could no longer use his tools or run a forge by himself. But Thomas knew better. He looked forward to the visits and cherished these moments of warmth and nostalgia, filled with boisterous laughter and refreshing smiles. At least until the troubles began. Now, with lines being drawn and war coming to his doorstep, Thomas could barely look at George standing in the cold with a single torch held in his one remaining arm.

"Sign the oath Appleby," Captain Coley shouted Thomas' last name with force and anger. He was not a neighbor, but he was one of the most respected leaders in the town and he had already lost two sons at Bunker Hill. Dressed in his Continental blue with his sword dangling menacingly at his side, he presented a commanding presence. He took a step towards Thomas and stared him straight in the eyes. "This is war. It's either our freedom or our enslavement. It's our lives, or theirs. Too many have died already," Coley looked back at the men around him. They were nodding in agreement. Coley wasn't the only one who had lost sons against the British. He turned back at Thomas and took another step closer. Their noses were almost touching and Thomas could smell the beer on his breath. "We don't want to hear your arguments," he said through clenched teeth, "we don't want to hear your pleas. You are either with us or against us. Now sign it!"

"Tory!" Someone shouted again.

"I am no Tory!" Thomas looked past Captain Coley and called to the crowd behind him. "I am no traitor. I am a free Englishman like all of you!" He turned back towards his children. Anne was hugging her little brother Isaac with both arms. Both of them were trying so hard to be brave. He stared directly at Samuel. His face was unreadable. Thomas knew by now that Samuel had joined the Patriot cause. Foolishly, impetuously, his son had ignored all his warnings and let his emotions rule him. Emotions of a teenage boy, Thomas remembered his own youth, were rarely guided by rationality.

Thomas held his son's stare and shouted back at the men although his words were really directed at his son. "But as free men, how can your first action as a nation be to take away my freedom?"

There was a sudden silence at Thomas' accusation. He hit a nerve.

"You are taking away the most basic freedom any man has," Thomas held his hands in open gesture towards his son then turned back to the crowd; "The freedom to choose; The freedom to live my life as I want to live it; The freedom to take care of my children and live our lives as we want to!"

"We are fighting against tyranny!" Paul rejoined the argument. He would not have his own principles thrown back at him especially by his own countryman.

"Are you not simply replacing the Tyranny of a King with the tyranny of the mob?"

Again the men were stopped by Thomas' words.

"My friends," Thomas changed his tone. He lowered his voice and stepped towards them. "I agree with you that the King has been a tyrant. He has taxed us beyond reason. He has sent soldiers to attack his own subjects. Do you not remember," he looked directly at Paul, "how I helped organize our town's relief efforts to help the citizens of Boston? Just because I do not pick up the rifle in rebellion, does not mean I do not agree with your cause."

The anger had subsided momentarily. Even the dogs had calmed. The torches flickered, the wind blew softly across the small farm and only the low screech of a distant owl could be heard somewhere in the trees.

"But in our zeal to defend our rights," Thomas should have stopped. He should have let the moment last but he could not control his own emotions. He was angry. Angry at his son for disobeying him, angry at his neighbors for invading his home, his privacy, angry at God for leaving him alone in the world with three mouths to feed and angry at himself for not seeing this coming sooner. "We fall prey to the propaganda and the rabble rousers. We let our emotions get the best of us and burn each other's homes and even torture people we once trusted and respected."

Some of the men shifted uncomfortably. Every single one of them had participated in tarrings and burnings.

"We have gone too far!" Thomas pushed further. "We take powers and rights even we do not have."

"We have every right!" Several of them shot back.

"Life, Liberty and the pursuit of happiness!"

"No taxation without representation!"

"Give me Liberty or give me death!"

"Join or Die!"

Thomas realized his mistake but it was too late now. He recognized all of those rebel quotes and knew their power.

"These are the times that try men's souls," Paul Knox quoted directly and stepped forward. Thomas Paine's *Common Sense* written that same year was the most popular book in America and its message had spread from New Hampshire to Georgia like wildfire in a dry forest. Its words, its arguments had convinced the rebels that their cause was right, that their cause was just and that men had to make a choice. "I have had enough Thomas." Paul held out the parchment and a feather pen. Black ink dripped from its tip into the snow below, "Sign."

"I will not," Thomas stood tall.

"Then you leave me no choice," Paul turned towards the crowd. All friendliness was gone. All memories of neighbors and friends were forgotten in the fire of rebellion. Thomas had made up his mind, just as every one of them had. Now he would have to pay for it.

"Burn the shop!" Paul commanded. "He will make no more tools for either Patriot or Tory."

"Wait!" Samuel jumped from his position at the door frame and ran next to his father. His hands were held high in the air. "Please, don't do this."

"He's made his choice," Paul turned his back.

"But he's my father! He's not some Tory aristocrat!"

"We are grateful for your Patriotism," Paul turned back to Samuel. The statement seemed more threat than gratitude. "And I feel for your loss, but we must carry out the orders of the government."

"Please," Samuel watched helplessly as the men took their torches held high and walked towards the blacksmith shed. He looked back at his father and over at his brother and sister. This felt like his fault. It felt like he had betrayed them. Of course he had tried to stop the Patriots before this. Of course he knew his father was no threat to anyone and repeated that in Patriot meeting after meeting. But he still felt like a traitor to his family. He had chosen a different side. He had broken with his father and none of them would make eye contact with him now.

The small shop went up immediately. The dark wood, already dry from the blacksmith furnace inside, took only a brush from the torches to ignite the walls. Everyone backed away from the intense heat and watched the orange flames leap into the air, snapping and crackling at the moon like angry wolves defending their young. Black smoke swirled away from the flames carrying pieces of ash into the air and darkening the night time stars from view. For the moment, all was still as the power of the flames and the level of destruction from the mobs' work took hold. There was no going back now. The act was done and all Thomas could do was watch in silence as the wood turned to ash and his life work disappeared.

"Do you still refuse to sign?" Paul finally turned to Thomas again. His face was clear in the light of the burning shop and Thomas saw nothing but stone cold resolve.

Thomas could give no answer. His convictions were true and he was in the right. He would not sign. Instead he watched in silence as the flames began to dwindle, the walls began to fall inwards and his ruined forge fell into pieces. He wondered what he would do now and prayed they would leave his home alone.

"You leave me no choice," Paul took Thomas' silence as continued protest and turned to the armed men. "Take him away!"

"Father!" Anne screamed from the doorway as she and Isaac ran outside.

"No!" Samuel stood firm between the men and his family. "You can't."

"We can and we will," Captain Coley approached, one hand was on the hilt of his sword; ready to draw it out if need be. "The Test Act is clear. The Connecticut legislature says we must swear allegiance to our new state government. If you refuse to sign the oath, your land is forfeit and trial is forthcoming."

"Father," Samuel turned around desperately and faced his father. "You've got to leave; Now!"

"But you can choose to exile him," Samuel swung back to the Captain and pleaded. "Please," he turned to Paul Knox. He looked over at George. He tried to look deep into their eyes. "My father is no threat. He is a good man. Just let him leave."

For a moment, the Patriots considered Samuels words. They had no wish to hurt Thomas any more than was necessary. They could see the pain in his face, the fear in his children's eyes. They were still neighbors, they had been friends.

"Father," Samuel turned back again to his family. "Anne," he looked at his sister. "You need to go."

"But where?" Anne wondered.

"To New York," Thomas answered quietly for her.

"It's just across the sound," Samuel told her. "And you will be welcomed there."

"What about you?" Anne's eyes opened wide in realization. She knew what had happened in New York. They all did. General Washington had been run out of the city like a rabbit being chased by wolves. The British had made New York their main base and Loyalists from all over the state and beyond flocked to them for protection. For Washington, he was lucky to escape with any of his army at all. It had been a humiliating slap in the face to the General and the entire army. Washington almost lost his command.

"You're coming too?" Anne pleaded with her brother.

Samuel did not answer. He looked in his father's lost eyes and watched him answer Anne's question for him.

"Your brother is not coming," Thomas said slowly and painfully. "He has made his choice and we all must learn to live with it."

Thomas turned away from his son and looked to his neighbors and friends. "Will this satisfy you?" He shouted slowly and painfully with outstretched arms. "Will you be content with destroying my livelihood, sending me into exile and taking my oldest son from me all in the name of Liberty and Freedom?"

No one spoke. There was no shame in what they had to do, but there was no pride either. It was, as a man named Cromwell said in an earlier English Revolution against another tyrannical king, "Cruel necessity".

"Are you sure Samuel? " Thomas turned one last time to his son. "Are you sure this is what you want?"

Of course Samuel wasn't sure. How could he be after just watching a mob destroy his father's livelihood and force him into exile? Samuel wondered if he would ever even see his family again. How could he ever be sure of abandoning his family in the name of a cause?

"This is war father." Samuel did his best to hide his emotions and the conflict inside. He wouldn't dare show his new friends or his father how afraid he truly was. "And I believe in what we are fighting for."

Two

"Thanks again for coming," Rob looked up over his black reading glasses and smiled. He placed another old yellow letter on the blue and white shag carpet floor in front of them. "I know how awkward it's been the last couple of days."

"No problem," Lindsey smiled back as she straightened one of her legs and grunted. It had been a long time since she sat cross legged on the floor. Maybe she should try those yoga lessons again.

Rob couldn't help but notice how tan and muscular her legs were. With the short black shorts Lindsey had on, her legs seemed even longer and a lot less like a hockey player's legs. How did she get them so tan in this short New England summer? Rob shook the thought away.

"Between the boys, the separation and now this," his head rolled around as he indicated the mess all around them, "it's just been crazy."

"No problem," Lindsey repeated. She was starting to question her decision to come. When Rob first asked, it seemed like a no-brainer. Rob was in need, she was free, why not? But now as she looked around the room and read the personal letters on the floor in front of her, she was not so sure. Rob's mother was a sentimental, personal woman. The house was filled with nick knacks, pictures, figurines and mementos. It had taken them almost an hour just to get to the letters because every time they passed a picture or a trophy from Rob's childhood, he stopped and told her the story behind it. She was learning a lot more about Rob's personal life than ever. *(Did anyone on the team know Rob wore reading glasses? It totally changed his demeanor from the rough and tough hockey center-man to the studious professor. Lou probably knew.)*

"And don't worry about my wife," Rob placed a wrinkled, worn picture of someone he didn't recognize in another pile, "she's going through a lot of stuff too."

"Shit his wife," Lindsey realized. She hadn't even thought about her. She thought that Rob and Deborah were getting divorced, not separated. Then there was that whole incident at Rob's house. It was the first time that being a woman on a men's team had become awkward. She hated it and she hated Deborah for making her feel that way. If she had not already committed to helping Rob out last week, she would never have come. "Is she coming?"

"No. I don't want her to. It was hard enough seeing her at the funeral." Rob glanced away. He could feel the tension and his blood rising. Just the thought of Deborah made him angry and he didn't want Lindsey to see that. *"Dammit! Why's everything have to be so friggin complicated?"*

He picked up another old letter, trying to lose himself in the task. It was yellow around the edges, like the other hundred or so sitting in front of him. The scribbly blue handwriting looked more like someone got a hold of one of those old fashioned Spirograph games he played with as a kid and let it loose across the page. He jumped to the end. Like most of them there was no date, all he could read was the signature. This one was from an Aunt Bettie. Another relative he never heard of. He dropped it in the pile.

"This is ridiculous," he groaned as he stood up to stretch.

"Oh it's not so bad," Lindsey admitted, as much to herself as to Rob. She really did enjoy all the family history investigating. It made her feel like some kind of detective. She looked up at Rob with another letter in her hand. "All this old stuff is living memories, stories, pieces of a puzzle of a time long gone."

Rob did not respond. He felt the same way Lindsey did, but it was just so much to take in. All those people at the funeral brought back so many memories, good and bad. Being in the house he grew up in, made it infinitely worse. He felt drained.

He gazed tiredly around the three room home. There were at least 20 boxes sitting in a variety of locations across this small living room. Some were open and sitting on top of the teak dining room table, others were sitting on the chairs, another was on the green ottoman and the rest were scattered on the fading throw rug in the middle of the floor.

"Why did she keep all this shit?"

"Who knows?" Lindsey looked up from the letter. She still could not find any pattern to any of these. "How long was she alone for?"

"How do you know she was alone?" Rob stopped in surprise and turned back to look at Lindsey. He had been headed towards the small white refrigerator to grab a beer.

"No one else could fit amidst all these boxes," she joked.

Rob grinned and turned back towards the kitchen. The house was so small that no room was truly separated from another. Only a small half wall separated them and Rob could still see Lindsey as he opened the fridge door. The nearly empty fridge sent a wave of sadness through Rob. He had always loved coming to his mother's and seeing all the food she kept in there for the kids and grandkids. Whether it was Rob's favorite jam or his kid's favorite brand of chocolate milk, there was always something for everyone in that fridge. Now there were just a couple of red and white six packs of Budweiser surrounded by the bright white light of empty steel shelves.

Rob twisted two cans free from their plastic holders and shut the door. "Seriously, how did you know she lived alone?"

"My grandma was the same way. She kept everything. She wrote letters to everybody and they wrote letters to her."

Rob tossed the can of Bud across the room and pulled the tab from the other one in his hand. The welcome fizz of carbonated air escaping from the top instantly put him at ease.

"Thanks," Lindsey caught the beer with her free hand and continued to explain. "Grandma started writing even before my granddad died but once she lived alone, the letters started to be her escape. She kept track of everyone and everybody. She wrote to me even though I was just a kid."

Lindsey cracked open her own beer and took a sip. So did Rob.

"Man!" Rob held the can out in front of him and stared at the label. "Why did you get this stuff? You know how much I hate this piss."

"Then why did you drink it?" Lindsey laughed.

"I was wicked thirsty. And I forgot how bad it tastes."

"Sorry Mr. Beer connoisseur," Lindsey continued laughing. This is how she loved to feel with Rob; Joking and drinking beer like buddies, "Not all of us are beer snobs like you."

"Heh," Rob laughed as he took another sip. He felt a little more relaxed now. "Life's too short to drink bad beer," he toasted her, then took another sip and grimaced.

Lindsey laughed one more time. "You're a riot!"

A loud crash came from around the corner followed by a shout, "You idiot!" One of the boys yelled. Rob had almost forgotten they were in their grandmother's room.

Rob ripped off the reading glasses, and in one swift motion placed them on the Ottoman nearby and jumped in the direction of the noise. Lindsey half expected him to rip open his shirt Superman style to expose the red and blue "S" underneath. She smiled and jumped up to follow Rob who only needed three of his large strides to bound into his mother's room.

"What's going on?" Rob commanded more than asked. The room was a mess. A cardboard box lay on the floor and the contents had spilled all over the green and white shag carpet. Letters wrapped in plastic sat close to the edge of the box, a few small white jewelry style boxes lay upside down and several figurines had rolled across the carpet. Rob moved his foot to the side. He had almost stepped on one. The only thing untouched was his mother's bed. Perfectly rectangular, perfectly made, the green sheets, pale yellow comforter and fluffy pillows had covered that bed for decades.

"This idiot dropped Nana's special box!" Bobby pointed at Adam in disgust. Bobby's black hair and tight white t-shirt added to his masculine confidence while Adam's blond hair, as usual, was in a mess and his shirt hung on his middle school body awkwardly. Standing next to each other and in front of Grandma's closet, they were a picture of opposites. Obviously they had been trying to get the box down from the top shelf of the closet when someone had lost their grip.

"It was an accident!" Adam snapped in defense.

"You're an accident," Bobby quipped as a smile grew from the corner of his mouth. He knew every button to push of his younger brother. That was one of the largest.

"Shut up!" Adam pushed his older brother onto his Nana's bed. He hated being called an accident. He didn't even understand it at first; only last year his father had taken him aside and explained "the birds and the bees" to him. Of course, neither Dad nor mom told him he was an accident. That was his brother's cruel idea. They denied it every time he asked but their firm denial only reinforced the truth. Every kid knew when his parents were lying and this was the biggest lie of all.

Bobby tried pushing Adam off of him but his younger brother was too big now. It was something Bobby was still adjusting too. He used to push Adam around effortlessly but now the twerp was almost his height and he had the leverage. He tried punching Adam's back but the bear-hug was too strong and Bobby's punches only landed on hard muscle.

"I hate you," Adam continued to push Bobby further into his grandmother's double bed. The perfectly straight, tightly tucked in green sheets that Nana loved so much were getting all wrinkled and pulled. Even the pillows had been pushed aside. That didn't matter. The boys were too upset.

Rob stood by the bed and watched. He knew the boys had a lot of tension and anger to work through and this fight might actually be good for them. More importantly, he still did not know how to handle this whole "accident" thing. After all, it was only partially true. Neither he nor his wife had any plans for another kid after Bobby but that didn't mean Rob did not want another son. He had always dreamed of birthing his own hockey line; three boys would make a center and two wingers and a girl or two could play defense. (Of course standing next to Lindsey, he was reminded that nowadays girls could play any position they wanted, not just get stuck on the blue line.) The problem was that his wife was perfectly content with one child. She had her exciting research at the hospital, lots of friends (even if they were on Facebook) and a husband she adored. Rob loved his job as an elementary school teacher as well. It was a unique job for a man, especially a "big rugged" hockey player like Rob. All the younger female teachers treated him somewhere between a celebrity and their big teddy bear. His wife was jealous of all the attention Rob got at work, but they had a great marriage. It could handle a little jealousy. It may have even made their sex life that much better.

Rob grinned a little, thinking of his sex life, the early years with his wife and his boys fighting. For a moment it washed away all the pain of the past few months. Then, suddenly, Adam managed to push himself up a little from his brother. It was just enough space for Adam to land a punch and he caught Bobby squarely in the eye.

"Asshole," Adam shouted as the force of his punch slapped Bobby's head to the right.

"Hey!" Rob sprang into action. His anger was instantaneous. (It was one of Rob's worst faults, he knew.) Before either boy knew what was going on, Rob had grabbed Adam by the scruff of the neck, lifted him effortlessly off of his brother and slammed his back against the opposite wall. "That's enough!"

Lindsey was right behind him. She jumped to the bed and held Bobby down by the shoulders before he could jump up and retaliate. She knew this was not her business, but her instincts just took over.

"Get off me," Bobby wacked at Lindsey's arms. She did not budge. Bobby swung again, this time much harder. "Get off me you bitch!"

Lindsey jumped back, more from the language and the hatred in Bobby's voice than from the punch.

"Bobby!" his father shouted, as much out of shock as anger. He taught his boys two things; respect and language. Treat everyone you meet with decorum and honor and talk to them in a civil tone. It was something he modeled just as much as he taught. Bobby just violated both his rules in one burst.

Bobby quickly rolled across the sheets and spun his body up so that he was standing across the tiny room from his father. With the bed placed strategically between them, he could safely challenge Rob while his brother was still pinned.

"What?" Bobby stared directly into his father eyes. His voice quivered a little but the challenge and the anger was obvious.

"You know what!" Rob held Bobby's stare while his right arm pushed the squirming Adam back harder into the wall.

"So?" Bobby shrugged his shoulders. "What are you going to do about it?"

Only the shock of the challenge kept Rob from instantly leaping across the room. His son had never before challenged him so openly. Of course there had been the usual talking back and disrespect that all young boys becoming men used on occasion, but this was an outright challenge. For a moment, Rob froze.

Adam broke free. Rob tensed. His body and his mind struggled to decide how to react.

"Hey," Lindsey said softly. Rob had forgotten that she was there. She took a step forward, reached out with both hands and slowly pushed down Rob's outstretched arm. "It's okay," she looked at Rob. His eyes were darting back and forth between his two sons.

Rob resisted. Anger flashed across his face again. "It's okay," she repeated. "Everyone's upset. Just let it go."

Rob looked down into her soft blue eyes. It was the first time he had noticed how beautifully bright they were. It was like a window into her soul and the message was warm and caring and soft. "Let it go," she said one last time.

The internal struggle was obvious to all. Rob's face was beat red in anger. The veins on his neck throbbed as his fists clenched and unclenched to their beat. Every fiber in him wanted to let loose; to smash and burn and destroy all the rage of the past few weeks. Only the horror of seeing himself let loose on his own sons was keeping it all at bay.

Slowly, agonizing slowly, Rob's shoulders finally loosened a bit. He nodded in agreement. Lindsey lowered her hands.

"Yeah let it go Dad!" Bobby suddenly broke the silence. Unlike his father, Bobby's anger was only getting worse. He was not sure if it was the disappointment in his father's weak response or the feeling of watching a woman who was not his mother have such a hold on Rob. Whatever it was, Bobby was not about to stand there and take it.

"Let it all go! Let mom go, let Nana go, let Adam go, and while you're at it, let me go!" He stormed across the room, opened the door to the porch and slammed it behind him.

"Bobby?" Rob called to him. He turned to look at his younger son for some sort of explanation. Adam just shrugged.

"Don't just shrug! Go after your brother!"

"But-"

"Go, I said!" Rob pointed towards the door Bobby had just slammed. "And don't come back until you have worked this all out!"

Three

"Sorry about that," Rob turned towards Lindsey after Adam had left.

"No worries," Lindsey smiled. Her long blonde hair was thrown all over her face and shoulders from the fight. "I can take a hit."

"Heh," Rob grinned as he turned back towards the other rooms. "C'mon." he waved.

Lindsey headed to her black purse lying on the floor of the living room while Rob strode straight towards the kitchen and the fridge. He needed another beer.

"They fight like that often?"

"Not really, no." Rob stopped for a moment to look over at Lindsey. She had grabbed her purse and was turning towards one of Grandma's full length mirrors.

"My hair is a mess."

"Didn't notice," Rob lied.

Lindsey chuckled as she took a brush from her purse and began straightening out her hair. It was not something Rob was used to. Lindsey had always kept her hair tied up under her helmet. To see it was so full and colorful was something new to Rob. He realized he liked it.

"Need another?" Rob opened the fridge and grabbed a Bud. "I am so stressed right now, even this piss tastes good."

"Sure," Lindsey put the brush away and reached out for the beer. She pulled at the top and the welcome fizz broke the tension.

Rob opened his beer as well. "To family," he toasted sarcastically.

"To family," Lindsey held the beer high and clinked Rob's beer so hard it almost spilled. Despite all the problems Rob was having, she knew how much family meant to him. More importantly, she knew how much it meant to her as well. At times like these she couldn't help but think of her mother, father and little brother all living back home in Buffalo. They could all be pains in their own way, but they were a tight knit family and always had been. Between her prep school life, her hockey, and going away to UCONN, it seemed like she had not spent any time at home in almost 15 years. She missed them all terribly.

Rob noticed Lindsey's mood but he was too much of an emotional mess himself to deal with it now. He decided to change the subject.

"Wanna hit the boxes again?"

"Sure!"

The two of them started back to the living room when Lindsey suddenly stopped. "Hey Rob, what was that special box the boys were carrying anyway?"

"Don't know," Rob shrugged. "That's what mom always called it. She said it was for her most special memories and keepsakes."

"Well why don't we start there?"

"You think?" Rob started to turn in that direction.

"Absolutely. If that is where the special stuff is, it should give us some idea of how all the other stuff is related. Maybe there is even some list or key. "

"Hey," Rob's face lit up as his pace quickened, "now that you mention it, I think there was something like that she had been working on."

The two of them hurried back into the bedroom, excited by the thought that all of their work could actually lead to something. Unfortunately, after the boys little escapade, the contents of the box were all over the floor. Any organization Nana might have had was completely lost. Rob stood over the mess, not knowing where to start.

"Hmmmm...," Lindsey thought as she got down on her knees and sifted through the pile. "There are all kinds of things in here; Figurines, booklets, more letters, pictures and stuff I don't even recognize."

"Well, "Rob sat down to join her, "let's see what we can figure out."

The two began sorting all the pieces first. Letters were placed to the right, pictures to the left, figurines on the bed so as not to break and anything they could not categorize went over in the corner. Rob recognized much of it from his childhood or from a story his mom told at dinner or bedtime. There were even mementos from his adult life or his own kids. Mom was a wonderful storyteller Rob remembered with nostalgia. As a boy growing up or as a man watching his own kids beg Nana to "tell more, tell more," Rob loved her stories. Sometimes she talked of family mishaps, other times it was about something Irish or even something supernatural. Rob had difficulty knowing what was true and what she made up. He pictured the many times that the entire family sat for over an hour at the dinner table just listening to one of her stories. It brought a smile to his face.

After almost an hour and three more beers each, they were beginning to make some headway. They were also getting a little buzzed.

"Oh my god, "Lindsey burst out with a laugh as she held up a picture. "Is this you?"

Rob laughed out loud as he reached for the picture. It was an official picture of him in full hockey gear that was taken by his college team. He was pretty proud of it too. The white jersey was straight and clean, he looked even taller in his skates and his shoulder pads made him look even stronger than he already was. His mother loved it especially since it was probably the only time his hair was ever straight while in uniform. "Whoa! I haven't seen that shot in years."

"How old were you?"

"About 20, I guess. That was the year we made it to the finals."

"At Tufts?" Lindsey remembered Rob telling them he had played division III hockey there.

"Yeah," Rob handed the picture back.

"You were hot!" Lindsey surprised herself and Rob with her bluntness. Rob was much closer to Lindsey's age in that picture and looked a little like the guy she used to date. It was the first time she thought of Rob as anything other than a father, husband and teammate. Maybe it was the beer.

"Guess so," He wasn't sure if he liked Lindsey's comment. He wasn't sure he didn't like it either. She was definitely hot, especially the way her hair was flowing seductively over her shoulders. Rob wondered if she realized how good she looked.

It actually pissed Rob off a little. He liked the way his life had been. He loved his wife and he loved his family. He loved his job and he loved playing hockey. Lindsey was a great teammate and a great friend. Any kind of relationship with Lindsey would ruin the entire team, not to mention what was left of his marriage and he wasn't ready to give up on that yet. He needed to control this.

"But," he quickly added, "I was already hooked up with Deborah by then."

"Really? When did you two meet?"

"Freshman year," Rob needed to change the subject. "What else is in there?"

"Let's see." Lindsey leaned forward to place the picture down in the pile and get another. Rob couldn't help but notice the enticing hint of cleavage she showed within his reach. *Fuck!* he swore to himself and looked away.

"Well," Lindsey fumbled through the pictures. She had noticed Rob's glance as well and felt equally uncomfortable. She also enjoyed it. "This one here looks like you and Deborah at a party or something."

"Oh my god!" Rob reached out and snapped the picture. "That's the party we met at. I had completely forgotten about that picture."

Again, an awkward tension filled the room. This was getting a little ridiculous. Lindsey sat quietly as Rob stared at the picture. His face somehow seemed to smile and squint and frown all at once. Lindsey even thought she caught the glimpse of a tear in his eye. After a few moments, she tried something different.

"How about these letters? They seem bound up pretty tight."

"Yeah, ok," Rob tucked the picture in his pocket. He was glad for the distraction. "Whatcha got?"

"A whole bunch of really old ones; But they seem to be much more important."

"How can you tell?"

"Each one is in a Ziploc bag," Lindsey held one up. "The others were all just thrown in boxes."

"Huh. Let me see one."

Lindsey handed Rob the Ziploc in her hands. "Be careful,"

Rob slowly opened the letter in his hands while Lindsey grabbed another from the pile. It was silent for several minutes while they each read the letters.

"Anything?"

"Not really. Just seems like a regular letter."

"Mine too," Rob folded it back up and returned it to the plastic bag. "Let's try a few more."

The next two letters were a little more interesting. There was a brief mention of owning some land up north as well as ties to some famous Americans. But there was no treasure map or lost wills like Rob had been romanticizing about. Lindsey suggested they put them to the side to read later.

"Wait a sec," Lindsey interrupted as she took out another letter. This one was in much better condition than the others. It seemed to be double bagged as well as wrapped in something like wax paper. Rob stopped what he was doing and waited.

Lindsey whistled. "Whoa."

"What?"

"No way!" Lindsey's eyes were fixated on the paper.

"What?!" Rob roared.

"The signature," Lindsey pointed to the bottom of the letter.

"What about it?"

"It says Franklin."

"Franklin. Who is Franklin?"

"You know," Lindsey's eyes grew wide. "Franklin!"

"Ben Franklin?" Rob quickly realized. Rob may have made it into Tufts on a partial athletic scholarship, but he was accepted for his academic credentials. He was no dummy. He knew what the Franklin name meant.

"No," Lindsey quickly corrected him. Rob's heart sank back down. "But I think it is from his son."

"What son? Ben Franklin had a son?"

"I think so. He talks about him like that."

"Let me see," Rob took the letter gently from Lindsey's outstretched hand.

"Look at the date," she pointed to the top of the letter.

"1785," Rob thought for a moment. "That's after the Revolution right?"

"I think so," Lindsey giggled with excitement. They both could feel they had found something big. "It's been awhile since high school history."

"Well I took some history classes in college and I am pretty sure this is after the Revolution."

"So?"

"So nothing," Rob shrugged. He kept reading.

"Look down the bottom," Lindsey pointed over his shoulder again. "See the signature?"

"William Franklin," Rob read.

"And notice right here in the middle," she pointed again. "He says something about his father."

"Would you let me read it?" Rob was getting a little irritated.

"Sure," Lindsey backed off. "Sorry."

Rob started reading from the top.

"He says he's writing from London."

"That's odd," Lindsey hadn't seen that. "What would he be doing in London?"

"And he talks about Canada and Loyalists."

"Loyalists?"

"Probably has something to do with the Revolution."

"Can you tell if he is related to Ben Franklin? If it is, it could be worth something."

"Not sure, not sure," Rob mumbled as he read further down. Lindsey watched Rob read. The anticipation was killing her.

"Wait, wait! Listen to this part."

"I have recently gathered in my possession, various documents and letters from my father concerning the most recent Treaty of Paris..."

"The Treaty of Paris?" Lindsey broke in.

"I think that is the Treaty that ended the war."

"With who?"

"England dummy,"

"Right, duh," Lindsey smacked herself in the head. "That's got to be his son."

"I think you're right," Rob grinned.

"Let's see if there are any other clues!" Lindsey turned back to the pile of letters. "Who knows what else is in there!"

Four

Rob slammed his black 2016 Toyota Camry's car door shut and walked to the trunk. He had no more time to think about letters or wills or Benjamin Franklin. Just as he and Lindsey had begun to get excited about the letter they found, the boys had returned from their fight and promptly reminded their dad that they had a practice to make. By the time he had got home from the rink, graded a few papers and thrown together a quick dinner, it was time for his own game.

Once a week, Rob got to be one of the boys again. The games were late at night, after the kids were already in bed or winding down. He never got enough sleep, but he also never took time away from his kids or wife. The only one who sacrificed was Rob and he was happy to do it. He had been playing hockey on the pond since he could stand and organized hockey since he was six. It was in his blood and he would have it no other way.

It wasn't glorious or for any trophy. Of course they did get a trophy if they won the championship but they were tiny twenty dollar trophies that made better book stands than anything else. Rob had a ton of them all over his house. Even after his wife made him throw some of them away, he still had what could only be called a clutter of silver, bronze and gold. It wasn't that Deborah had been against his playing hockey. After all, the boys were starting to bring home their own trophies and she had been an athlete herself. She just didn't want the house to turn into one large trophy case.

Hockey was like the family religion and Deborah knew that her husband needed that time to be one of the boys. She had even liked it. It gave her a little peace and quiet once a week when he kissed her goodbye at nine or ten o'clock at night. In some strange, back to high school sort of way, she even liked being married to a tough, athletic guy who got in the occasional fight. The bruises Rob came home with on a regular basis were her own little trophies that she would brag about to her friends whenever she got the chance.

Winning was always great. In the championships, the competition level was fierce. The game was faster and the hitting was harder. The rink even let the winner skate around the rink hoisting a beer keg over their head like it was the NHL finals. They jokingly called it the "Stanley Keg" and Rob had lifted it over his head many times in the past ten years. Still, the reason Rob never missed a game of late night beer league hockey was not because of the winning or the drinking.

It was the only place left in his life where he was still a boy. In the locker room, he was just Rob; not Mr. Callahan or Dad or husband or teacher or even son. He could be himself, let off some steam, joke with the guys and escape all the trappings of the everyday world.

Rob pulled his hockey bag out of the trunk, grabbed his sticks and slammed the trunk shut. If he hurried, he might have time to get his skates sharpened.

"Hey," a voice called from behind. Rob turned to see Lindsey jogging through the parking lot carrying her own bag and sticks. She was wearing a Buffalo Sabres shirt (for which she never received any peace. Most of the guys were Rangers or Bruins fans and they never let Lindsey forget that Buffalo hadn't ever won a cup or made it to the finals more than twice!) Her hair was tied up and she was wearing very little make-up. It was the way Rob was used to seeing her and he felt relieved.

"Hey," Rob replied as Lindsey matched his stride.

"I got a few minutes at home to look into this Will Franklin thing."

"Really?" Rob had almost forgotten this afternoon and just wanted to focus on the game.

"Yeah. I Googled his name and it came up right away."

"What did it say?"

"I'm not sure I believe it and I don't think you are going to like it."

"What?" Rob stopped walking, placed the butt end of his stick down on the ground and leaned on it. Then he hiked his hockey bag back up onto his shoulder and stared at Lindsey with acute interest.

"Well the good news is he is Benjamin Franklin's son," Lindsey explained as she too stopped and placed her stick perpendicular to the ground.

"Great! Then maybe it is worth something!"

"Maybe."

"Excuse me," a guy with a hockey bag interrupted. Rob and Lindsey realized they were standing directly in front of the rink doors. They moved to the side.

"Sorry," Rob said, turning back towards Lindsey. "What's the bad news?"

"They hated each other. It's almost unbelievable."

"Wait. What?"

Lindsey sighed. "I don't really understand why, but it seems that Will Franklin took the British side in the American Revolution and his father hated him for it."

"What?" Rob gasped. That made no sense at all. He knew enough American History to know what an important man Benjamin Franklin was. To think that he had a son that was a traitor, Rob just couldn't believe it. "You've got to be kidding."

"Don't think so," Lindsey shook her head. She did not know as much history as Rob did, but every kid in America knew Ben Franklin. It didn't make any sense to her either. "I'm not sure anyone is going to want a letter written by a traitor."

"Shit!" Rob slammed his stick down and started walking into the rink. Lou, the captain of his team was standing right at the front counter talking with the rink manager.

"Hey big guy," Lou said with a friendly smile, "something wrong?"

"Nah," Rob grumbled, smiling back at Lou. The sight of his old friend wiped away Rob's anger immediately. He and Lou went way back. Their kids had played together since mites and they had even coached a little together as well. They were like brothers in many ways. "Just some shit," Rob smiled wider as he patted Lou on the back, "nothing that a few hits can't clear out."

Lou smiled again as Rob walked past him. "Locker room 3," he called to Rob. "Hey Lindz," he turned to Lindsey as she passed by as well. "Ready?"

"Always," Lindsey smiled.

L3

1779

British Occupied New York City

William Franklin was in a good mood.

It was the perhaps the strangest feeling he ever had and it made no sense whatsoever. All around him were signs of depravation and suffering. Refugees from Connecticut, New Jersey, Pennsylvania, even as far away as the Carolinas crowded the streets of New York City. They suffered disease and malnutrition. They lived in crowded tenements and thrown together homes. The streets were dirty, the buildings still being rebuilt from the many fires that had plagued the city. Vagabonds and drunks roamed the city, buildings had been converted into warehouses and churches turned into hospitals as New York fell under the Martial law of the British Army.

What had once been a thriving economic bastion of energy and excitement had become a fortified Loyalist slum surrounded across the rivers by Patriot raiders. After George Washington had been run out of New York by the British Army, the city had emptied out of anyone with Patriot sympathies or leanings. In a city where rebels had torn down King George III's statue and melted it down into lead after July 4, 1776, now mighty British warships brought in thousands of soldiers. They were quickly followed by thousands and thousands of desperate Loyalist refugees who had been kicked off their land and were looking to the British to protect them from Patriot mobs, the war and their neighbors' reprisals.

Franklin knew exactly how his fellow Loyalist refugees felt. Just a few short years ago, they and the Rebels all lived together in peace and harmony. They all were members of the mightiest empire on earth and not only benefited from the protection of the British Army and Navy, they prospered under its economic might.

And now, suddenly they were hated, vilified in their own country. From the

Aristocrat who was protecting his position, to the veteran of colonial wars, to the farmer trying to support his family, to the slave hoping for the British promise of freedom and to the ardent Loyalist believing in King and Empire, no matter the reason, no matter the motive or lack thereof, they all were hated by their neighbors. And no one was hated more than William Franklin. He had become the ultimate symbol of Tory Loyalism. Governor of the colony of New Jersey and son of the famous Patriot Benjamin Franklin, William himself had originally benefited immensely from his father's fame. He had worked with his father in the famous kite experiment; he had worked with him on western land expansion and in politics. He had taken advantage even of his father's name to help himself become Governor of New Jersey. The two of them were not just partners, not just father and son, they were also friends.

But where his father had seen it to be his duty to defend the rights of the colonists, William had seen it to be his duty to uphold his office as Governor. The split had been slow at first; both men agreed that King and Parliament had made major mistakes in how they dealt with the colonies. But as the colonists became more extreme in their actions, Ben went in one direction and William in the other.

Stubbornly holding onto his power even after most Governors had abandoned their posts, and even after the war had begun, William not only refused to budge, he even began to inform the British government of the actions of the rebels. Finally, the Continental Congress ordered his arrest.

Now, two years later, William Franklin's defeat had been complete. Humiliated, arrested, imprisoned, he had lost so much weight, he was as he described himself to friends, "considerably reduced in flesh." He was bitter, angry and alone. Most of his peers had run away to England. His wife, never that healthy had died of a broken heart while William was in prison. His home had been taken. His only son, William Temple Franklin, had been stolen away by the grandfather Benjamin and worked with him for the Rebel cause. He had no job, no salary, no family, no future.

So why was he smiling? He wondered. As he took a left off of King Street and breathed a sigh of relief from the swollen crowds, he realized how free he actually was. An enormous weight had been lifted off his shoulders, as if the hand of the angel Gabriel had swept down and gently removed a sack full of immense stones from his back. No longer must he balance his sympathy for the plight of the American colonists with his duty to his King. They had destroyed any sympathy he had with their mobs and the destruction of everything and everyone he held dear. For the first time maybe ever in his life, he had one purpose and one purpose only; to win this war for the King.

He knew of the power of the Loyalists. He knew how many men and families had suffered under the Patriot mobs and he knew that with the proper leader and direction, they could become a powerful force.

William Franklin was that leader, he realized. He had influence, he had connections, and he had thousands of loyalists living in the city that he could recruit. With a little time and a little luck, he could gain back everything he had lost.

He knocked lightly on the door of the Blacksmith shop. This was not his first stop in his recruitment drive but it was an important one.

"Thomas Appleby?" William asked as the door opened slowly.

"Yes," Thomas replied opening the door just enough so he could see. The years of worry and stress had not been kind to Thomas. His hair had begun to gray, his hands had grown even more calloused and cut and he seemed to always be stuck in a permanent hunch.

When Thomas had lived on the farm, and worked in the open fields, the fresh air and sunlight kept him alive and moving. The work was just as hard of course, but when he tired of one chore, there was always another. He could even take a break now and then and lie in the grass or take a short walk to the nearby stream.

Having left that all behind now, Thomas worked only as a blacksmith and even though the money was good and the work regular, it had taken its toll on his body. Worrying about his eldest son Samuel and the rest of the family took its toll on his mind.

He had not heard from Samuel in over a year. At first, letters had come fairly regularly. He knew most of them were being read by both sides, and that it was dangerous to even correspond with his son, but he had to know.

The last letter they had received had been a few months after Washington's incredible victory crossing the Delaware at Trenton. Even though they had taken the British by surprise and captured over one thousand Hessians, Samuel was still in great danger. That had been Washington's first real victory and most critics pointed out that it was only because he had taken them by surprise on Christmas day. No one expected that band of farmers and shopkeepers to stand a chance against the mightiest army on earth. It was only a matter of time, Thomas feared, before he heard of his son's capture, or even worse.

"Can I help you?" Thomas stuck his head out slowly, staring through the partially opened door at the stranger in front of him. William Franklin may have been neatly dressed in his red Gentlemen's overcoat, matching knee breeches, stockings and black silk cravat perfectly woven around his neck, but after two years living in occupied New York, Thomas had learned to trust no one. Of course most of the city was bound together in their common loyalism, but there were spies and immoral people everywhere. Everything you said was suspect. Every action you took, questioned. It was a paranoid fearful time where friend and neighbor could become enemies in a heartbeat. It was dangerous to have an opinion and dangerous to become known.

"Governor William Franklin," he introduced himself. The title was still his. No rebel Congress could take that away. "May I come in?"

"Of course," Thomas nervously swung the door wide. He quickly brushed his hands on his brown burlap apron and shook the Governor's hand. He had met many important men in the city, officers and men of power, but this was his first Governor.

"T-take a seat," Thomas let go of Franklin and waved in the direction of his small square, dark oak kitchen table. It was surrounded by four wobbly light brown chairs that in no way matched the table. Obviously it was a mismatched set. That didn't bother Thomas anymore. Just having a home, a kitchen table, was an accomplishment in this day and age. He grimaced slightly as he looked at the fourth chair. It of course still had never been used. One chair for himself, one for his daughter Anne, one for Isaac and the fourth one was for Samuel for when he returned from the war. "Can my daughter make you some tea?"

"Tea?" the Governor repeated with a smile. He knew what a treat that was. After all, tea had become the drink of pride for any loyalist in America. While the rebels refused it as a matter of protest, for men like Franklin it was just one more way he could show his support for the Crown. He was surprised Thomas even had some. In New York, any provisions were hard to come by. Inflation had spiraled almost out of control and famine was often around the corner now that the French, Spanish and pirate fleets had begun raiding British trade. "I would love some." He placed his fancy walking cane next to the kitchen table legs and pulled out a chair.

"Anne!" Thomas shouted to his daughter.

"You needn't shout," Anne scolded as she quickly appeared from around the corner. There were after all only three rooms in the home; a bedroom that Thomas, Anne and Isaac shared, a kitchen and a dining/living area. The home had been a Patriots home before the British occupation and Thomas had been lucky enough to keep it. Most of the other abandoned homes had been given to officers and soldiers but whether it was because Thomas had become an important Blacksmith in town or they just had overlooked him, he had managed to keep it for a year now.

"Oh," Anne noticed the Governor sitting in the chair. "I am sorry. I did not realize we had company."

"Anne," her father introduced them, "Meet Governor William Franklin of New Jersey. Governor Franklin, my daughter Anne."

"Pleased to make your acquaintance," Anne curtsied nervously. Her dirty white gown bent awkwardly and she felt ashamed dressed so casually in the Governor's presence.

"The pleasure is all mine," Governor Franklin smiled as he ignored her discomfort and quickly rose to kiss Anne's hand. She may have been dressed poorly but even through her work clothes her beauty was stunning. In the two years in New York, Anne had changed even more than her father. The lanky, incomplete teenager had grown into a full figured, beautiful woman. From her free flowing auburn hair, to her perfectly shaped breasts, to the long muscular legs, Anne was a sight to behold. Even dressed as she was, she took the Governor's breath away.

"I am honored to meet such a beautiful, talented woman such as yourself," The Governor quickly recovered. "Your father must be very proud."

Anne looked at her father in sudden confusion. What was the Governor talking about? Her father just shrugged his shoulders.

"Your reputation precedes you," The Governor sensed their confusion.

"Reputation?" Anne repeated. "I was not aware I had a reputation."

"It is nothing to be ashamed of," The Governor could see that Anne was drawing the wrong conclusion. "I talk only of your talent for singing." He smiled and turned towards Thomas. "Your beautiful voice is the talk of the Army," he explained. "Even though I have only been in the city a short time, I have heard of it already."

Anne blushed. This was the first time she had ever heard any of this. Most of the men she encountered in the theater were drunk and condescending. They stared at her breasts or even grabbed her legs when she strayed too close to one of them. They complimented not her voice, but her body. It made Anne feel dirty and ashamed.

She never would have taken the job in the first place if her father had not suggested it. They needed money now more than ever and with Anne being almost twenty, she was more than capable of taking care of herself. Besides, her father was hoping to get any news on her brother Samuel. The theater was not only attended by officers and soldiers, many of the actors themselves were members of the British Army. As both a singer and a servant, Anne would be able to find out lots of information about what the army was doing.

"That is kind of you to say," her father said quickly. He was not sure how he felt about his daughter's new found fame. He was both proud and afraid. Anyone of notice in these dangerous times could become a target or worse, accused of spying. "Would you mind making the Governor some tea?" he turned back to Anne and asked softly, trying to change the subject. He still had no idea what Governor Franklin wanted with him.

"Of course," Anne replied as she returned to the kitchen in search of some tea.

"So," Thomas turned to the Governor and indicated the chair again, "what can I do for you sir? Do you need some tools or something for your horse perhaps?"

"I am not here for your smith skills," the Governor sat down again. The chair squeaked loudly on the wooden floors and strained visibly under the Governor's weight, "at least not in manufacture. I am here for your knowledge of the city."

"The city?" Thomas frowned. He had hoped the Governor was there as a customer. A rich gentleman like Franklin would be great for his shop. "What do I know of the city that can be of help to a man like yourself?"

"Let me be more clear," the Governor leaned forward. Despite his weaker state and frail frame, he could still be intimidating. His eyes held an intensity and a passion that made Thomas feel uncomfortable and even nervous. He was not completely sure he trusted the man.

"I am recruiting men like yourself to help his majesty win this war."

"Men like myself?"

"Friends of the King," the Governor waved his hand, "Loyalists; who the rebels so inaccurately call Tories."

Thomas nodded in understanding.

"This unfortunate misunderstanding is at a critical juncture," the Governor began to explain. It sounded almost like a rehearsed speech but it did not lack for passion. Thomas chuckled ironically at the phrase "unfortunate misunderstanding". It was always the Gentleman's way; to take horrible consequences and tragedies that destroyed everyday lives, ruined families and refer to them only as unfortunate misunderstandings. Would these men ever understand how the games they played affected the common man? Thomas had often mused. "Rebels and Loyalists attack each other in the countryside with barbarity," the Governor's voice rose, "destroying homes and livelihoods. The Rebel army is in disarray, despite their successes at Trenton and our withdrawal from Philadelphia. George Washington and his men barely made it through the winter at Valley Forge alive and their illegal Continental Congress can do nothing to aid them. Their currency is practically worthless and the colonies fight and argue with each other almost more than they unite against us."

"But what of Saratoga?" Thomas returned. He knew of the incredible blow the rebels had struck in upper New York State. A British victory would have ended the war right then if not for Benedict Arnold. Instead it helped convince the French and others that maybe they should aid this new United States.

"A setback to be sure," the Governor admitted, "but the King has more than 30,000 troops here in the colonies and Washington's army is filled with worthless boys and inexperienced farmers. It will only take one capital stroke to finally end this foolish enterprise."

"Do you really think so?" Thomas wondered. One of those "worthless boys" the Governor was talking about was his own son Samuel. He had not even allowed himself to envision an end to all of this suffering. It tore him in so many directions. After all, if they won, what would that mean? Would he be allowed to return home? Would the King forgive all that transpired? And what of Samuel? Would he be hanged if he even survived?

And what if they lost? What would happen to Isaac and Anne? Where would they go? Would the Patriots let them leave or would they be killed by some mob. No matter how Thomas saw it, any end was a horror too awful to imagine. His greatest wish was just to see it all stop and for things to go back to the way they were.

"I do," Franklin affirmed. "But not without Loyalist help."

"Here is your tea Governor," Anne interrupted as she walked slowly across the room with the small plain teacup in hand. "I hope it is too your liking."

"I am sure it will be," the Governor smiled as Anne placed the warm cup and plate in front of the Governor and waited for his approval. Steam was still rising from the tea. The Governor bent over and breathed the warm aroma into his lungs. He smiled and placed a hand gently on Anne's side.

"People like you and your daughter are the key to this entire war," the Governor continued, looking up into Anne's innocent blue eyes for a moment. Despite everything Anne had seen, and everything she had lived through in her short life, the beauty and hope of youth still burned inside her. Through her eyes and into his own, Franklin could feel her frustration, her anger and her passion fueling his own determination to win the future. "You are the heart and soul of the very meaning of why we fight!" He clenched his fist as his voice rose. He looked at Thomas for a moment. "Indeed, of everyone involved, you and I have the most to lose even after we have lost so much already. Anne, my dear," he looked into her eyes again, "what have you lost in this war?"

"I have lost my brother," Anne said immediately. The anger in her voice bit the air.

"My sympathies."

"Not to war, at least not that I know. But to passion."

"Passion?"

"You know of what I speak," Anne explained. "The passion of the mob, the passion of teenage boys who think they are men."

"I understand," Franklin realized. "Your brother joined the other side."

"He is a good boy," Thomas interrupted. He did not want anyone judging his son or worse the rest of his family. "But he fell prey to the voices of discontent."

"No one is more aware than I," Franklin frowned angrily, unconsciously clenching and unclenching his fists. He recalled his famous father, the death of his wife and the loss of his son, "of the power of those voices and the pain of family torn apart by it."

"But," he threw off the dark thoughts and almost shouted, "let us talk of the future instead and what we can do about it." He pointed to the empty chair next to him. "Anne, my dear, please join us."

Anne looked nervously at her father who simply nodded.

"Thank you Governor," she said, folding her dress behind her legs and sitting down.

"My friends," Franklin's voice was soothing and gentle for now he felt a common bond with the Applebys; the bond of lost family. "I am putting a group together, a board if you will, of associated Loyalists. Its purpose will be to not only help the many of us who are displaced and wanting, but to recruit able bodied men to form regiments and fight for his majesty."

"Aren't there Loyalist units already?" Anne asked.

"Yes, yes of course," the Governor quickly replied. "But this will be different. The numbers in New York City alone dwarf the size of Washington's army and with a united leadership, they will turn the tide."

"There certainly are thousands of refugees," Thomas agreed.

"And more every day," Franklin added.

"And with the Dunmore declaration," Anne said, "even more escaped slaves are joining the ranks."

"Of course my dear," Franklin smiled. He agreed with the British strategy of promising freedom to any slave who escaped. He knew as a politician himself that the promise was about winning the war and not about any moral high ground. While slavery was illegal now in England, the slave trade itself was still in effect and British colonies worldwide still used slavery as the basis for their economy. But if the British promised the escaped American slaves their freedom it would not only add to the ranks of loyal subjects it would decimate the Southern economy. "This is a war in which all manner of people; aristocrat and slave, farmer and shopkeeper all have a stake. We will prove to the King that Americans know how to behave. We are not the rabble these rebels show to the world."

"I cannot fight," Thomas broke the mood. "I swore to my son that I would not be pressured by the rebels, and I will not be pressured by you either. I am a free man."

"I am not asking you to fight," the Governor corrected Thomas. *How stupid of this man to think I wanted an old, bent man such as himself in the first place,* the Governor thought to himself. Still, he was clearly disappointed in Thomas' attitude and pressed on. "I am simply asking you for some names."

"Names?" Thomas repeated.

"That is why I am here," the Governor sat back as if he had just announced the secret to a mystery. "I know of your feelings towards fighting. I know of your past in Connecticut. I always make sure I know who I am talking to before I enter any conversation."

Anne was nodding her head in understanding. The Governor noticed.

"That is why I knew of your daughter's singing talents," he smiled at her again, "and how I know you can help me in my cause."

"What kind of names are you looking for?"

"As a blacksmith you know many quality men and you know what kind of occupations these men have when you fix their tools and weapons."

"I do," Thomas agreed.

"Well then would you tell me which ones may be willing to aid our majesty in this war?"

It was Thomas' turn to sit back now. He looked at his daughter. She shrugged in confusion. The Governor took a slow sip of tea. Thomas was still not sure how much he trusted Franklin. He didn't like the man much; he didn't like any Gentleman much. Franklin represented much of what he hated in the King's government. Still, he knew of the man before he had walked into his home. The Franklin name was known all across America of course, both father and son. Never in all the years before the war, had William Franklin done anything that could be dishonorable. He appeared to be a patient, fair man who listened to his constituents and tried to understand their concerns. His stubbornness to remain loyal even reflected Thomas' own stubbornness. He could clearly see that Franklin was a man of principle and conviction, much like himself, who would not be bullied into choosing a side unless he himself believed in it. And most importantly, he understood the pain of broken families.

"Of course," Thomas finally said. He could think of no reason not to. He was only giving the Governor names of people who had publicly professed their love for the King. No trouble could come of that.

"Wonderful," the Governor smiled. He looked at Anne who was smiling as well. She was glad the conversation would be an amicable one. Anne held no misgivings about helping the King as her father did. She resented everything the Patriots stood for and felt only anger towards them and what they had done to her brother. His abandonment of the family had placed her in a role she never wanted and a role she hated. She was no longer the innocent daughter, protected and sheltered by her father and big brother. She was the second in command, the confidant of her father and in some ugly way she resented, the substitute for her dead mother. All Anne had wanted ever since she was little was to have a close, loving family where they could work hard and laugh together every night at the dinner table. The Patriots had stolen that all away from her. They had stolen away her future.

"What of John Adams?" she immediately suggested to her father.

"John Adams?" Franklin almost spit out his tea.

"Ha!" both Thomas and Anne laughed joyfully. "He gets that all the time," Thomas explained through chuckles. "Not *that* John Adams."

"Heh," Franklin joined in. "I understand. I spent enough time in New England to learn that there are more Adams families than there is corn on their cobb."

"We may think it is funny," Anne said. "But John doesn't. Sharing your name with one of the most famous rebels in America is quite an inconvenience."

Anne realized immediately the error or her words and blushed. Thomas blushed as well.

"No worry my dear," Franklin waved off the comment and smiled. He had more than gotten used to being the son of Benjamin Franklin. "I completely understand."

"Tell me of this John Adams," the Governor suddenly looked like a cat that caught the canary. Having a Franklin and an Adams fighting on both sides of the revolution was an irony he would love to exploit.

"He is from Connecticut," Thomas began.

"Fairfield," Anne interrupted.

"And he has already enlisted in the King's army," Thomas continued.

"But he is quite discontent," Anne interrupted as she saw the look of confusion on the Governor's face.

"They do not treat him well," Thomas went on, "nor do they carry out their promises."

"Of course," the Governor nodded in understanding. "I have seen too many times how the British officers look at us. They often do not treat us as equals and constantly refer to us as colonials."

"He also has an infant son and his wife is pregnant with another."

"But could he leave them to help the cause?"

"He also has an older son Jonathan who can help out."

"He is seventeen," Anne added.

"And if father is not interested," Franklin finished, "maybe son would be."

"Hey, hey cut it out," a young voice and sounds of struggle could be heard from outside. "Leave me alone!"

Anne turned to her father. "That's Isaac's voice!"

"Isaac?"

"My son," Thomas got up quickly and headed towards the door.

"Settle down boy," an unidentified voice could be heard from the other side of the door. There were more sounds of pushing and shoving and then there was a series of angry knocks on Thomas' front door.

"Thomas Appleby!" the voice called.

Thomas opened the door immediately. In front of him was a uniformed British soldier, rifle holstered over his shoulder, holding Isaac by the scruff of the neck. The soldier had a smug look on his face and his uniform was dusty from the roads and muddy below the knees from what, Thomas could not tell.

"Is this your boy?" he asked, pulling Isaac in front of him as the teenager continued to struggle. Isaac's blonde hair had grown darker over the years and it hung all over his face like a mop. Dirt had dried together several strands of hair as well as spots on his face as if he had been swimming in mud. Indeed his boots were still dripping water and his brown trousers were darker below the knees as if he had been wading in the river.

"Let me go!" Isaac shouted as he grabbed the soldier's arm in vain. Still a young teen of thirteen, Isaac had not yet had a growth spurt and his strength was still more of a boy's than a man. It had frustrated him even more now that his older brother was gone and Isaac was expected to sometimes act older than he truly was. Yet one more reason for him to be angry at the rebels for taking his brother away.

"Let me go!" Isaac repeated as he fell forward. The soldier chuckled as he purposely let the boy fall to the dirt from his efforts. He looked again at Thomas. "Is this your son?" he repeated.

"He is," Thomas made no attempt to help his son up. This was not the first time the boy had gotten into trouble. "What's the boy done?" Thomas thought about adding "this time" but he did not want to give the soldier any more information that might lead to his son's arrest, or worse.

"We found him spying on the prison ships."

"Spying?" Thomas looked in shock down at his son who was only now getting up and wiping the dirt off his brown trousers.

"I wasn't spying," Isaac quickly protested. "I was looking for Samuel."

"On the prison ships?" Thomas looked past his son to the street beyond. Neighbors were starting to congregate around his home. He tried to ignore them.

"Not on the ships," Isaac was annoyed. His father knew even if he could get near the prison ships, he would never go on them. They were a mass of disease and pestilence. Dark, dank, overcrowded and filled with way more rebel prisoners of war than they could ever carry, these converted British ships had rightly earned the nicknamed "Hell ships". If Samuel was on one of those ships, he wouldn't last long anyway.

"I was just on the shore watching the ships," Isaac looked up at the British soldier again, repeating what he had said four or five times already. "I thought maybe I might hear something."

"Precisely what a spy would say," the soldier said.

"No, no," Isaac's voice shook. He knew spies were hanged, regardless of their age. "I was hoping to hear something about my brother."

"Your brother who fights for the rebels," the soldier added. Now it was sounding even worse.

"It's not like that," Isaac protested.

"Sir," the soldier turned to Thomas. "Your son was caught spying in a secure area. He can give no good reason for his actions and the fact that his older brother, your son, is a known soldier for the Rebels, dictates I must take your son in for questioning."

"No!" Thomas protested. "You can't. He is just a boy."

"He would not be the first boy found to be a spy."

"Maybe I can help," Governor Franklin came to the door.

"G-Governor Franklin sir," the soldier recognized him. "What are you doing here?"

"This is the home of a loyal subject of his majesty," the Governor answered formally. "I was talking with him about ways in which we can help the cause and defeat these rebels once and for all. You can take him at his word. If his son was not spying, he was not spying."

"B-but sir," the soldier protested. He was disappointed that he would not get the satisfaction of turning in a spy and worried that he had somehow made a mistake with the Governor as well.

"Do not worry," the Governor sensed the man's conflict. He had been in politics and war enough to read men quickly, "I will make sure your superiors know of your diligence. Now please, leave the boy with us."

"Yes sir," the soldier said as he saluted awkwardly then realized the Governor was not military. He frowned.

"You may go," the Governor commanded.

"Th-thank you sir," the soldier said as he slowly turned and headed back towards King Street. The crowd of neighbors parted to let him through and turned their gaze towards the Governor. He ignored them and turned back towards the home and the kitchen.

"That could have been very ugly."

"Thank you Governor, thank you," Thomas shook the Governor's hand vigorously then closed the door behind them. He pushed his son to the front of the room. Isaac almost tripped but managed to stop himself before hitting his head on the table.

"Of course," the Governor smiled and returned to his tea. It had stopped steaming by now but it was still drinkable. "I know what a loyal subject you are. Now," he said as he took another sip and gestured for Thomas to sit down. "Tell me some more names like John Adams."

Five

The rink was like every other rink in North America. The white ice had the standard three red and two blue lines, the red circles, face off dots and nets were all standard issue and even the boards had the same ads that just about every rink in New England had. A sign for Friendly's, Jordan's furniture and USA Hockey along with a "Head's UP Hockey" logo all covered the puck marked boards. Only the empty wooden bleachers told the occasional fan that this was a beer league game. During the day and especially on weekends, there were always moms and especially Dads standing by the glass or sitting in the bleachers drinking coffee or hot cocoa, complaining about how much the equipment cost or commenting on the lack of eyesight from any referee. However, by 9:00 at night no one was interested in watching a bunch of adults try to recapture their lost glory on a frozen sheet ice.

So no one was there to see Rob sitting in the penalty box again. He didn't care. None of the guys did, especially his teammate Stevie who was sitting right next to him. They didn't play this game for the fans or the attention. And the last thing Rob would want would be to have to explain to his wife again why he almost got in another fight.

"Thanks for getting my back," Stevie turned to Rob as the referee shut the penalty box door in front of them.

"It's what I do," Rob grinned and slid to his right. There was barely enough room for them on the small bench. He would have to tighten up just to let Stevie in.

Penalty boxes were of course not designed for comfort or style. Sandwiched in between your team's bench and the score keeper, they isolated the player from everyone else in an attempt to make him feel some sense of community disapproval. That never worked with Rob however. Maybe the first time he was penalized, when he was five or six years old, he might have felt some sense of shame. He still remembered the shouts and threats from the other team, the screams from parents in the stands and the look on his mother's face just before she turned away in disapproval. Who knows, he might have given up hockey in that one moment until he turned towards his own bench and saw his teammates and coaches smiling at him.

"Nice job son," his father had explained after the game. "You stood up for your teammates and protected your friends."

It hadn't taken Rob long to understand what his father was getting at. Hockey was a violent game. Emotions ran high as people hit one another at alarming speeds. In a split second, you could deflect a pass and launch the puck into the net or find yourself face down on the cold ice with your head ringing in your ears. It was raw instinct and almost instantaneous reflex. Rob loved it.

But more than anything, hockey was a team sport. As sticks and pucks and bodies flew all over the ice, the only thing that protected you was the guy sitting next to you. The enemy, boys just like you in another sweater, would do anything to knock you over and go right through you to score that goal. Rob had once heard the term "cold warriors," applied to his sport. It was the best phrase he had ever heard.

Rob's coaches knew he had the skill to go far. He had the reflexes and the strength to stick handle and shoot. He had the size to park himself in front of the net despite the enemy whacking him and slashing him with their sticks. He had the leg strength and stride to move from blue line to blue line with grace and style. And most importantly, he had heart.

Despite his many visits to the penalty box over the years, Rob never thought of himself as a fighter. He never went out of his way to pick a fight and never hit a man when he was down. It was simple to Rob; protect your team, stand up for your friends. As one of the biggest guys on the ice, Rob knew that job fell to him. Whether he was knocking an enemy away from his goalie or jumping in to protect one of his smaller teammates, Rob was there.

"And you do it so well," Stevie grinned back through the black helmet cage covering his face. He loved having Rob on the team. It made Stevie's job as an agitator so much safer. He lost count of how many times when he was about to get jumped on by two, three or four guys; that Rob skated over and smashed his way into the fray. It was strange, he realized; how he and Rob seemed to be so much alike when they physically were so different. Stevie was the shortest guy on both teams. He did not have Rob's skill or his strength. But he had Rob's passion. No matter where the puck was or who was carrying it, Stevie would be there. He skated around the ice like a gnat or a fly buzzing around the enemy and annoying the crap out of him. Guys liked to joke that he only had two switches; on and off.

"This is your second time in the box right?" Stevie watched his teammates on the ice defending their own goal. Their penalties meant that the team had to play with one less player, so they had to collapse into the middle of the ice for protection. It was like the way settlers on the Oregon Trail had formed a circle when being attacked by Indians, except in hockey, they formed a box.

"Yup."

Lou stuck out his stick, intercepted the enemies pass then shot the puck down the ice towards the goalie. The delay allowed him to skate towards his bench. Rob saw Lindsey jump on the ice to replace him.

"Nice play Lou!" Rob shouted through the glass partition.

"We still got two more periods," Stevie reminded him.

"I know," The league had a three penalty rule. Rob would be kicked out of the game with one more.

"Don't get another one; I need you to cover my back." Stevie punched Rob's shin pad with his gloved hand. Neither player felt anything through their equipment of course but both understood the gesture.

The play on the ice changed. Rob tensed as he watched. Stevie started to rise. "Fuck!" He slammed his stick on the plexiglass in front of him.

"That go in?" Stevie's body had blocked Rob's view of the net.

"Fuck yeah," Stevie lifted up the rusty metal door lock and opened the penalty box door. The bar gave out the loud "clunk" it always did. "Friggin point man just ripped a slap-shot past Timmy."

"Shit."

Stevie stepped back onto the ice. The score was now 2-1 against and the power play was over. "See you in a few," he closed the door behind him. The boards slammed into place and the Plexiglas vibrated back and forth for several seconds. Rob would have to finish his match penalty regardless of the score.

The game continued on with the same level of intensity. Once Rob got out of the box, he picked up where he left off and took over the center of the ice. His size allowed him to protect the puck from most of the opponents' stick checks and his speed kept them off balance. By the middle of the second period, he had managed to take a pass from Lindsey and tie the score.

Lindsey had the best hands on the team. One instant the puck would be on her stick, the next it was speeding towards a teammate or whizzing over the goalie's shoulder. It meant that most of the men in the league treated her with respect. They had to. Her skill was too great. But every team seemed to have one asshole who hated being beat by a woman. Lindsey had to keep her head up all the time to avoid a shot to the head or a cross check in the back. Nothing upset those guys more than when Lindsey deeked past them and scored a goal.

"Watch number six," Rob warned Lindsey during the short break before the third period. "I think he has it in for you."

"I know. He already slashed my ankle twice."

"Guys a dick," Stevie said. "He cross checked me from behind and I was nowhere near the puck."

"Yeah but you're Stevie," Rick joked.

The guys all laughed, Stevie gave Rick a look and the buzzer went off to signal the start of the third period. Lindsey and Rob jumped over the boards and lined up at center ice. "Watch this," Rick said to the guys on the bench. He had noticed that "the dick" was out on the ice and lined up next to Lindsey.

Even before the puck was dropped, Lindsey and "the dick" were going at it. They pushed and shoved each other, trying to force themselves into a better position before the puck drop. They whacked each other's skates with their sticks. The referee had to break them up twice.

As the play developed, Rob found himself heading towards the opposing net while Lindsey chased the puck down the side of the ice and into their corner. A defenseman from the other team was standing practically still along the white and yellow boards struggling to get control of the bouncing puck. Lindsey saw her opportunity and rushed towards him. In one swift motion she lifted his stick, pulled the puck away from him and turned to make the play. At that exact moment, "the dick" took advantage of Lindsey's exposed position and skated full speed towards her.

Rob could see what was about to happen but could do nothing to stop it. Frustrated and shocked, he glared as "the dick" came up from behind Lindsey, held both hands on his stick and shoved her violently head first into the boards. Her body crumpled.

In two strides, Rob was on top of him. His speed and anger hit "the dick" hard into the boards. He was shocked but he did not fall. With a wave and a snap, Rob's hockey gloves slid off his hands and fell to the ice below.

"You fuckin' asshole!" Rob punched him with the full force of his fist squarely in the nose. Fortunately for Rob, "the dick" was not wearing a facemask or a cage; otherwise Rob's fists would hurt more than the other guy's head. Without any protection for his face, "the dick's" nose flattened under Rob's hand and quickly started to bleed. He fell backward onto the ice.

All hell broke loose. The defenseman on the other team grabbed Rob by the shoulders. Another of Rob's teammates rushed in to help. Two players from the enemy jumped in. Lindsey managed to get on her feet and swung at the guy on Rob. She loved the fact that Rob and her teammates were there for her, but she wasn't going to let them fight her battles for her. Even the goalie from the other team jumped in.

As with all men's league hockey games, the referees stood back and watched. They were not paid enough to get in between two grown men (or women) trying to destroy each other. They blew their whistles a few times and waited for everyone to get tired. By the time it was over, Rob had managed to flatten two of the other team's players while "the dick" skated off the ice, hands covering his face trying to hold back the blood coming from his nose.

"Out you go," the ref placed his hands on Rob's shoulder. It was Nick. He and Rob went way back. Nick and he even used to play on the same team for a while before Nick decided he liked the money from reffing more than the money he paid to play. He gave Rob a smile as he pointed towards the locker room. "That's your third one Rob; Plus a game."

"A game?" Rob protested, "For what?"

Nick was not going to even dignify that with a response, he just rolled his eyes and watched Rob skate towards his bench.

"Way to go Rob," Lou handed Rob his extra stick and water bottle. "Been waiting awhile to see that asshole get what's coming to him."

"Thanks," Rob took the stick and water bottle. "Finish this one off for me guys," he said as he turned and headed off the ice. He would have to watch the rest of this from the other side of the glass.

Six

Rob was still sitting in his equipment. He had taken off his helmet, shoulder and elbow pads, jersey and gloves and was sitting shirtless on the bench in the locker room. Some of the other guys were already undressed and heading into the showers. A few were half dressed like Rob, sitting back and drinking the beer the rink had delivered after the game. Their pants, hockey socks and skates were still on and steam rose from their bodies despite the coldness of the rink.

Rob leaned back against the cold blue concrete locker room wall and sipped his beer. Sweat was still dripping down his hairy chest and the coolness of the wall felt good on his warm back. He loved these surreal moments when his senses were still on high alert and he could feel and taste and smell everything. The high of hockey still held back the real world and as long as he stayed in this moment, kept on his skates, sipped his beer, leaned back and watched, he felt like time itself slowed down.

He always felt completely drained after a hockey game, fight or no fight. The emotional high and the intensity with which he played slowly dissipated amidst the laughter and beer in the locker room. Everyone to a man agreed that the joking and drinking after the game was just as treasured as the game itself.

"Good win boys," Rob held up his plastic cup of beer.

"Fuck yeah," Timmy held up his empty cup from the corner he took over. As the goalie, Timmy was always given space. Heck his shoulder pads alone took up the space of two guys. "You made my job easy," he stepped over his equipment and held out the empty cup to Lou.

"You kept us in it till we woke up," Lou picked up the pitcher, stepped over all the equipment bags and hockey crap laying all over the rubber matted floor and refilled Timmy's cup.

"I thought it was Lou's stellar defensive play," Marty quipped. He and Lou had been a defensive pair longer than anyone remembered. They didn't dominate like they used to, but they played like they always knew where the other was.

"Someone had to get your back."

"C'mon Lou," Stevie picked up his towel and wrapped it around his small naked body. He grabbed his shampoo and headed towards the showers. "Marty had a good night. He only tripped over the blue line, what four or five times?"

"Six," Mary corrected him with a smile.

"Hey Rob," Billy walked out of the showers carrying his towel in his hand and dripping water on the floor. His large naked body was still soaking wet. It seemed that Billy always had something to say the moment he finished showering and could never wait long enough to dry himself off or cover himself either. "Nice fight."

"Thanks."

"No I mean it," Billy insisted. He stepped over his own equipment bag and finally began toweling himself off. Billy was another passionate, big player like Rob. At first, Rob had found Billy to be a chippy, dirty player. He spent more time in the box than anyone on the team. But over the years, Billy proved to be the man everyone went to when they were in trouble. No matter what happened, no matter whether you were right or wrong, Billy was there to hurt the other guy and defend his teammates. He also had the biggest smile of anyone on the team. When Billy smiled, an almost sinister smile sometimes, the tension in the room just drained away.

"That dick caught Lindsey totally from behind." Billy looked over at Lindsey and smiled his famous smile. He looked back towards Rob. "If you hadn't dealt with him, he would have answered to me."

Lindsey smiled back at Billy. "I wouldn't wish that on anyone."

The comfort level in the room still astounded Lindsey and made her feel immensely welcome. Here she was, in a locker room full of naked and half naked men, toweling themselves off and walking back and forth to the shower with their ass and penis in full view, and no one acted any differently with her there. Billy, always the most open and honest of anyone, hadn't even bothered to cover himself up as he talked to Lindsey. His square shoulders, wet hairless chest, slight beer belly and even his "junk" were a mere five feet away. That's just how he talked to everybody. There was no better proof that they all considered her an equal part of the team.

Still, Lindsey remained in her equipment. Like Rob, she had shed her top layers and sat on the bench in a sports bra and hockey pants. When she first joined the team, she had dressed in another locker room. But Billy would hear none of that. If she was going to lay it all out on the ice like the rest of them, she belonged with them. The only compromise Lindsey had made, (more with herself than anyone on the team), was that she waited until all the guys were done with the shower before she went. Showering with the guys was not a line she was ready to cross yet.

Billy laughed, wrapped the towel around his waist and turned back to Rob. "Seriously Rob," Billy's tone suddenly changed. "You really went at that guy. I haven't seen you that wound up in a while."

"Yeah," Stevie poked his head out from the showers. He was covered in soap and dripping but that didn't seem to bother anyone. "You jumped in to help me pretty quickly. Can't remember the last time you had two fights in one game."

"Yours wasn't a fight. If it had been, Ref would have thrown me out the first time."

"Roughing then."

"Something wrong Rob?" Lou leaned forward. He was still in his full equipment, somehow more relaxed in it than not. "You seemed pretty steamed before the game too."

"Nah," Rob lied. He bent down and began untying his skates. It was a clear sign that he was not interested in talking. "Just shit from the funeral is all."

"That was a nice spread," Rick headed towards the showers. "Didn't expect anything edible at an Irish funeral," He laughed. Rob tried to whack him as he hurried past.

"Yeah," Stevie rinsed off, stepped out of the way and switched places with Rick, "Just thought there would be lots of booze."

"His ex is Jewish," Billy said. He had finally sat down and started dressing. "That's where all the bagels and shit come from."

"She's not my ex. We're still married." Rob threw his skate in the bag with more force than was needed. It made a thud sound as it hit the black burlap. The guys all looked at each other. Stevie shrugged his shoulders. No one said a word.

"Fuckin' eh," Rob broke the silence as he finished undressing, grabbed his towel and headed to the showers. "Someone pour more beer." He had enough of the conversation.

After about ten minutes, Rick, Rob and Timmy had finished showering. (Timmy was always last in the shower. No one knew whether it was because it took him longer to get undressed from his goalie equipment or just natural inertia. It was just another one of those locker room constants that made it feel like home.) Lindsey could finally take her turn.

"Don't finish the beer on me," she wrapped a towel around herself and headed towards the showers.

"No worries," Rob looked around the locker room. A quiet calm had begun to take hold now that they were in stage two of the post-game ritual. The rush of showering, changing and heading home to bed was over. Anyone who was left had already decided they would sacrifice any chance at a good night's sleep and hang around until the beer ran out. After all, the wife and kids were asleep and no matter how tired you were in the morning, there was always coffee.

Rob smiled a little as he thought about how he would feel in the morning. As an elementary school teacher, you never woke up slowly. Those sweet, cute, beautiful little children were about the noisiest phenomenon on the planet. Every morning it was like getting woken up by a bucket of ice thrown in your face. It was another reason Rob stayed late and drank with the guys. He needed to just sit, hang around and chill with his buddies. Besides, whether he got five hours or six hours sleep, he would feel the same when the ice bucket hit.

As he sat quietly and watched Timmy pour himself another plastic cup full of beer, he wondered for a moment if there would be enough beer for Lindsey. There were only two pitchers left and even though more than half the team had left, Lou, Stevie, Rick, Timmy and he were all big beer drinkers. But if it wasn't, he thought, they could take it out to the parking lot since Timmy often had an extra cooler of beer in his trunk for just such an "emergency". *No worries.*

"How are the boys?" Lou asked Rob. With the group getting smaller and Billy having left, the ribbing and joking dwindled down a little and the conversation usually became a bit more mellow.

"Ok," Rob topped off Lou's beer and then his own. "I had to break up a fist fight this afternoon."

"Really? What about?"

"To be honest, I'm not sure. Lindsey and I ran into the room and the boys were already going at it."

"Lindsey was there?" Lou looked puzzled, "At your house?"

"No. We were at my mom's house going through her things."

"Why was Lindsey there?"

"I needed her help. She knows a lot about family history and shit."

"Oh," Lou sat back and sipped his beer again. The questioning seemed to be over and an awkward silence hung in the air. Rob did not know if Lou was reading anything into Lindsey being there and he didn't like the feeling of his actions being questioned. Even if he wasn't sure they were.

"Anyway, the boys were already going at it, so by the time Lindsey and I got in the room all we do could was break it up."

"Who was winning?" Timmy smiled.

"Heh," Rob chuckled. "Actually Adam was."

"Heh, heh," Timmy laughed. Everyone on the team loved it when the little guy took the big guy down a notch. "I was hoping so."

"Yeah. Gave him a pretty good shiner."

"Chip off the old block."

"What's so funny?" Lindsey returned to the locker room and walked over to her hockey bag. She was wrapped in her plain blue towel which covered her almost completely. All Rob could see was her bare shoulders and legs. It was about the only time when he and the guys could see just how short Lindsey was. On skates, in full equipment, Lindsey was about the same size as Stevie. She skated with speed, grace and power. No guy would ever guess she was the petit woman standing in front of them now.

Of course she was still a hockey player. Her smooth bare legs clearly showed the strong muscle beneath and her shoulders were as broad as any man's. She even had a scar on the base of her chin where a stick had once come up and cut her deep. It gave her almost a cleft chin look. This was not the first time that Rob had noticed just how sexy that was, but this time the thought scared him.

"I was just telling them about how Adam clocked Bobby this afternoon."

"Oh yeah," Lindsey took out another towel and began vigorously drying her long blond hair. "Your kids know how to punch." She rubbed the shoulder Bobby had hit in mock pain.

"Sorry." Rob chuckled.

"No worries," she smiled as she sat down in her towel and reached out with her empty cup towards Stevie. "Did you tell them about the letter?"

"What letter?" Stevie leaned over with the pitcher and filled Lindsey's cup.

"No," Rob said with a frown. He didn't want to tell the guys about it.

"What letter?"

"Rob just found an old letter in his mom's stuff that we thought might be worth something," Lindsey looked over at Rob apologetically and mouthed *"Sorry."*

"Really? What kind of letter?"

"It was from Ben Franklin's kid," Rob explained. If the news was out, he might as well tell them himself.

"You mean the kite guy?"

"Yeah, the kite guy."

"Ben Franklin had a kid?" Lou had been nursing his beer quietly ever since Rob had mentioned being at the house with Lindsey.

"Yeah. But not one he was proud of."

"Huh?" Stevie said. "What do you mean?"

Rob looked over at Lindsey and nodded for her to take over.

"I googled him this afternoon. Turns out he joined the side of the British during the war and his dad practically disowned him. Guy was even Governor of New Jersey. He almost makes Benedict Arnold look small time."

"Whoa, Franklin's kid a god-damn traitor! And you're related to him?"

"Don't know, could be. Might just be a friend of the family. That's why I brought Lindsey along. She knows about this shit."

"Hey I'm no expert. I just traced my own family back a couple hundred years. I don't know anything about the American Revolution."

"The strangest part," Rob added, "was some mysterious phrase he mentioned about documents and his dad and the Treaty of Paris."

"Treaty of Paris?"

"It ended the American Revolution, gave us our independence, you know, nothing real important." Rob grinned. A few of the guys chuckled.

"What's it all mean?" Lou said.

"We still don't know," Lindsey answered. "It could be meaningless or it could be fucking huge."

"I got a guy who could help ya," Rick had been so quiet in the corner that Rob had almost forgotten he was there. That was typical Rick of course. He spoke only when he had something brilliant to say or annoying. All others times he waited like a wolf amongst the sheep. It sometimes gave Rob the creeps. "Buddy of mine teaches up at UCONN," he walked over to the last pitcher, held up what was left and poured the remainder into his empty glass. Everyone else eyed the end of the beer with solemn regret.

"He's a professor of history up there. I even think he's a specialist on the Revolution."

"Really? How do you know him?"

"Oh this and that. When you're my age, you get around."

"Think he'll see us?"

"Why not? What else does an old history professor have to do?"

Everyone laughed at that. Rob and Stevie took the last gulps of their beers. They looked over at Timmy wondering if he would offer to go outside.

"Wait a minute," Timmy was in his corner shaking his head slowly. The beer was still in his hands but he had not taken a sip. He looked confused. "Wait a minute. I'm just trying to wrap my head around all of this. Are you saying that Benjamin Franklin had a son who was a traitor?"

"Yeah," Lindsey did not like the tone in Timmy's voice. It sounded like an accusation. "I guess."

"The. Benjamin Franklin. The. Benjamin. Franklin! Founding father; constitution guy, face on the fifty, Benjamin Franklin?"

"Yeah."

"The Benjamin Franklin had a son who was a fucking traitor and you might be related to him?"

No one said anything. The air was tense and tight. It was rare for anyone to raise their voice in the locker room, especially towards fellow teammates and especially coming from Timmy. He had to be the most lovable simple guy there was. Rob and Billy may have had a big heart, but Timmy wore it on his sleeve. He was always offering to help out the guys, loaning someone a few bucks, even coming over on a Saturday to help with some chore. Yeah he could get a little intense at times, especially with his politics, but no one ever spoke politics in the locker room. The only reason anyone even knew Timmy's politics was because of his Facebook page. It was littered with patriotism and quotes from the constitution. But he never promoted his views in the locker room. Hopefully this was just some beer related reaction and he would calm down in a second.

"No fuckin way," he suddenly smiled and looked right at Rob. "I'd bet my left tit you ain't related to no traitors."

The tension left the room like air rushing from a balloon. Laughter replaced the tightness as Lou, Rick and Lindsey all gulped down the rest of their beers. "C'mon," Timmy crushed the plastic cup in his hand and threw it in the trash, "my cooler is waiting."

L4

1783

British Occupied New York City

"You have to write him father!" Anne shouted as she slammed the paper and ink well down on the table in front of her father. Her face was worn and wrinkly like a woman twice her age. The young vibrant woman William Franklin had been so impressed with just five years ago was gone. Only her passionate blue eyes and her silky smooth auburn hair remained.

The war had taken a large toll on Anne, on everyone. She, Thomas and Isaac all had wrinkled faces and achy muscles. Most of the fat was gone from their bodies and their bony faces showed the lack of good food from years of boycotts and raids. Time, worry, stress and lack of nutrition had turned them into shadows of what they once were. "You must let Samuel know we are leaving!"

"He knows!" Thomas shouted, snapping his head back towards his daughter and standing up so fast he knocked the chair down on the floor. He was almost fully gray by now and the hunch on his back had become permanent. "How could he not know? The whole world knows!"

For the first time in his life, Thomas Appleby did not know what to do. His convictions had failed him, his faith had failed him, his loyalty had failed him and his King had failed him. The war was lost.

The battles had ended almost two years ago now, at Yorktown, when the British army under General Cornwallis had been trapped between the American George Washington and the French Navy. But even after that disaster, the Loyalists still held out hope that the King would continue the war using more Loyalists or even the thousands of black slaves that were still running to the Empire for help. They could not imagine the King would abandon them.

But they had been abandoned. They had been abandoned and perhaps even betrayed. There would be no protections. There would be no compensation for their losses. There would be nowhere for them to live. The news had just come in with the new Treaty of Paris, ironically negotiated almost entirely by Ben Franklin. The King was unable to get anything from the new United States that would help or protect the Loyalists. State Governments were already taking everything from the Loyalists and running them out of town. They were enemies in their own land.

The entire war replayed in Thomas' mind; The news of victory and defeats, the letters from Samuel, the mobs, the prison ships, the fear of spies, the anguish over his children's safety, even William Franklin and his false hopes. Every hope and dream and nightmare, every choice he had ever made, it all came flooding in.

He had to sit down.

"When did it all go wrong?" He cried to Anne as he buried his hands in his face. "What did I do wrong?" How could I have fixed this?"

"You didn't do anything wrong father," Anne placed a hand gently on his shoulder. She did not know what to do either. Like her father, Anne had always expected the King to win. She had always hoped that when it was over, they would all return to the farm in Connecticut, she would finally marry and have her own family, just like her father had. Now nothing was certain. She had no hope, she had no future.

"What now?" Thomas vocalized what Anne was thinking. "What do we do now?"

It was the emptiest Thomas had ever felt. His entire life had always been clear; marrying Sarah, moving to Connecticut, starting a farm, a blacksmith shop, even a family. These choices had always been easy. His future, almost completely laid out for him and his family. Even his decision to stay out of the war had been an easy one. He had to protect his family and he would not be bullied.

But nothing was easy now. No decision made sense. How could he stay in a land where he was an enemy? How could he protect Anne and Isaac in a world where they were hated and vilified? But how could he choose to flee? How could he leave everything behind, abandon his son forever and start all over again?

"All over again," the words swam in his head. *"All over again,"* He felt dizzy and weak. He couldn't do it. He could not lose it all and start all over again.

"Samuel has to know that we have no hope," Thomas abruptly stood back up, almost pushing Anne over as tried to make sense of it all. He paced around his small kitchen waving his arms. "He has to know that the King has left us to the mob; that state governments can do anything they want to us."

Thomas remembered what he had read about the treaty. Article VI of the

Treaty of Paris gave no protection to Loyalists at all. The King had tried, to be sure. Many people in the British government felt a sense of debt to the thousands of supporters who had endured so much for so long. But, none other than Benjamin Franklin himself had made sure that the Treaty gave the Loyalists nothing; no protection, no land, no hope. Some people claimed that Franklin was taking out his anger at his son on them all.

"Damn them!" He slammed his fist on the table. "Damn politicians and diplomats! They have left us nothing!" He stopped and looked directly into Anne's blue eyes. They were no longer innocent but they were still so beautiful.

"And that is why we must leave," Anne held his stare. Her calmness surprised Thomas. So much like her mother, he managed to think. It was always his wife Sarah who calmed him down, who took the bad and managed to find the good. "Leave like the thousands who have already left."

Many neighbors and fellow Loyalists were saying that Canada was a wonderful place. They said that it held hope and opportunity for all. They said that in Canada they could again be Loyal British subjects and enjoy the blessings of Liberty and Empire away from the mobs of Patriots and zealots who destroyed everything, especially freedom, in the name of liberty.

Thomas stopped pacing and looked at his daughter. Her beauty amazed him every hour of every day. He felt such joy staring at her soft full lips, her passionate blue eyes and her silky smooth auburn hair. It shocked and pained him deeply that amid all this war and heartache that she still had not found a husband. He would do something about that. He stood taller and took a deep breath. *"Finally,"* he thought, *"a purpose again."*

"You are correct daughter," Thomas said with determination. "We must leave before it is too late."

"Winter will be here soon father," Isaac suddenly spoke up. Thomas had forgotten his son was even in the room. As the youngest child, Isaac was often ignored, even with Samuel gone. If Thomas was not careful, he would lose this child as well.

"There is one more fleet left," Anne reminded her brother.

"There is plenty of room on board the ships," her father added.

"I want to go on the Clinton," Isaac said quickly. "It's a frigate!"

"I know," Thomas chuckled. "I know."

"Father," Anne scolded him, drawing his attention to the paper and feather pen that were still on the floor.

"But first," Thomas nodded to Anne as he bent down to pick up the materials, "I must write your brother."

Seven

Rob walked briskly across the parking lot. It was a beautiful Connecticut spring day. The air was still a little crisp, the sun was shining brightly in the clear blue sky and the wind carried the scent of pollen and promise. Students from every part of the UCONN campus were outside enjoying the weather. Some were sitting on the grass studying, others were playing Frisbee, still more were walking between classes and all of them wore short sleeves and shorts as a kind of unspoken celebration to the end of the cold New England winter.

None of that mattered to Rob. He just wanted to get home.

He took his key to the Camry out of his pocket and aimed it in the vicinity of his car. The musical "beep beep" and flashing of the car headlights pointed him to the right.

"Over here," he nodded.

Lindsey hurried to keep up. Rob hadn't said a word since they left the professor's office. Again Lindsey started to wonder if perhaps she had made a mistake accepting Rob's invitation to come along. She couldn't afford to miss work and she was still not sure if getting this close to Rob was a good idea. But she couldn't help herself. Her curiosity about the Franklin letter was too great and she couldn't pass up any time she got to visit her alma mater.

It had been years since she walked on campus even though it was only just over an hour away from home. It wasn't that she had a bad time at UCONN. Life, as usual, just seemed to get in the way. After graduation she had jumped right into "real life". An administrator in a small robotics firm in Milford had been a fan of the UCONN women's hockey team and had offered Lindsey an internship there. Within six months she had a paying position and six months later a full time salary. She hadn't even been able to spend any quality time after graduation back at home. One week to pack, visit some of her favorite hangouts and the friends who were still in town were all she had. Mom didn't even get a chance to make her famous tuna noodle casserole.

Six years later, things hadn't gotten any slower. Her current project of developing robots to aid and even hopefully take over surgery was something she truly believed in. Yes she worked more than fifty hours a week either in the lab or doing paperwork but it was work she loved. By the time she got home, took care of bills, cleaned up, went shopping for groceries and any other errands, her weekend was shot. She barely had time for a social life or even a boyfriend. In fact the one real boyfriend she had left her after two years because "you're just never around." Thank God she had hockey to get out all her aggravations or she would go crazy.

Lindsey turned her head and looked southwest. The athletic facilities were a short drive in that direction. "Hey Rob want to swing by the rink?"

Rob stopped and looked at his watch. She couldn't believe he still wore one. It was one of the little quirks he had that Lindsey thought was cute.

"Maybe for a few minutes; But we should be heading back to Milford soon. I don't want to get stuck in traffic."

"Great!" Lindsey smiled as she jogged up to the car. The double "beep" had gone off so she knew Rob had unlocked it. She opened the door to the passenger side and slid into the seat. "It will only take a few minutes, I promise."

About an hour later they were finally on the interstate headed west.

"Only a few minutes," Rob grumbled once he had set the car on cruise control.

"Sorry," Lindsey apologized. She knew Rob was mad but what could she do? At first, being in the beautiful NCAA division one rink had cheered Rob up. Lindsey showed him the personalized locker rooms, the work-out room, the hang out room and of course the ice. It brought back his own memories of playing at college. But then Lindsey saw an old friend, then another, then another. Rob had started to look at his watch every few minutes and Lindsey could tell how irritated he was getting. By the time they left the rink, Rob was actually more upset than he had been before. Unfortunately, Lindsey had no idea why he was in a bad mood in the first place.

"What a waste of time," Rob complained shaking his head.

"Sorry. I really thought we could just pop our heads in."

"Not at the rink," Rob turned his head to check traffic in the right hand lane. Interstate 84 was getting busier by the minute, "at the professor's." He put on his blinker and gently edged the steering wheel right.

"What do you mean?" Lindsey thought Professor Gross was great. He knew so much about the Revolution, and Franklin and Loyalists. She could have listened to him for hours. "I thought we learned a lot."

"We did. But nothing that can help sell the letter."

"Sell the letter? You want to sell the letter?"

"Of course."

"But it is a part of your family's history."

"Not a part I'm proud of."

"But, but," Lindsey was truly stunned. "I-I thought you, I thought you understood what the Professor was saying about the Loyalists; about how they were thrown in the middle of it all and were just trying to protect their families."

"Of course I understood it," Rob swerved the car to the left suddenly to avoid a slow driver. Traffic was getting heavy. "That's not the point."

"Okay, now you've lost me."

"Did you see Tim's face the other day in the locker room?" Rob realized he was losing his temper and driving recklessly at the same time. He needed to ease back on Lindsey and on the gas pedal.

"When?"

"When he was thinking that I was related to Loyalists."

"Yeah, so? He laughed it off."

"You don't know Tim like I do," Rob looked in his rearview again and moved back into the right hand lane. "He is a big time Patriot, USA-USA guy, right wing, tea party whatever you want to call him."

"Yeah I kind of figured. I just never really cared."

"None of us do. The locker room is no place for politics. Never has been."

"Again. So?"

"So, let me explain." Rob looked again in his rearview. "But while I am doing that, would you pull out your phone and check the traffic. We are getting close to Hartford now and I don't want to get stuck in a jam."

"Yeah, sure."

"The only reason Tim did not blow his cool and yell at me," Rob explained as Lindsey looked at the app on her phone, "is because we were in the locker room. If we had been anywhere else, who knows what he would have said or done?"

"Traffic is getting pretty heavy near Hartford," Lindsey interrupted; "Looks like there might even be an accident on I-91."

"How's 84 West?" Rob tried to sneak a look at her phone from the driver's seat.

"It clears up pretty nice after Hartford. Why don't you stay on that and you can turn south either at Waterbury or Newtown. It's not the usual way but it avoids the accident."

"Sounds good; Let me know if anything changes in the traffic."

"Will do."

The decision to detour had released some of the tension. Rob could drive a little easier now that he knew the traffic would dissipate soon. "So anyway, can you imagine what other people will do once they hear about this letter?"

"What other people?"

"Any people; Friends, strangers. No one is going to take the time to drive up to some UCONN professor and get the full story on the loyalists. This is New England. You know how the Patriots are viewed."

"The football team?" Lindsey said half joking. She regretted it the moment she said it.

"No! Be serious Lindsey! No one wants to hear that side of the story. We live in the land of Paul Revere and Sam Adams and John Hancock. Those guys are gods."

"People aren't that bad."

"Lindsey, listen, I know you didn't grow up in New England. Neither did I. I was born in Michigan. But we both went to college here. My kids go to school here. You know that nobody is interested in Loyalists or the other side of the story."

"Okay. I will grant you that for many people that is true. But there are just as many people who want to hear the other side. Not everyone is a die-hard Patriot."

"Doesn't matter; It's not something I want to deal with. It's not something I want my kids to deal with. We all have enough on our plate. I just want to sell the letter and move on with our lives."

"But," Lindsey stopped. Rob had a point and she had no idea what it was like to be going through all the shit that he was going through right now. What was it like to have two kids and a wife separated from you and a mom who just died and a job that doesn't pay the bills? Was some old letter really worth all this hassle? Maybe it was better to just sell it and let her and Rob return to normal.

Lindsey looked back at Rob. His eyes were focused on the road but she could see the tension in his shoulders. *"Why put him through this?"* She thought. She sat back in her seat and looked out the window. "Shit," she swore softly.

October 1783

My dearest son,

I write this last letter to you in the hopes that it will finally get through. I have no idea if you have received any of my earlier letters or if you are even alive. But with God's grace and blessing, I pray that these words find you happy.

Let me begin by saying I bear no ill will towards you. You are my son and always will be. If you are at fault in anything it is for being as pig headed and stubborn as your father is. While I will always believe that my course was the correct one for our family, you must follow your own path. I pray that you will find happiness and peace in your new country.

Your sister, brother and I must leave. It is no longer safe here. I am sure you have read about mobs in Charleston rounding up Loyalists and torturing them and taking their property. Already we have Patriots returning to New York City and I fear that it is only a matter of time before they come after us. It is rumored that George Washington himself will be here soon, and while the General has always been the utmost in honor and integrity, I fear that even he will not be able to control the hatred that surrounds us.

There is no safe place left for us in your new country. New confiscation laws are being written by the states and we must take whatever we have that we can carry to safety.

I am sure you realize we will go to Canada. We do not have enough money to go to England and we have been told by his Majesty's government that we will receive land upon our arrival. I do not know for sure where this land will be, whether it will be Halifax, the river St. John or elsewhere. Just know how much it breaks my heart to leave you this way, but we both made our choices long ago.

I will begin anew. Your sister, God willing, will find a husband, and your little brother Isaac will help me start a new farm and hopefully even another shop.

I leave you with this my son. Always remember that what you fought for and what I refused to give up on was the freedom of all men. While this was taken from me by your friends, I forgive them for it and pray that you will now turn your efforts towards protecting that freedom. Build a nation my son that truly protects all men's freedom. Take your hero Jefferson's words to heart and create a land that will be worth the horror and devastation we have been through.

Above all my son, never forget that your mother and I love you with all our heart, with all our soul. And while I am sure, we will never see each other again, have faith that we will indeed meet again in the Happy Kingdom.

God bless you my son,

With Love and admiration,

Father

Eight

"You getting hungry?" Rob broke the silence. The traffic had calmed down now that they were past Hartford.

"Famished; haven't eaten since seven."

"Sorry about that."

"Nah it's my fault. If we hadn't stopped at the rink, we wouldn't have gotten stuck in traffic and we would be almost home by now."

"Yeah but I still feel bad about all this." Rob looked in the rearview mirror, turned on his blinker and moved from the fast lane. A black Mazda roared past.

"Bad about all what?"

"Me snapping at you earlier; dragging you up here, just being a dick."

Lindsey chuckled. He had been a dick, but she didn't feel like saying that. Instead she let the silence speak for itself and stared out the window some more. She knew enough about men by now to know that silence was sometimes more powerful than words.

Rob got the message and let the silence return as well. His frustration and anger from earlier was beginning to dissipate into a mellow reflection that made him feel closer to Lindsey. It often happened on long car rides. Sitting alone, listening to the hum of the engine, and watching the world outside pass by eventually calmed him like a warm blanket on a cold winter's night. It was at times like these that he and his wife Deborah usually had their best conversations. He was pretty sure it was on the long drive home from a Bruins game in Boston that they had decided to have children. He sat back a little and placed one hand softly down on the console between them.

"You've helped me more than you could know."

Lindsey smiled. She too was enjoying the soothing energy enveloping their senses. Looking out the window she could see the tall dark green oak trees in full bloom lining the highway. The grass on both sides of the road was a continuous line of unbroken sod except for the occasional clump of ferns. With the smooth black asphalt and the low hum of the a/c fan, it created an almost hypnotic, calming effect. It had been a long time since she had this kind of quality time with anyone, especially a friend. She placed her hand gently on his. Rob softened.

"Ever since Deborah started drifting apart, I've not known what to do."

"When did it start?"

"I don't know, months, maybe years. It's hard to explain." Rob turned to look at Lindsey for a moment.

"You don't have to."

"We did everything together," he looked back at the road. "I mean everything. In college we were like Siamese twins. Our friends used to hate that they could never get either of us alone."

Lindsey smiled. One of her best friends in college had been stuck to her boyfriend's hip too. They were married the day after graduation.

"Every decision I ever made, every important thing I ever did, was done with Deborah."

Rob grew silent again. The road continued to pass them by. Lindsey wasn't sure if he was trying to say more or if he was done. She read some of the road signs, waiting for him to continue. One big blue sign showed the restaurants at the next exit. Friendly's, Subway, even the McDonalds looked good right now. Her stomach grumbled at her.

"So having you around has made it so much easier," Rob broke the silence again. Lindsey could tell he was leaving out a lot of thoughts in between. That was okay. She couldn't expect to hear his entire life story all at once. Just hearing this small amount made her feel special. No one knew much about Rob, not even Lou. He was a private man, proud and sort of old fashioned. Sure they bullshitted and joked in the locker room, but they rarely talked about anything that mattered. It always amazed Lindsey how much men could talk without really saying anything.

"Hey!" Rob shouted and pointed out the front window. "You see that sign?"

Lindsey looked in the direction Rob was pointing. There was a small brown sign with white lettering on the side of the road. It was one of those tourist signs that told people where all the parks and sightseeing points were along the highway. She never paid much attention to them.

"Connecticut Antiques Trail exit 15," she read aloud. "So?"

"So who better to sell the letter to than an antiques dealer? Why don't you google that?"

"Ok. But I don't think,"

"Quickly," Rob interrupted, "the exit is coming up fast."

Lindsey pulled out her phone. She still thought selling the letter was a bad idea. There was something in her gut that was telling her the letter was a lot more important than they realized. If only Rob had let the professor look at it.

"Heh," Lindsey chuckled as the website came up.

"What?" Rob slowed the car down. The exit was just up ahead.

"You weren't kidding about New England. The slogan on the top of this tourist website is 'Revolutionary Connecticut."

"See!"

"Anyway," Lindsey didn't want to give Rob any more help with his theories. "This trail looks like a whole bunch of Antique dealers. The next exit takes us to the town of Woodbury, the quote antiques capital of Connecticut."

"I've heard of Woodbury. It's supposed to be a quaint old town." He put on his right blinker as the sign for exit 15 grew closer. "We can grab some food first then check out the dealers."

It only took a few minutes driving on Route 6 to get into town. Even before they saw the sign on the side of the road for Woodbury, "the Antiques Capital of Connecticut," they had already seen an antiques store. By the time they had driven up and down main street looking for a place to eat they must have counted between ten and twenty different shops, each one with a different style and specialty.

"Where do we start?"

"I have no idea." Rob slowed the car as he approached a small green and yellow sign that simply read "Hazel's" as if everyone should know what or who Hazel was. Rob assumed it was a restaurant with all the cars in the small parking lot. "Let's pull into this place and see if we can get a bite to eat. Maybe the owner can help us."

They had picked the right place to stop. The little yellow café with bright white trim had to be the most unique, eclectic restaurant Lindsey and Rob had ever been in. It had so much character that it was no wonder that all it needed was the name out front and everyone would know what it was. There were only about eight indoor tables covered with the matching yellow tablecloth, a few of the white trim outdoor tables, a daily menu with specials usually reserved for five star restaurants and even an art gallery. Rob and Lindsey chose to sit outside and take advantage of what was left of the beautiful day.

A woman introduced herself as the owner (Hazel of course.) and led them to their table. She was dressed in a flowery green and red dress which somehow matched the theme of the restaurant without being too loud. Her hair was a mix of gray and black and she could not have been more than four and a half feet tall. Yet, her energy and warmth was twice her size and half her age. Within minutes they were captivated by her personality and after an awkward moment in which she assumed they were a couple, she was telling them everything they wanted to know and more.

She had lived in Woodbury for more than 30 years and she knew everything about everyone. Once she had gone over the specials and they had ordered, (Rob got the turkey Rueben and Lindsey got the chef's salad.) she went on to give a history of the town, her café and most importantly where she thought they could go to find someone who specialized in colonial era antiques. By the time she had finished, their meal had arrived.

"She reminds me of my mom," Rob smiled and picked up his sandwich.

"Mine too," Lindsey dove into her salad. She could not believe how hungry she was and once the food was in front of her, it took all her will power not to shovel it all in at once.

Rob barely noticed. He was too busy eating as well and this had to be the best turkey Rueben he had ever had. For several minutes, the only sound that could be heard was Lindsey's stabbing of the fork and the occasional crunch of Rob's home baked potato chips.

"Rob," Lindsey looked up from her salad and broke the silence. Rob's comment about his mom had got her thinking again. Something had been bothering her since the funeral and she had to get it off her chest.

"Yeah?"

"Uh, well, uh, I know this is kind of awkward, but uh,"

"What?"

"About your mom,"

"What about her?"

"I've just been wondering. Uh, how did you say she died again?"

Rob stopped in mid bite and looked up at Lindsey. He did not know whether he was angry, shocked or relieved at her question. He had been wondering about it himself ever since he found his mother slumped over her chair.

"Doctor said it was a heart attack."

"Wasn't she in really good health?"

"Mm-hmm," Rob nodded as he took another big bite. He did not want to voice what he had been thinking. It just seemed so crazy and desperate. And what good would any of it do? It wouldn't bring his mother back.

"Nine times out of ten, a heart attack is a reaction to something else."

"You're not telling me anything I don't know."

"It just seems odd." Lindsey shook her head. She was not sure where she was going with this. Ever since they found the letter, her imagination had started going in all kinds of weird places. If the letter really was worth a lot of money and someone knew Rob's mother had it...

"I know what you're thinking. I've been thinking it too."

"Really?"

"Of course, how could I not?"

"So you think,"

"No. I don't. I did, but I don't anymore."

"Why?"

"It's just too crazy. We live in the real world, not some Hollywood movie. Things like that just don't happen."

"But,"

"Lindsey c'mon; Don't. Let's just not go there."

"Okay. I guess it is a pretty crazy idea."

"Thanks," Rob returned to his sandwich. They both sat silently for a few minutes. It was easy to say they weren't going to think about it. It was much harder to do it. Rob's mother had not only been in good health, she had been in great health. She walked twice a day. She ate all the right foods. She was active socially and she had the mind of someone half her age. No one could believe that she just slumped over one day and died.

Lindsey wiped the last bit of dressing from around her plate with a piece of bread. Whatever that dressing was, she could not get enough of it. She was tempted to order seconds. "Are you sure you want to do this?"

"Yeah I'm sure," Rob gave no hint of doubt or certainty though. His shoulders neither slumped nor rose. He was so hard to read sometimes. Lindsey decided to press the issue.

"It's eating at me though. Something about what Franklin said to your relative that makes me think there's more."

"More what?"

"I don't know. It was something in the way he talked about his father."

"You mean at the end of the letter?" Rob reached into the bag where he kept his notebook and began opening up a sealed folder.

"You have it with you?" Her voice was so loud the couple next to them turned and looked.

"Of course. How else are we going to sell it?"

"But," Lindsey lowered her voice and sat back in her chair. The couple turned their heads away and returned to their meal. "Why didn't you show it to Professor Gross?"

"I don't know. There just didn't seem to be any good moment. He was going on so much about Loyalists and Revolutionaries and Connecticut and the war and all, I could barely get a word in."

"But he could have told us something about that last paragraph."

"I just didn't trust the guy. There wasn't anything wrong with him, I just got a feeling that maybe we should keep the letter close to our vests."

"Yet you want to sell it to some stranger," Lindsey snapped. She was pretty upset with Rob now. The main reason she had come along was that she knew there was something about that letter. She could feel it. Franklin was hiding something and he didn't want anyone to know what. She could tell by the mysterious phrases he was using.

Rob ignored Lindsey's comment, took out his reading glasses and scanned down the page for the phrase that he too thought sounded ominous. "I have recently gathered in my possession," he read aloud once he found it, "various documents and letters from my father concerning the most recent Treaty of Paris..."

"That's the one," Lindsey leaned forward again. Her heart almost skipped a beat every time she heard that phrase. "What do you think he meant about 'various documents in my possession'?"

"Who knows?" Rob shrugged. He put the letter back and glanced at the check sitting on the table.

"The Professor would have," Lindsey said angrily.

"Let's go." Rob stood up, ignoring Lindsey completely. He took out his wallet and threw some cash on the table. "Lunch is on me."

Nine

"This the one?" Rob asked as he slowed down and put on his blinker.

"Francois' Antiques," Lindsey read the sign. "That's what she said."

"He's got to be better than the last two," Rob steered the car into the parking lot. The popping and crunching of the tires on the dirt driveway forced him to slow down a little as he pulled in. This was their last chance. It was getting late in the day and the two of them were exhausted. Two other antiques stores had been a complete waste. The owners knew less than nothing about Canadian antiques or the Revolutionary time period. But Rob had thought it was a good idea to go to a few other dealers first before they hit the one recommended to them by the café owner. They would have a better idea what to expect and how to bargain if they knew what their options were. Unfortunately all it had done was left them tired and desperate.

"Well she said he was an expert on New Brunswick and Nova Scotia," Lindsey unstrapped her seatbelt and opened the car door. "And that is where the Loyalists ran away to during the war."

"I know," Rob locked the door. The "beep" and flash of the headlights replied as he turned towards the short brick path leading into the shop. "Let's hope he knows more than furniture."

Lindsey chuckled as she followed Rob into the store. She was still not sure how to handle all this. Her anger at Rob and the frustration at his desire to sell the letter were still there. But now her curiosity at how much money the letter might be worth combined with her exhaustion from this long day was giving her a little hope that this shop might be able to help them. Add to all that her mixed feelings for Rob and she was a total mess.

"Good afternoon," a small, skinny man greeted them from behind a glass display counter. It was filled with various assortments of jewelry, toys, dolls and many more knick knacks neither of them recognized. He was dressed awkwardly, as if he could not decide what era he belonged in. His white fluffy shirt was clearly colonial in style but his blue Levi jeans and snake belt buckle not only seemed out of place, they did not even fit him well. He smiled warmly but the twitch over his right eye disturbed Lindsey enough to make her turn away. Only the gold trimmed wire glasses which sat precariously on the end of his nose seemed like they belonged in an antique shop.

"Are you Francois?" Rob asked as he looked around the store. It was by far the neatest antique shop he had ever been in. The living and dining room furniture was in one corner, bedroom and personal items in another and statues and artwork in another. The organization was both scientific and artistic at the same time. Rob was impressed.

"I am."

"We were told you are an expert on British and Canadian Colonial antiques," Rob said as he approached the glass counter. It too was organized perfectly with the small rings and other jewelry on the top shelves and larger figurines and busts below.

"I am that as well," Francois held out his bony hand. His fingers were long and pale while his arm was strangely short and bulky. The man's entire body seemed to be a mess of contradictions: long legs, short torso, firm chin, soft eyes, large ears, thin graying hair. He was the strangest looking man Rob had ever seen. Even his handshake somehow started strong and quick and ended with a limp.

"Rob Callahan. And this is my friend Lindsey."

"Pleased to meet you," Francois looked at Lindsey. Again, the twitch over his eye made her shiver.

"Hi," Lindsey waved.

"What can I do for you? You obviously seem to know what you want."

"It's not what we want," Rob hesitated. He looked at Lindsey. She blinked and waited. Rob turned back to Francois. "It's what we have."

"Oh?" Francois raised an eyebrow. The twitch stopped momentarily. "That is interesting. We do sometimes purchase certain items, if they are something we feel we can resell. What is it you have?" Francois looked beyond them as if the item might be behind them somewhere. He glanced out the window at the parking lot to see if something was in the car. Seeing nothing, he looked back at Rob.

"It's not anything big, not furniture or anything."

Francois frowned. He looked at the tan bag strapped over Rob's shoulder. Rob was holding it with both hands.

"And I am not even sure you will understand it," Rob fiddled with the bag some more. Just the feeling he got from Francois staring at the bag made him uncomfortable, as if some stranger was going through the family closet.

A wave of panic rushed over him. That is exactly what was happening. This man, this stranger was about to be shown the family secret. Rob was opening a Pandora's Box he could never close. His heart began to race along with his mind. What should he do?

"What do you know of the Loyalists?" Lindsey blurted out. She could see the internal struggle going on and she knew that if they were going to show this man the letter, they better check his credentials.

"Quite a lot actually," Francois smiled as the twitch returned. "I have several contacts in New Brunswick and Nova Scotia who specialize in that time period. It's quite fascinating how they lived and survived in such brutal conditions. That is why their collections are so valuable to me. So much hard work and personal attention went into everything they did. You can see evidence of Colonial, French and English style in so many of the works."

"Not the furniture. How much do you know about the people?"

"As much as anyone and quite a lot more. You cannot succeed in my line of work unless you know the history behind the pieces and the stories of the people who used them."

Lindsey looked at Rob again. His arms were back at his sides and his calmness had returned.

"Now please, why are you here? It is getting late."

"I found this letter," Rob began as he reached into his bag and pulled it out, "In the belongings of my grandmother. It was written to one of my ancestors back in 1785."

"1785? That was right after the war."

Lindsey and Rob looked at each other and smiled. This guy did know his stuff.

"Unfortunately," Francois continued as he reached across the glass counter to take the letter, "thousands of people wrote letters at this time. After all, it was a confusing, horrific time for so many families. The value of them therefore, is quite low." He had the letter in his hand now and was gently unfolding it. "While I am sure that this letter holds a lot of sentimental value for you," he continued as he pushed the reading glasses further up his nose (which to Lindsey's relief, hid the eye twitch), "they very rarely are of any interest to anyone beyond immediate family."

"It's from William Franklin," Lindsey interrupted. Francois' eyes looked over his glasses and at Lindsey. The twitch returned.

"William Franklin?" Francois looked back at the letter, "The son of Ben Franklin?"

"The very same."

"Well then, I stand corrected. You may indeed have something of value."

Lindsey and Rob watched Francois read the letter. They could barely contain themselves. They both felt a mixture of pride and anxiety as they waited. Rob could feel sweat forming on his brow.

"What does this mean?" Francois pointed at the bottom part of the letter and held it out to them, "I have recently gathered in my possession various documents and letters," Lindsey's heart began to race as she heard those words again, "from my father concerning the most recent Treaty of Paris..."

Francois lowered the letter quickly and looked at them in amazement. "Do you know what the various documents and letters are?"

"No."

"Do you know anything at all about them?" Francois almost shouted. "Perhaps another letter that mentioned them?"

"No," Rob shook his head. The question and Francois' sudden change unnerved him.

"As I said before," Francois tried to slow down a little. He could tell Rob and Lindsey were on edge. "I have several contacts in New Brunswick. Let me call one of them," he took out his cell phone. It was a new one, perhaps the latest one and it seemed out of place, almost inappropriate surrounded by all these relics from the past. "Perhaps I can get an idea of the letter's value."

Francois held the phone out and waited for a reply. Rob and Lindsey were still confused but neither of them could see any reason to not keep going.

"Uh, Ok," Rob shrugged.

"I'll be right back," Francois hurried to the back of the store. Lindsey and Rob could still see him in the darkened corner. His back was to them and he was standing next to what looked like his desk.

"Strange little man," Rob said to Lindsey, still watching Francois' conversation.

"Yeah, kind of gives me the creeps."

"Me too."

"Did you see his eye twitch?"

"No."

"It stops when he's thinking," Lindsey took another look at Francois. He was waving his arm in the air as he talked.

"Lots of people have twitches," Rob replied. He was feeling a little guilty that they were judging the man so quickly. "I have a couple of students in my class with twitches. It's no big deal."

"I know. It still gives me the creeps."

"Let's give the guy a chance. Strange doesn't mean evil."

"That what you tell your students?" Lindsey laughed.

"Yeah," Rob laughed too.

"Sounds like something right out of the manual," Lindsey ribbed him.

"Probably is," Rob kept smiling, as he glanced back at Francois. He was heading back to the front of the store. Rob turned and waited.

"Where did you say your grandmother's family was from?" Francois asked. He held the phone away from him but it looked like it was still on.

"Canada."

"I know that," Francois snapped. "What part of Canada?"

"Uh, I'm not sure, somewhere north of Maine." Rob frowned. "What does this have to do with the letter?"

"How far north of Maine? New Brunswick; Nova Scotia, Newfoundland?"

"Uh," Rob frowned some more.

"New Brunswick," Lindsey interrupted. Rob looked at her.

"I saw it on one of the other letters," Lindsey explained. She had a sheepish, apologetic look on her face.

"North or south of St. John's?"

"Um," now Lindsey was confused.

"Look," Rob said firmly. "What does this have to do with the letter?"

"Never mind," Francois turned away. "It doesn't matter. Excuse me again."

"Definitely New Brunswick," Francois said into the phone as he returned to the back of the store. Rob and Lindsey watched him closely. He seemed even more agitated now.

"Never mind," Rob turned to Lindsey again. "I don't like him."

"That was weird," Lindsey agreed.

"Listen," Rob lowered his voice. "Don't tell him any more about my family."

"Sorry,"

"No, it's not your fault. Just don't tell him anymore."

"Ok,"

"What did you say your name was?" Francois returned. He was still holding his phone.

"Rob Callahan." He had already told Francois that.

"No, I mean your grandmother's family."

"Look, I am not trying to be rude here, but I don't see what this has to do with the letter. Are you interested in it or not?"

"I have to determine its credibility. This item could be of tremendous value."

"Tremendous," Rob repeated. His eyes lit up and he glanced at Lindsey, "How tremendous?"

Francois frowned considerably. He was angry he had let that slip. "You said this was part of a larger collection of letters."

"That's right. How tremendous?"

"I can't say yet. What was the family name?"

Rob and Lindsey looked at each other unsure.

"This is critical to determining its value," Francois urged.

"I am not one hundred percent sure, but I think it was Appleby."

"Appleby," Francois immediately repeated into the phone. The person on the other line raised his voice in reply but they could not tell what he said.

"Can I see the letter again?"

Rob hesitated.

"Please," Francois begged.

Rob slowly pulled the letter back out and unfolded it carefully on the counter in front of Francois. This time however he kept his right hand on the corner, just to be safe.

"Yes, yes," Francois was saying into his phone. "It's right here." He leaned down and read the line aloud: *"I have recently gathered in my possession various documents and letters from my father concerning the most recent Treaty of Paris..."*

He paused and listened for a moment. He looked up at Rob over his glasses. Rob saw the eye twitch. It gave him a shiver.

 "Are you sure you don't have any idea where these various documents and letters might be?"

"I'm sure."

"But you did say this was part of a larger collection."

"Yes, but..."

Francois held the phone back up to his ear. The other person was shouting again. Rob looked at Lindsey.

"I don't like this," he mouthed to her.

"Me neither," she whispered back.

"Hey!" Rob shouted as he ripped the paper out from Francois' grip. The phone was turned sideways and aimed at the letter. "What are you doing?"

"I was just going to take a picture," Francois backed up a little, trying to distance himself from Rob's anger. "I meant no harm."

"You're not taking a picture. This is my personal property! C'mon Lindsey," Rob waved as he turned away from Francois and headed towards the door.

"Wait," Francois called out. The voice on the end of the phone was practically screaming now. "Wait!" He called again, giving chase and waving his arms.

There was no way Francois could keep up with Rob. In a matter of seconds, he had crossed the walkway and reached his car. A press on the remote, a beep from the horn and a flashing of lights and Rob was already inside and starting the car up.

"Do you believe that guy?" he turned to Lindsey.

"Unbelievable," she agreed as the sound of the tires on gravel announced their departure. She turned her head and looked back at the shop. Francois had stopped waving his arms and was holding his phone in his hands.

"What's he doing?"

"Nothing," Lindsey lied as she watched Francois take a picture of their retreating car. "Just get us out of here."

L6

British Occupied New York City

Thomas Appleby stood outside his home and stared at the closed wooden door. Memories of 1776 and leaving his son behind swirled in an unreal painful flow. For a moment he was not sure where he was or when. This was the second time in less than ten years that he left everything behind and abandoned his home. It was not a feeling he enjoyed.

"Do we have everything father?" Anne stood right behind. She was dressed with coat and hat, preparing for the cold sea journey ahead of them. She too remembered the day they left Connecticut. At the time, she always believed they would return. The move to New York, she told herself, was just temporary. Once the madness was passed, everything would return to normal.

But of course it hadn't returned to normal. Nothing had. Anne was beginning to wonder if she would ever know what normal felt like. Each day of the war brought a new surprise, a new shock, and more bad news. The only good thing about leaving this New York house, she realized, was that there were not many good memories to leave behind.

"Everything we can carry," her father replied. He too was frozen in the surrealism of the moment. For Thomas Appleby this wasn't just abandoning a home, it was failing his family. It was his job as its leader to provide and protect, yet he not only had lost two homes, he had lost his wife, he had lost his son and he had lost his faith. What was left?

"Did we get much at the auction?" Isaac asked. As always, Isaac was the curious one. While Anne and Thomas were melancholy and brooding, Isaac was wondering what they got out of the deal. He had been questioning his father ever since the decision had been made to leave; what would they bring, where would they go, and what would they leave behind?

"Of course not stupid," Anne hated Isaac's obsession with material things.

Couldn't he just once, let them feel a moment? "How could we get any real value for anything when everyone knows we have to sell?"

"Vultures," Thomas swore under his breath.

"What father?" Isaac leaned in.

"Nothing," Thomas replied as he swung the burlap sack over his shoulder and turned away. "Let's head to the wharf."

The streets were more crowded than Thomas had ever seen. Many people, like his own family, were dressed in warm clothes and carrying their belongings. Others wore rags, moved quickly with heads down and empty hands. Some people were locked in final conversations, saying goodbyes, exchanging pleasantries and long held embraces. It was like nothing Thomas had ever seen.

Refugees from all over the continent had swarmed into New York City. Despite the fact that thousands of Loyalists had already left the city, thousands more were heading there for safety. It was not only the last place in all of America that British troops could be found, it was also the point of departure for every Loyalist leaving the country.

The King had promised to protect all of his loyal subjects, and that meant all of them. Sir Guy Carleton, the King's man in charge of the city, had made it clear to General Washington that he would not leave until every last Loyalist and soldier had safely made it out of New York. With the Treaty of Paris being signed and the United States of America officially a recognized nation, Washington was getting impatient to end the war and get home to Mount Vernon before the end of the year. In a moment's notice, the United States Army could be in the city.

"Watch yourselves children," Thomas warned as he avoided a broken wheel cart in the middle of the crowded dirt street. Even though Anne was 23 and Isaac was 19, Thomas still called them children and watched out for their safety. He had to. New York had become a dangerous place.

It wasn't just the return of the Patriots to the city and the threat of mobs that made it dangerous. The refugees coming into the city were desperate and poor. They had lost everything in this war, many of them coming with nothing more than the shirt on their backs. They slept in the churches and in the warehouses. They made space wherever they could and their mess spilled into the streets as well. It was chaotic. Filth was everywhere. Street lamps were broken. Trash littered the gutters and the wharves were in disrepair. Thieves stole from homes and shops and the overworked British Army was in no mood to protect every subject from all the treachery rampant in the city. The city was on the edge of anarchy. They would be lucky to get out intact.

"Thomas!" A voice called from somewhere behind him. Thomas turned in the direction of the sound. "Thomas Appleby!" the man called again.

"John?" Thomas thought he recognized the poorly dressed fellow. It was not so much that he was wearing rags, Thomas had seen much worse today. It was that he was wearing so little, and it was all so dirty. In this cool October air, everyone should be wearing a jacket. Perhaps he did not own one or maybe he was just so sweaty from carrying the burlap sack over his shoulder that he didn't want one. "John Adams?" Thomas smiled as he saw through the dirt and dust on the man's face. He was a handsome man. Soft cheeks, firm chin, broad shoulders, John Adams was a man that would have no difficulty with the ladies. He was still athletic, despite his years and he carried a friendliness and genuine warmth that made him easy to like. Only the sadness in his brown eyes gave away any of the complexity of the man.

"Ha-ha!" John began laughing as he jogged towards the family. He leaped over the broken wheel and dodged a young boy before reaching them. "Are you heading out as well?" he almost shouted.

"Yes," Thomas looked at the group following behind Mr. Adams. There was another young man, probably his son Jonathan, a small boy and far behind was a very pregnant woman. They were all dressed poorly and mismatched, like so many of the other refugees in the streets. "We are," Thomas returned his gaze to John. "Is this your family?"

"It is," John said with a smile. He put his hand on the shoulders of the young man standing taller next to him. "You have not seen my son Jonathan in a few years."

"This is Jonathan?" Thomas gasped. He was more handsome than his father, with none of the sadness in his eyes. Instead, those burning green eyes looked angry and passionate. "How old is he now?"

"Twenty One," John said with a broad grin.

"That is almost the same age as my daughter," Thomas realized as he looked over at Anne. She had lowered her burlap sack to let it rest on the dirt street. Isaac was still carrying his but he was smiling broadly. He had always liked the Adams'.

"Hello Jonathan," Anne smiled at John's older son. She did not know him well, but he was quite handsome. Maybe, she wondered, she would get to know him.

"Hello," Jonathan replied. He turned away slightly. Anne did not know if it was shyness or something else.

"And this is my little boy Sturgis," John continued with the introductions, "and my wife Sarah."

"Oh my," Anne gasped. It was strange enough that this woman shared the same name as her mother, but to see a woman as pregnant as her about to embark on a dangerous sea voyage gave her pause. "How far along are you?" she asked.

"Seven months," Sarah answered softly. She was holding her belly for support with both hands and still trying to catch her breath. Her face was quite pale and her legs were shaky as if simply supporting the weight of the child inside had become unbearable. She looked exhausted.

"I was hoping we would see a friendly face," John tried to change the subject. He was worried sick about his wife. It was difficult enough giving birth, especially in this dirty city, but to ask his wife to embark on this trip to Canada with winter around the corner was on the edge of madness. If the alternative had not been so much worse he would never even attempt it. But this was the last fleet out and if they did not leave now, who knows what would happen to them?

"What ship are you on?" Isaac of course chimed in, practical and curios as ever.

"The Clinton," John answered as he and Thomas picked up their burlap sacks again and started forward.

"The Clinton?" Thomas repeated. "That is our ship as well."

"Wonderful!" Anne exclaimed. She was relieved that she would know somebody on board. There were so many unknowns. Where would they land, what would they do when they got there, where would they sleep, how would they eat and most importantly, who could they trust? Knowing at least one family would make the trip a little more bearable, especially if she could spend time with Jonathan.

"The papers said the ship is leaving soon."

"Tomorrow I believe."

"Well then we had best hurry up!"

The ship did not leave tomorrow. Nor did it leave the next day or the day after that. Thomas did not know if the delays were caused by more refugees, politics or weather. All he knew was that he wanted to get going.

"It has to be tomorrow," John Adams broke the long silence. It was the middle of the day and despite the chill in the air, the bright October sun warmed their faces. Autumn was one of John's favorite seasons, especially as the leaves began to turn. But today, amidst the stench and the noise of the evacuation, it was difficult to even notice. He and Thomas had been standing on the dirty wooden deck, a little off to the side of the main mast by themselves for over an hour in a spot they found on the rail. From there they could watch the loading and unloading, the yelling and crying, the confusion and madness without being bothered by another passenger asking them for help or directions. They could also try to watch to get a clue about when they would finally leave. The kids had been driving them crazy with the questions.

It had to be soon. The East River was filled with British ships. Thomas could count at least five or ten in his direct line of sight and he knew there more anchored in the harbor beyond his vision. This entire enterprise was simply incredible. No matter where he looked, on board or on the docks beyond, there were people of all different classes and distinctions. Most of them were poor and many of them were women, but he could also see many Loyalist regiments that had volunteered to fight for the King. There were men from New Jersey, Connecticut, Long Island and beyond. There were white men and black men. There were slaves and freedmen.

It was confusing to Thomas, dealing with these black men. He of course knew several of them personally but this war had made race much more confusing than before, despite how hard that was to believe. During the war, the British promised to free any slave who ran from his rebel master to fight for the King. Many had answered that call, thousands in fact. But the King also protected the rights of Loyalists who owned slaves. After all, if you were a loyal British subject in Virginia and you owned slaves, why would you support the King if he took away your slaves?

How then was one to know if a man who escaped from slavery was running from a master who was Loyal or Patriot? Was he freed slave or fugitive? Who could answer his claims? And how was Thomas supposed to interact with them personally? To him, all men were free and the politics of the war were over now.

"I think you are right," Thomas agreed. It would have to be soon. How nice was it, Thomas was thinking to have a man such as John Adams that he could talk to, a man who was similar in needs and lifestyle as himself. Both of them of course were Loyalists. Both had children depending on them and both had no idea what lay in their future. They had never really been friends much before, more like acquaintances, but as they spent these tense, nervous days together, they began to form a bond. It had been a long time since he had such a friend. It would be nice to know him better.

"How did your time with Governor Franklin work out?" Thomas suddenly remembered how John was the first name he had given the Governor.

"It didn't."

"Oh?" Thomas knew that the Governor had been quite successful in recruiting men and forming his Board of Associated Loyalists but beyond that, he knew little. He had heard of raids and plots and whispers of impropriety perhaps even barbarism but Thomas stayed as far away from it as he could. Governor Franklin was too radical for Thomas' tastes and shortly after their first meeting, he stopped dealing with him altogether.

"I did not care for his methods."

"They never should have hanged that man," Thomas added, referencing the famous Lippincott affair in which Franklin's men hanged a rebel soldier in retaliation for a Loyalist being hanged. It had taken place after the surrender at Yorktown and caused an international incident involving not only George Washington and the British Parliament but even the King and Queen of France.

"Agreed."

"Ironic though," Thomas continued, "that Franklin is now in England representing all of us."

"Father represents the rebels," John chuckled. It truly was an incredible irony, "and son the Loyalists."

"Let's hope he is as skilled in politics as his father if we are to ever receive any compensation from the King."

"He left last year, right?"

"Yes."

"And what has he accomplished in that time?" John pointed out bitterly. No Loyalist had much hope left and the lack of progress from William Franklin did not help. Thomas' silence in response made it clear, he felt the same.

"You think," John changed the subject, "we will ever see this land again?"

Thomas did not answer right away. He looked out at the city in all of its chaos. He remembered when he had first seen it as a lad more than twenty years ago. It had been a beautiful shining example of the glory and prosperity of the British Empire, a beacon to the world. He remembered how excited he was when he finally got his first shop up and running and he dreamed of taking advantage of the growing trade in the colonies. He wondered now how this new country, this new government would manage. Would they trade with England? France?

Spain? Would they prosper at all? Would his son be living in a land of opportunity or a land ruined by war and unable to compete with the global power it had just thrown off?

And what of Anne and Isaac? What would happen to them? Would Anne marry? Would Isaac stay with him or run off as Samuel had done? Would Canada be a land of promise or would it be a struggle to survive? Would the King honor his promise and give them land? Would the land be any good? Already many of the emigres were talking of deep dark forests and reptiles everywhere. There was only one thing Thomas could be sure of in these uncertain times. The world had changed forever and nothing would ever be the same again.

Ten

"What the hell is this shit?" Rob joked as he held the bottle of beer out in front of him. It was hockey night again and he needed the release more than any time in recent memory regardless of how the beer tasted. He squinted a little more at the bottle. Its label was barely visible in the pale yellow street lights of the ice rink parking lot. It didn't help that it was after midnight and he had already had several beers in the locker room before he and the team retired to the back of Timmy's S.U.V.

"Hell if I know," Timmy laughed. "Had a BYOB for the Rangers game the other night and there was some left-overs. I just emptied the fridge into the cooler."

"Beggars can't be choosers Sam," Billy teased. The boys called Rob "Sam" whenever he complained about beer. It had started years ago when Rob started bitching that the only American beer worth drinking was the beer brewed by a real American, Sam Adams. All the others, Rob claimed, tasted like different versions of piss.

Rob chuckled at the tease. The irony did not escape him that with all this Loyalist crap going on, that the boys nicknamed him "Sam" after one of the most famous American Patriots in history. "Guess not," he agreed as he twisted the top off the bottle and took a sip. It had a woody almost oak flavor and was tinged with just enough hops to keep it from being too bitter. "Hey," he held the bottle out again and re-read the label. "This stuff ain't bad."

"Is it enough to make us forget that game?" Lindsey said. She was standing directly across from Rob in the small circle the boys had formed around the cooler. Every one of them had a beer bottle in hand and was dressed in old shorts and t-shirts. Of course they all were wearing various kinds of hockey t-shirts from the usual Rangers and Bruins ones (Lindsey of course had on a Sabres t-shirt.) to the Adult League champs and USA Hockey MVP shirts that only were worn to the rink. It didn't matter what they wore of course. This late at night, no one was around to see and even if they had been they never cared. This was hockey, not fashion. If the games were early enough, they were joined by guys from other teams or even the rink manager. But tonight they did not even get on the ice until eleven and the parking lot was empty except for their own cars and the pile of Zamboni snow in the back. With only six of them remaining, they could easily fit under the opened trunk of the S.U.V. Its backlights and the yellow street lights were just enough illumination to see each other and the cooler between them.

"That was a stinker," Lou said.

"Yeah I let you down boys," Timmy got the only spot on the back of the opened S.U.V. He was the goalie and it was his car, so he got to sit on it.

"You friggin goalies always think you're so important." It was nice to have Billy there. He almost always went home after the games. "It's kind of hard to win a game when you don't score any goals." Billy turned to his left and pointed to Rob with his thumb. "If anyone is at fault, it's this guy."

"What the fuck?" Rob laughed. He almost spit out his beer.

"Yeah Rob. What was wrong with you tonight?"

"What the fuck?" This time Rob didn't laugh.

"You're good for at least a goal a game; Or at least a fight."

"Guess I am just tired boys, dealing with a lot of shit lately."

"Need to change your tampon?" Rick suddenly jabbed. As usual Rick remained quiet until he could go on the attack. This time however, he did not hit the target. He turned suddenly in realization of his goof. "Sorry Lindsey," he said sheepishly.

 "No worries," Lindsey laughed as she held up her beer and tapped it against Rick's in a little salute, "I'm used to you being a dick."

Everyone laughed at that one as a quick silence filled the air. A change of topic was needed.

"Hey Rob," Rick realized suddenly, "You never told me how your meeting with my Professor buddy went."

"Oh yeah," Rob hadn't said anything about the meeting to anyone. He was still freaked out by the antique dealer. "Sorry. It went well thanks."

"Learn anything?"

"Shitloads. Guy's a fucking genius."

"You still a traitor?" Timmy smiled.

"Guess so," Rob hid his reaction behind another gulp of beer.

"Leave him alone Tim," Lindsey came to Rob's defense. She knew it wasn't necessary. Maybe Timmy was just teasing Rob but she couldn't help herself. This Loyalist stuff was really beginning to get to her. She had been doing more reading ever since they got back from UCONN and what she was learning was upsetting. The last thing she or Rob needed was more ribbing from Tim; even if it was harmless.

"Yeah Tim," Lou added, sounding more like a father than a captain. "Lay off."

"What the fuck guys? Since when can't Rob handle a little jab? He's the fucking Sam Adams of the group."

"No worries Tim," Rob put his empty beer bottle on the edge of Tim's S.U.V. Suddenly he didn't feel like hanging out anymore. "I'm getting tired anyway and the little kiddies are going on a field trip tomorrow."

"You heading out?" Billy figured with him staying, everyone would make it a late night. The disappointment in his voice stung.

"Sorry Jim," Rob swallowed the guilt of letting Billy down, picked up his hockey sticks and slung his equipment bag over his shoulder. "Duty calls."

"I gotta go too," Lindsey placed her beer next to Rob's. "Thanks for the beers Tim."

"What's up with those two?" Lindsey heard Tim saying as she hurried to catch up to Rob.

"I don't know," Lou admitted. "But I don't like it."

"Rob!" Lindsey called up to him. "Wait up."

Rob turned back to Lindsey just as he was pressing the remote for his car trunk. The black Camry opened up in response. "Yeah?" he said.

"Have you had any luck?" Lindsey asked as she laid her Bauer bag and sticks on the black asphalt next to Rob's car. Like all the guys on the team, Lindsey refused to use one of those wheeled hockey bags. Those were for wimps. She carried her bag over her shoulder like they did in the old days.

"Nah," Rob admitted. He put his hockey sticks in the trunk, threw his bag on top of them and slammed the door shut. "I can't figure out what to look for."

"What do you mean?"

"That Antique dealer, he said that it was worth a lot of money."

"Yeah. So?"

"Well what exactly is worth a lot of money? Is it the letter itself or is it the various documents and letters that Franklin refers to?"

"Uh, I'm not sure. I just assumed it was the letter that was worth something."

"Maybe or maybe not. If it's the other documents, then all this is a clue to some kind of hidden secret somewhere."

"Like what?"

"I don't know," Rob turned and headed towards the driver side door. He was too tired and buzzed from the beer to think about this now. "And right now I don't care."

"Wait! Maybe this will help," Lindsey bent down and reached into her hockey bag.

"What?" Rob took his hand off the car door and turned back towards her. His voice perked up a little.

"I found something," she opened the skate pocket of her hockey bag and pulled out an envelope. It was double zip locked and pressed between a manila folder. Lindsey was making sure it would not be damaged.

"I've been going through that box you gave me," she explained. Rob had decided that before they could continue exploring the Franklin letter, they should see if there were any more clues in Nana's stuff. Last weekend he had gone through almost everything and divided up all the letters, pictures and keepsakes into possible clues and other crap. It had taken him hours, but he had managed to get all of what he thought was important into two large boxes. He had taken one and given Lindsey the other. Unfortunately, he had no more time this week to do anything else.

"What did you find?"

"It's not a letter," Lindsey opened up the envelope and handed him the item. It was still in a Ziploc but Rob could see through it no problem. "It's a newspaper clipping."

Rob looked up at her and raised an eyebrow.

"I almost missed it. Your mother kept so many newspaper clippings of you guys and current events and hockey games and there was even one about some dog being found."

"Anyway,"

"Anyway, this one here is a really old one. It couldn't have been one she cut out."

"How old?"

"1783." Lindsey paused to let the date sink in. That was at the end of the Revolution. Rob stood up a little straighter.

"What's it about?" he looked at the clipping for the first time.

"A whole bunch of things; those newspapers back then were really funny. They just listed all kinds of news and announcements all over the front page. There were even some ads for escaped slaves-"

"Anyway," Rob said again with some anger in his voice.

"Anyway," Lindsey laughed. "Sorry, this stuff is just so cool." She looked at Rob and smiled. He smiled back. She was pretty cute with all of her passion for this old crap. Her eyes lit up like a school girl and Rob stopped that thought right there.

"Someone circled this notice about Loyalists in the middle of the page." She pointed to the paper in Rob's hand as he held it closer to his face.

"I can't see it in this light and I don't have my reading glasses. What's it say?"

"It's a notice about a Loyalist commission being set up."

"Loyalist commission?"

"Yeah, but here is the kicker," Her voice rose a little. "It was being set up in London to give Loyalists compensation for what they lost in the revolution."

"So?"

"So, it's obvious that someone in your family was trying to get money or land or something from London to pay for what they lost in the Revolution."

"Did they get anything?" Rob's heart was beginning to race.

"I don't know yet. But that is not the cool part."

"Then what is?"

"The guy who represented the Loyalists; The one who was in charge of getting money for them; The one who would be writing letters back and forth to Loyalists in America."

"Yeah?"

"Guess who it was."

"I have no fuckin' idea."

Lindsey couldn't help but smile. "It was William Franklin."

Eleven

"What are you doing here?" Deborah ripped open her apartment door after seeing her husband through the peep hole. "Are the kids okay?"

"They're fine," Rob held both hands up and stood in the open doorway. He was dressed in a Rangers t-shirt and jeans. He wore a USA hockey hat on his head. He was either on his way to a game or coming back from one. Days had passed since Lindsey had shown him the newspaper article and neither of them had made any more progress. It was time to change tactics. "Can I come in?" He asked before he could change his mind. He still wasn't sure this was a good idea. Deborah looked absolutely stunning standing at her apartment door, holding a big glass of red wine and wearing her hospital pajamas. It didn't matter that it was the end of a long work day or that her make-up was mostly worn away. Despite all the fights and anger and hurt feelings, Rob still was turned on every time he saw his wife.

"I suppose," Deborah stepped back slowly to let him in. "It's pretty late."

"I know," Rob stepped into the spacious apartment. "Sorry. I've got a game tonight and I knew you would still be winding down from work, sipping your wine and watching your T.V."

Deborah looked at the glass of red wine in her hand and smiled. Rob knew her so well. It felt good. "Take a seat," she waved toward the couch.

Rob looked in the direction she waved and smiled as well. Sitting on the small glass coffee table was a half full bottle of Cabernet. The T.V. was muted but still on. It comforted him more than he realized to see she still kept all the habits from their years together. "Thanks."

"Want a beer?" Deborah offered as she walked towards her kitchen. The knowledge worked both ways.

"Just one, please. Game starts in an hour."

Rob looked around the apartment as Deborah disappeared into the kitchen. It was the first time he had ever been inside and it spoke volumes. Where Rob and Deborah had been reserved, family oriented and even a little old fashioned, this apartment was modern, contemporary and decorated. The walls were a bright red, the hardwood floors were polished and clean and the T.V. hung prominently from the living room wall. Rob wondered who she got to hang it up. He sat back in the two person couch and felt the sticky black leather beneath him. They would have never dared get that with the boys around. Nor would they get the glass coffee table in front of him, or the Picasso style coasters supporting Deb's wine glass. It was like nothing Rob would ever live in. It was the home of a stranger.

Again the doubt resurfaced. Seeing the life his wife was now leading made it so much more real. There were paintings on the wall and knick-knacks on the table he did not recognize. A few furniture pieces from their own house were mixed with high end items that she must have bought from Pier One. It was her favorite furniture store that Rob hated. It seemed the moment Deborah left Rob that she went out and bought everything he had always resisted. It screamed, "I am free of him".

"You like the place?" Deborah returned with a Sam Adams and handed it to him.

"Yeah," Rob smiled. His feelings flipped back to comfort and relief. She still kept his favorite beer in the fridge. "Don't recognize a lot of it."

"Well," Deborah had seen the hurt on Rob's face and recognized it for what it was. It bothered her even more that her first reaction was satisfaction that she hurt him. She couldn't hold back all the anger she was feeling, despite the comfort she felt being with Rob again. "It's amazing how quickly you can buy things when you don't have to ask for permission."

"Yeah I guess," Rob took a big sip of his beer. He glanced at the fancy digital clock on the wall. (It was another item he would never have had in his house. He liked the old fashioned clock faces.) It was getting late. He had better hurry.

"Listen Deborah, I know how awkward this is for both of us."

"No shit," Deborah took a sip of wine.

"But I don't want it to be,"

"You can't have everything the way you want it," Deborah interrupted angrily. "That's the reason we broke up in the first place."

"I know, I know," This was not starting the way he wanted. He tried again.

"What I am trying to say, is that I feel really bad for how I hurt you last week."

Deborah didn't say a word. She took another sip of wine. Rob took a gulp of beer. This was harder than he thought.

"Everything is just screwed up," he blurted out. "Mom dying, the boys all pissed at us, this crazy letter-"

"What letter?"

"Uh," Rob wasn't ready to talk about that yet. It was why he came over but there was other stuff he wanted to say first. Oh well. "Uh, a letter from one of my ancestors; we found it in Nana's special box."

"The special box?" she emphasized the word "THE" as if to give it even more special status.

"Yeah, that box," Rob was relieved that Deborah remembered what a big deal this was. "Oh," he reached into a small plastic bag he was carrying and pulled something out. "I also found this," he said, handing it to Deborah.

Deborah reached across the couch and took the picture. "Oh my god!" She smiled and covered her mouth with her right hand. She almost dropped the glass of wine. "The party we met at!"

"Yeah, I can't believe mom kept that."

"I haven't seen this in years," Deborah's voice cracked a little as she held the picture closer to the light. Rob could see her eyes getting moist. He wanted to reach out and hold her, or take her hand at least. The fact that he couldn't was like a knife in his chest.

"Keep it."

"Really?" She looked up at him. It was the first time tonight their eyes met. Deborah could feel the tears starting to swell up. This was too much too fast. *"What was Rob trying to do?"* She wondered. *"Was he really just being nice or did he want to sleep with her?"* The thought made her angry. She didn't like being manipulated and confused.

"Is this why you came?" She said a little coldly and sat back in the couch again. She put the picture down on the coffee table. She was not sure if she wanted to keep it, give it back, or throw it away.

"Yes and no. I really do feel bad about this whole mess. I know it's not your fault-"

"Damn right," Deborah interrupted harshly. That made Rob angry. He only said that to be gentle. Of course some of it was her fault. *"Shit,"* he swore to himself. A lot of it was her fault.

"And I wanted to show you that I still care."

Deborah softened a little. She still was unsure what this was all really about, but no matter how angry she was, she could never hate Rob. He was the greatest love of her life and her best friend. That would never change.

"Thanks."

The room fell into silence in that awkward moment. Rob played with the lip of his beer bottle and glanced around the room. Deborah took another sip of her wine. The T.V. was still on and Rob could see that Deborah was watching one of her favorite cop shows. That reminded him.

"Did I ever tell you how I found mom?" Lindsey's comments were still bothering him and he needed to share it.

"No," Her voice had a hint of both anger and hurt. "I was already out of the house; remember?"

"Oh yeah,"

"I found out about it in the newspaper," Her temper was beginning to get the better of her. Rob could have at least called. Yes, they were in the middle of a horrible fight, but he should have known how much Nana meant to her and done the right thing.

 "She was just slumped over in her chair."

"That's odd."

"I actually thought she had fallen asleep with her letters. You know how she is with them."

"Heh," Deborah chuckled. She did know. Nana could work for hours on her letters and newspaper cuttings. It was unreal how much time she spent writing relatives and friends and sending them clippings from the newspapers. Even after her and Rob starting fighting, Nana continued to send Deborah little inspirational articles about couples or basketball (Deborah's favorite sport) or even a clip from the comics. A wave of sadness washed over Deborah. Nana would be truly missed by everyone.

"But then I tapped her and nudged her and called her name and she didn't budge."

"My god,"

"I panicked and called 911. But there was nothing they could do."

"It was a heart attack right?"

"That's what they said." He let that thought hang in the air.

"What do you mean 'what they said'? You think it was something else?"

"I don't know. You know what good health she was in."

"Yeah, so?"

"So what if it wasn't a heart attack?"

'What are you getting at Rob?" Deborah was losing patience. Her emotions had been going all over the place since Rob got here and she still did not even know why he was here in the first place.

"Nothing," Rob stopped. He realized how crazy he was sounding, especially since Deborah knew nothing about the letter or anything else. He needed to get to the point.

"Never mind," he waved it all away as best he could and glanced over at the clock. "That's not why I came." He really needed to move on. It was only about 45 minutes before puck drop and the rink was still a few minutes away.

Deborah just waited. What the hell was he here for?

"The major reason I came is to ask a favor."

Deborah almost blurted out, *"A favor!"* She wanted to scream. *"After all this, you have the nerve to ask me for a favor?"* Only her respect and deep understanding of Rob kept her in check. Rob may be an over protective, possessive pain in the ass, but he was never petty or trite. If he needed something, it had to be something important and it had to involve more than just him. She still wasn't going to make it easy for him though.

"What kind of favor?" She said instead.

"It goes back to the letter," Rob sat back in the couch. This would take a minute or two. "It's not just an old letter from a random ancestor of mine. It's from William Franklin."

"William, don't you mean Ben?"

"No, I mean William. He was the bastard son of Benjamin Franklin."

"Bastard?" Deborah leaned forward and put her empty wine glass down on the table. She thought about pouring another glass. She certainly needed another glass. But she didn't want to interrupt. "I didn't even know he had a son, never mind a bastard one."

"Yeah well don't worry much about the bastard part. The Professor told me that Ben was a bastard too and it didn't change how he felt about his son; probably made him love the kid more."

"The Professor?"

"Yeah," Rob chuckled a little bit realizing how much had happened since the funeral. "Lindsey and I visited a history professor up at UCONN last week."

"Lindsey," Deborah repeated icily. "What was she doing there? I thought you said she was just a friend."

"Shit," Rob swore to himself again. *"I meant to break that in slowly."*

"She is just a friend. Really." He didn't dare tell her about the dream he had the other night of he and Lindsey in the locker room showers. That was intense. He had to change and wash the sheets twice before the boys noticed. It was embarrassing and exciting and it made Rob angry that he wasn't in control.

"A friend."

"Yeah. A friend."

Deborah kept his gaze. It really wasn't her business anymore was it? They were separated. She had her own place. She was making her own life. She had moved on.

Only she hadn't. She hadn't accepted her new life yet. Maybe that's why she kept his favorite beer in the fridge. "Fuck it, I need a refill." She got up from the couch and grabbed her wine glass. "You want another?"

"Sure," Rob knew it was a bad idea to have a second beer right before the game, but what the heck. This shit called for beer.

"So," Deborah called from the kitchen, "what's this whole Franklin thing about anyway?"

"We're still not sure," Rob was glad to get past all the Deborah, Lindsey bullshit and get back to the story. "But the guy at the antique dealer said it might be of enormous value."

"Now there's an antique dealer? How many people are in this story?"

"That's just the thing, too many people know about this already. I've got to get right to the source and stop beating around the bush."

"What do you mean?" Deborah handed Rob another beer, took a sip of her wine and sat back down on the couch. She crossed her legs and flung back her hair. Rob could easily see the outline of her breasts through her hospital pajamas. Damn she was hot. Damn he was fucked up.

"Lindsey has been doing some more research and she found some pretty crazy things."

"Like what?"

Rob laid it all out for his wife. He told her about the about the Loyalists, about Canada, about the possibility of more secret documents and even about the relationship that Ben and William Franklin had. He didn't tell her how much the antique dealer gave him the creeps. No need to worry her.

"Wow," Deborah finished off her Cabernet in one large swig when he had finished his story. "That's some crazy shit! But what do you need me for?"

"I've got to go to Philadelphia. I can't ask any more experts and Lindsey has hit a dead end. Everything out there is about Ben Franklin, Ben Franklin, and Ben Franklin. You ever hear of too much information? Holy Shit. I can't sort through it all to find anything more on his son or what he did after the war. This letter is either some really valuable part of American History and may be worth a lot of money or it's a worthless piece of junk. I need to show it to someone who can sort through all the Ben Franklin stuff and get me on the right track."

"Who is in Philadelphia that can do that?" Deborah was feeling a little light headed having downed two full glasses of wine.

"I don't know. But that is where the Ben Franklin museum is, and Independence Hall and the Liberty Bell and everything you would ever want to know about the Founding Fathers. It's the best place to look for someone or something to sort this all out."

"And you need me to watch the kids," Deborah suddenly realized. She was both excited and disappointed at the same time. As Rob had told his story, she had become genuinely interested in it. She was no dummy. Yeah she was a science major but she knew her history too. This could be a really big deal. She also knew Rob's mother really well and she cared deeply for her. The funeral wasn't just painful for Rob. Deborah was pretty upset as well. To hear that her role in this whole affair was just to watch the kids, made her realize that she was not a central part of the family anymore and that hurt her. At the same time, she was looking forward to spending time with her sons.

"I will just be gone for a long weekend. I already got a friend to cover my afternoon classes for Friday. That gives me plenty of time to drive to Philly and be back late Saturday or Sunday."

"Don't they have games?"

"Yeah. But I already got Lindsey to cover Bobby's game and Adam has a bye this weekend."

"Oh," Deborah frowned. *"There's Lindsey again."* She thought bitterly. *"Rob may think Lindsey is only a friend, but it sounds like he wants more."*

Rob saw the frown. "I knew this would be a sudden imposition. And I don't even know if you have any plans. So I wanted to make this as easy as possible for you."

"I don't have any plans."

"Well that's great then," Rob smiled. "You'll get to spend some time with the boys, and even get some alone time with Adam while Bobby's at his game."

"Great," Deborah tried to recover quickly. She smiled and glanced at the clock. It was time for Rob to leave; the way she felt she would either pass out from the wine or have sex with him. "Shouldn't you be going?"

"Shit! Yeah," He grabbed his empty beer bottle and held it up. "Where you want this?"

"Just leave it."

"Thanks," Rob hustled towards the door and reached for the knob. Something felt wrong.

"Really," he turned back to Deborah and caught her stare, "Thanks a lot; for everything."

Deborah smiled. The room got really quiet and really still. Rob wasn't sure what to do next. He spent his whole life hugging and kissing and making love to Deborah and now he wasn't even sure how to say goodbye. He thought of reaching for her hand, or giving her a hug, or just turning and going. *"Fuck it,"* he thought suddenly as he just went with his instinct.

"Thanks," he said one more time as he kissed her on the cheek and ran out the door.

Twelve

"Just a minute!" Deborah shouted from the kitchen towards the front door as the bell rang a second time. She still couldn't believe she was back in her old house. How could Rob do this to her? Didn't he have any idea how painful it would be staying here? Everything was different. The glass cookie jar with old Oreos had been emptied and placed on top of the white 1990s era refrigerator. The pictures of the boys playing hockey and Adam's honor roll certificate had been neatly placed on the fridge doors. The dark brown wooden cabinets, the bright green tile floor, even the plain white circular kitchen table looked polished and shiny.

"He'll be right there!" she swung around the center counter, went down the hallway littered with family photos, swung around the corner of the stairs and peeked over at the door. Lindsey's face was pressed up against the small window pane to the right of the door. She had turned her Sabres hat around rally cap style and her blonde hair fell loosely on her shoulders and around her face. With a swipe of her hand, Lindsey pushed the hair to the side and turned her blue eyes towards Deborah. She nodded in understanding.

"Adam!" Deborah turned away from the door and called up the stairs. She had no desire to see Lindsey any more than she had to. "Have you seen your brother?"

"No," came the simple response from Adam's room. Deborah almost marched up to scold him. She knew he did not even register her question. His head was in his video game as usual. What could she possibly do with him today?

"Bobby!" She screamed, grabbing the wooden railing and walking up a step or two. "Your ride is here!"

"Just a sec!" Bobby shouted from across the house. Deborah turned back in the opposite direction. The voice was coming from the garage. He must be putting his equipment bag together.

"Hurry up! You'll be late!"

"Can you grab me an energy bar?" Bobby dropped his large black hockey bag on the tile and ran through the kitchen. He had on his blue and white game jersey but was still wearing his underwear. His long legs looked even more muscular in contrast with his outfit. His thick black hair was a mess all over his head, probably because he knew he would be wearing a helmet soon and his brown eyes were focused so much on his goal that he almost knocked his mother down heading back up the stairs.

Deborah smiled at the usual chaos of getting ready for a game. She could hear things being thrown about in Bobby's room and swearing as he looked under his bed and in the blue unfolded laundry basket. He probably lost his garter again. He could never keep his stuff together.

"Ok," Deborah turned back into the kitchen and looked towards the brown pantry door. *"Where are the energy bars?"* she thought to herself in frustration. She couldn't believe what Rob had done to the house. It actually was more organized than before. The counters were clean. The floors had no clutter. The dishes were put away. The sink was clean. The only messes were the boys' rooms. Was she the reason the house had always been a mess?

Deborah stopped and stood in the middle of the kitchen. The moment had become surreal. Moments of the past; Adam playing video games, Bobby yelling from across the house, her frustration at her boys, merged with the craziness of the present; the unfamiliar kitchen, the girlfriend at the door, being a stranger in her own home. Everything began to spin. Memories turned, merged and warped. She saw Rob screaming at her but Lindsey was at his side. The boys were crying and laughing at the same time. Her work office and her new apartment melded into one. Late nights and sales reps wined and dined her. A hockey mom yelled in her face. Even her parents and their synagogue managed to make their way into her visions. She staggered.

"Mom, are you okay?" Bobby was suddenly at her side and holding her shoulder. He was her height now and could easily hold her steady. He was holding the black garter belt he finally found in one hand and his hockey sticks in the other.

"Yeah," Deborah shook it off and placed her hand on the brown and white marble counter for support. She shook her head to clear the visions and quickly wiped her eye to hide the tear. It was nice having her son worry about her. "Yeah," she repeated. "I'm fine."

"Did you find my energy bar?" Bobby asked as the teenager in him asserted itself. After all, if there was anything certain about teenagers it was that they were almost always focused on themselves. Bobby stopped worrying about his mother immediately.

"No. I don't know where your father put anything."

"They're over here." He opened up the pantry and reached directly for the third shelf. Deborah was shocked again at how neat and organized the food was. "Where's my ride?" he ripped open the energy bar and slung his hockey bag over his shoulder.

"Waiting outside."

"Uh, Ok." It wasn't like his mother to leave someone waiting at the door. It took him only a second to realize why but like a good son he did not say a word and headed towards the door with his hockey bag over his left shoulder and his sticks in his right hand. He almost knocked three family pictures off the wall with his bag. Deborah followed behind and held the top of his sticks together to prevent any other possible damage in the narrow hallway to the front door.

"Ready to go?" Lindsey said with a smile and a wave as Bobby stepped outside. She was dressed in a black Ramones t-shirt and green athletic shorts. Bobby tried not to notice how good she looked while Deborah shook her head silently in disgust.

"Yup," Bobby replied. He walked right past Lindsey and headed towards the driveway.

"What time will you be back?" Deborah stepped out onto the red brick patio and joined Lindsey. All the pleasantries were ignored.

"Not till early evening," Lindsey pointed the remote towards her neon blue Hyundai. The lights flickered, the horn beeped and the trunk popped open. "He's got a double header today."

"I know."

"Do you need me to grab him some dinner on the way back?" Lindsey was just as uncomfortable as Deborah. Lindsey hated being thought of as some kind of "hottie" or seductress. She was a woman, a professional and a hockey player. Of course she realized she was pretty, but so was Deborah. In fact if anyone was intimidating it was Deborah. She was a full head taller than Lindsey, just as well built and her piercing green eyes reminded her of magical creatures from fairy tales. Worst of all, Lindsey knew Deborah thought she wanted to sleep with Rob. In fact she probably thought they already had. The last thing Lindsey wanted was to get in between a husband and wife. She hated that Deborah assumed she was some kind of slut.

"That would work. I still don't know what Adam and I will be doing."

"Sounds good; I can just swing through a drive thru or if we have time, maybe we will sit for a few minutes."

"Ready!" Bobby called out as he slammed the trunk door shut and walked around towards the passenger side. He took a huge bite of the energy bar as he waited impatiently for the women to join him.

"Guess I should go," Lindsey turned away and headed towards the car. Deborah followed.

"Bye son," Deborah stepped in front of Lindsey and kissed his forehead. It was suddenly comfortable again. How many times had she done this when Rob was driving off with the boys to a game? The memory made her feel warm. "Good luck," she added.

"Thanks," Bobby reached around and gave his mother a hug. He could tell she needed it. He really was a perceptive young man.

"Hey," Deborah turned to Lindsey. The moment had her feeling more generous. "Do you need any money?"

"No thanks. Rob already gave me some."

"Figures," Deborah smiled. "He thinks of everything."

"Yeah, he does." Both women felt suddenly uncomfortable at the mention of Rob's name. There was an awkward silence and a tension as they were both reminded of what side in the fight each was on. Even Bobby could sense it.

"Time to go," He opened the car door to get in.

"Hey," Deborah noticed something up the street. She turned to Lindsey. "You know that guy?"

Lindsey turned her head in the direction Deborah was looking. There was only one thing she could be staring at. The rest of the street was as typical as any neighborhood in America gets. Houses lined both sides, each one with a manicured lawn and a small white fence. They all had short driveways with the same white mailbox at every entrance. Green oak trees lined the left side of the street and a concrete sidewalk lined the other. The small gray, slightly damaged old station wagon parked about 100 yards up the street stood out like a sore thumb. Whoever the man was sitting inside was not good at hiding. He looked directly at the two women.

"Oh my god," Lindsey turned pale as the man suddenly ducked down. A chill ran deep down her spine. "Oh my god," her hand instinctively rose to cover her mouth.

"What is it? Do you know him?"

Lindsey turned back to Deborah. She swung her head back again to the strange car. The man was still crouching out of site. She swung her head back and forth twice. Deborah looked at Lindsey desperately waiting for an answer.

"Oh my god," Lindsey said one more time. "It's him."

"Who?"

"The antique dealer!"

"Antique dealer?"

"Yes! I thought Rob told you."

"Told me what?" Deborah was trying to sort it all out. "You mean-"

A loud screech burst through the air. Both women turned to see the gray blur roar past them and head to the end of the street. Lindsey managed to grab one last glimpse of the driver as he ripped around the corner and disappeared. It was him. She was certain.

"What the fuck?" Lindsey sprinted several steps after the car and down the sidewalk in his direction then stopped in futility. She turned back towards Deborah. "Why would he be following me?"

"How do you know he is following you?"

"Why else would he be here?" Lindsey waved her hand in the direction the car had gone. "And why else would he speed away the moment I saw him?"

"I don't know."

"You better get out of here." Lindsey turned back to the car with determination.

"Get out of here? Why?"

"It's not safe."

"Why?" Deborah was annoyed now, "Because you saw some guy? What does that have to do with me?"

"Not you," Lindsey snapped. Her nerves were on edge. She fumbled through her pockets looking for her phone, "With Rob; with this whole letter thing."

"Don't yell at me," Deborah snapped right back. The last amount of reserve she had was gone. No more pretending to like this little slut. "And don't pretend you care about me or what happens to my kids."

"Huh?" Lindsey found her phone and looked up. Where did that come from?

"Listen you bitch. You can't just walk into our lives, have your little adventures with my husband and act like you're my friend or something."

Lindsey stepped back. She was not prepared for this hostility. She knew in the back of her mind to expect something like this of course, but that didn't mean she was ready for the backlash.

"Just go on playing your little game," Deborah stepped forward and puffed up her chest. It was the first time she realized her physical advantage over Lindsey. On the ice, Lindsey might be a power to be reckoned with, but toe to toe, Deborah was much bigger. "Pretend that you're some kind of expert or detective or whatever you're trying to be."

"Listen," Lindsey held up her hands in defense. She had to try to take control of this. She had to back off somehow and get in touch Rob. "I'm sorry you feel this way and that you think this of me but you have to listen-"

"I don't have to do anything."

"This guy is bad news." Lindsey tried to change tactics. "Your kids may be in danger."

Deborah paused for just a moment. She glanced at Bobby still sitting in the car and playing something on his phone.

"This letter must be really valuable," Lindsey pressed. "He wouldn't drive all the way down here for nothing."

"Do you think he wants to steal it?" Deborah's demeanor had suddenly switched as the mother in her took over.

"I don't know, but he might. Why would he be sitting in a car outside your house?"

Both women paused at that thought. The creepiness took over. A stranger was watching them. How long had he been out there? What was he doing now? Would he be back? A chill ran down Deborah's spine.

"You better get Bobby to his game," She said abruptly.

Thirteen

"And right over there," the National Park Ranger pointed, "is where Benjamin Franklin sat."

The hairs on the back of Rob's neck stood up as he followed the Ranger's direction and looked across the perfectly preserved colonial style room to the small green tablecloth covered table. He edged his way to the front of the crowd and placed both hands on the wooden railing by his waist. Just 10 feet in front of him was where it all happened.

It was the most famous room in America, the room where both the Declaration of Independence and the Constitution were written. Two rows of rectangular, green tablecloth covered tables in the center of the room faced the one table at the front where George Washington himself sat. There were candles on every table, papers and booklets and even a feathered pen. To the right and left of Washington's chair were gray marble fireplaces and more colonial chairs lined both sides of the room. The ornate crystal chandelier hanging from the center ceiling was not needed as sunlight streamed through the two large windows on each side of the room. No matter how many historic places he visited, whether it was New York, Boston or here in Philly, it was always the Revolution and the Founding Fathers that gave him that sense of power and history. *"This is where it all began,"* he thought to himself.

Philadelphia was only about a three hour drive from his home in Connecticut. Rob could have made this into a day trip if he wanted to push it. He had even considered trying to somehow make Bobby second's hockey game. But he needed the escape. He needed to get away from family and his conflicting emotions with Lindsey and Deborah. This wasn't just about the Franklin letter.

He had left Friday after recess, made a stop in Jersey for dinner and found a hotel in downtown Philly. That would give him all day Saturday and even Sunday if he needed it to explore the historic area. He hadn't been there since he was a child and he was looking forward to walking the entire downtown all by himself. Everything he wanted to see, from Independence Hall, to Congress Hall, to the Franklin Museum and even the Liberty Bell were all in a relatively small area. He could easily walk to them all and still have time for his research.

Rob woke up bright and early after having yet another disturbing and somehow sexual dream about Lindsey and Deborah. A few cups of the hotel coffee however quickly got rid of the cobwebs and Rob was able to get to the center of the colonial city before the crowds got there.

Philadelphia of course was one of the most visited cities in America and probably the world. It was rivaled only by Boston in Revolutionary history and was preserved better than any colonial town outside of Williamsburg, Virginia. If Rob could get on the first tour, he would be able to avoid the massive crowds and wait times that would occur soon enough and maybe get a word or two with one of the Rangers.

The National Park Rangers of course looked like all the other Rangers from every other park in America. They had the green pants, gray shirt and badge and of course the greenish wide brim hat that topped off the uniform. With so many of them walking to and fro on the red brick paths and standing next to and in front of every conceivable statue and monument, it gave the feeling of importance and reverence, as if the city were a priceless treasure, which of course it was.

"Where did Thomas Jefferson sit?" a young boy wearing a cheap, black colonial triangular hat that all the tourists were buying called out. He and about thirty other people from the tour group surrounded Rob. There were mostly families with young children, a few teenagers with headphones on that made Rob grimace and an elderly couple. He felt like a sore thumb standing there all by himself.

"Over there," the Ranger pointed to another table nearby. "Even though Thomas Jefferson was from the South, he was no stranger to Franklin." The Ranger explained. "Both men already had quite the reputation by 1776. Indeed it was Franklin who asked Jefferson to write the Declaration of Independence."

"Is this exactly how the room looked in 1776?" The father of the boy asked.

"Indeed it is," The Ranger answered as he swung his arm slowly around the room. "The green tablecloths, the wooden chairs, even the pens, are all exactly how everything looked when these men began the struggle for our freedom." The Ranger paused for a minute as he let his words settle in. For several quiet seconds, the group looked in various corners of the room and took it all in.

"Just think of it," He continued with a wave of his hand, "everything we all learned in grade school happened right here over two hundred years ago."

Rob's mind drifted away from the Ranger's words as he looked around the room. Washington, Hancock, Adams, Jefferson, Franklin, the names descended upon him like the Olympic Gods. Every story he ever heard as a child, every book he had to read for school and the ones he read on his own, every lesson he ever taught to his own students about the birth of the United States and the bravery of these men, and even the stories he would tell to Bobby and Adam all started in this very room. He took a deep breath, looked at the chair where John Hancock himself had sat and smiled.

A knot formed in his stomach and grew. He shook his head and shivered. Could his family really have been the enemies of these men? Was he indeed a traitor? He reacted instinctively and shoved the thoughts away but they would not leave. It was more complicated, he told himself. Bravery takes many forms, he added. He shook his head again. He did not want these thoughts. He wanted to revel in the power of freedom and heroes and everything that made him feel great about his country.

"Dammit!" he swore as he stormed out of the room and shoved his way through the tour group. He rushed through the hallway, into the open air and stopped.

The tour was ruined. Rob could not settle down. Everything the Ranger said, every question that was asked by the group was colored by what he had learned about loyalists and his family. He grew angrier with every passing moment and could not find a way to get rid of it. He needed a drink or to hit someone. He needed all of this to be over.

"Excuse me," a man dressed in colonial clothes, top hat and cane said as he gently tapped Rob on the shoulder. Rob stepped to the side to let the man and his tour group pass. He turned back to look at the awesome red brick façade entrance of Independence Hall again. There were tour groups and families everywhere. In the short time he had been inside, the numbers of tourists skyrocketed. Private tours, national park tours, men and women dressed in period costumes, and even horse and buggies filled the large cobblestone courtyard. On a bright spring day like this, it seemed that every family and school child in the Northeast was here.

"And directly down that street," Rob overheard a nearby tour guide shouting over the chaos. About thirty people surrounded the tall man dressed as a town crier. He held a black walking cane with a gold eagle knob and was pointing it down Chestnut Street, "is where Benjamin Franklin spent much of his time."

"Franklin, Franklin, Franklin," Rob shook his head in annoyance. *"Is everything in this town about Franklin?"*

"Did Benjamin Franklin have any children?" A woman in the group asked. Rob's ears perked up as he was reminded why he came here.

"Three," the guide replied. Rob turned and took a step towards the edge of the group, "two sons and one daughter. One son died young, the daughter married Robert Bache and is buried in Christ Church Burial Ground over in that direction with her father," the guide pointed, "and the other son eventually left the country and moved to England."

"Now let's move over here," the guide gestured towards the large free standing statue of George Washington on a pedestal, "and discuss 1776!"

"That's it?" Rob thought angrily as the tour group wandered away. *"That's it? No mention of William Franklin being a Loyalist? Or that he was the governor of New Jersey? No mention that he was a bastard like his father and that the two of them hated one another?"* The shame and embarrassment Rob had been feeling the entire tour suddenly washed away in the face of this slap. Rob knew these tours were all about the Revolution and the heroes, but to not even mention the controversy? Of course Rob was no loyalist, no traitor, but he wanted honesty. He didn't want the story just white washed and thrown away. He shook his head in disgust.

"Excuse me," someone tapped Rob on the shoulder. "Is everything all right?"

Rob turned to see the National Park Ranger from inside Independence Hall. He was much shorter than Rob (even with the Ranger hat) and his eyes looked tired and worn.

"Uh, yeah," Rob was caught by surprise and embarrassed. "Sorry," he apologized. "I didn't mean to disturb the tour."

"You didn't," The Ranger smiled. He was a pleasant little man, Rob realized. His gray uniform and badge made Rob feel instantly at ease and he had no idea why. Maybe it was just that it was nice to see that not every uniformed government official was a soldier, a police officer, an FBI agent or even an IRS man. This man's job was just to help his fellow American learn history.

"Good," Rob replied honestly. He was relieved to hear his outburst did not cause a scene. "It had nothing to do with you."

"Are you feeling alright?" the Ranger's official responsibilities took over. "Do you need a doctor?"

"No," Rob chuckled. "I'm fine; just needed some air."

"Well as long as you are okay," the Ranger began to turn away.

"Actually," Rob stopped him. "I could use some help."

"Really?" The Ranger said with some curiosity. The energy came back to his eyes as if he were relieved to have a little variety in his day.

"I need to find someone who can help me with a little research," Rob began.

He did not know why he trusted this man so. Maybe because in essence he was a teacher like himself.

"What kind of research?"

"On Benjamin Franklin."

"Well you certainly have come to the right place," The guide chuckled.

"No kidding," Rob smiled back. A part of him wanted to complain about the Franklin this and the Franklin that and all the Franklin, Franklin, Franklin he had been hearing but he wisely kept those thoughts to himself.

"I have a letter written by his son," Rob pulled the drawstring bag off of his shoulders and began to reach into it, "and I need someone to help me understand what it means."

"His son?" The Ranger repeated.

"William," Rob said.

"William Franklin?" the Ranger looked surprised. "You have a letter in there from William Franklin?"

Rob immediately stopped fumbling through his bag and pulled his hand away empty. He was suddenly reminded of the value of the letter hidden inside. He needed to be more careful. "Do you know someone who can help me? I was thinking of heading over to the Franklin museum."

"No," the Ranger corrected him. "I wouldn't head to the museum. The best person to help you is our Chief Curator," the Ranger answered. He could sense the sudden awkwardness as well and subconsciously took a step back. "She has been studying Franklin and his life for years and is the curator for all of the facilities in Independence National Historical Park including the Franklin Museum. If anyone can help you, she can."

"That would be great," Rob smiled.

"In fact," the Ranger went on, "She is at the Visitor's Center this morning. I was just on my way there. Why don't I introduce you?"

"Super," Rob smiled again and threw the drawstring bag back onto his shoulders. He took a few steps to catch up to the Ranger who was already moving briskly and followed him through all the crowds and across the courtyard.

It was a short walk back towards the visitor center but during that time Rob had already become much more comfortable with the Ranger. The man's knowledge and enthusiasm were remarkable. He talked of the buildings, the streets, even what the weather was like back in 1776. By the time they made it to the Visitor's Center, Rob could picture the entire scene.

"Why don't you wait out here?" The Ranger pointed to some brown wooden benches on the edge of the walk outside the Center. "It may take me a minute to find her and it's such a beautiful day."

"Alright," Rob agreed as he took a deep breath of the early summer air and sat on a bench. Despite the fact that they were in the middle of a huge city, the open air and smaller buildings of Independence Park allowed the fresh air to settle in. With the cloudless blue sky, warm sunshine and slight breeze, it could not have been a nicer day.

Rob stared up into the sky, let the sunshine warm his face and took another deep breath. He closed his eyes and allowed himself to relax. The sounds of the city; buses, cars, traffic, could still be heard from several blocks away but the brighter sounds of children laughing and parents trying to direct them drowned out most of it. He even heard a few birds. It reminded Rob of school and his own kids. He wondered how Bobby's games were going. He would be getting on the ice soon.

Thinking about Bobby made him think about hockey which made him think about his own team which made him think about Lindsey, then his wife, then the funeral, then his house and back to his kids again. He shook his head and opened his eyes. His life was all screwed up. He needed to take care of this Franklin stuff and get control again.

The phone in his back pocket buzzed. Rob had put it on vibrate during the tour and forgot to change it. He pulled it out and looked at the text. It was from Lindsey.

"Get home ASAP. We are being followed."

Rob read it again. *"Being followed?"* He wondered, "By who?" He texted back.

"Who would follow us?" Rob thought again. *"Did Lindsey mean she and I were being followed."* Rob instantly looked up. He scanned the entire park looking for strangers. He stood up abruptly and looked around. There was no one suspicious. He sat back down but still looked back and forth.

"Wait!" he realized. *"Did she mean she and the kids were being followed?"* He looked down at his phone; Still no reply. *"Why didn't she reply? The kids; my God the kids! What have I done?"*

"Excuse me," a woman's voice interrupted Rob's thoughts. Rob looked up to see a curly brown haired woman about his age standing over him. She was dressed in a plain green suit that somehow reflected the color of her eyes. They were so striking and beautiful that for a moment Rob was lost in them. "Are you the man who needs help with some research?" she said.

"Umm, umm," Rob shook his head trying to clear his thoughts. He could not get the text out of his mind. "Yes," he finally replied as he took a look behind the woman for some stranger that wasn't there.

"I only have a short time in between meetings," she explained. "May I sit down?" the woman asked as she looked in the direction Rob was staring. She shrugged her shoulders slightly and looked back at Rob.

"Of course," Rob said quickly as he stood up and waved his hand at the bench to invite her. He felt a little foolish and tried to regain his composure. He sat back down.

"Alan tells me that you have a letter from William Franklin," she said quickly as she sat next to Rob and crossed her legs. Her boldness took Rob by surprise. He had expected a little small talk first.

"Umm," he stuttered again. He needed to calm down. He was coming across like an idiot. "Yes," he said. "Yes I do." He made no movement for his drawstring bag. It was too early for that.

"Where did you get it?" she said quickly. Her green eyes grabbed Rob again. There was a passion and an excitement in them that gave away her calm, reserved approach. Rob could see why she was the Chief Curator here. She had a commanding presence driven by a passion for her work.

"I found it in my mother's keepsakes." He still was not ready to trust this woman, especially after the text from Lindsey.

"Figures," she smiled. "I can't tell you how many times I have heard something like that."

Rob smiled back. "Robert Callahan," he said abruptly as he stuck out his hand. It was time to break the ice.

"Denise Karie," she shook Rob's hand. It was a solid, firm handshake especially from someone with such nimble fingers.

"Mom passed away last month," Rob began.

"I'm sorry."

"Thanks," Rob acknowledged. "And shortly after that, my friend and I were going through all of her keep sakes." Rob looked back and forth one last time for any strangers. He felt more comfortable now and decided to forget about the text.

"What kind of keepsakes?" Denise asked. If she was going to have any idea whether the letter was authentic, she needed to know everything about how it was found.

"You name it she had it," Rob laughed. Denise smiled politely. "To say mom was a pack rat would be giving pack rats a bad name," Another chuckle. "She had letters from family members, old photos, mementos from my life, my kids' lives, and newspaper clippings. Oh, speaking of that," Rob reached into his drawstring bag now and pulled out the envelope. "She had this one right here."

Rob handed Denise the clipping that Lindsey had found about Loyalists. "The Pennsylvania Journal," Denise read the heading. "I have seen hundreds of these."

"Oh I know it's not valuable," Rob said quickly. "It is more interesting because of the article in the middle," he reached over and pointed about halfway down the page.

"The circled one?"

"Yes," Rob answered. "But I didn't circle it. Someone in my family must have; someone who was either a Loyalist or interested about Loyalists."

"And that is where you think the connection is to William Franklin," Denise finished the thought for him.

"We've traced my family back to Canada," Rob could see he was getting her interest so he pressed on. "And I know that William was a staunch Loyalist."

"That's for sure," Denise agreed. "It's what tore him away from his father."

"Do you know much about William Franklin?" It was time to see if she could help him.

"Oh quite a bit," Denise assured him. "You may think everything here is about Ben, but when you study the Franklins, you study everything. As the Chief Curator here, I have access to just about everything in Ben's life, including his relationship with his son. If I can't help you, I will be able to direct you to someone who can."

Rob smiled and let out a breath of fresh air. Finally, he felt like he could get some answers.

"Did they ever talk again?" He asked quickly. It was the biggest question he had. Sure the Revolution and Loyalists and the revelation that the most famous American of all time had a son who was a traitor was incredible stuff, but the burning question in Rob's mind was a simple one: forgiveness. With his own family falling apart and his kids choosing sides in the battle between mother and father, he had to know if the bond of father and son was torn forever by war and politics.

"Once," Denise replied. "But it was not a very cordial visit." She could sense Rob's passion for the question. She felt it too. She knew that Ben had adored his son, had schooled him in all the ways of politics and press and helped him land his governorship. Perhaps no one in history felt more betrayed by William Franklin's Loyalism than his own father. Did he ever forgive him?

"Why?" Rob asked.

"Franklin," she paused and corrected herself. It was not often that she had to clarify which Franklin she was talking about, "Ben was not doing well both physically and mentally. He suffered from gout and old age and was in no condition to travel across the Atlantic. In addition he had just finished negotiating a difficult Treaty with the British and had been venomously attacked by Adams both publicly and privately. He was an old, lonely man who had lost his son to war, had been questioned by men he thought were his friends and had been away from home far too long."

"Wow," Rob whispered. He hadn't seen that coming. These men had all seemed to be such heroes and so noble that even he, a teacher and college educated professional, had fallen under the spell of their majesty. To hear how difficult Ben's life was and how painful his last years was; it was remarkably sad.

"I'm sorry," Denise broke the silence. "But I don't have all day," she reminded him. "My meeting starts soon."

"Oh," Rob took the hint. He was still nervous. He looked around one last time. If anyone could help him, he reminded himself, it was this woman. He reached back into his drawstring bag and pulled out the sealed envelope.

"We found this in her special box," Rob slowly took out the letter.

"Special box?"

"Where mom kept her secrets," Rob smiled as he handed it to Denise.

"Heh," Denise smiled back as she gently took the letter into her hands. The way she handled it and the intensity in her eyes, proved to Rob that this was a woman who knew how to handle valuable documents. She took a pair of white gloves out of her purse before actually touching the letter. Then opened the sealed plastic Rob had placed it in and slowly unfolded it. Rob waited patiently as she read. There was no shock or surprise on her face at all. If she thought there was something important in this letter, Rob could not tell.

A few minutes later she looked up at Rob. Her green eyes bore into him for several uncomfortable seconds. Then without a word, she looked back down at the letter and read it again.

Rob got nervous. The silence and her intensity were too much. He began to panic.

"It is real isn't it?" he burst out.

"Oh it's real alright," Denise stopped reading and assured him. "I've seen enough Franklin letters to at least know that." Her head returned to the letter.

"Whew," Rob exhaled. "You were beginning to make me nervous."

Denise did not respond. She was reading again, stopping, skipping down to the bottom and reading again. Her eyes darted all over the paper.

"What does this mean?" she suddenly asked. "I have recently gathered in my possession, various documents and letters from my father concerning the most recent Treaty of Paris..."

Rob smiled. "That's the phrase that everybody asks about."

"Everybody?" a look of worry suddenly appeared on her face. "Have you shown this to a lot of people?"

"N-no," Rob replied. He did not like her tone, "Just a few. Why?"

"Items like this are very valuable," Denise answered. Her voice became monotone, as if this was something she had said many times in the past. "And once the general public finds out about their existence, it becomes difficult to deal with responsibly."

"What do you mean responsibly?" Rob could tell she was not telling him the whole story.

"Letters like these are priceless," she explained. Again the monotone voice, "They are the gateway to understanding who and what we are as a people and as a nation. Treasure hunters, pawn shops and many other less than respectable people try to exploit these items for their own profit."

An instant of revelation hit Rob. She wanted this. Or at least she wanted it for her museum or some museum. She was afraid that Rob was just looking to sell it on e-bay or something. He felt almost dirty, partly because she was not completely wrong.

"I'm not looking to sell it," Rob half lied. The passion Denise had for history and the magic of Independence Park was starting to rub off on him. He was not sure what he wanted now.

"That's good to hear," Denise smiled. "Because something like this could cause real trouble."

"Trouble?" Rob repeated. "What do you mean?"

"The Treaty of Paris was highly controversial," Denise explained. "Among so many other things, it set the border between Canada and the United States."

"My family is from Canada," Rob reminded her.

"But the borders were unclear," Denise went on. "It took another Treaty and the War of 1812 to begin to settle the issue."

"Begin?" Rob repeated.

"I don't know that much more," Denise cut the conversation short. "Do you have any idea what he means by *"various documents and letters from my father concerning the most recent Treaty of Paris..."*

"No," Rob admitted. "Not really. That's why we came to you."

"Franklin was in Paris for years," she thought aloud. "And by the end of his stay he was quite ill."

"Really? I never heard about that."

"Very few have," Denise replied. She took great pride in her knowledge of Ben Franklin's life and seized on the opportunity to talk about the lesser known Franklin. "Everyone has heard about the Constitutional Convention and the Declaration and of course the Kite. But most people are completely unaware of how painful the story becomes once he gets to Paris."

"What happened?"

"Everything," she shook her head. "Everything happened. Congress turned on him. John Jay and John Adams constantly attacked him. His health almost completely destroyed him. He became bitter and angry and trusted almost no one."

"My God."

"There were many days when Franklin could not even get out of bed. He had urology problems, he was almost paralyzed on his left side, and he could barely walk or ride in a carriage. The only time the pain was bearable was when he lay down."

"And during all of this, he was being attacked by his friends?"

"They were frustrated with him. They wanted France's help and later they wanted the Treaty finished. They felt that Franklin was slow and incompetent. They didn't trust him. Congress even threatened to recall him."

"Did they?"

"No. But Franklin was so paranoid from all the attacks that he began keeping separate notes from Jay and Adams."

"Have you read these notes?"

"Many times over."

"Did he ever mention a secret stash?" Rob was getting excited. The clues were starting to add up.

"No," Denise answered. Rob slumped on the bench.

"But he wouldn't" Denise continued after a moment's thought. "It would have been too dangerous. He knew his correspondence was being read."

"So maybe," Rob's energy came back even stronger.

"If there really are various undiscovered documents and letters written by Benjamin Franklin about the Treaty of Paris, they could be an incredible find."

"Really?" Rob's eyes grew wide.

"Really," Denise repeated.

"What kind of a find?" Rob asked.

"I don't really know," Denise said honestly. "But I know someone who might."

Interlude

Oval office

Dr. Edward Randolph, official Historian for the State Department, walked into the Oval office and stopped. He had been fighting so much traffic and dealing with so much security and being escorted by so many important people that he had almost forgotten where he was heading. Now all of a sudden he was in the most famous room in the world. He consciously breathed deep and took it all in. He stared down at the Presidential Seal of the Eagle with the Olive branch and arrows woven into the carpet at his feet. He read the "E Pluribus Unum" in the center and smiled. He looked ahead towards the three large almost floor to ceiling windows and their view of the South Lawn beyond. Two flags, the United States flag and the Presidential Flag straddled the left and right of the center window. In between he and the windows was the famous ornate mahogany *Resolute* desk given to President Hayes by Queen Victoria of England where the President himself sat. He turned his head to his right and admired the gold framed portraits of Lincoln and Washington. He imagined the overly plain couches and chairs in front of him occupied by famous foreign leaders. And everywhere he looked a bust or a picture frame of famous historical people decorated the white bookcases set back into their niches, the various chests and tables and even the President's desk. He recognized every one of them.

"Come in Dr. Randolph," Martha Fairfax, the President's chief of staff urged him forward. She was standing to the President's left and dressed in a beautiful purple, blue and black pencil dress that was cut above her knees. Her shoulders and arms were covered by a more reserved black business cardigan. The dress perfectly accentuated her slim figure. The cardigan jacket made it clear that she was a woman of power. It was a wonderful merge of business formal and strong femininity that spoke directly to the kind of woman she was. President Custis had chosen her as his chief of staff for that very reason. She was a bold woman who was not afraid to be herself while at the same time, respecting tradition and style.

The President was a mirror of his Chief of Staff. Elected last year as the country's first true independent, President John Custis was a breath of fresh air that the country needed so badly. Years of in fighting, back stabbing and party loyalty over country had so splintered the Republicans and Democrats that the country looked to an outsider for help. They needed a normal, everyday American they could relate to and trust again.

He had actually been discovered on YOUTUBE. A veteran of the Afghan war (he still walked with a limp from an IED explosion), Custis had been organizing a fundraiser for some cancer survivors that drew lots of media attention. As people got to know him, they began to trust him and to like him. He was warm, caring and intelligent. He had a strong moral center. He was good looking. He loved his country and more importantly, he loved his countrymen. There wasn't a hateful, ambitious bone in Custis' body. And after decades of hate in American politics, people were ready for a little love.

Dr. Randolph had originally thought that was a weakness. Randolph himself had served in the military for over 20 years and in the Federal government for another 20. He had seen his share of Presidents and politicians. He didn't think Custis could cut it. But as the campaign went on and Custis maintained his composure and integrity after countless attacks from the left and the right, Dr. Randolph's opinion of him began to change. By November he was won over, and Dr. Randolph happily voted for him.

Of course that made this moment even more powerful. Not only was Dr. Randolph standing in the room of the most powerful man on earth, not only was he surrounded by historical figures, busts, paintings and statues, he was also crushing like a school girl to meet the man he voted for. He hesitated. He had only been in the Oval office twice before and never alone.

"Hello Dr. Randolph," President Custis stood up and held out his hand. Randolph noticed the limp.

"Mr. President," Randolph resisted the urge to stare and shook the President's hand. He had a firm grip. "It's quite an honor."

"The honor is all mine," The President released his hand and pointed over at his Chief of Staff. "Martha has been telling me all about you. You've got quite the resume'."

"Thank you sir," Randolph blushed slightly. At the same time he wasn't going to waste this opportunity. How many times did you get to meet the President of the United States? "I am pretty proud of my service to our country."

"Not just your military service," Martha took a step forward as well. She held out her own hand, "but your services as the official Historian to the State department."

"Author, advisor, researcher," the President took a step back to allow Martha to shake Randolph's hand, "faculty at VMI, advisor to the D.O.D. , Department of State in 2014 and a Doctorate in History from George Washington University." He turned to Martha. Did I forget anything?"

"Associate Dean of Faculty at Georgetown," Dr. Randolph smiled. They had done their research.

"As I said; impressive. Would you care to join me in my living room?" The President waved his hand at the furniture in the middle of the room. He had purposely chosen couches that were like his living room back home. Dark brown and suede they were on the edge of embarrassing for a President but the voters loved Custis' laid back attitude and down to earth personality. He had almost put his Kansas City Chiefs football chair in the room but Martha wouldn't allow it.

"Absolutely," Randolph grinned as he followed the President past the couches and to the more formal mahogany and black colonial wooden chairs. Custis' love of American history made sure to have something colonial in the room and the chairs seemed the best option. They were similar to a set President Obama had used.

"I must confess," the President turned slightly and sat in the left chair while leaving the right one for Randolph, "while I know about you, I do not know why you are here."

"Sorry sir," Martha began to explain. She had remained standing in her position in front of the President's desk. "There was just no time. This is a matter of the utmost urgency and I had to squeeze Dr. Randolph in at the last minute."

"Sound serious," the President glanced back at Randolph.

"I've asked select members of your cabinet to meet us here," Martha headed towards the door Randolph had entered through. "They should be here by now."

"Not the full cabinet?" Custis said.

"No sir," Martha stopped momentarily. "This is too sensitive."

"Too sensitive?"

"Yes sir. That is why we are meeting here instead of the Cabinet room. It gives the impression of a relaxed, casual conversation."

"Relaxed and casual," The President slumped in his chair and smiled at Randolph. "I can do that."

Martha rolled her eyes and reached for the doorknob. "Sally," she called to the President's secretary in the anteroom beyond. "Are they all here?"

"Yes ma'am,"

"What the hell is going on?" Secretary Lewis burst into the room. He was followed immediately by the Press Secretary, the director of the CIA, and the Secretary of Energy. It was an odd mix of officials that was obvious.

"I don't know any more than you do Tom," The President said to his Secretary of State. He had been President Custis' first choice for State and it had been a slam dunk. True, having an African American as Secretary of State was nothing new. Secretaries Rice and Powell before him had both been highly respected in their jobs. Like his predecessors, Tom Lewis was a highly intelligent, logical man. Graduate of Harvard, ambassador to the U.N. and even a brief T.V. celebrity, Lewis was also a grandson of the first civil rights marchers and was one of the most popular men in Washington. He more than offset Custis' emotional, even irrational Press Secretary Alex Johnson. She had been Custis' best friend in Afghanistan and had helped him organize the first cancer fundraiser that made him famous. The appointment to Press Secretary sat on the edge of cronyism but no one could deny Alex's skill at her job.

The two of them, Lewis and Johnson were constantly at odds. Lewis arguing for reason and logic would often point out that Press Secretary was not an actual cabinet position and try to get her excluded. Johnson however never ceased to impress the President with her skill at realizing in a heartbeat how their actions would be perceived by the public and how they should best proceed. President Custis found both their arguments flawless and would sit back quite often and listen to them battle it out before making his decision. If it wasn't for the constant back and forth almost child-like insults, Custis could listen to them every day. They were the Spock and McCoy to his Kirk.

The presence of CIA and Energy was less obvious. Custis did not know either of them nearly as much. Bill Donovan, head of the CIA and Al Grant, Secretary of Energy were both recommendations of Martha's. Both men were career politicians who had served different presidents for over 20 years. But both were highly respected in D.C. and beyond and both did their jobs well.

"Let me get right to it," Martha remained standing as the four officials took their seats on the suede couches. Alex took her usual spot, on the end of the couch nearest the President while Tom, predictably, sat opposite her on the other couch. Bill and Al filled in the remaining spots. Bill chose Tom's couch perhaps because CIA and State worked together on occasion while Al chose to sit next to Alex there being no real connection between Energy and Press that anyone could think of.

"Dr. Randolph has brought to my attention something that could have major National and International ramifications and could become one of the greatest border crises this country has seen since the Revolution."

"The Revolution?" Secretary Lewis looked directly at Dr. Randolph, back at

Martha and again at Dr. Randolph. His face had grown dark and his large black eyes bore into Randolph, searching for some answers. "Why wasn't this brought to my attention first? Randolph works for me."

"I tried sir," Randolph pushed back in his chair. His boss was famous for his anger. It was his second greatest fault, not far behind his rampant sexism. He had already been involved in several close calls that almost became major scandals. Only Alex Johnson's quick work as Press Secretary behind the scenes managed to save him. It was yet another weird quirk in their stormy relationship.

"It's not about you Tom," Alex predictably interrupted.

"I should have been notified."

"There is a memo on your desk," Dr. Randolph quickly explained. "But no one was taking me seriously and this is a time sensitive manner."

"What the fuck is this all about?" The President was losing his patience. "Cut all the bullshit and get to it already Martha."

"It would be better if I let Dr. Randolph explain." She looked directly at the Dr.

"OK," Dr. Randolph paused. He had plenty of public speaking and command experience but this was still an intimidating situation. For a moment he was afraid that he had made a mistake. Maybe this wasn't the big deal he thought it was. "Last week I was contacted by a friend of mine in Philadelphia. She is the director of the National Park Service over there. We've known each other since graduate school days and we had even collaborated on some historical research."

He paused for a second to see if there were any questions. All eyes were on him.

"She informed me that she had just come across a most startling discovery."

"How did she come across it?" Lewis asked. He was still fuming about Dr. Randolph going over his head but would not let his anger get in the way of his job.

"A tourist at Independence Hall showed her."

"A tourist!" Lewis was about to lose it. The President put up his hand immediately to signal him to be quiet.

"This man had a letter with him that was clearly written by William Franklin."

"William," the President said. "Don't you mean Benjamin?"

"William Franklin was Benjamin Franklin's first born son. He is also the most famous traitor in American History."

"I thought that was Benedict Arnold." Bill Donovan, CIA, said. He was leaning forward intently. Anything dealing with letters and traitors and border crises definitely held his attention. His brown eyes focused directly on Randolph trying to read the man.

"At the time," Randolph was a little uncomfortable with Donovan's stare, "it was William Franklin. While Arnold had started on our side, Franklin was the highest ranking, most well-known Loyalist of his time."

"What did the letter say?" Donovan pressed.

"I won't go into all the details as they are not necessary. The issue is that near the end of the letter Franklin references some mysterious documents that he has in his possession concerning the Treaty of Paris."

"Treaty of Paris?" The President asked.

"The Treaty of Paris," Secretary Lewis answered, trying to take some control of the situation, "was the Treaty ending the American Revolution."

"That is correct," said Randolph. "And this letter makes it clear that Benjamin Franklin may have hidden away some letters or documents regarding that Treaty."

"How?"

"About three quarters of the way into the letter, William Franklin says.

Randolph stopped and consulted his notes. He placed his finger on a spot on the paper. "I have recently gathered in my possession, various documents and letters from my father concerning the most recent Treaty of Paris..."

"Holy Crap."

"The Treaty of Paris was ratified more than 200 years ago," Lewis continued to bait Dr. Randolph, "and has been upheld ever since. How could some papers written by Franklin have any effect on that?"

"Actually sir, the Treaty was quite controversial."

"In what sense?" the President asked. He was fascinated by the Revolution and colonial time period and this was all news to him.

"In regards the ending of the war and independence of the United States, the treaty was quite clear."

Lewis rolled his eyes.

"But in the negotiations on the border with Canada, there was quite a bit of controversy."

"Canada?" Lewis had heard enough. "This is what this is all about? Who gives a flying fuck about Canada? I'm dealing with terrorism, war, famine, third world crises, money laundering by Latin American dictators and you waste our time with a bunch of hockey playing, moose hunting Canucks?"

"Well now we know why Randolph went above your head," Alex quipped. She had been listening quietly, trying to see what her role in all this might be.

"Screw you Alex," Lewis said. "I don't even know why you are here."

"I don't know why any of you are here," the President shouted at both of them. "Would you just shut the heck up and let the Dr. finish? God I don't know why I put up with you two. And Martha, would you grab a friggin seat? You don't need to be standing over all of us. I thought this was a friendly conversation."

"Yes sir," Martha pulled one of the non-descript brown wooden chairs from next to the President's desk towards the group and sat down. She crossed her legs and placed her iPad down on her lap.

"Dr. Randolph," the President waited for Martha to settle, "would you please continue?"

"Believe it or not," Randolph said, "the border with Canada is still not settled."

"What?" Lewis gasped. The President gave him a look.

"Machias Seal Island at the entrance to the Bay of Fundy is under dispute and has been for decades. The United States and Canada have never really made it an issue but both sides still claim it as their own."

"I've never heard of this island," Alex said. She prided herself on her knowledge of anything controversial that could hit the newspapers or the on-line junkies but in all of her constant surveillance of the news, she had never once come across anything like this.

"It is quite a small island and houses only a light house. No one cares much about it other than some ecologists and lobster men but this is merely the tip of the veritable iceberg. The island sits right at the entrance to the Bay, one of the greatest resources in North America if not the world. It is the gateway to Canada."

"But you've already said this has been in dispute for decades."

"It has," Randolph explained patiently. "And both sides have never pushed the issue. Unfortunately Franklin's letter could change the entire dynamic."

"How?"

"The Treaty of Paris was quite vague about the border and there have been many disputes, even violence. During the War of 1812, one of the major issues was the unsettled border. Smuggling was rampant and so was piracy. Even after the war, disputes continued. It was only after the so called Aroostook war that the 1842 Webster-Ashburton Treaty seemed to settle the issue."

"Seemed?"

"There is still disagreement about how the lines are drawn to and from the river St. Croix, the original source of the border dispute in the 18th century. The Unites States and Canada have never bilaterally agreed upon their own set of baselines."

"And you are saying," Martha tried to sum it up for the group. She already understood much of this. Dr. Randolph had explained it to her privately just two days ago. But she needed the President to hear it from the State Historian's mouth. "That if there are documents and letters written by Benjamin Franklin about the treaty, then the entire border with Canada could come into question again?"

"It's not just some small island," Dr. Randolph pressed. "If there are documents out there which describe or contradict the treaties made afterwards and the lines that were drawn, then everything in New Brunswick and Maine comes into question."

"Again," Lewis could not stop himself. "So?"

"TransCanada is currently trying to build an oil pipeline that would transport oil across Canada to almost the exact point of contention in the Bay of Fundy."

"Oh shit there is oil involved?" Al suddenly realized why he was there. As Secretary of Energy anything dealing with oil or coal or any other resource fell under his department. He knew of the TransCanada pipeline. He was involved in discussions of the earlier Keystone pipeline which also transported oil from Western Canada. The difference with this new pipeline was that while Keystone went into the United States, this one was entirely in Canada and not under any U.S. laws. At least that it was he thought, until now.

"I've never heard of oil in eastern Canada," the President said.

"There isn't any," Al explained. "But this pipeline will bring oil to Eastern

Canada from the west and potentially to all of the Eastern Seaboard when it is finished. There is also an oil refinery in St. John's, a big one."

"It's the biggest refinery in Canada," Randolph added, "and the tenth largest refinery in North America."

"And where there is oil," Alex was beginning to see her role in all this, "there are protesters."

"That's right," Randolph was pleased they were beginning to understand. "There are two Canadian organizations that I know of that are already protesting the pipeline."

"And if word gets out to our side of the border,"

"Especially after all the Keystone problems,"

"This could get really ugly."

"Hold on, hold on," the President interrupted. "I am no historian, but I know enough American History to know that Benjamin Franklin was not a man of secret's and conspiracies. This is Ben Franklin we are talking about."

"Actually sir," Randolph corrected, "he was. All of the Founding Fathers were. Indeed the entire Constitution was written in secret."

"It was?"

"Yes sir. But more to the point is why he would write the documents alluded to in the letter."

"That is what I was wondering," said Lewis.

"And so was I," Randolph was looking for some common ground with his boss. After all, at the end of the day, he had to answer to Lewis. "So I did some digging and what I found not only gave credence to the possibility of these documents, it makes it likely."

Randolph let his words hang in the air for a moment. He realized the chilling drama of what he was saying and could not stop himself from enjoying it. Everyone waited for him to continue.

"We all know the famous Ben Franklin, the man revered throughout our country; the kite story; the Declaration, the Constitution, the dear old grandfatherly like sage who advised Jefferson and even Washington. Unfortunately, the myths of Franklin and all of our Founding Fathers being some kind of gods has been built up and propped up for decades if not longer."

The President had a frown on his face. He did not like where the Dr. was taking him. He grew up on those myths. He signed up to serve based on the beliefs in those myths.

"Franklin, Washington, Jefferson, Adams, they were all men like you and I filled with emotion, jealousies, political ambition and ego. They fought constantly and agreed rarely. Once Franklin had been sent to Paris, his enemies had begun to talk and plot behind his back. There were attempts by Congress to recall him. Adams and Jay, who had been sent to Paris to join and possibly replace Franklin, were frustrated with how the negotiations were going. Adams was an outspoken critic of Franklin. He criticized him regularly."

"Well that much I could guess," the President smiled. "I saw the John Adams mini-series. He could be quite the ass hole."

"You have no idea sir," Randolph again opened the small notebook he had been carrying, "and neither did I." He glanced at the open notebook page and placed a finger on the words he was about to read. "Listen to what Adams said about Franklin during the Treaty Negotiations."

"I can feel no other sentiments than contempt and abhorrence."

"About Franklin?"

Randolph did not respond. He moved his finger further down the page. "And,"

"He is lazy, despotic, controlling, untrustworthy, villainous."

"Where did you find this shit?" Lewis gasped.

"These were in letters Adams wrote during the Treaty negotiations."

"Holy Fuck," The President reacted.

"There's just no way." Donovan said.

"I am as shocked as you are," Dr. Randolph tried to get hold of the group again. Their disbelief was leading to their own little rebellion. "But there is no denying it. I have spent the last few days reading everything I could about the treaty and about Franklin and Adams and Jay."

"Why was there so much animosity?" Alex was beginning to realize that this could approach a whole new level of crises that no one had yet realized. She needed to understand everything.

"Well without going into too much detail," Randolph was glad for the question. "The Treaty of Paris was intensely complicated and the tensions could not have been higher. I remind you that the 13 colonies were trying to free themselves from the most powerful empire in the world."

"It took almost two years just to write it," Lewis added. He at least knew that.

"That's right. Franklin was having financial problems, he missed his daughter intensely and he was no spring chicken anymore. He was an old man, suffering from physical pain and personal loss."

"Like his son turning traitor," The President added.

"And an angry, bitter, victimized man like Franklin may have kept secrets."

"To protect himself from Adams' attacks," Alex broke in. The light bulb had gone off. Her skill in public relations was clear. She explained to the group. "If Franklin was being attacked publicly, and in the press," she looked to Randolph for approval. He nodded and gave her the floor, "then he just may have kept certain letters and documents secret to protect himself in case Adams attacked him again."

"And if his son William got his hands on them,"

"Holy shit," the President swore again.

"Kind of like how Hamilton and Jefferson went at it," Bill Donovan added. He of course had not only seen the Hamilton musical, he had read all about Hamilton's affair and Jefferson and the slave girl. He knew how people of power acted.

"Exactly," Randolph agreed.

"Guys we've got a lot more than a potential border crisis on our hands," the wheels in Alex's head were still spinning. "This could become a public relations nightmare."

"Explain," the President ordered. He was still wrapping his head around the whole thing.

"OK, hear me out," she said. "Ben Franklin has a son who is a traitor. He keeps secrets about Adams, the man who will become the second President of the United States. The founders turn out to be everyday men like you and I who fought against each other and even fought amongst their own family members. The Revolution was not a story of heroes and a united front against an evil enemy but a time of chaos and mistrust when we were at each other's throats."

She stopped for a moment to let her words sink in. "How will the American public react to this information?"

"They will deny it," Donovan said quickly. "They will accuse whoever releases the information of fraud and disloyalty."

"Some of them," Randolph hoped for the more rational side to win out. "Many of them will accept it and be fascinated by it. They will appreciate the power of the truth."

"Correct," Alex agreed. She too had faith in the vast majority of Americans. "But let's not forget the power of our story, of our founding. We have a great heroic story of men who stood up against all odds and brought us freedom and democracy against an evil enemy. There are people in America who use that story for their own gain. What about them?"

"They will attack it."

"And they will attack us."

"Why?" The President asked.

"We are now involved. We know about it. Information like this will not stay secret forever and you will eventually be asked when you found out about it."

The President put his thumb under his chin and his forefinger on the side of his nose. He leaned forward, making sure he understood every nuance. He took Alex's words quite seriously.

"You will then either tell them the truth or be forced to lie."

"You know I won't lie."

"In addition, discussions about the border with Canada will come up. Perhaps your own beliefs on the founders will be questioned; Then your own Patriotism."

"You've got to be kidding me."

"We live in a 24 hour news cycle sir. The talk shows need something to talk about. Your enemies or perhaps some demagogue who likes to hear his own voice will attack the President of the United States for his Patriotism. He will question if you really believe all this nonsense about Franklin and Adams or if you think the Loyalists were victims."

"Stop it."

"As an Independent," Alex ignored the President. "Republicans and Democrats will see this as a moment of weakness. Republicans will probably appeal to their bases' love of country and Patriotism. Democrats will wonder why you kept it a secret for so long."

"Ben Franklin is like a God," Randolph chimed in. "Everywhere I went in my research, he is praised and admired."

"He's on the fifty,"

"Not just that," Randolph continued. "I did a quick search of things named after Ben Franklin. There are 32 counties, 50 towns and cities, three mountains, a lake, six colleges and universities, 23 high schools, eight middle schools, 14 elementary schools , countless businesses, streets, parkways and a bridge. There was even a state temporarily named after him and in 1964 a Broadway Musical opened titled "Franklin in Paris."

"Jesus," the President shook his head. He knew Alex was right. "What do we do about it?"

"Obviously we keep it a secret as long as possible. If it turns out to be a hoax, then no harm done. You have protected the Republic. If it turns out to be true, you were acting in the Nation's best interest. But if word gets out before we know for sure-"

"That'll be my job," Donovan said. "I'll also put a tail on this tourist you mentioned."

"You'll need to coordinate with the RCMP," Lewis added. He still chuckled every time he thought about the Royal Canadian Mounted Police. He couldn't ever get that Dudley Do Right cartoon from childhood out of his head.

"You think we should tell the Canadians, Tom?"

"Yes sir, Mr. President," Lewis said formally. He was always a stickler for protocol and now that decisions were being made, he took on his role as Secretary of State seriously. "Alex is right about the public relations nightmare. We need to get a handle on it immediately. There can be no question at all that we informed Canada immediately. After all the Canadians are our best friends."

"Even though, they are a bunch of hockey playing, moose hunters," Alex could not resist the jab.

"Deserved." Lewis took the blow in stride.

"Alex you've got to keep control of this," the President turned back to her. "You've got to keep an eye on every rumor, every innuendo and you have to keep track of everything that we say and do in this room and beyond. I will not be accused of being some kind of a traitor or weakling or having my loyalty questioned. This cannot become a scandal."

"And what is my role in this?" Al asked. It was obvious why he was in the room as Secretary of Energy however what he could do about it was not so clear.

"Keep your eyes open and your mouth shut," Martha finally spoke up. She had been quiet during the meeting when it was all review. Now that plans were being made, she took charge. It was one of the qualities the President liked most about her. He could just sit back and let her do the work while he waited for those rare times when he disagreed with her. "You need to watch TransCanada as quietly as possible. Look for any indication that they are aware of even a rumor of a border dispute. Once big Oil finds out about this, there is no way we will be able to control it."

"Of course."

"And Tom," Martha turned back to the Secretary of State, "you had better prepare for any kind of border dispute. Draw up best and worst case scenarios, get a handle on what impact even the slightest border change could cause including this Matiaz Island."

"Machias Seal Island," Dr. Randolph corrected her.

"Thank you Dr. Randolph for your diligent research and for bringing this to our attention," Martha concluded the meeting.

"What's your security clearance?" Donovan had to ask.

"Not high enough," Randolph chuckled.

"That's for sure," Lewis agreed. "Randolph I want you answering only to me. Do not do any more research, do not make any more contacts with this National Park service person unless you get explicit orders from me. Do you understand?"

"Absolutely sir."

"I can't say it's been a pleasure," the President stood up and stuck out his hand. "But thank you for bringing this to our attention so quickly Dr. Randolph."

"It's been an honor sir," Randolph shook the President's hand and took a step forward to leave, "A real honor."

"Randolph," Bill Donovan stopped him. "What did you say was the name of this tourist who found the letter?"

"Callahan," sir, "Robert Callahan."

Fourteen

Rob stood outside of the Starbucks and stared in the window. He could see Lindsey sitting in the back. She was wearing her blue Sabres cap and looking down at the coffee mug in her hands but he could tell it was her immediately. Her beautiful blond hair flowed out of the hat and over her shoulders. Her pink shorts contrasted perfectly with her tan legs and her breasts firmed up tightly against her black Nike work out shirt. Damn she was hot.

"Fuck," he couldn't let this happen. But after that phone call, when he thought Lindsey might be hurt, his emotions betrayed him. He realized he was falling for her and that it would ruin everything.

"Fuck," he swore again as he opened the coffee shop door and headed in.

"Hey," he tapped her on the shoulder.

"Were you followed?"

"Hello to you too," Rob put his keys, phone and an expandable binder down next to Lindsey, then headed over to the cash register to make his order. "And no, I wasn't followed."

Despite his bravado, Rob was nervous too. He pulled his own cap (New York Rangers of course), down over his forehead and looked around the coffee shop before he made his order. It was like any other Starbucks; some two person tables and chairs, a few comfy recliners, a display case with healthy snacks and a shelf selling coffee mugs. Even the newspaper stand carrying the New York Times and Wall Street Journal was where they always were, near the front entrance. The patrons were just as regular; a young couple right next to them, a group of students studying in the corner and a woman reading a novel near the window. No one and nothing was suspicious.

"Sorry," he returned from the register with his coffee after a long two minutes and sat back with Lindsey. "I know it's been tough."

"You have no idea," Lindsey glanced around again. She could not settle down. "The entire drive back to UCONN, I was a bundle of nerves. I almost went off the road twice looking in my rear views to see if anyone was behind me."

"What did you find out?" Rob tried to get her mind off the Pawn shop dealer. He could feel it too. At school yesterday, he could swear he felt someone watching the kids at recess. Three times he almost asked the principal for a lockdown drill.

"Some pretty cool stuff," Lindsey's eyes lit up. Rob loved the way her passion for this family tree stuff just took over and washed everything else away. "The Professor knew a lot more about Loyalists and Canada than we gave him credit for."

"Really?"

"Yeah, you should have given him more of a chance the first time," Lindsey scolded him.

"Hey," Rob reminded her. "It was my idea to send you back."

"True."

"Anyway,"

"Oh yeah," Lindsey laughed. "He said that hundreds, maybe thousands of Loyalists were left with nothing after the war. The King was pretty slow to give them anything and when he did, a lot of times it was worthless land."

"So what did they do?" Rob took another sip of his White Chocolate Mocha and stole a glance around the shop; Still no one to worry about.

"Some of them gave up. Some of them moved around. Some of them petitioned the King or even hired lawyers."

"Like Franklin," Rob added.

"Like Franklin," Lindsey confirmed.

"That backs up what I found in Philly." The nerves in his back were getting excited as things began to fall into place. "After I left the visitor's center, I spent a little more time looking around-"

"After you got my text?" Lindsey frowned.

"Yeah," Rob lowered his head. "I knew another hour or two wouldn't make a difference at that point, and who knew when I would have time to come back there." Rob paused for a moment to see if Lindsey would scold him some more, but she just sat in silent anger.

"So after the war," Rob continued, "William moved to London and spent years representing Loyalist families."

"Like your family?" Lindsey perked up again.

"I still don't know," Rob took another sip of coffee. One of the teenage students in the corner suddenly burst out laughing. Both he and Lindsey jumped in reaction.

"Sorry," the student said through stifled laughter as he held up his hand and waved. His face was covered with freckles and he was wearing a "Geek Out" t-shirt. He held out his other hand to stop the coffee from coming out of his nose as the girl and two boys sitting with him lost control and laughed at him. It reminded Rob of school. He smiled and returned his attention to Lindsey.

"I went to the D.A.R. right after school," he said over their laughter. He even chuckled himself, "Just like you suggested."

"And?"

"They gave me some ideas."

"Some ideas?"

"Yeah."

"Like?"

"It was pretty uncomfortable. They had paintings of the Revolution everywhere, flags in every room and even a few mementos from the Revolution itself. It was like a shrine."

"Sorry." Lindsey knew it would be uncomfortable for Rob. The Daughters of the American Revolution were all women who could trace their lineage directly back to the veterans of 1776. Here in Connecticut that meant that most of their ancestors fought with either George Washington or Henry Knox or both. They were probably the most patriotic group in America. But they were also the best genealogists in the area and they had a meeting house right in Fairfield. If anyone could help Rob trace his family back to the Revolution, it was them.

"I couldn't bear to tell them I might be from a Loyalist family."

"No surprise," Lindsey nodded. Her head swung to her left. A small older man walked into the coffee shop. For a moment she thought it was the Pawn shop dealer. She had to force her heart to slow down.

"But you know," Rob quickly continued, "it is quite possible I have a member of my family who did fight for the rebels."

"Oh?" The older man went on to order his coffee. Lindsey turned away.

"Sure. One of my great uncles or a cousin could have joined up. All the families around here were pretty large."

"True," Lindsey agreed. "The Professor did say that the rebellion split up families-"

"I probably had relatives on both sides," Rob added emphatically.

"Probably."

"And," Rob smiled. It was time to get to the point of all this. "I also found this." He pushed a piece of heavy paper across the table. It was yellow around the edges and had a corner broken off but Lindsey could tell it was covered in writing.

"What is it?" Lindsey glanced up at Rob as she pulled the paper over to her.

"Just look," Rob smiled as he sat back in the chair and sipped his coffee.

Lindsey picked up the paper. It was heavy, almost like cardboard. Someone obviously wanted to make sure it did not get ruined.

"I almost missed it," Rob interjected. "It was lodged against the back of the box and I thought it was just a broken piece."

"Is this?" Lindsey began as she turned the paper over.

"Yeah," Rob smiled again. "It is."

"The Index!" Lindsey almost shouted then panicked. She looked all around to see if anyone reacted to her shout.

"Yeah," Rob whispered and laughed.

"Are you sure?" Lindsey scanned the names. It was not what she expected. When she first suggested to Rob that they look for it, she was hoping it would be an itemized list or a drawing of a family tree or some other kind of key. This was just a list of names.

"Well no. But it is the closest I could find." He paused for a minute as Lindsey looked it over. She took another sip of her drink. The loud slurp of a straw looking for more liquid escaped from the cup. It was almost empty except for the ice.

"But I recognize some of those names," he added.

"Which ones?"

Rob paused for a minute and reached back into his bag. Lindsey watched him take out a small yellow glasses case, open up the black frames and slide them on. *"You know, I think I like them,"* she thought to herself, *"they add a mysterious whole other side to him."*

"Appleby," Rob looked down at the list and quickly added. He had no idea Lindsey had been looking across the table at him. "That is my grandmother's maiden name, and I think I heard of the name Garrison before."

"And there is an Adams," Lindsey shook her head slightly and pointed to the name at the top of the paper.

"I saw," Rob nodded.

"Any relation to John Adams?"

"The President?" Rob guessed, "Maybe." He shrugged. "That would really be messed up huh?"

"We should try to match this up with some of the letters I found in my box," Lindsey said. She took the last sip of her iced coffee and started to get up.

"Right now?" Rob remained seated.

"Yeah! Who knows what we can find out now?"

"Like what?"

"I don't know," Lindsey grabbed her purse off the chair. "But I have all kind of notes and even a book of names from the area that I found on the internet. There is a whole section on the Adams family!"

"Wait a minute," Rob grabbed her arm as he stood.

"What?" Lindsey quipped. Rob's grip was pretty tight.

"You're making a scene," Rob lowered his voice.

"Me?" Lindsey frowned as she stared down at her arm. Rob was still holding it.

"Sorry," Rob quickly let go. "You know what I mean. "

"Ok," Lindsey rubbed her arm where Rob had grabbed it for a second to get the blood flowing again. "Why don't we take our own cars and then meet at my place?"

"My place," Rob repeated in his head. He knew what those words universally meant. Panic rushed through him as he suddenly thought Lindsey wanted to have sex. *"Don't be an idiot,"* Rob laughed at himself. That is not what she meant at all. He hoped Lindsey did not see him blush.

"Makes sense," Rob tried to hide his ridiculous thought with logic. "I will wait a few minutes then head out."

Fifteen

Finally the doorbell rang.

Rob stopped pacing in the kitchen. "Thank God," he let out a large sigh at the same time as his pulse started to race. "Took forever," he almost ran to the front door.

"Hi," Rob greeted his wife with as big a smile as he could muster. Deborah was dressed in a Celtics t-shirt and jeans. Rob didn't know if she was trying to look sloppy casual on purpose or if she was trying to tease him. Rob always loved how tight her ass looked in blue jeans, and she knew it.

"Hi," Deborah did not return the smile nor did she make any motion to walk into the house. She would rather be any place other than here, with him.

"C'mon in," Rob stepped back to allow his wife entrance. He realized how strange it was treating his wife like a visitor. He had never had to open the front door for her. She just always walked in, usually through the garage door entrance near the kitchen.

"Thanks for coming," Rob said as he walked into the kitchen. "Want some coffee or something?" Again, how strange it was offering his wife a drink in her own house. But it wasn't her house anymore, was it?

"No," Deborah said coldly, following him into the kitchen and placing her purse down on the kitchen table. "Let's just get this over with."

"Ok, ok," Rob agreed nervously. No sense in prolonging this. He was certainly not enjoying this either. But it had to be done. "The box is in the bedroom." He turned away from the kitchen and towards the stairs.

"In the bedroom?"

"I didn't want any chance that the boys would see it," Rob explained. "And it's the only room they don't dare go in."

Deborah smiled at that thought. It only took one time for Bobby to walk in on his parents having sex that the bedroom became a forbidden zone. He was only eight years old at the time and he screamed all the way down the hall and down the stairs as he ran outside in total horror. The memory was a good one at least for Rob and Deborah. "Where are the boys?"

"Over friends' houses," Rob reached the stairs and swung his hand over the banister as he turned. "I didn't want any chance we would get disturbed or that they would see us together."

"Good idea," Deborah followed a few feet behind. She hated the thought of sending her boys away because she and Rob were too embarrassed to be seen together. And now, with the two of them heading up to the bedroom it was just too much. She felt bile in her throat and a little dizzy. *God-damn you Rob,* she swore to herself.

"It's in the back closet," Rob headed deeper into the bedroom while Deborah stood by the bed. It was a full king size bed, with Tempur-pedic pillows and a firm mattress. Deborah eyed it with longing. She had so many great sleeps on that awesome mattress, and so much great sex. That is why they had bought a king size. In the old bed, she and Rob had destroyed several lamps and even a picture frame she had on the night table with a wild leg kick or a swing of an arm. Even with the new large bed, she smiled and closed her eyes in thought; Rob had fallen off more than once.

It was perfectly made as well. The mattress cover was tucked in, the red sheets barely noticeable underneath. The pillows had their covers on and even the red pillow hearts were propped up perfectly in the center. Why hadn't the bed ever looked like that when they were together? She wondered.

"Here it is," Rob broke her mood as he placed the box down gently on the bed. "Everything I could find at mom's that I think needs to be safeguarded."

"And why are you giving it to me again?"

"I need you to keep it safe while we are in Canada."

"Canada." Deborah repeated. She knew he was going there. He had explained it all over the phone, about how they needed more clues and that there were families up there that Nana wrote about, but she still didn't get it or like it. It was all happening to fast.

"And why are you taking the boys?"

"To keep them safe," Rob didn't want to tell her it was also to get them away from the whole separation stuff and to give them time with their dad. He was actually looking forward to going to the birth nation of hockey, seeing some minor league games and maybe even getting into a rink or two with the boys. It would be a little vacation that was so long overdue.

"From what again?" Deborah remembered the whole scene with Lindsey and the creepy Pawn shop dealer but that was it. She didn't see why they had to run away with the children.

"I don't really know Deborah," Rob admitted. "But Lindsey and I both feel-"

"She's going?" Deborah raised her voice and her shoulders.

"Y-yeah," Rob took an instinctive step back. Deborah's temper was almost as bad as his. It may take longer to get going, but when she was upset, she threw things. "She knows so much already. She found the land clipping and she has this great book-"

"Land clipping?"

"She thinks we may have land up there."

"Oh she does? How convenient."

"Hey," Rob took a step forward now. His temper was starting to rise as well. He didn't like what Deborah was insinuating, especially because it might be true. "Back off. This has nothing to do with Lindsey and nothing to do with you. It's about my mother and my family. I got Lindsey into this mess and I need to make sure she is safe."

"And what about my safety?" Deborah was not backing down.

"You weren't followed. You weren't at the Pawn shop with me. The old guy doesn't know where you live. He only knows our house and Lindsey's house and probably mom's. You will be safe at your place."

"And how do you know I will be safe?"

"He hasn't seen you that much." Rob was getting pretty upset. He had hoped to stay away from all this jealously crap that fueled their anger.

"But he has seen a lot of Lindsey,"

Rob wondered if she was going to say it. The thought hung in the air between the two of them as their eyes locked. It didn't need to be vocalized. They both could hear it loud and clear. *And you have seen a lot of Lindsey too.*

"Just admit you want to sleep with her Rob,"

"Would you cut this shit out?" Rob was almost yelling now. "How many times do I have to tell you I don't want to sleep with her?"

"It doesn't matter how many times you tell me, or how many times you tell yourself. You know it's true. You can't lie to me about that kind of shit."

"So what? Even if it were true, we are not together anymore." Rob was trying his best not to admit to himself or to his wife just how right she was. It would ruin everything; the team, his friendships, and any last chance he had with his wife.

But it was true. How could it not be true? She was so damn hot, and he had already had that dream.

"Are you sure you want to do this Rob?" Deborah's tone suddenly changed. She realized the path he was going on, that they both were going on, and she wasn't ready to go there. Maybe they could still salvage this marriage. Maybe they could still keep the family together, if nothing else for the kids' sake. "You can't walk away from something like this."

"I don't know what the fuck I want," Rob's anger and passion was growing out of control. He was also getting turned on. A good percentage of the sex he and Deborah had, started with fights. It was one of the reasons their sex life was so good. They both were already emotionally out of control and on edge even before they had their clothes off. It didn't help that he was also unable to shake the memory of the threesome dream he had of his wife and Lindsey and he.

"Well you better decide quickly," Deborah was feeling it too. They had both stepped closer to each other and their eyes had been locked the entire time. She could feel her body starting to tingle and the warmth rising. "Don't let your goddamn prick make your decision for you!"

"I won't!" Just the mention of his prick got it moving. Rob could feel it rising as his passion grew.

"You better not," Deborah stumbled over the last word. Her throat was getting dry. Her body was aching for Rob. It had been so long. Their eyes connected like they had so many times before.

No more words were needed. Rob grabbed Deborah with both hands and pulled her against him. She could feel how turned on he was immediately. Within seconds, they were expertly reaching for each other's buttons and snaps and zippers and seconds after that, they were on the bed.

Sixteen

"That was a mistake," Rob rolled off his wife and swung his legs over the edge of the bed.

"I know," Deborah agreed, rolling to the opposite side and reaching for her clothes that still lay in a pile at the edge.

"Couldn't help myself," Rob grabbed his red cotton briefs and slipped them on.

"You never could," Deborah smiled as she headed into their master bathroom to clean up and change.

"Hey it takes two,"

"Always does."

"Or sometimes three," Rob grinned as he thought again of his dream. The sex had done nothing to make that image go away.

"Mom! Dad!" Bobby's voice rose up from the front hallway.

"Fuck!" they both shouted together. Rob grabbed his pants. Deborah did the same.

"Just a minute!" Rob answered.

"Is mom there?" this time it was Adam. "I saw her car in the driveway."

"Shit," Deborah cursed as she walked back into the bedroom half dressed. She slipped her Celtics t-shirt back over her head. "I knew I should have parked down the street."

"You had no idea," Rob defended her. He turned towards his still open bedroom door. "She and I are going over some things," he called down the stairs. "Be right down."

"Damn it, damn it, damn it," Deborah was pacing back and forth. "They can't see us like this."

"They won't," Rob quickly shut the door.

"You and your fucking prick," Deborah became suddenly hostile.

"What the hell?"

"It's always getting us into trouble!"

"This ain't the time Deb," Rob could feel where this was going. They had never really had it out. The fighting, the arguing, the tension between them was always dodged, avoided, distracted. The real issues between Deborah and Rob never made it out into the open and Rob could feel it coming now.

"You think with your dick more than with your head!" Deborah didn't care. She was tired of being the outsider. Tired of feeling like she was the one who did something wrong while Rob lived in the house and stayed with the kids and cooked their meals and went to their games. She was tired of living alone and asking for permission to see her own children.

"I know," Rob kept his head down and refused to look in her eyes. He knew she was right. He knew that his jealousy was a large part of the problem. He knew that he had made too many accusations; that he had asked too many questions; that he had ripped and tore at the trust a husband and a wife are supposed to have. "I couldn't help myself."

"If you had only trusted me!" She screamed. She didn't care if the kids heard. She didn't care if the whole world heard.

"I tried," Rob said meekly. He did try. He really did. All those nights when she came home late, all those meetings with Doctors and sales reps and parties she was invited to. He tried to pretend it didn't bother him. But it did. And whether he trusted his wife or not, he didn't trust the men she was with. Rob knew how beautiful his wife was. He knew how men were around her and whether she wanted to admit it or not, those men were after her. It didn't matter whether she was interested in them. They were interested in her. "But you never even heard what I had to say."

"That's because you should have trusted me!"

"I did trust you! It was all those men I didn't trust!"

"Oh!" Deborah threw her arms up in the air. This part of the discussion they had already had, over and over again. She wasn't about to relive that. "Just give me the stupid box," she grabbed it off the bed. "And let me get out of here."

"Fucking eh," Rob swore. As usual his temper did not disappear as quickly as Deborah's. He wanted to keep talking. He wanted to tell Deborah that it didn't help that she made all the money and that she was being wined and dined by all these men with money while he was an elementary school teacher. He wanted to hear her reaffirm that she still loved him and that the money didn't matter. But none of that would happen now. The kids were still downstairs (hopefully not at the bedroom door) and this would have to wait until later; or perhaps never.

Rob opened the door for Deborah so she could carry the box and tried to smile like she was doing. "Coming boys!" He called.

"Are you guys back together?" Adam called up the stairs as soon as his parents appeared. Both boys had stood at the base of the stairs listening to the screaming, afraid to move, afraid to do anything. Bobby looked athletic and tired, as if he had been playing a sport. He had some color in his face and sweat still gleaned off his nose. Adam was dry. He was wearing a Warcraft t-shirt and his lanky body looked almost ridiculous next to his brother's. He had probably been playing video games. Both of them however, were at complete attention, ears yearning to hear their parent's hoped for response.

"No," Deborah answered Adam quickly. Her heart ached for her son. His face was bright and filled with hope. His eyes pleaded, even his body leaned up the stairs, begging to hear good news. Deborah could barely get the words out. "I was just picking something up for Dad is all."

"B-but, I thought," Adam protested.

"Shut up loser," Bobby smacked Adam in the back of the head. He was just as upset as Adam was but he hid his disappointment with violence (much like his father, Rob knew.)

"Hey," Rob ignored the slap and stepped right past his boys to reach for the front door. "Give your mother a kiss boys. We have to start packing."

"Packing?" Adam kissed his mother on the cheek while he looked at his father.

"For Canada idiot," Bobby managed to give his mother a hug around the box that was still in her hands. "Remember he told us about it last night?"

"Oh yeah; is mom coming?"

"Oh Jesus," Bobby shook his head.

"Goodbye boys," Deborah took that as her cue to leave. "Have a safe trip."

<h1 style="text-align:center">Seventeen</h1>

"You really didn't have to come," Rob looked away from the highway for a minute and glanced at Lindsey. Her Sabres cap was again turned around rally style and her hair was tied up underneath. Rob could see that she was concentrating on the book in her lap.

He put on his left blinker and moved the Camry back into the center lane where he would not have to keep worrying about some idiot tailgating his butt like they had been doing ever since he left Hartford. No matter how long Rob had lived in New England, he could never drive the way they did. It must be something in the blood, he had long ago realized, that made them all drive like race car drivers, gangsters and soldiers as they darted and weaved and practically rammed into any car that was in their path. Rob had lost track of how many times some angry driver had given him the finger.

Driving just wasn't his thing. He didn't hate it, or fear it, he just didn't really care for it. Maybe it was his demeanor, maybe his Midwestern roots. If he could take the train or the subway, he would always prefer that. At least there, he could read or look at his phone. For whatever reason, the motion of a car made him woozy whenever he wasn't driving.

He turned and looked back at Lindsey in envy. She obviously didn't have any trouble reading in the car. "I said," he raised his voice a little. "You really didn't have to come."

'Huh?" Lindsey looked up. "Oh sorry. What did you say?"

"How did you get off work?" Rob moved the conversation on. He realized he didn't want to have the whole, *'you didn't really need to come, but I wanted to, but you really didn't, but I am glad you are here'*, conversation anyway. They were way past that point and he was tired of dealing with his feelings about Lindsey and the new love/sex triangle that had formed in his life. He just wanted to break the silence. Lindsey hadn't said a word in almost an hour.

"I had a ton of personal time built up," she answered. The book remained open on her lap. Apparently she hadn't gotten the hint. "I never realized how many late nights and weekends I must have worked. Guess I'm finally reaping the reward of an overworked no social life professional."

"Not much of a reward," Rob glanced in the rearview and looked at his boys.

Neither one of them had said a word since they left the house. They had just turned on their phones, stuck their headphones in their ears and sat on opposite sides of the car as if each one of them had the plague. *"So much for time with the boys,"* Rob lamented to himself.

"Sure it is," Lindsey argued. She hadn't interacted with the boys or Rob either. Her nose had been in the book since they left. "This stuff is fascinating." She held up the cover. The blue and white title *"Passamaquoddy,"* flashed into Rob's vision.

"Find out anything?" Rob asked half curious and half frustrated. He could barely read the book. The first part was fairly straight forward but the second half was just a list of families and genealogy charts. Even the title confused him.

"A ton," Lindsey's eyes lit up as she finally closed the book and laid it down on her lap. "There is so much information on every family that settled there."

"In Passama whatsis?" Rob still could not pronounce it.

"Passamaquoddy," Lindsey laughed. "The bay that your family comes from was a haven for Loyalists. The entire index from your mom's box seems to have settled there. Adams, Coley, Lawless, Whittaker, Appleby,"

"My mother's family,"

"And Garrison too," Lindsey added. "Do you know yet what your relationship is to all of them?"

"Not completely yet."

"Well the Garrison connection is big,"

"Really?"

"Yeah. Remember any of your Civil war history?"

"Of course. It's part of the curriculum."

"Well then," Lindsey smiled. "Remember William Lloyd Garrison?"

"The abolitionist?"

"THE abolitionist," Lindsey emphasized "The". "He started the newspaper *'Liberator'*, worked with Frederick Douglas. Was basically a pain in the ass to all the slave owners."

"Yeah, yeah. What about him?"

"You're probably related."

"No shit!" Rob swore. "What about John Adams?" It made Rob feel good that he was finally seeing relationships to some of the "good guys" in history.

"No sign of that yet," Lindsey frowned. She knew how much Rob needed some vindication.

"Franklin?"

"Definitely not. This book is about the people who moved to Canada and settled just north of Maine. I did see somewhere that Franklin owned some land up there but no signs of anyone moving there."

"He stayed in England?"

"Think so."

"So what exactly are we looking for then?" Rob frowned. He knew they had to do this. It was his idea. It was his family. Hell it was even his car they were driving. He just didn't really understand where exactly they were going.

"Letters, documents," Lindsey looked out the window and saw the blue and white welcome sign. They had just entered Massachusetts. It was still another four hours to Portland. "We need to find other families who talked to William Franklin. Get an idea what he was talking about."

"And you think we can find them?" Rob wondered again. He had heard this several times from Lindsey before they left. It is how she convinced him to take the route they were taking.

"Franklin wrote to a lot of people. He was the representative of all the Loyalists in America. Anyone who needed help must have written a letter to him."

"But you said the letters burned in that fire."

"The letters he kept in New Jersey," Lindsey corrected Rob. "Not the ones that other people kept."

"Like mom's family," Rob finished.

"Like your mother's family."

"And you think some of those could be in the archives up there?" Again, Rob knew the answer. He just needed to hear it one more time before he took his boys on this crazy journey. They still hadn't budged, Rob noticed. Other than the occasional grimace or smile, the boys showed no other signs of life. Rob could not believe how easily their phones occupied their attention. He thought they would rebel against taking a five hour car ride to Portland and a ferry ride just as long. He hadn't even mentioned how long the journey would be until the last minute, afraid they would never get in the car. But when they heard about it they just shrugged their shoulders, double checked their battery power and climbed in.

They didn't even question the whole idea of the trip when Rob first explained it to them. Of course Bobby complained. He complained about any idea his father had. At least that part of the teenage years was still the same. But they didn't show any interest in the family history, in the exploration of another country and culture, even one that was the heart of their favorite sport. They just made the usual whining noises and quickly gave in.

It astounded Rob how different his boys were than he. When he was young, he had spent his free time playing outside with the neighborhood kids or on the pond for hours playing hockey. His boys were chaperoned all their lives. Whether it was in the rink or in school, on the field or in a club, there was always an adult chaperone telling them what to do and how to behave. They had no time to just be boys; to laugh and play and fight and solve their problems on their own. It just didn't seem right to Rob. How would they ever learn creativity or leadership if every moment was controlled or planned? It tore at his gut and frustrated him at every turn. Maybe he could use this time to change some of that.

He looked back in the rearview mirror again for any signs of life, shook his head and thought, *"and maybe not."*

"Halifax, Fredericton, even St. Andrews keeps an archive," Lindsey went on. She had no idea of the inner struggle going on inside Rob. "Only some of it is on-line but if we show up, they should be able to help us."

"Should?" That was the first time he heard her use that word. He wasn't dragging his kids to another country for a "should".

"Th-there's no way to know for sure," Lindsey could sense the anger in Rob's voice. "But even if those don't pan out," she quickly continued, "when we get to Passamaquoddy Bay and the island your mother's family is from we should learn a ton. Maybe even about the land you may own."

"Wait!" Adam burst out. Rob almost veered off the road. "We own land?"

"I thought you were listening to your phone!" Rob shouted angrily. His pulse was still racing from the shock as he tried to settle back behind the wheel.

"I was," Adam admitted. "That doesn't mean I completely tune you guys out."

Rob smiled. A little of his faith in his son was renewed.

"What do you mean we own land?" Bobby took his earplug out of his right ear and joined the conversation. "I thought you said we were just going up to play some hockey."

"That is not what I said," Robert was amazed at the selective listening skill of his older son.

"We're not playing hockey?" Adam interrupted. He placed his phone down on the seat next to him and pressed what looked like the pause button.

"I didn't say that either."

"You said we were going to Canada, to the land of hockey to play some games and see some sights." Bobby argued. He leaned forward, grabbed onto the headrest from his father's seat directly in front of him and spoke right into his ear.

"And," Rob's temper was starting to flare. "I said we were going to look into some stuff about Nana's family."

"What kind of stuff?" Adam leaned forward as well and glanced at the book on Lindsey's lap, "Genealogy stuff?"

"How much did you hear?" His father said angrily. He was relieved that his son was not the empty video head that he suspected but upset that he was also eavesdropping.

"I don't know," Adam shrugged his shoulders and sat back down. He instinctively could sense his father's anger and got as much distance as he could from him. It would not be the first time his father slapped him while they were driving. "I didn't understand most of it."

"Well I did," Bobby admitted boldly. He did not have the same fear of his father that Adam did. Or at least he refused to admit he did. "I just didn't care."

"Well you should care," Lindsey couldn't help herself. She knew to stay out of family matters, especially after the fight at Nana's house. But she had spent too much time invested in this. She had spent too much energy wondering and planning and reading. She wanted to be involved, she needed to be involved and it was beyond her belief that Rob's own sons showed no interest in this. "Don't you have any curiosity about your grandmother?" She almost shouted. "Don't you want to know more about your family?"

"Family!" Bobby shouted right back at her. He still couldn't believe Lindsey was even here. What did she think she was doing? What was she trying to do? The other day when Lindsey had given him a ride to his games and even taken him through the drive-thru, Bobby had tried to get an idea what she was all about. All he could figure out though was that she was really nice, really knew her hockey and was really hot. To Bobby's testosterone overdosed brain that meant only one thing. She wanted to sleep with his dad. If that happened, there was no way back. His family would be ruined and his mother would be devastated. He couldn't let that happen. "Who the fuck are you to be telling me about my family? You're not even in it! You're just some hottie trying to sleep with my dad!"

"Bobby!" Rob's deep bellowing shout tore through everyone and his body jerked backwards so hard he almost lost control of the car. What the hell was his son doing? What was he saying? Rob had never in his life heard anything like that from Bobby and it set him off like Vesuvius destroying Pompeii. Bobby and Adam jumped back in abject terror and Lindsey pushed herself against her side door in shock.

"How dare you!" Rob continued screaming. He had lost all rational thought. His every fiber was on fire. No child of his would ever, ever, ever talk like that! He swerved the car right across two lanes into the brake down lane in a massive screech and pressed so hard on the brakes that the boys were thrown forward into the seats in front of them.

In one motion, Rob threw the car into park, jumped out and opened Bobby's passenger door. A car in the right hand lane swerved out of the way in the last moment. Rob ignored it and reached into the car as his son pushed himself away towards the other side.

"Come here!" Rob grabbed his son's shirt and effortlessly tossed him like a rag doll into the weeds next to the highway. Bobby landed hard on the grass but to his credit managed to get up to his feet. He backed away, sliding down the slight grassy incline toward the trees below. He had never in his life seen his father this angry and he had no idea what he would do.

"Rob don't!" Lindsey jumped out of the car and grabbed Rob's outstretched arm with both her hands. "Don't!"

Rob shrugged Lindsey to the ground in a heartbeat. "Stay out of this Lindsey!" He growled.

"No!" Lindsey got up quickly. She knew this was her fault. It wasn't just what she had said to Bobby. It was everything. She had come between Rob and his sons. She had put herself in the middle of this family when she knew it was wrong. Of course she did not sleep with Rob. Of course she never tried to seduce him. But she didn't stop it either. She knew Rob had interest. She knew he was vulnerable. And she knew she was enjoying that interest. Maybe she even encouraged it.

"I won't stay out of this!" She got in Rob's face. "I won't let you hurt what you have left of your family!"

Rob stopped for an instant. The words barely made sense in his rage.

"Look at them Rob!" Lindsey waved her arms. "Look at the terror in your sons' eyes. Is this how you want them to see you?"

Rob turned back to the car and looked at Adam. His face was pressed up against the car window, his eyes were wide in terror and tears were starting to form in his eyes. Rob turned back to his older son. Bobby was visibly shaking. His fists were raised in defense ready to face his father. Rob could not tell if it was anger, fear, hurt or hate coming from his son, probably it was all of them and more.

"Is this the father you want to be?" Lindsey pressed. "Is this how you want your children to see you?"

Rob needed no more evidence. His boys saw him as some kind of monster. "My God," he collapsed onto the grass and hung his head in between his knees. The intense rage immediately transformed to a grief and humiliation just as powerful. "My God, what I have done?" He began to sob.

No one moved. No one dared. The cars raced by on the highway, oblivious to the anguish consuming Rob.

"How did this happen?" Rob continued to sob. He held his hands over his forehead. "How did I let my life get so fucked up?"

Lindsey took a step towards Rob and stopped. Bobby waved her off. But this time, there was understanding and gentleness in his eyes. He approached his father.

"You didn't do this dad," Bobby placed his hand on his father's shoulder. "We all did."

"Yeah dad," Adam said as he opened the car door and stepped onto the grass. "You, me, mom, Bobby, we all had a role in this."

Lindsey watched in awe as the two boys knelt down beside their father and hugged his still sobbing form. "*Maybe,*" she thought," *they had finally turned a corner.*"

Eighteen

"This good?" Agent Foster turned to his partner. "I can barely see them in my rearview."

"Yeah," Agent Saltman pushed the wire rim sunglasses back on his nose. He had started to sweat. This was supposed to be an easy job. *'One last play in the field to end on a good note'*, his boss had said. It better not get fucked up all ready. "Pull off to the side right here."

"You want to get out the jack and make it look like we broke down?" Foster quickly turned the blue Ford Taurus into the brake down lane and off onto the grass. The car kicked up some dirt and smoke but none of the other drivers on Highway 84 seemed to care or notice.

"Nah," Saltman shrugged, "we might attract some random do-gooder. Let's just lay low and look like an abandoned vehicle."

"You gunna show the badge if the staties arrive?"

"If I have to. Hopefully they'll be too busy setting up their freakin' speed traps. Those guys are obsessed with it."

"I heard. Even down south they talk about the troopers here."

"No surprise. Sometimes I forget we are on the same side." Saltman sat back and made himself comfortable. He glanced in his side-view mirror at the black Toyota Camry they had been following since Fairfield. They almost lost it when it swerved off the road.

Agents Matt Foster and Daniel Saltman were one of the stranger pairs the CIA had ever put together. Foster, a young man of 28 years old, was an Afro-Canadian who had only recently been granted American citizenship and was one of the greenest agents in the entire D.C. area. Saltman, twice his age, was a Massachusetts native with so much experience he was not even considered a field agent anymore. He spent most of his time in the Boston office consulting with the many businesses and academic institutes that had relations with the agency. He had to be given special dispensation just to be put on the case.

Yet each was chosen for a specific reason. Foster was probably the most athletic man Saltman had ever seen. Good looking, well built, with a perfectly formed buzz cut hair top and goatee, he looked like he could be a cover boy for

GQ. He ate right, worked out, and broke just about every record the office had for speed, push-ups, chin-ups, you name it. After serving in the Coast Guard, he had turned his attention to the CIA, completed the requisite course work at G.W. and was granted special agent status just last year. His knowledge of the maritime issues as well as his dual Canadian-American citizenship fit the unique needs for this case.

Saltman countered all that. He wasn't out of shape or weak. He had kept to standard agent health protocols despite being out of the field for years. He was thin, wore glasses and blended in perfectly with the academics and engineers he constantly worked with. However just last year, he had completed his second Boston Marathon. But by now, at age 55, he was clearly showing his age. His jet black, stringy hair showed spots of gray. His face showed signs of wrinkles and worry and if he grew tired or lazy, he walked with a distinct limp, probably from some injury years ago. There was no one however, who understood CIA protocols better, knew when to invoke them and more importantly, when to ignore them. He more than made up for Foster's inexperience. In addition, Saltman had an undergraduate degree in American History from a local almost Ivy League School, (Brandeis University in Waltham) as well as a PHD in criminology from Northeastern. His local connections and time spent in the Boston area gave him a unique knowledge of the American Revolution and all things Patriots. Indeed, he spent almost two days a week working with companies in the Lexington area where the first shot of the war had been fired.

Still, this case was an odd one. Their orders were both specific and vague at the same time. Carry your guns, but don't use them. Work with the Canadians, but keep it close to the vest. Follow the Callahan guy but keep your distance. "Observe and report," his boss had said. "And do not engage."

"What's going on?" Foster shoved the car into park and leaned back as well.

"Guy just jumped out of the car," Saltman turned his head to look directly at the family. There was no danger he would be noticed. "And he's grabbing his kid and throwing him out of the car."

"Must be some fight." Foster turned around as well.

"None of our business," Saltman turned back and closed his eyes. "Wake me when it's over."

"But," Foster started to argue, and then shrugged. His partner was probably right. What did he know about any of this stuff? His own kids were only infants and he himself had grown up without a father as well. Family dynamics were above his pay grade.

"Might as well catch up on my research," he grinned as he reached behind Saltman to his small briefcase sitting behind the seat. "I was right in the middle of this when we left Fairfield."

"Research?" Saltman sat up and opened his eyes. "What kind of research?"

"Just some light reading," Foster placed the black briefcase on his knees, clicked the small silver handles on the edges and opened it up. "Want one?"

"Comic books?" Saltman laughed. "That's your research."

"We stand on Guard," Foster showed him the title. "It's a future story about a war between Canada and the United States."

"A war?"

"Yeah," Foster's eyes lit up. He had always been a fan of comic books. Ever since he was a little kid, he would hide out in his room and get lost in all the adventures of his favorite heroes: Spiderman, Thor, Superman, Captain America. Maybe it was his childhood need to have to replace his absent father with some kind of adult male role model or maybe it was the adolescent boy who loved the way the women were always drawn. It didn't really matter. Foster loved the comics especially with all the movies about them now. He had strolled into the local comic store in Fairfield just before they left and his eyes caught these books. It seemed like more than a coincidence.

"It takes place in the future," he explained, "but the attitudes between the Canadians and the Americans are so current."

"You're wasting your time."

"Really?" Foster snapped. "You haven't noticed how much American Canadian relations have soured in the last few decades."

"You haven't been alive for decades."

"You know what I mean. Heck you have been alive for decades. You can remember when Canada and America were best buds."

"Yeah, I can."

"Well this comic here is a sign of the times," Foster pressed, "terrorism, 9/11, the war on drugs and even the war in the Middle East. Canadians not trusting Americans, booing each other's anthems at the hockey games, thinking of the U.S.A. as some kind of military threat." He waved the covers at Saltman. "There are six issues here and man you should read the letters page. There are some angry people out there."

"You know," Saltman took the first issue out of Foster's hands. "Whether I think this is bullshit or not, the fact that so many people want to read this stuff makes it relevant." He opened the book to the first page. "And if nothing else, it will pass the time."

About ten minutes later, Foster looked up from the comic book and into the rearview mirror. Callahan was still on the side of the road, sitting on the grass it seemed. Foster sighed and turned to Saltman. "Man, what if it's true."

"What if what's true?"

"This whole Ben Franklin thing."

"No idea," Saltman put his face back into the comic book. It really was scary.

"Yes you do," Foster pressed. "If anyone has any idea it's you."

"Yeah," Saltman continued reading.

"C'mon man," Foster gently reached over and pulled the comic down so he could see Saltman's face. "What if it's true?"

"It ain't." Saltman tried to pull the comic book back up.

"But what if it is,"

"What do you think this is," Saltman's lips formed a sarcastic grin, "National Treasure part three?"

"Nah man," Foster laughed. Saltman continued reading.

"It could be true," he put the comic back down again.

"Ya think?"

"No, but it could be."

"So what if it is?"

"Whew, wow," Saltman let out a large breath and closed the comic book. "If it is, it would be the biggest news since shit, I don't know, Watergate."

"You think it's a scandal of some kind?"

"Not a scandal, no, but you know the media today."

"They'll make it one," Foster finished for him.

"President hates that shit, hates unknowns, hates people judging him."

"He'll take it personally."

"Well it's our job to make sure he is ready for it when it all blows up."

"But do you really think anyone will give a flying fuck about something over 200 years ago?

"You're Canadian right?"

"And American." Foster hated when guys brought that up.

"Yeah but you went to Canadian schools right?"

"Yeah,"

"So you never learned all the Patriotic crap we did."

"Crap?"

"Don't get me wrong," Saltman quickly explained. He didn't want Foster getting the wrong idea. The kid seemed sincere and had a good heart. He didn't want his own cynicism ruining Foster's love for his newly adopted country. "I love this country. I truly do. Otherwise I wouldn't have dedicated my life to serving it for all these years and through all these dickheads who have been running it for so long."

"Dickheads," Foster chuckled.

"You know what I mean," Saltman went on. "We do the job. We serve. "

"Yeah,"

"But what I meant about the schools was that you got no idea how much Patriotism is thrown at us. Hell in kindergarten they dress us up as little Pilgrims and Indians and we all get off on Patriots day and the fireworks on the fourth and even a mountain with our Presidents' heads on it."

"Yeah," Foster smiled. "Canada ain't got nothing like that."

"Well you guys have a different story."

"Yeah."

"So trust me, when news gets out that the greatest founding father next to Jefferson and Washington is fraught with scandal and had a son who was a traitor you bet your ass people are going to care."

Foster just nodded and turned back for another glimpse. The family had finally returned to their car. Either that or they had walked further away and he had missed it.

"And it will involve the President, the P.M. of Canada, heck even the British and the French could get involved."

"Why them?"

"The Treaty was written between the U.S. and England and it was brokered by the French."

"Shit. But do they really care?"

"Everyone always cares," Saltman started to sound like the consultant he had spent years being. "Number one lesson in the field, everyone always has a stake, even when they don't."

Foster nodded.

"Plus with oil being involved–"

"Yeah, damn."

"And lawyers,"

The Black Camry sped past them.

"There they go!" Saltman pointed. Foster calmly placed the car in drive and pulled back onto the highway. He may have been green but he was never one to panic.

"So what's this Callahan guy's stake in all this?" Foster continued the conversation once he was the perfect distance behind the Toyota, "He in it for the money?"

"He's not after money."

"How do you know?"

"A, the guy's a teacher."

Foster chuckled. He knew what Saltman meant.

"B, he has made no attempt to sell it. No pawn shops, no antique dealers, just one search on ebay."

"You keeping tabs on his computer?"

"Sometimes."

"I thought the boss said just follow."

"This is following."

"So where's he headed now?"

"Portland."

"Portland?"

"He bought a ferry ticket for the four of them to Halifax via Portland."

"Halifax? Why there?"

"Not sure," Saltman admitted. "But we knew he had to head to Canada at some point."

"Well if we know he is headed to the Portland Ferry, why are we following him?"

"Good point," Saltman realized. "Let's put our time to better use."

"Yeah," Foster nodded as he hit the accelerator and sped past the Camry. He hated following, especially guys like this Callahan dude who barely went past the speed limit. There were much better uses of their time. "Let's go."

Nineteen

"I'm so fucking bored." Bobby looked out at the bright blue cloudless sky and raised his voice over the wind. The boat engines were not that loud but between the waves crashing against the side and the wind whipping through his hair, it was difficult to hear much. Bobby leaned further onto the Ferry railing and stared into the deep blue Atlantic water. Nothing to look at there either, not even a damn fish.

"Dad said we would see dolphins," he tried to engage his brother again. He knew Adam couldn't hear him over the headphones. "Maybe even a whale if we were lucky."

"Huh?" Adam finally took an earbud out and looked at his brother. His pale baby face and bright blond hair were already beginning to show signs of sunburn. "You say something?"

"I am so fucking bored," Bobby repeated. "You really think dad knows what he's doing?"

"Of course," Adam answered. His unquestioning loyalty of his father instantly annoyed Bobby.

"But all this talk of Patriots and Loyalists and Ben Franklin and land in Canada, it's like a bad Disney movie."

Adam chuckled. "Yeah, it is kind of."

"You tell any of your friends?"

"Yeah, they thought it was kind of cool."

"That figures," Bobby turned away for a minute and looked out at the water. He actually thought for a second he saw a splash. Maybe there was some life in there after all. "They're all a bunch of kids."

"Fuck you," Adam shot back.

"Hey no offense," Bobby grinned and slapped his brother playfully on the side. "You can't help your age."

Adam made a face.

"You see that splash," Bobby quickly pointed.

"Yeah," Adam looked in the direction Bobby was pointing. "That's the second one I've seen."

"Second what? Splash?"

"No, dummy; Second whale."

"You didn't see no damn whale."

"Did too."

"I've been looking out at this boring water for over an hour. There ain't no whales."

"Of course there are. Dad even said so."

"Dad said so."

"What you got against Dad anyway?"

"I don't want to talk about it."

"Seriously."

"I don't want to talk about it."

"You shouldn't have gotten into that fight with him."

"I thought we were over that."

"We are," Adam gave in. He had no desire to relive the fight on the side of the highway either. It might have ended up opening up some conversations that needed to be opened but that didn't mean he wanted to relive any of it now; especially in the middle of the Atlantic Ocean with his big brother.

Both boys turned away and looked at the water again. Adam put the earbud back in. By now, the sun was starting its downward trend. Bobby wondered if they would make it to Halifax before dark. It would be cool to see a sunset out on the ocean. His father had promised that the trip would be exciting and that they would see all kinds of wild sea life out here. A blazing red sun disappearing into the water could make up for the missing whales.

"Still don't see no damn whales."

"Huh?" Adam took the earbud out again.

"My friends gave me a lot of grief," Bobby returned to the earlier conversation.

"What did you tell them?" Adam asked.

"Not much," Bobby admitted. "Just that Dad found some cool letter from Ben Franklin."

"So why did they give you grief?"

"They didn't make fun of me or anything."

"That's good."

"They just didn't care."

"Really? My friends thought it was kind of cool."

"Again. Kids."

"Cut it out."

"Sorry." Bobby meant it.

"Do you think Dad is nuts?" Adam opened his eyes wide and stared at his younger brother. He would never tell Bobby this but he really did look up to him. He couldn't believe the way Bobby stood up to Dad and refused to back down. Dad was pretty scary when he was angry.

"No way." Bobby answered firmly. He might have a lot of problems with Dad, not the least of which was how he screwed up his marriage and their family, but he knew his Dad was no idiot. "There is definitely something to all of this."

"What?"

"I don't know." Bobby turned back towards the water and hung over the red railing again. He could feel the pressure of the railing right under his rib cage. "I don't care about any of this Patriot and Loyalist bullshit. It's all just a bunch of dead guys getting mad at each other."

"Me neither." Adam turned and looked over the water as well. "They both had a point."

"Score!" The hockey announcer shouted through Bobby's phone. It was his personal text alert and it had gotten him in trouble in class more times than he would care to admit. Bobby looked down at the text and smiled. "LOL" he typed back.

"Who's that?" Adam leaned over to see the text.

"No one," Bobby tried to turn away.

"Are you texting mom?" Adam shouted.

"No!"

"You are!"

"Back off!" Bobby gave Adam an elbow in the gut.

"Dad will be pissed." Adam forced his way back.

"I said back off," Bobby shoved Adam down to the deck. "What I do with my mother is none of Dad's business!"

"She's just going to cause trouble," Adam scrambled to his feet and tried to grab Bobby's arm. "What is she saying?"

"None of your business," Bobby held the phone high in the air to avoid Adam's reach. He did not know why he was being so private with his mom. They weren't talking about anything special or giving away any secrets. Yes he had talked to her about the fight on the highway but it wasn't headline news or anything. He just knew that talking to his mom made things feel normal. It made them still feel like a family, like he still had two parents. He missed his mother deeply but he didn't want his brother to know that. Adam was totally on dad's side and that pissed Bobby off. "Stay away!" He shoved Adam again.

"Let me see!" Adam grabbed Bobby's arm and swung it towards him. The phone flew out of Bobby's hands and towards the ocean below. "No!" Bobby screamed.

"Got it!" A large black man suddenly appeared out of nowhere. Neither Adam nor Bobby had any idea who he was or where he came from but the phone sitting safely in his outstretched arm was all they cared about.

"Thank God!" Bobby ran forward.

"Nice catch," Adam joined him.

"Everything all right boys?" the man said as he handed the phone back to Bobby. "You boys were getting a little rough out there."

"Y-yeah fine sir," Bobby found it strange that the man seemed to have been watching them. He couldn't believe how fast the man was, his speed was almost inhuman. How close had he been? Bobby hadn't seen anyone nearby. Bobby looked down at the phone to see a new message from his mother. He quickly put the phone back in his pocket. "Thanks a lot Mr."

"You can call me Matt." The man reached out his hand in greeting. Bobby thought it was strange that he was dressed in a suit and tie for a Ferry ride. His perfectly formed buzz cut hair top and goatee made him look more like a businessman than a tourist. Maybe he was a hockey player! Bobby smiled.

"Thanks Matt," Bobby waved the suspicion away and stuck out his hand. "You're a life saver."

"No worries," Matt turned away quickly and returned to wherever he had come from, "just glad I was close by."

Twenty

Deborah stirred slowly in her bed. The early morning sun was just beginning to poke through the blinds in her bedroom window. She rubbed her hand over her forehead, through her long black hair and down along the back of her neck. She wasn't ready to get up.

A gentle snore came from the left side of the bed. Deborah's eyes burst open in shock as she glanced to her left.

"Oh god," she closed her eyes again and put her hand over her face, "what did I do?"

The figure next to her didn't budge. Deborah could at least be thankful for that. It would give her time to figure out what had happened and what she should do next. "Shit, shit, shit," she swore to herself as her mind raced back over the last 12 hours.

His name was Mark. He was one of the many sales reps who had been flirting with Deborah for several months now. Despite her constant denials and arguments with her husband, it turned out Rob was absolutely right. There were many reps who wanted to sleep with Deborah.

She knew that. She had always known that. From the flirting to the obvious stares, to the crude jokes and outright propositions, Deborah could not go more than a day or two without feeling like she was some kind of steak hanging up in a butcher store. It had actually made it easier to say no all those times because it had disgusted her so much.

Still, she was shocked at how easy it was to grab someone once she decided to go after it. Mark, (it was Mark, right?) had practically jumped out of his pants the minute she flashed just a little tit. It almost turned her off completely. If she hadn't been so mad at Rob, she probably wouldn't even have gone through with it.

They always say it. She'd always known it. Don't have sex when you're mad. But those who say it are never mad when they say it. And Deborah was fuming! She was angry. She was hurt. She was a mess. How could Rob do this to her? How could he ignore her feelings so much? How could he run off with that little bitch and leave her to take care of the house as if she was a servant or a maid or something? If he really wanted the marriage to end, he could have at least had the guts to say it to her face.

"Ohhh," Mark began to stir.

"Shit," Deborah swore again. She still hadn't decided what to do about him. She couldn't just throw him out of the condo; she had to work with him. Office romances; yet another thing she was supposed to avoid.

Of course this wasn't a romance. It was all about the sex. Mark was, in every definition of the word, an ass. God, how she had humiliated herself! She threw off the sheets and stealthily ran into the bathroom. She needed a shower.

As the hot water flowed over her face and cleaned away the sweat and grime from the night, Deborah slowly started to gather her thoughts. "Damn," she realized. That had to be the worst sex she ever had.

It amazed her how bad Mark had been. After all she had chosen to go after him because he was young, relatively attractive and had a self-declared plethora of experience. For whatever reason, Mark always thought that the constant bragging about all the women he slept with would impress Deborah when of course all it did was turn her off. He was everything Rob wasn't and maybe that should have been a warning sign. She should have trusted her instincts more. It wasn't just that the guy was one dimensional and boring; it was that he was so self-absorbed. He focused on himself, he talked about himself. Hell after last night, Deborah felt like he had sex with himself and Deborah was just along for the ride.

She never realized how great Rob was, and not just in bed. Rob's whole demeanor was about giving and caring. He wore his heart on his sleeve and always thought about others first. That had to be what made the sex so great. Rob wasn't some kind of martial art sex master. He fumbled around and was clumsy. He wasted time in the wrong spots and sometimes even talked too much. But his caring, his attention to detail and most importantly his desire to make Deborah happy was truly something special.

Deborah shut off the water and leaned her head against the shower wall. *What the hell was she going to do?*

"Hey babe," Deborah jumped and almost slipped in the shower. Mark was standing on the bath rug totally naked and smiling. His hard on was starting to form.

"Oh," Deborah groaned, trying to hide her disgust. She quickly grabbed the white towel off the bar and flung it around herself. "You startled me."

"I was hoping I could join you."

"Not now," Deborah brushed past him, out of the bathroom and back into the bedroom. "I have to get ready for work."

"Are you sure?" Mark followed her, still naked and smiling. God Deborah felt like she was going to vomit. "It's probably been awhile."

"What's that supposed to mean?" Deborah snapped around. If Mark had been much closer she might have slugged him.

"N-nothing," Mark backed away. Deborah's anger caught him off guard. "Not a thing."

"I've got to get to work." Deborah turned away again and headed to her hall closet. Hopefully Mark wouldn't follow.

"Christ, Christ, Christ, Christ, Christ," Deborah tried to lose herself in the mundanity of choosing her clothes. It would need to be something old and boring that was for sure.

"Is this him?" Mark called from the bedroom. At least he had put on his white boxers.

"Yeah," Deborah glanced over at the picture frame and then turned towards her dresser. "That's my husband," she said a little louder than necessary.

"Husband?" Mark placed the picture of Rob and the kids back on the mantle. "I thought you guys were divorced."

"Separated."

"Same thing."

"Not at all."

"Ok, whatever. Long as we can still do this," he grinned.

Deborah tried to smile. She needed to cut Mark some slack. Yes he was a self-absorbed asshole with no concept of his own actions but he did try to do the right thing once in a while. He wasn't a crook or a swindler. He never went after her until she opened the door. And he didn't force himself on her this morning like he obviously wanted to. God she had set the bar so low.

"Sorry," she honestly said. "I've just got to get to work."

"Hey babe I get it," Deborah hated the word babe. The bile began to rise in her throat again. "We can pick up where we left off another night."

"Sure," Deborah couldn't believe she said that. What she meant to say was, 'Oh god never again'.

"Sunrise, sunset," her phone suddenly sang. It was the old *Fiddler on the Roof* tune. "Sunrise, sunset; swiftly flow the days," The musical had always been one of her favorites, ever since she was five years old and saw it at her synagogue play. The song reminded her to grab every day as if it was her last.

"Uh oh," she looked at the text alert.

"What?"

"My house alarm is going off."

"House alarm? I don't hear anything."

"Rob and my house,"

"Can't Rob take care of it?"

"He's out of town."

"What about the cops?"

"Rob and I both agreed to not pay for that service. It is a false alarm so many times."

"Let me go with you."

"No need. It's probably just the wind; wouldn't be the first time."

"And it might not be."

"Really, it's ok."

"I insist," Mark stood up and began to get dressed. Whether he truly felt the need to help or had some warped sense of chivalry that could help him sleep with Deborah was unclear. Deborah almost laughed at the way he stuck out his chest and got all tough guy with her. "It could be something dangerous."

"Ok," Deborah smiled, trying to make it look more like gratitude than laughter. "I'll drive."

It was about a 20 minute drive to her house through the worst traffic of the day. When Deborah had first moved out, she wanted to make sure she could still visit the kids easily without Rob suddenly appearing at her door (like he had done just last week, she realized). Now she would have to pay for that decision. Traffic would be annoying and slow and she would probably have to sit through some lights two or three times. It would give Mark plenty of time to ask more questions.

"Where did Rob go? Beantown?"

"No," Deborah slammed on the brake as the silver BMW in front of her decided to not run the yellow. She almost honked her horn but thought better of it. "Canada."

"Canada? Wow. What part?"

"I'm not sure actually; Nova Scotia or New Brunswick."

"Really? I've got a couple of friends up there."

"Oh?"

"Fishing buddies; met them on a deep sea jaunt out of Maine."

"I didn't know you fished." Deborah admitted. Actually she knew very little about Mark at all. She knew he wasn't an athlete like she or Rob. That much was clear. Mark wasn't out of shape or anything and of course he was good looking, he just didn't have that edge to him Deborah had found in all the athletes she knew.

"Big time," Mark's chest puffed out again; yet another chance for him to brag, "Done a lot of it off the coast and into the Bay of Fundy. There's some great mackerel, pollack, flounder, and cod. But my favorite is the haddock. Rob go up there to fish?"

"No," The light finally changed to green. The BMW took its time moving. Deborah almost screamed. "He brought the kids up there to look at some land."

"Land? In Nova Scotia?"

"Actually I think it is New Brunswick," Deborah may as well tell Mark something about it. She had no interest in lying and needed something to pass the time. She wasn't going to say anything about Franklin though. That was for sure.

"What kind of land?"

"He's not sure." The BMW took a left down a side street thank god, and Deborah was able to pick up some speed. They were almost there, "There's some questions dealing with his family history."

"What kind of questions?"

"Legal, border, ownership; I don't really understand it all."

"You know," Mark tried to impress her again. "One of my fishing buddies is a realtor up there."

The stop sign appeared. Deborah put on her right blinker.

"I could give him a call for you. He works with new and old deeds all the time."

"Old deeds?" Deborah's ears perked up, "How old?"

"Oh I don't know. Could be anything I guess. He told me once of a plot of land he was dealing with that went back a couple hundred years."

"Really?"

"Yeah. Didn't come to much but he made a killing on fees."

"Oh," Deborah was let down; yet another man of questionable motives.

"But he is really a good guy," Mark sensed her disappointment. He wasn't a total idiot. "He helped a lot of families keep their land when some big companies wanted to buy it all up. It even made the local papers."

"What kind of companies?"

"Not sure. Lumber, Oil, hell maybe it was Walmart." He laughed.

Deborah laughed too.

"You sure you don't want me to call him?"

"No thanks. It's Rob's business." Deborah looked ahead towards her house down the street. Everything looked ok.

"I am sure he could help." Mark ignored her. "He knows all the big names, does commercial and residential. If there is any land worth anything, he would know."

"No thanks."

"It would save Rob a lot of trouble," Maybe if Mark made it innocently look like he wanted to help Rob, Deborah wouldn't think it was all about sleeping with her; which of course it was. "One quick call and you could be days ahead of anything Rob is doing."

That gave Deborah pause for a minute. Maybe helping out Rob was the first step in getting him back. Or, maybe it would come across as desperate and pathetic. Or maybe she didn't want him back in the first place.

Deborah could hear their burglar alarm still going off.

"He could save you a lot of time and aggravation."

"No. Thanks." Deborah said firmly as she pulled the car into the driveway and pressed the garage door opener. The garage looked spotless, even the trash had been emptied out just before Rob left town. God he had changed, Deborah realized again.

She pulled the car in, put it in park and shut off the engine. "Rob can take care of himself."

"Wait." Mark grabbed Deborah's arm. The suddenness surprised her.

"What?"

"Let me go first."

"Jesus," Deborah pulled her arm free in one easy motion. "I'm fine." She stormed out of the car, walked briskly up the two stair platform and opened the house door. Mark quickly followed.

Deborah stepped into the main foyer and stood still in shock. The alarm was still blaring and she could see into the kitchen and living room beyond. Furniture was pushed around in odd formations or turned over completely. Drawers were left open and papers were scattered on the floor. The pantry door was wide open and one of the plastic shelves was dangling by a single screw. Someone had broken in.

"My god," Mark stood next to Deborah.

Picture frames were crooked. The television was pushed to the side. Jewelry and other knick knacks lay on the floor. Even a cushion on the couch was upside down.

"Someone was looking for something," Mark realized. Why else leave all the valuables behind? "What could they have been looking for?"

"I don't know," Deborah lied. She knew exactly what they must have been looking for.

"Lucky no one was here."

The boys, Deborah realized. *What if the boys had been here?* Deborah instinctively ran down the hall and to the edge of the stairs. She looked up towards the boys' room. Their doors were open as well. *Lindsey had been right.* She turned back towards Mark. *They were in danger.*

"Who is that realtor friend you have in Canada?" Deborah suddenly said to Mark.

"I'll get you his number."

Part II

Oh Canada!

Twenty One

Deborah stood in the middle of the Pub and gawked. She had never seen an Irish Pub like this before. The dark wood circular bar was freshly polished, almost glowing, the wooden barstools, made of the same material, looked sturdy enough to hold a 500 pound Irish man and the tan colored oak hardwood floors were so clean she could almost see her reflection. There were Celtic signs carved into the walls and the pillars and a wall of multi-colored liquors that stretched from one end of the pub to the other. It was ornate as well. Golden paint adorned all the walls, pillars and bar stools. Two by two square tile artwork was interwoven throughout the hardwood floor and even the bar stools and booths had fine blue fabric seats. It was as if every piece of carved wood, seat, and bar stool was straight from a pub in Ireland. And indeed it was, she quickly learned from one of the signs on the wall. *Durty Nellies*, the sign had read, *an authentic Dublin Pub built in the city itself and then shipped directly to Canada.* It was, according to the man she was supposed to meet, a must visit drinking hole for anyone who was visiting Halifax.

She knew the minute she stepped in that it was mistake. First and foremost, it reminded her of Rob. He loved Irish Pubs, as much as for the Guinness as for the atmosphere. The Pubs were so much more than a bar, he claimed, and she eventually agreed. They had a sense of community, almost family to them beyond just the friendliness natural after a few pints. For as long as they had been together, Rob would drive the extra mile or two downtown to Grace O'Malley's every Friday and come back a little sloshed and a little horny. It put a smile on Deborah's face remembering how he staggered both his words and his walk after an evening at Grace's.

And second of all, she knew the minute she walked in, that Rob would have to come there. There was no way, her big adorable husband would miss a Pub like this. *An Irish moth to a wet damp flame*, Deborah giggled. Either he had already been there, or he would be soon. She would need to find a spot at the bar where she could eye the entrance, just in case.

"What'll you have?" the bartender leaned towards her. He looked like a mix between a skin head and a sage. The top of his head was shaved clean yet the dark, brown beard covering his chin must have been the result of years of growth. The smile he flashed however was authentic and real. Deborah instantly felt at ease.

"Irish whiskey," she approached the bar and smoothly took a seat. Who cares

193

if it was Wednesday afternoon? She needed a drink and this was the closest to a vacation she had had in years.

"Brand?" the bartender looked back at the multitude of colored bottles on the wall. The mirror behind them made the collection that much more impressive.

Deborah eyed the whiskey section. She had never seen so many varieties or even so many colors. She had always been a Jameson girl, but this was the place to try something different.

"What do you recommend?"

"How about Teeling?" He reached behind him and grabbed an oddly shaped, barely rectangular decanter bottle. It was the most golden color whiskey Deborah had ever seen. "This is their Revival," he took out a glass from beneath the bar, "brewed right in Dublin. A little pricey, but it's worth it."

"Sounds great!"

"Rocks?"

"Neat," Deborah watched him pour her a generous portion. She had noticed over the years that male bartenders usually poured her larger portions than the female bartenders, especially when she was alone. She had a pretty good idea why but wasn't about to complain. Maybe that did make her a hypocrite but with the price of whiskey, who cares?

"A pro," he smiled referring to her opting for no ice, "you a tourist?"

"Not exactly," Deborah waved the glass under her nose and enjoyed the unique aroma. Was that citrus? Chocolate? It was so smooth and so complicated. She could already tell this was the finest whiskey she had ever had. "Wow."

"That's real Dublin whiskey," he placed the bottle on the bar next to Deborah.

"Sure is," Deborah took a slow sip, then a gulp.

"So, not exactly a tourist?" The bartender stayed put. The Pub was relatively empty. Only a few couples sat at the tables across the way and two older men in suits at the end of the bar.

"Sort of business,"

"Sort of?"

Deborah finished off the whiskey in a large gulp. She glanced at the entrance for her contact or worse, for Rob. "Give me another please."

The bartender's eyebrow rose. That was expensive stuff. Lady must either need it bad, be loaded or both. He lifted up the bottle and gave her another generous portion. He could tell Deborah didn't want to discuss her business. "Been to the Citadel yet?"

"No," Deborah was a little more comfortable with the small talk. The warm feeling in her chest from the whiskey helped as well, "Just got here a couple hours ago."

"From where?"

"The states."

"A Yankee?" Of course he knew that already.

"What's this Citadel you mentioned?" Deborah changed the subject again.

"National Historic site, a fort, an army museum; they even do cannon demonstrations. If nothing else it's got one of the best views of the city and it's just up the street."

"Sounds like my husband would love it," Deborah didn't mean to say that.

"Everybody goes there," the bartender straightened up a little as another customer approached the bar. "It's the center-point of Halifax." He turned to the new customer and reached for a pint glass. "Hey Jim," he smiled, "Guinness?"

"You know it," the man smiled and turned his attention to Deborah. "Mrs. Callahan?"

"Yeah," Deborah swung around and placed the whiskey glass down in front of her harder than she intended to. The liquid bubbled a little and swirled around the rim, but it remained in the glass. She let out a small breath of relief. "I'm Deborah Callahan." She still used her married name.

"Jim Watts," the man smiled and stuck out his hand. He was a darker skinned man, possibly biracial, with white sideburns and jet black hair. His gray business suit was impeccably neat, with crisp corners and even a white handkerchief in the lapel pocket. The man was either rich and powerful or conniving and sleazy. Maybe he was both. "We spoke on the phone."

"Hi Jim," Deborah shook his hand. His grip was firm and their eyes locked. Deborah hoped he didn't notice just how sweaty her palm was. "Thanks for agreeing to see me so fast." Deborah noticed him checking her out. She was glad she had chosen to wear just a regular green t-shirt today.

"No problem," Jim sat down at the bar. The bartender was still working on his

Guinness. "Any friend of Mark's,"

"We're not really friends," Deborah said a little too fast. She still was having trouble getting rid of the memory of the other night. God, what a mistake sleeping with him was. At least it got her here though.

Jim awkwardly turned towards the bar tap and eyed the foam settling in his dark beer. It would take time for the Guinness to settle before the bartender would finish the second pour.

"But we've worked together for a long time," Deborah added quickly as she reached for her whiskey.

"You in sales?"

"No, medicine," Deborah waved the glass under her nose again. That aroma was just unreal. She decided to nurse this drink a little more.

"A doctor eh?"

"More like an engineer."

"Robot surgery?"

Deborah raised an eyebrow. The guy was sharp. "I'm impressed."

"Not as much as I am." Jim watched the bartender place his hand over the tap again. He topped off the Guinness and slid it over. Deborah ignored the come on.

"Here you go Jim."

"Thanks John." Jim admired the dark Guinness sitting in front of him. The tan foam sat comfortably on top like a soft cork guarding the preserved black gold beneath. Bubbles rose towards the foam at incredible speed and a single drop of perspiration glimmered down the outside edge of the glass. John knew how to pour a Guinness. "Now I see why Mark knows you so well." He turned back to Deborah.

"He's sold me a lot of great stuff we use in surgery."

"Well then," Jim grabbed his beer and held it in front his face, waiting patiently for the right moment to drink it. The bartender headed down to the other end of the bar. He knew Jim didn't like him around when he was conducting business. "I guess it is my turn. What can I do for you?"

"I need some help sorting out an old deed."

"How old?"

"Probably the 18th century."

"Probably?"

"I don't have the deed in hand."

Jim finally took a sip of the Guinness. He continued to stare at Deborah while he did so. "What do you have in hand?" He wiped off the brown foam mustache with a napkin.

"Just some letters referencing land," Deborah looked away and took another sip of the whiskey. She realized how pathetic this sounded.

"Some letters?"

"Well, a letter." Deborah corrected him again. "And I don't actually have it with me."

Jim took a large gulp of the Guinness and slowly placed the half empty glass on the bar between them. "Mrs. Callahan, what exactly do you want from me?"

"I need help," Deborah blurted out. The whiskey was getting to her. Jim instinctively backed away from the sudden announcement.

"My husband is off on some crazy adventure, trying to find land his family once owned over 200 years ago and he's dragging my kids all over your country with him."

"OK," Jim sat back slowly and looked directly at Deborah, "why don't you start from the beginning?"

Twenty Two

Deborah couldn't tell him everything. She didn't know everything. She didn't have everything. The Franklin letter, the index, the genealogy research Lindsey had done, all of it was with Rob. The only thing Deborah had was a letter from one of Nana's uncles that Rob had missed. It referenced disputed land and a claim that went back to the Revolution.

Jim was clever. He was experienced. He had been dealing with real estate in Nova Scotia and New Brunswick for over a decade now. First as a local realtor out of St. John's, then working for corporate and investment clients, Jim had seen his share of land disputes. Whether it was lumber, fishing, oil or even real estate brokerage firms, Jim had dealt with them all.

Deborah of course did not completely trust him. He had still not even told her who he worked for. It seemed that he had his hand in so many buckets that he worked for everyone. It only took a few minutes for her to realize that Jim worked for Jim. He was just like that sexually immature sales rep Mark, but a lot smarter and self-aware.

Jim quickly realized the Loyalist connection. That part had been easy. Many of the land disputes in the area, Jim had told her, went back to the Loyalist days. King George III had been so vague, so impotent with carrying out his promises to the refugees that some issues lasted for decades. The Loyalist themselves had claimed so much land and changed the population of Canada so quickly, that the entire province of New Brunswick was formed just a year after the Revolution was over.

She hadn't said a word to Jim about Franklin either. Jim mentioned his name anyway. It wasn't clear whether Jim was trying to just show off his knowledge to impress her or if he knew a lot more than he let on. Perhaps Deb's poker face was not as good as she thought and she had given something away. She noticed his eyes lighting up the more he talked about disputed land claims. His knowledge came not only from experience but personal research he had been doing for years. The entire area fascinated him; so much wonderful land, so many people, and so much controversy. You had to know your history in this part of the world to make any money as a realtor or as an investor. Franklin, Jim had told her, had his hand in land disputes from as far north as PEI (Prince Edward Island, he explained. It was north of Nova Scotia but all the locals call it PEI.), to south of the Maine border. If there was a land dispute that went back to the Loyalists, Jim explained, there was a good chance William Franklin had his hand in it.

That didn't mean there was still a dispute. Jim dashed her hopes. Two hundred years was a long time. Every issue Jim had come across since before he got his license had been settled by Canadian courts long ago. It would have to take an act of God to change anything now.

"An act of God or an act of a man worshipped like a God," Deborah had thought to herself. She couldn't believe what Rob may have stumbled into.

"Your husband is on a wild goose chase," Jim said once he had been brought up to speed. He finished his second Guinness and waved at John. "I wouldn't worry about him."

"It's not him I am worried about," Deborah took a large sip of water. Jim had offered to buy her another round but she decided to take a break after the second Whisky was done. This was not the time to lose any control. "It's my kids."

"Well that part I still don't get." He waved at John again. The bar was a lot busier now that the early after work crowd was starting to arrive. "What is there to be worried about?"

"Well," Deborah frowned. This was the hard part. What did she tell him? She wasn't sure herself why she was there at all. The entire plane ride to Nova Scotia she spent second guessing herself. Was this really about the kids? Was this about her and Rob? Was it about Lindsey? Was this some pathetic attempt to win Rob back? My God, what would he say when or if he saw her?

"Mrs. Callahan?"

"Well," Deborah frowned again. Did she let Jim know that their house was broken into and that she was probably being followed? Deborah looked around nervously for a brief moment. The crowd was a mix of tourists and business people; no one suspicious except maybe Jim himself. How did she get his help without giving anything away? "My husband found something valuable that other people might want."

"What did he find?" Jim stopped looking down the bar and fixed his eyes on Deborah.

"I don't know." She lied.

"Who might want it?"

"I don't know." She lied again.

"Well why do you think it's dangerous?" He waved at John again. Finally the bartender noticed him.

"Because I know it's valuable." Deborah finished the water in one large nervous gulp. She had to give Jim something.

"How?"

"Rob took it to a pawn shop and they were very interested."

"Do you know which one?"

"No." That was the truth.

"Do you know what your husband is doing with it?"

"From what I understand, he is trying to find others like it."

"Other what? You still haven't told me what it is."

"Another Guinness?" John returned. He already had the glass in his hand.

"And another for the lady," Jim did not even look at Deborah for an answer. He wanted her to drink more.

"It's something he found in his mother's keepsakes," Deborah thought about refusing the drink but thought better of it.

"And his mother has family up here." Jim concluded. He really was quick.

"Exactly."

"Do you know where exactly?"

"Near Eastport."

"Maine?"

"Yes. His great grand parents lived up there."

"Well that's right near the border," Jim passed the whiskey over. The bartender started pouring his Guinness. "What are you doing in Halifax?"

"Rob took the ferry and I flew." Deborah lifted the glass to her lips and immediately took a sip. No time for enjoying the aroma right now. "It was the quickest way to get to Canada."

"Is he here in Halifax now?"

"Probably; He promised the kids a vacation and I know there's a lot to do here." She smiled at John who was still working on Jim's drink, "Something about a fort?"

"The citadel," Jim smiled at her and John.

"I actually was afraid he might have come in here," Deborah looked around again just in case. "He absolutely loves Irish bars."

"Who doesn't?" Jim took the Guinness John had just finished pouring.

"What did he look like?" John asked. "I was working all day yesterday."

Deborah took out her phone and quickly found a picture of Rob and the boys. They were all over her phone.

"Sure," John said quickly. "I remember the guy. He was with a good looking blonde girl." Deborah frowned. "They talked a lot of hockey and drank a lot of beer."

"That's them."

"Did they say where they were going or what they were doing?" Jim asked quickly. Finally he had something to go on. It was why he always chose to meet new clients in bars. No one knew more about who was doing what than the local bartenders.

"Well the boys were all excited about the Citadel."

"No surprise there." Deborah smiled, "Guns, explosions, forts, teenage boys; Duh."

"But the lady asked me if I knew where the archives were."

"The archives," both Deborah and Jim repeated in unison.

"You know," John looked at Jim, "the one down at the University Medical district."

"The archives," Jim said more to himself. "Did they say where they were going after that?"

"No," John started to turn away. He did not like giving out information on other patrons. That could cost him his job. "I wasn't asking; just giving advice on what to do in Halifax."

"Thanks John,"

"What does it all mean?" Deborah asked as she watched John return to another part of the bar.

"They are looking for something," Jim answered. "What, I am not sure. But I am confident we can get ahead of them."

"We can? Why?"

"Because my dear," Jim smiled from ear to ear as he stood up and threw some colorful Canadian cash down on the bar. "You have me."

Twenty Three

"When are they going to fire?" Bobby complained to no one in particular. It was one of his perfected teenage traits; complaining. No matter what Rob did, Bobby always found something to complain about, and it was always in the same tone, even the same pitch. "It's taking forever!"

Rob just ignored him. It had taken him many months to get to this point and he had needed help from both Deborah and even Adam, but Rob was finally beginning to accept that it was just a part of being a teenager. No matter what anyone did, Bobby would complain. It didn't matter if Rob spent hours planning it, it didn't matter if it cost a lot of money, and it didn't matter if it was Bobby's favorite thing on earth he would find something to complain about.

At first, Rob thought he would be spared. Bobby and Adam had actually woken up on their own and at a decent hour. Usually they slept right through the free hotel breakfast and had to eat the cold leftovers Rob had managed to stash. Some bagels, cream cheese, a yogurt or two and some bananas was the usual fare. But not only were the boys awake in time for fresh waffles and powdered eggs they even had a chance to see Lindsey off before she disappeared to the archives. A day at the fort seemed to be all they could talk about.

Bobby had always had a thing for fighting and for war. As a young boy he would play chase out in the woods, army ranger with his friends and even a few role playing games. If his mother would have let him have one of those video games he would have played that too. Even chess, which Rob had taught him, held some fascination for Bobby. At least until he hit puberty. So of course Rob thought that the Citadel, with its redoubts and its cannonade and its fortifications and its re-enactors dressed in military period costumes would be eye candy for Bobby. And at least for the first hour and a half, it was.

They had arrived with plenty of time to spare before the cannon demonstration. Rob parked the Toyota in the public lot at the base and the boys immediately jumped out of the car. The air was fresh and clean, with a smell of the not too distant sea around the edges. With the deep blue sky and the white cumulous clouds, it could not have been a nicer, summer day.

Of course the boys could care less about the weather. They immediately began to race up the steep green hill and pointed out to each other the various fortifications protecting both the town and the people inside. Meanwhile, Rob tried to walk slowly up the asphalt path and take it all in. The boys had already run away from him, directly towards the first wall and would get stuck at the ditch anyway. He could take his time and enjoy the scenic views of downtown and the harbor. From where Rob stood he could see the downtown office buildings, the shops nearby, the wharf beyond and the boats docked in the harbor. There was even a cruise ship on its way towards the Atlantic. It was by far the best vantage spot in the city. No wonder they built a fort here. Not only could you see an enemy approaching from land and make his climb miserable, you would also be able to fire upon any naval ship approaching the city.

Rob took a deep breath of the crisp, Canadian summer air and turned back towards the fort. The boys had disappeared into the ditch. Rob wondered if they would remember how to get out. He knew from looking at the brochure pictures that the fort was built in the shape of a giant star, with angled walls and a deep ditch running all the way around it, but you couldn't tell that from the outside. The massive fort was too big to be seen all at once.

The ditch itself was also deceptive in its appearance. It was covered in grass both on its top edge and inside. Young excited teenage boys had probably not even noticed they were in it until it was too late. It had to be at least 30-40 feet wide and just as deep and it butted up right against the walls, forcing any invaders to be sandwiched in between dirt and stone. The impenetrable, thick walls were built of almost perfectly rectangular grayish blackish stone, like the ones Rob had seen at the Bunker Hill monument near Boston. With the angled walls, it would allow the fort occupants to rain down a heavy fire upon any invader trapped inside.

At least Bobby and Adam realized that. By the time Rob caught up with them, they were talking and pointing at the defenses and realizing just what a mess any invader would be in if they were foolish enough to get trapped. Rob was proud to see his boys working it all out together.

Unfortunately the camaraderie hadn't lasted. Bobby of course got bored and complained once they were inside and looking around at the soldiers' quarters. He pushed Rob on anytime he wanted to talk with one of the re-enactors or read one of the signs. By the time they had made it to the cannon demonstration, Rob was ready to burst.

A small crowd of about 25 people had already started to gather by the edge of the inner fort. The cannon stood about 30 feet in front of them, sitting on a sturdy iron base with thick metal wheels. Its cylinder was jet black like the other cannon in the fort and was about six feet long. The entire mechanism rested on a long wooden platform that allowed for the cannon to be rolled forward into place and then rolled back when not in use as it was now. The noon time signal shot it would give off, was a tradition in Halifax that everyone, soldier, sailor, businessman and tourist depended on. Here Rob could lose himself amongst his fellow tourists and get a good view of the century old tradition the Citadel was famous for. He placed himself a little off to the side so as not to block anyone's view and instructed his boys to do the same.

The tourists were as generic as any other group Rob had seen before. Mostly families with small children and a few retired couples, they all were either engaging in small talk or had their heads in their phones. One older man dressed in a Canada t-shirt with a large red maple leaf in the center was even trying to go old school with a black JVC video camera at the ready.

"Noon, right dad?" Adam took out his cell phone and pressed the small clock face on the screen. He wanted to see if they got it right.

"Yeah."

Adam pressed the stopwatch symbol and began the countdown. The big white numbers flashed on the screen. He flashed it at Bobby with a smile.

"Ugghh," Bobby sighed. He had no patience for Adam's techno-phone electronic obsession. *Didn't the kid realize what a geek he was sometimes?*

Bobby looked out at the rest of the graveled courtyard. The same kind of high, gray stone, sturdy walls enclosed the inner courtyard as those outside. These inner walls however were different in that there were all kinds of little alcoves and windows cut into the stone. Bobby and his brother had already explored half of them on their way over. They would stick their head into the darkened room, look for a moment or two, then decide there was nothing interesting inside. A little left of the center was a huge stone building, at least four or five stories tall that probably contained more stuff their dad would want to look at. Around the outside edges of the courtyard were military and historical items scattered randomly and there was even a set of about 10 dark black cannons without their bases just lying side by side on the ground near the back corner. Other tourists were milling about, taking pictures or just walking casually under the noon day sun. Either they didn't know about the imminent cannon demonstration or they didn't care.

"At least Lindsey's not here," Bobby muttered under his breath. He knew Adam would hear him but he didn't want his dad to hear. They were just starting to get along again. There had been no heart wrenching conversation, no come to Jesus revelation or intervention between them, but father and son at least were beginning to exchange smiles again. It gave Bobby a little bit of hope that things would get better.

"What do you have against her anyway?" Adam stood up a little straighter in anticipation. Five soldiers, all dressed in black uniforms had started marching two by two over to their position. They wore black circular hats, not helmets, with a black chinstrap that made them look more like bellhops than soldiers. They had a tight red collar around their neck and a matching red stripe length ways all the way down their trousers. One of them, the lone soldier in the front, looked to be carrying a small wooden bucket.

"Here they come," their dad pointed. Mumbles and whispers ran through the crowd. Several people began recording with their cellphones.

"Everything you idiot," Bobby continued the conversation. Adam's countdown was still reading more than five minutes.

"Shut up."

"You just don't get it do you?" Bobby lowered his voice. His father looked at them for a moment then turned his attention back towards the soldiers. "Lindsey's the one keeping mom and dad apart. She's the one dad has the hots for now."

"You're the idiot," Adam turned on his video feature on his cell phone as well. He noted the countdown reading of five minutes and pressed record at the precise moment. The cannon should go off at precisely the five minute mark on his recorder counter. "Dad and mom already were separated long before Lindsey showed up," Adam kept the phone pointed at the soldiers but was looking at his brother. He had had enough of Bobby's antics. "Besides do you really think Dad would do something with one of his teammates?"

Bobby didn't answer. The soldiers had reached the cannon and were making a formation around it. One of the men stood off to the side to give orders. From somewhere nearby, bagpipes began to play.

"You're just so pissed at Dad that you are blaming him for everything."

"No I am not."

"Yes you are. You took mom's side even before the break up." As if on cue, Bobby's text alert went off. "Score!" the announcer shouted. Bobby hurriedly reached for the silent button. His father gave him a glare.

"See!" Adam pointed at the screen. "Mom" appeared in the text reception box. Bobby looked down and read.

"She's just asking what we are doing today."

"She's not asking me."

"That's cuz you haven't texted her."

"And I'm not going to."

"You're just as mad at mom as I am at dad."

The soldier in command suddenly barked out an order that Bobby did not understand. The other men began loading the cannon. Their movements were sharp and precise as if they had been practicing this for years, which of course they had. Both boys watched for several moments, content in letting the conversation die. They both knew which side they had taken and they both knew their brother had taken the other side. To hear it out loud though made things different. It sounded silly, childish to both of them. It was the first step towards them getting through this together.

"You still don't need to be mad at Lindsey," Adam said.

"I know."

"And you gotta admit she is kind of hot," Adam grinned. It was a knowing smile and it spoke volumes. Adam knew Bobby thought she was hot. He had tried to hide it but Adam was not as young or as naïve as his brother thought. He really was a smart kid, Bobby had to admit.

"Uh-huh," Bobby smiled right back at his brother. It was one of those smiles men and especially boys exchange when discussing a sexy woman. It was immature and silly. Both the boys suddenly burst out laughing.

"That's the sponge," Rob suddenly took a step next to his boys and pointed at the long mop like stick in the soldier's hands. The man was ramming the soft end into the muzzle of the cannon. "They use that to clean the cannon before they fire it."

Both boys continued to giggle and smirk as their father attempted to explain the actions of the soldiers. He didn't understand everything they were doing but it was fascinating watching their speed and precision. Bobby thought the way they moved the cannon forward by placing long pieces of wood under each wheel and smoothly rotating them was the coolest.

Adam's video counter was at 4:55. The soldier in charge had his face in his pocket watch. One second, two, three, "Time number one!"

"Fire!" the soldier at the cannon yelled. The cannon roared. Everybody jumped as the concussion vibrated through them. Somewhere below, a car alarm began to sound. The smoke rose up, the crowd clapped and Adam and Bobby both looked at each other. "Awesome!" they shouted as one.

Twenty Four

"We're going to have to separate," Agent Saltman turned to Agent Foster. He felt out of place in his New England Patriots t-shirt and dark blue jeans. It had been years since he had done anything resembling a vacation or dressed comfortably or even gone to see a movie, he realized. When was the last time he was working and not wearing a tie?

Agent Foster on the other hand was much more relaxed. He was wearing his favorite weekend outfit; a blue and white U.S. Coast Guard t-shirt and black athletic shorts. The shirt was just tight enough to show off his bulging muscles but comfortable enough to let him breathe. The outfit was perhaps a little lite for the crisp Canadian summer air but it felt wonderful and free and reminded him of his days on the cutter. Matt always thought back to his days in the Guard with nostalgia and even longing. Of course he loved his work in the Agency, but it was with the Guard that he truly felt like he was making a difference. He could see the immediate results of his work, whether it was rescuing a stranded surfer or clapping on the cuffs to a drug dealer.

Despite the agents' best efforts, the two of them did not blend in. Saltman could just not relax and kept playing with his shirt collar, stretching it out at the imaginary tie. Foster could not keep his eyes off the boys, turning away as quickly as he could whenever they seemed to look his way. He still had not gotten the knack for field work. Perhaps, Saltman had suggested, with everyone watching the cannon demonstration they could be a little more out in the open.

"Separate?" Foster looked away quickly. *Had one of the boys noticed him?* "When?"

"Now," Saltman replied. He took out his phone and double checked the time. "You're going to have to hustle to make the meeting in Campobello."

"I still wish you were going."

"I was." Saltman pushed his glasses back up on his nose. You would think after decades of wearing them, he would have found a pair that didn't slide down all the time. "But your little phone rescue blew that out of the water."

"Any advice?" Foster consciously ignored the not so subtle reprimand from his senior partner. He knew he had blown his cover, he didn't need another reminder. Saltman had already scolded him on the ship immediately after it happened and in the hotel in Halifax. It must have been some kind of record for the quickest blown cover.

"Honesty," Saltman took a step backwards. He too felt as if the boys were looking their way. "The Canadian agents are just as good as we are. They will pick up on anything you don't say and everything you do. Plus, they are our allies, our friends in this. The boss wants everything on the up and up."

"Well this should be easy then."

"Not necessarily," Saltman reminded him. "Don't forget how serious this could get. If it gets out in the open, if the press finds out, this could explode."

"I get it." Foster looked down at the tourist crowd. They had started to disburse. The boys headed away with their father. "I screwed up once. I won't do it again."

"Just stay in contact." Saltman turned in the direction the boys were heading. "And meet up with me as soon as you can."

"Did you see him?" Bobby whispered to his brother as they walked on the asphalt path down the grassy hill. It was just wide enough for both boys to walk side by side with their father about 10 feet in front. Bobby was relieved that his father headed right to the exit after the cannon fire and did not want to go into the museum or see any more of the Citadel. In fact, Rob seemed to be in a hurry to leave.

"Who?" Adam hurried to keep up. His father was walking quite briskly.

"The guy from the boat."

"The black guy who caught your phone?"

"Yeah."

"No."

"He was standing by the ramparts, dressed like a tourist this time."

"When?"

"During the cannon firing."

"You sure?"

"Can't forget that cool goatee."

"So? Maybe he's a tourist too. The guy at the pub said everyone comes here."

"Maybe."

"C'mon boys," Rob made his strides even longer. It took more energy stopping yourself than walking as they hurried down the steep incline from the top of the Citadel. "We'll have just enough time."

"For what?" Adam was having trouble controlling himself. He was going almost at a jog just trying to keep up with his father. Gravity was pulling him even faster.

"It's a surprise!"

"S-s-surprise!" Adam began to laugh. He was losing control. Every step he took, his foot slammed onto the asphalt as the acceleration pulled him downward. Bobby was caught in it too and took advantage of the opportunity to step off the path and onto the much steeper grassy side. He let gravity take over.

Rob stopped on the path, smiled and watched his boys run straight down the hill. Their arms were flailing, their legs whipped forward and back, forward and back, like something out of a Bugs Bunny cartoon. It was wonderful watching them lose themselves in their age. Rob gasped when Adam almost ran over someone laying in the grass and reading. Then, seconds later, Adam stumbled, then Bobby and the two of them rolled all the way down to the bottom. They ended in a heap of laughter and grass stains.

"Have fun?" Rob laughed when he finally reached the bottom and helped them up.

"Yeah!" Both boys grinned. Each of them had bright green grass stains on their jeans right at the knees. Bobby was trying to wipe his off while Adam just stood there grinning. "That was awesome!"

"C'mon then!" Rob grinned as well. "The surprise is right across the street!"

"What surprise?"

"You'll see," Rob waved them to cross the street. On their left was some blue clay tennis courts and on their right a rotary with some flowers in the center. Traffic was relatively busy and people were walking in all directions so the boys were concentrating too much on crossing the street to look far ahead.

Rob stopped suddenly and looked at his boys. They looked at him; then in the direction he was nodding. "Whoa!" both cried in unison, jaws open and eyes focused forward. "What is this place?"

"Halifax Commons," Rob answered with a sly grin. "That there is the Oval."

Rob watched his sons' heads turning back and forth and smiled. This was a great choice! Halifax Commons, he had read on-line, was much like any city park. There was green space everywhere, paths to walk your dogs, a fountain, a ball field and even a skate park. People of all shapes, sizes and ages were enjoying this beautiful day playing Frisbee, strolling with the baby, or laying on the grass reading a good book. What had caught Rob's attention immediately was the big brown ellipse on the outskirts. It was called "the Oval" and it was designed like a race track. This one however was not for cars, it was for people. It had been built back in 2010 for the Canada Games and was originally constructed for speed skating. About three times the size of an NHL rink it had become a mecca for ice skating even after the games were over. In the winter, Rob had seen the pictures with envy, the locals skated around on the frozen ice, but in the summer it was used for any form of wheeled transportation. At the moment there were about five kids on bicycles and a single teenager on roller blades. The rest of the Oval was wide open for the taking.

"Want to go skating?" Rob started walking towards the benches off to the left.

"Skating?" Bobby jumped to join his father. "But we left our rollerblades at home."

"They rent here."

"No way!"

"C'mon," Rob pointed to the brown glass and brick building ahead, "we can get skates in there!"

It only took about ten minutes for the boys and Rob to find Rollerblades that fit. "Only in Canada," Rob remarked to the boys, "can you find so many kinds of skates."

The three of them sat outside on the gray wooden benches and tightened up their skates. Bobby ran his hand along the wheels, noticing how well they spun. "These bearings are pretty smooth," he grinned, "especially for rentals."

Rob smiled and bent down. He was enjoying the freedom to work on his own skates while letting the boys take care of themselves. For too many years he had been in the locker room with them, tying their skates up and any other kid who needed help. It wasn't like the old days when your old man just flung a metal t-shaped skate tightener at you and said, "Here kid."

"Ready boys!"

All three of them jumped up in unison and headed for the brown concrete style track. Bobby quickly jumped in front with Adam right behind him and Rob bringing up the rear. Rob was amazed at how smooth the surface was. One of the reasons he did not roller blade much at home was that the sidewalks were filled with cracks and were unsafe, the streets had too many cars and even the bike paths were made of some kind of gravely asphalt that vibrated your feet painfully. This track was smooth and wide. The bearings on his skates were well maintained and there was hardly any vibration in his feet at all. He could skate here all day.

The boys were easily able to avoid the few bikers on the track. It had to be at least 20 feet wide. All three of them could easily skate side by side with outstretched arms never touching if they wanted to. Of course they were too competitive for any side by side skating. The track was perfect for getting up some real good speed on the straightaway before you had to do the tight crossovers around the bends. Bobby and Adam took turns sprinting and coasting, sprinting and coasting until they had lapped their father twice.

"Hey you guys!" Lindsey suddenly called from the edge of the Oval. She held up several clear plastic "Subway" sandwich bags with both arms. "Hungry?"

"Yeah!" The boys leaped forward into a hard skate around the Oval and made their way back towards the benches. Rob laughed, peeled off and coasted next to Lindsey. He towered over her, especially in his skates.

"Thanks Linz," He took one of the bags from her, dragging his left foot to slow himself down and keep pace with her. "Your timing is perfect."

"You guys have a good time?" Lindsey took the manila folder tucked under her armpit and held it with her freed hand.

"It was great!" Rob noticed her documents folder was much bigger than it had been when she left this morning. "Find anything?"

"Some," she said mysteriously. "I'll tell you after lunch. Over there?" She pointed to a picnic table standing alone just a little bit away from the benches and next to some strange 20 foot high rope like artistic sculpture that somehow looked like hockey laces.

"Sure."

The boys came screaming around the turn of the oval, through the benches and did perfect 360 degree stops right next to the picnic table. "What did you get?" Adam said.

Rob gave him a stern look. Adam frowned. "I mean, thanks for getting us lunch Lindsey. What did you get?"

"Ham and cheese, Roast beef, tuna, turkey," she placed the bags on the table.

"I figured each of you would find something you like."

"We're in Canada and you got subway?" Bobby whined. His father glared.

"Well I know it's all 'America corporate invasion' and all," Lindsey smiled. She did not want to get subway either. One of the things she loved the most about traveling was experiencing new cultures and new foods. She had wanted to find a local shop or maybe even a Tim Hortons, but she was afraid the boys would complain. She should have known Bobby would complain anyway, "but I wanted to play it safe until I got to know you boys better."

"It's fine," Rob reassured her. "The boys eat subway almost every weekend."

"That's why I wanted something different," Bobby pressed. He really did not know when to quit.

"You pick first Lindsey," Rob rolled his eyes and took an effort to ignore his son.

"Ever the gentleman," Lindsey smiled and reached out for one of the subs. "Anyone mind if I take the tuna?"

"I got the ham," Adam grabbed.

"Roast beef," Bobby snapped.

"And I guess the turkey is mine," Rob laughed.

The boys whipped open their subs and each grabbed a bag of chips. Lindsey just got four bags of regular chips in case the variety of subs did not work out. It was silent for a moment as everyone dug in. Rob held the turkey sub up, opened his mouth, then stopped and stared. This was all too normal. All of sudden they were a family again, except Lindsey was suddenly in Deborah's place; the boys eating ravenously, the blue sky, the white clouds, the families laughing and playing in the background. It was like so many other days over the last 10 years. A swell of emotion surged in Rob's gut. He was sad, angry, nostalgic, melancholy and bitter all at the same time. *"Deborah should be here,"* he thought. *"Lindsey was great. The boys seemed to be taking it all in stride. I want this back. This is what it's all about. What the hell had happened?"* A tear started to form in his left eye. He quickly wiped it away with a napkin.

"Can we skate more when we're done?" Adam said in between bites.

"Sure," Rob was thankful for the interruption. He couldn't handle moments like these.

Once the boys were done, had cleared up their mess and skated off to the Oval again, Rob was finally able to ask Lindsey about the archives.

"They were really friendly," Lindsey began. "And they had literally millions of documents."

"Millions?"

"Yeah, but thank god they are all so organized."

"What did you find?"

"It took a while," she did not want it to seem too easy. The work was painstaking. All the documents in the archives were catalogued but very little of it was on-line. That is why Lindsey had to go there personally. She had to look at microfiche readers and computer entries and get some personal help from the librarian herself. "And Lauren was really helpful."

"Lauren?"

"The Librarian. She suggested I do a search for the specific families from our index."

"And?"

"Well I didn't find any of the big names: Appleby, Garrison, and Adams. But I did find a book and some letters from the Inglis family."

"I don't remember them."

"They're on the index."

"Hey dad!" Adam screamed as he raced by.

Rob waved.

"Hey Lindz," Bobby raced by a second later. The sandwich must have slowed him up. It was the first time Adam had any kind of a lead.

"Hey," Lindsey smiled at Bobby and waved. That was nice. "The family is a pretty large one," Lindsey returned to the story, "and it took me a lot of reading to get anywhere. But here is what I found." She pushed the folder across the picnic table to Rob and opened it to the first paper inside. "It's just this one letter."

"What's the rest of this stuff?" Rob fingered through all the papers underneath. There was close to 50 photocopies of various letters and documents.

"Just near misses; I had to print off any clue there was. Any mention of Loyalists or the border I thought might help."

"So what's this?" Rob held up the front paper. It was a letter written to someone named Rob Inglis.

"It's not a big revelation," Lindsey cautioned him. She didn't want Rob to get his hopes up. This was not going to be easy. "It's no smoking gun, like they say in the movies."

"Then what is it?"

"It's a letter that mentions William Franklin?"

"That's it?" Rob's face fell.

"No," Lindsey said quickly. "It is much more specific than that." She pointed to a spot in the letter about half way down. Rob reached into his pocket and took out his Clark Kent style glasses. Lindsey couldn't help but notice the transformation. "It discusses William Franklin representing many Loyalist families."

"So?"

"They match the names on your index."

"They do?" Rob began to read the names over. "Adams," he called out, "Appleby-"

"And Garrison and Lloyd and Lawless. It matches perfectly!"

"But what does this tell us?"

"It tells us that we are not crazy Rob!" A few kids nearby turned their heads towards them. Lindsey lowered her voice. "This proves that your family joined together with a bunch of other Loyalist families and had correspondence with William Franklin."

"Great!" Rob smiled; then frowned. "But where does that leave us now?"

"The librarian said that we would find much more information in New Brunswick. As soon as the provinces split, the records from where your family went were handled by the new province. That's probably why I couldn't find Appleby and Adams. We just got lucky that someone in the Inglis family must have moved to Nova Scotia shortly after the war."

"Hey dad c'mon!" Adam raced by again. "Stop talking already."

"Be right there!" Rob got up. His feet rolled forward and he had to steady himself on the picnic table with his left hand. He almost forgot he still had his roller blades on. "Want to join us Lindsey?"

Map Courtesy of Curtis Rindlaub and *A Cruising Guide to the Maine Coast*

L7

May 1790

Deer Island, New Brunswick

"Please father, sit down," Anne pleaded. It was starting to become a pattern for her and again she wondered if she should have ever left him alone with Isaac. It wasn't that Isaac was irresponsible; quite the contrary. Over the last seven years he had grown into an impressive young man, bigger stronger and even wiser than their older brother Samuel (who they still hadn't heard from!) It was Isaac himself who had convinced Anne to move out of father's home in the first place.

She had married the young Jonathan Adams almost the moment they had stepped off the crowded refugee ship. Whether it was the physical attraction, their shared experiences, their similar age or just their need for something good in their lives, Anne and Jonathan had fallen head over heels in love. And for that first horrible winter, it was only the richness and innocence of that love that kept either family going.

Near starvation, bitter cold, crowded refugee camps and the constant competition for resources flooded every day of that winter of 1783-84. Of course the King had done his best to provide rations and protection for all his loyal subjects, but there was no way even an international empire could provide food and shelter for thousands and thousands of wandering refugees. They would have to build their own homes from the earth itself amidst the merciless Nova Scotia winter all the while wondering if their neighbors were men of character and honor or scoundrels who were about to claim the very land under their feet.

Tragedy had struck them even before their ship had reached the shores. Sarah, Jonathan's mother, had lost the baby. The journey from New York to Nova Scotia had just been too much for her. She miscarried in the middle of the night, waking everyone on deck with her terrified screams. By the time the ship docked, she was in such a weakened state that she had to be carried off the ship with a stretcher by both husband and son. Within a month, she was gone as well. John, Anne's new father in law, never recovered. "It was all his fault," he cried, day after day. He should have stayed. He should have left earlier. He never should have gone to New York, or to Canada, or stayed loyal or even come to America. Every decision John Adams had ever made came into question and was at fault for his wife's death. He was broken beyond repair.

They had hoped their wedding would help. It certainly made Thomas Appleby happy. Finally one of his hopes had come true after years of disappointment and heartbreak. As he walked down the aisle of the packed Halifax church, (The wedding was attended by many of the Loyalists from the ship ride and even beyond. Everyone needed some good news in these difficult times and there were few occasions more joyous than a wedding.), Thomas' heart had been light and warm. Anne was such a wonderful young woman; so beautiful, so caring, so responsible, god-fearing and wholesome. Her mother would have been proud. She deserved this happiness. She deserved Jonathan. He was a good man as well and Thomas was sure that he would take good care of his little girl.

But when Thomas had looked up the aisle at the groom and his father John standing at the altar, his heart skipped a beat. There was just no escaping the dark cloud hanging over his old friend John Adams. Not even the wedding of his oldest son could break the hold of blackness encompassing his heart. As all eyes in the church had turned from Anne and towards the men standing at the altar, the cloud of tragedy descended like the infamous London Fog and permeated every soul. The wedding had become more like a funeral.

"Please father," Anne repeated. "You need to sit."

Even before arriving in her father's home, Anne knew she would find him this way. Thomas Appleby had become a ghost of the man he once was. What was left of his thin hair was completely gray. His eyes were dark and so deep set into his wrinkles that Thomas needed to turn his head to look left and right. The hunch in his back had grown to encompass his right shoulder as well and the imbalance in his weight forced him to walk with a limp whenever he took more than a few strides. Anne could not believe he had survived as long as he did.

The years had been tough on all of them. Loyalist Canada had not been the Garden of Eden they all hoped for nor had the King carried through on all of his promises. Oh to be sure there had been plenty of land available. Nova Scotia had filled up with so many Loyalists that an entire province had been broken off to form this new one named New Brunswick. But just because there had been land did not mean that the land was useful. Some of the land was too rocky, some of it was too far from any water or too deep in the woods. So the competition for the best land had been fierce. Veterans, soldiers and officers, government officials, merchants, farmers, families who had always been loyal, families that had become loyal during the war, and even families who chose neither side but were forced from their homes or lost everything during the war, they all had been in competition for the best land that could be found. Unfortunately, not all these families were treated the same way. There was a hierarchy that put some in front of others and forced the Parliament appointed Loyalist commission to enforce all kinds of rules, some fair, others not so much. Everyday Loyalist families, including the Applebys and the Adams, were forced to abandon their worthless plots and move out of Nova Scotia further south to places like St. John's or the Passamaquoddy area.

Fortunately, Passamaquoddy was a real gem in this rugged land. Somewhat sheltered from the open waters of the Atlantic and not as vast as the Bay of Fundy to the north, the bay was in many ways the perfect compromise. Indeed it was even set in the exact middle of the hemisphere, halfway between the North Pole and the equator. It meant of course that the winters were intensely frigid and dangerous, but the summer days were long and productive, with the sun's last rays lasting to near midnight. When Anne first set eyes upon the many islands and blue waters of Passamaquoddy, she had felt hope for the first time since the wedding.

The problem (or at least one of them) had been that they were not the first ones there. Large tracts of land had already been claimed by powerful men along all the rivers heading into the bay. While the border was still in question and no one was quite sure which river was the actual border between the new United States and Canada, everyone could still see the value in the deep forested cedar, pine and maple trees. Their ancient limbs and towering trunks covered every inch of the land creating a carpet like green canopy from the coast to as far as any man could walk for weeks. Nothing was more valuable to an international empire with one of the largest fleets in the world, than lumber. By the time Appleby and Adams had even arrived in Passamaquoddy, more than a dozen sawmills had been built.

Even the islands closer to the eastern mouth of the bay were starting to see disputes. Both nearby Campobello and Moose islands had significant numbers of Loyalist settlers who were beginning to argue. American Governor John Hancock of Massachusetts was taking advantage of the border dispute and eyeing Moose Island in an attempt to extend his state's border as far North as possible while Campobello was filling up quickly with veterans from both the Royal Fencibles and Argyll regiments. Fortunately, Deer Island, sandwiched between the two, was still largely undeveloped.

The Adams and the Applebys had been some of the first settlers on Deer Island. But while that meant they had an eye on some of the best land, it would all have to be cut, cleared and forged not only into a home that could shelter them in the frigid winters, it would also have to provide them with a livelihood. They would get nothing from the King. Ships only arrived sporadically and even then they could only afford the bare necessities; salt, spices and hopefully some tea. There certainly would be no luxuries. Everything they had, everything they used would have to be made by hand. Chairs, furniture, beds and tables, it all would have to be carved. For food, they would hunt and fish and if they were lucky, one day they could afford to buy a cow, a pig or at least a chicken. If disease struck or a storm lasted too long or did too much damage, they were doomed. Life was lived on the edge.

Fortunately, at the time of their arrival, Isaac, Anne and Jonathan had been in the prime of their lives. Thomas was still a powerful man from his lifetime of being a blacksmith and a farmer and even little Sturgis could lend a hand. John Adams, Anne's father in law while being empty in soul was still healthy in body. After the wedding, they were not even sure he would make the trip but the responsibility he felt for his sons and new daughter in law kept him going. He went through the motions, cleared the land, worked hard with Thomas to build each of their family homes and labored intensely but there was no spark left in him at all.

Now, as Anne stared into her own father's eyes more than five years since their arrival on the island, she was heart-broken by how much the struggle had cost him and wondered if she would lose him as well. He may have arrived on Deer Island a powerful man, but their survival had come at a high price.

"I can still take care of myself," Thomas shouted in protest. Anne smiled in relief. Her father still had his spark. It was almost tragic that the spark was lit by the fire of his anger, but at least the passion was still there. The old man may be falling apart physically, but he still was burning with anger.

It was an anger they all felt. Anger at the King, anger at the commission, anger at Parliament and anger at the men still preventing them all from receiving legal title to the land they had struggled so hard to maintain. It had been five years damn it! Five years of clearing land, building homes, surviving on salted meat and fish with only the occasional British ship sending supplies and aid. They deserved to be compensated. They deserved to legally own that land. The King and Parliament had promised, they had sworn to protect and take care of the Loyalists!

The meeting was Anne's idea. She knew the families all gathered together regularly anyway to worship or socialize. What else was there to do? But this time they needed to plan. They needed to take some action. It had been too long and they had been to patient.

"Of course you can take care of yourself," Anne pointed to the soft aspen wood rocking chair Thomas had built last year. She still did not understand how he had time to make it or how he was able to carve it so beautifully with the limited tools they had, but she wanted to make sure he sat in it before someone else did. "But

I can't sit until you do." She smiled.

"What did I do to deserve you?" Thomas smiled back as he made his way slowly to the chair. Anne had to steady it for him as it rocked beneath his weight.

"The same back at you father," Anne was relieved he did not protest her holding the chair for him. The old man hadn't turned into a complete grump.

"When will the others arrive?" Isaac walked into the room with a piece of salted pork in his hand. It was the last one left from the winter. Thank goodness the warm weather had arrived before it ran out.

"Any minute now," Anne smiled. Isaac still hadn't change. No pleasantries, no chit chat or small talk, he was practical as ever, always getting right to the point. "John is waiting for his little brother so he may be late."

"Is your father in law coming?"

"No," Anne offered no further explanation. None was needed. John Adams had not socialized since they arrived in Passamaquoddy. He didn't even attend prayer meetings. Neighbors had started to complain and grow suspicious until Thomas and Anne explained. It was just as well he did not come today anyway, Anne realized. No need for the darkness to fill the room. This meeting would require, hope and resolve. Those were two things John Adams had lost forever.

The first knock occurred a few minutes later. Isaac and Anne had barely enough time to arrange some crates and the few chairs they had in a circle. All the homes on the island were of course plain and simple, almost Spartan. There were no amenities and no extra chairs or cushions. Log homes, some caulk or tar to fill in the gaps between boards, were the only materials they had to work with. In winter the frigid air swept right through the home and the sheets and blankets they covered themselves with barely provided enough cover to survive. In summer the rain and even occasional hail could leak right through the roof. With no separation between rooms, kitchen, fireplace and bedroom were all in one place. If she hadn't decided to serve food and drink, Anne would have held the meeting outside.

Anne put some water on the fire for tea and even broke open a package of biscuits they had been saving for a special occasion. The neighbors would be there any moment and the tiny tea pot she had managed to bring with her from New York would have to be used and reused several times to serve them all. Her hard working neighbors were always prompt, always exact, sometimes annoyingly so. This time though, Anne was relieved for their promptness. She was too nervous to wait much longer. Within minutes, all eight families had arrived, including her husband Jonathan and his younger brother Sturgis. Anne could barely move around enough to serve the tea in the crowded home.

The purpose of the meeting was clear to everyone. Something had to be done. As long as they held no title to this land, anyone could come along and force them to leave. All the hard work and years of cutting, sawing, lifting and building would be an utter waste. None of them had the will power left to start all over again. As Anne scanned the room, she realized even more just how true that was. Every man in the room looked tired, regardless of their various ages or physical condition. Their heads moved slowly up and down as they talked, their hand gestures were reserved and their voices subdued. That would change soon though, Anne realized. Once they started talking of the land and of the King, the shouts would begin, the voices would rise and the blood would boil. Anne hoped she could control those passions long enough to convince them of her plan.

"Thank you all for coming," Anne announced once the last of the tea had been poured. It was still a little odd taking a leadership role as a woman alone amidst all these men but fortunately, the norms and constraints of society were often ignored on the island. Here the sexism was less, the needs were greater and no one really seemed to mind when Anne or any of the women spoke their mind or gave an order. The needs of survival superseded everything else. At least there was one small thing she was grateful for.

"What's this all about?" Joseph Lawless quickly spoke up. He was perhaps the most impatient man in the room and definitely the most blunt. The other 10 men had pulled a crate from the pile, taken seats in the semi-circle and were carefully sipping their tea or nibbling on a biscuit. Joseph had not even sat down yet. He was not going to waste his time socializing when there were more important things to be done.

"Sit down Joseph!" Lieutenant Karlson commanded in his usual deep bark. There were thousands of veterans all over Passamaquoddy and throughout the Canadian Provinces. Three of the men in the meeting in addition to Karlson himself were veterans. However, only Karlson was still called by his rank. His edginess, his commanding tone and presence, even his tiny, intense green eyes boring a hole through your soul all commanded attention. No one was even sure what his real first name was. They all just called him Lieutenant.

Joseph immediately lowered his balding head and sat upon the last crate left in the room. As a veteran of the New Jersey Volunteers himself, he naturally bent to Karlson's commands, even with the cessation of hostilities. Sheepishly he settled down and grasped the edges of the crate to sturdy himself. The other men smiled. Only Karlson could quiet Joseph like a whipped dog they all were thinking.

No one really liked Joseph Lawless. He was an odd man, aloof and self-centered. Yet they accepted him as their neighbor as they accepted everyone else. Joseph, like the rest of them, was a hard worker. He was trustworthy and he was reliable. They all were. They had to be. It was the only way they could survive here.

It was an odd collection to say the least. The only thing the eight families had in common of course was their loyalty to the king. Some again, were veterans. Yet none of them had served together with even the action they had seen being at different locations and under different commanders. Two other families were strictly refugees. William Stuart, was from the already infamous Penobscot Loyalist group. Their entire Loyalist settlement, nearly 500 strong, had been located near the old controversial border between Massachusetts and Canada. After all their struggles in the revolution and in relocating, they were still forced at gunpoint to retreat further north. William was the only one of the Penobscot group to settle on Deer Island. The others were on Campobello or Moose Island or on the mainland to the west. Lawrence Brawn, another refugee, shared little about himself and was the only Irishman in the room. The Irish and the Scottish were all over the area, having been both heavily recruited by the British Army as well as a significant percentage of the colonial population. Brawn was neither veteran nor official, New Englander nor New Yorker. Perhaps, most of them thought from his darker skin tone, he had lived in the Southern Colonies. He either spent a lot of time in the warm sunshine, or was of mixed race. It didn't matter. He was the kindest man amongst them, always sharing his time and his wares with anyone who needed them. Of all the men in the room, he was the only one they all generally liked.

Only Oliver Rockwell stood out. Like Thomas Appleby and John Adams, he had lived in New York City for a time. Like Karlson, Brawn and Lawless, he had war experience although he never said what unit he served in. Unlike everyone else though, he was alone. He had no wife or children. He brought no companions or friends with him. No one even knew if he had once been married, fathered any children before his new life, or even what his occupation had been. The man was a mystery.

And he was the perfect man for Anne's plan. She needed someone who had no one depending on them. She needed someone who was as desperate as the rest of them and understood what was at stake. Oliver was all those things and more. He had worked with William Franklin.

"As you all know," Anne stood in the center of the semi-circle to command their attention. It was time to let the figurative cat out of the bag. She spoke quickly, trying to calm her nerves and get to the point before she could be interrupted. "Parliament's original Loyalist relief act has expired and a new far stricter one has taken its place."

Mumbles and sworn oaths immediately filled the room. Joseph Lawless almost stood up again. Anne rushed on. "This new act shows even less promise for us with its requirements and investigations."

"How are we supposed to prove our losses?" Anne's own father Thomas was the first to interrupt her. Anne was not surprised. He still thought the meeting was his idea. "We have no papers from my burnt shop or my lost home!"

"They treat us like criminals!" Lawless shouted. Most of the men nodded their heads in agreement.

"It's as if my service means nothing," Brawn snapped his fist forward in anger, "Nothing!"

"How many of us fought for the King?" Lawless fed on Brawn's anger. He had seen the most action in the group. Having joined the King's army shortly after Washington's retreat from New York City, he had been in almost every battle in the east, including the humiliating surrender at Yorktown. It was a wonder he had even survived. For six years he had served King and country and had nothing to show for it, less than nothing. When he returned home after the war, his home had been burnt down by his neighbors and his family had already fled to New York City.

"Or lost our livelihoods?" Thomas Appleby knew Lawless' anguish. He had felt it as well of course. No he had not fought in the war, nor lost a son and a daughter to the Old Sow, but Thomas had lost his home, his shop and of course his son trying to stay out of it all. "I have not seen my son since he left over ten years ago. I do not even know if he is alive or dead."

"It's not even about the border anymore," Jonathan placed a sympathetic hand on Thomas' shoulder. He knew more than most how much Thomas Appleby had suffered. "The Nova Scotia government has made it clear Deer Island belongs to the King, not the United States. Who cares whether the river is the St. Croix, Schoodic or Digdeguash?"

"Even their own President Washington, has told Congress he wants the border issue settled."

"Let's be fair," Lieutenant Karlson countered. He was a little better off than they were. He had proof of his service. The military kept meticulous records, especially for officers. Still, like the rest of them, he held no title to the land. "To them we are all like salmon swimming up-stream with all the other refugees. How are they to know we are honorable men? We all have met swindlers and tricksters over the last few decades."

"Like Farrell," Jonathan cried bitterly. He looked at his right hand bitterly and remembered how he lost his index finger to an axe in the first year of their arrival.

How much work had he done to build his home and protect his family? How much had he lost; his mother, her unborn child, and his father John who had become a ghost of a man that was more dead than alive? And what did he have to show for it? Nothing! Nothing! Farrell owned the land. Farrell controlled everything. They did all the work, and Farrell was the one who benefitted! Only Anne filled his life with joy and hope. Jonathan stared directly into his wife's eyes, knowing what the purpose of the meeting really was. "He is the reason none of us have any land."

"That's right!"

"The son of a whore!" Brawn swore in his thick Irish accent. No one knew how to curse and insult more than Irishmen and Brawn was all Irish at times like this. "He and the other bastards like him want all the land for themselves."

"Yes, yes," Anne put up her hands and locked eyes again with her husband. She needed to keep control. "Farrell is the problem. We all know that."

"That motherless devil," Brawn was still in a groove. Anne grimaced at having lost control again, "never even shows his face here. He's a coward like all the others."

"I saw him once," Lawless stood again. "He was walking the land and caressing the tree trunks like they were lovers."

Everyone burst out in hearty laughter, even Anne.

"I don't think he even knows how to hold an axe!"

More laughter.

"Or a shovel!"

"He knows how to screw us though," the laughter changed in tone and quickly dissipated. That cut too close to their nerves.

"Listen," Anne used the awkward moment and tried a third time to take control. "I have a plan to get back at that bastard." Perhaps if she used harsher language like them, the men would listen better. She glanced nervously at her father. He wasn't sure what to think but he couldn't help but smile. "Oliver," she turned away from her father and looked directly at Oliver. He had not said a word the entire meeting. Even when Anne called him out, he continued sitting perfectly still with hands placed gently on his lap, making no reaction whatsoever to suddenly being the center of attention. His calmness was almost unnerving. "You know William Franklin don't you?"

"Franklin?" Lawless shouted. Did the man ever sit still?

"Isn't he dead?"

"No, his father is."

"Really?"

"Last month, do you not read the papers?"

"Not all of us have free time."

Anne looked again at Oliver. The man was sitting calmly, waiting for the chatter to die down. His black eyes never moved, his lips didn't curve in either a smile or a frown. There was no twitch in his scarred face or motion of any kind. He was unreadable. "Yes I know William Franklin." He finally responded. "Don't most people?"

"You worked with him," Anne pressed. That much she knew. It had been one of those rare moments of peace and quiet a few weeks ago, standing under the sunset and watching a flock of gulls disappearing into the horizon. She had finally gotten Oliver to open up a little. He had not said much. He didn't share any feelings or details, but he did discuss his relationship with the Governor. "During the war, right?" she added.

"Yes," Oliver remained stoic. Anne was not sure if she had broken a trust but it was too late now. "We worked on several campaigns together."

No one knew what he meant by campaigns. The Governor had become famous, maybe infamous by now for the methods he had used near the end of the war. He had never recruited enough men to form any kind of Loyalist regiment, but he did form his Association. They had performed raids, sometimes at night, captured soldiers and of course there was that whole ugly affair after Yorktown with Lippincott that had so upset most reasonable men, including General Washington and even the King of France.

"Do you remain in touch with him?"

"Not really."

"But can you get in touch with him?" Anne's blood pressure was starting to rise. Oliver was more frustrating than she had imagined. She knew she was not the only one in their association to write the Governor. But no one had made any progress. They needed a face to face. "Perhaps even arrange a meeting?"

"Yes," Oliver replied thoughtfully, "If Odell will help."

"What does this have to do with us?" Karlson interrupted. He did not like Franklin. Lippincott had been too much for him. The war was over. Revenge served no purpose and was the act of brigands and thieves, not honorable men. Yes, there were two sides to the story and yes Franklin was legitimate in his anger at the rebels for all the transgressions, but that was still over the top in his mind. He had no interest in working with a man such as this.

"Franklin has connections," Anne turned to the group and explained. "He can cut through much of the paperwork and take our case directly to Parliament or the King."

"He has no real power anymore," Lawless argued.

"We don't need power right now," Jonathan added. He needed to help his wife. Things were not going as well as they had hoped. He even considered telling them of the letter his wife still had locked away. It was clear from his language, that Governor Franklin had something in his possession that did indeed give him some kind of power over the King; if he wanted to use it. "We need connections and Franklin has those."

Anne was a little annoyed that her husband had felt the need to speak up. For a moment, she was afraid he would even mention the letter she still possessed, written years ago in a moment of desperation. She had contacted the Governor sometime after the war, hoping he would remember their brief encounter with them in New York. Maybe he would feel some compassion for their plight and know how to help them. But his reply was cryptic and frustrating, making vague promises and strange references. And then all communication stopped. She was frustrated and embarrassed that it had come to nothing. Thank goodness her husband had not humiliated her so.

The room had grown silent as the idea began to take hold.

"No one of consequence knows of our plight," Thomas pressed as well. He was the only other person who knew of Anne's plans in advance. At first, he was furious with her for even writing Governor Franklin. But once he got over the humiliation and realized that no one would ever know, he calmed down and listened. She had discussed with both her father and husband almost two weeks ago how if they sent an emissary of sorts to Franklin, representing all of them, it would be more respectful and proper. After all, they had already contacted just about every lawyer they could in Canada and come up empty. They needed help from someone in London. Someone with power, and clearly that was Franklin. He just needed to use it. "Only Farrell and his wealthy lumber friends have any idea what is going on here." Thomas added. "Franklin can bring us the attention we need."

"He knows everyone in London," Anne said.

"His years as representative for the Loyalists have not been good to him," Oliver spoke again. This time however, there seemed to be a spark of passion in his eyes. Anne could not tell if it was anger or hope. "And he has grown even more bitter and angry with each failure." Anne's heart sunk. Many of the men shook their heads slowly. The list of families denied fair compensation grew longer by each passing day. Yes, of course, thousands of people were helped by the King. It had been perhaps the largest aid ever given to refugees in history. But no matter what, there were stories of despair and tragedy. There had to be. Nothing like this had ever been seen in the British Empire since the Vikings attacked almost a thousand years ago. What could one man do, even if he was the most famous Loyalist on both sides of the Atlantic?

"Yet he still presses on," Oliver's voice began to rise and so too did their hopes. "The man is unstoppable in his passion for justice."

"Would he meet with you?" Anne pressed. This had to work! Her eyes lit up and she almost stood on the tip of her toes leaning towards Oliver.

"I will see what I can do."

Twenty Five

A man with a New England Patriots t-shirt and dark blue jeans held the glass door open for Lindsey.

"Thanks," Lindsey said as she walked into the dark tan brick main building. The man walked in slowly. behind her and wandered off to the side, looking confused, while she headed straight to the skate rental area. She was excited to join the boys on the Oval and paid no attention to anyone or anything, friendly or unfriendly. It wasn't just the prospect of skating outside in the summer air on that incredible track; it was also finally beginning to feel just a little welcome by the boys. A bomb would have had to go off to get her to notice anything out of the ordinary and Agent Saltman had no trouble hiding in plain sight with Lindsey so hyper focused. Within minutes, she had rented her skates, taken off her shoes and headed out the door.

Rob was coasting just ahead and the boys were rounding the Oval in the distance. "Hey Rob," she jumped onto the Oval and caught up to him easily. "This place is great!"

"I know," Rob started to skate a little faster. His stride was natural and smooth. Even on Rollerblades, skating had to be the freest movement a person could make. Free from the friction of dirt, grass, floor or street, you could turn forward or backward, spin a 360, glide, jump, or even move yourself simply by swinging your hips. He could look at the boys, swing around and talk to Lindsey or simply glide next to her with barely a thought. It was a unique freedom that only people raised on skating could truly appreciate. He loved it. "The boys haven't slowed down yet."

"Hey dad, Hey Lindsey!" They both whizzed by as if on cue. Rob and Lindsey both sped up a little. Their natural competitiveness began to surface. "Think we can catch them?" Rob smiled.

Lindsey just smiled back, hopped forward on her skates with three quick sharp strides and broke into a half sprint. Rob did the same. The fresh, open air whipping through him and blowing his hair around made him feel the speed even more than when he was in the rink. Plus, with such a long straightaway, he could gather a lot more speed before he would have to turn. Within seconds they were passing the kids on bikes and making their way to the turn. Lindsey made a hard right crossover and hugged the turn right where it met the green grass in the center. Rob copied her move and was a half stride behind to her right. He bent a little more to get more strength. "Let's catch them before they make the lap."

Three more hops as they came out of the turn and the two of them could pick up speed on the straightaway. Bobby and Adam were so intent on racing each other that they had no idea they were even being followed. They rounded the turn at the other end of the Oval but were taking it much wider, with much more casual crossovers. It would be child's play to catch them.

Lindsey pulled to the right, Rob to the left. They would pass the boys on either side. Lindsey just raced by Bobby's side, keeping a safe distance between the two of them but Rob could safely tease his younger son. He gave Adam a sharp poke in the ribs just as he passed, "Gotcha kiddo!"

"Hey!" both boys snapped their heads forward and jumped into a sprint, trying to catch up. It would not be easy though. Both Rob and Lindsey had powerful strides from decades of skating. Bobby and Adam were both great skaters too, having started about the same time they learned to walk. Unfortunately for them, they both had been skating for a while and still were feeling their subway lunch in the center of their gut. A good fifteen feet ahead, Rob and Lindsey looked at each other in triumph as they skated down the straightaway. Their eyes met, they smiled and Rob whispered "sandwich".

They approached the turn. This time however, both Rob and Lindsey took the turn at its widest. In fact they waited so long to begin their turn that Bobby and Adam both thought their father would run right into the grass. At the last moment however, Rob turned with an incredibly tight turn of his inside leg into an almost 90 degree turn while Lindsey widened her turn to remain on the outer edge. It allowed a huge space in between them, with Rob on the inside edge and Lindsey on the outer one. The boys would be able to fit in between easily.

Both of the boys sprinted even more and dashed into the wide space. As the four of them made the final part of the turn, they were all evenly matched coming into the straightaway. They exchanged glances and grins. Bobby and Adam tried to pull in front. Before they could however, both Lindsey and Rob started to tighten the gap between the skaters. Lindsey inched towards Bobby. Rob inched towards Adam. Both boys were forced closer together.

"Hey no fair!"

Now they were all touching shoulder to shoulder. It was a classic rub out. If they had been on ice, Lindsey and Rob would have given a final shove and knocked the boys flat, but concrete and stone did not give like ice did. There was no way they would do that here. It was slowing them down though.

Adam started to fall back. He did not have the strength to keep up. Bobby on the other hand grinned and pushed back. He thought he had a better chance against Lindsey than against his father so he leaned his shoulder into her. Lindsey smiled and leaned back.

"Whoa!" Bobby exclaimed almost losing his balance. Lindsey was a lot stronger than he gave her credit for. She could skate great. Her form was perfect and her butt looked really good in those jeans. "Whoa!" Distracted, Bobby almost got his skates caught in Lindsey's. He wheeled off towards the right suddenly, spun into the grass and landed in a heap.

Rob and Lindsey immediately swerved off the track and jumped onto the grass nearby. Their momentum forced them to hop a little towards Bobby. Adam joined them as well.

"You alright?" Rob lent a hand down to his son.

"That was tricky," Bobby accused as he extended his hand out towards his father. He took a side glance at Lindsey, hoping she never noticed his extended stare at her butt.

"You could have thought of it," Rob teased.

"You're always doing that," Bobby pulled away from his father's grasp and hopped back to his feet.

"Doing what?"

"Treating me like a kid."

"I'm not treating you like a kid."

"Yes you are." Bobby was angry. His face was red and he was pumping his fists. For a moment, Rob thought he might take a swing at him. Falling in front of Lindsey had upset him a lot more than he cared to admit. "You have been since before the trip began."

"What are you talking about?" Rob was defensive and getting angry as well. He was tired of these fights with his son. He had bent over backwards to try to make this a fun trip for the kids. The Citadel, the Oval, ignoring Bobby's constant complaining; what else could he do?

"Do you think we're idiots?" he nodded at his brother.

"Again. What are you talking about?"

"We know something else is going on." Bobby looked to his brother for agreement. Adam rolled his eyes and nodded but did not give any gesture to indicate he wanted to join Bobby in his accusations. "We know you have been keeping secrets from us."

Rob tried to stop himself from looking at Lindsey but he couldn't help it. A look of concern washed over her face.

"See," Bobby pointed. "You guys give each other looks like that all the time. You think we are just a couple of dumb kids who don't notice anything."

"We don't think-"

"Well did you know we are being followed?" Bobby blurted out. He surprised even himself with that statement but it was something that had been bugging him ever since the boat ride and the way his dad had been acting made it even worse. They still had not even told him why Lindsey went to the archives in the first place. It was a good thing Bobby hadn't noticed Agent Saltman following Lindsey earlier or he would have lost it.

"Followed?" Lindsey panicked. All the fears she had back home with the Pawn shop dealer and the creepy way he spied on them immediately resurfaced. She nervously scanned the entire Oval and beyond into the park. He could be anywhere, "By who?"

"Some black guy."

"How do you know you were being followed?" Rob said. He did not know whether he was relieved that it was not the pawn broker or more worried that it was someone else.

"Cuz the guy was spying on us on the boat and I saw him again at the Citadel."

"Is he here now?" Rob looked all over the commons as well. No sign of a black man anywhere, except that guy playing Frisbee with his dog. "Is that him?"

"No. He's not here now."

"Well he could be just a tourist," Rob tried to reassure himself as well as the boys.

"That's what I said," Adam finally spoke. "Lots of tourists do what we're doing."

"Your brother is right," Rob said firmly. He had to nip this in the bud. "The man was probably just a tourist. There is nothing to worry about and Lindsey and I are not keeping any secrets from you guys."

"Yes you are!"

"Listen Bobby," Rob reached out to comfort his son.

"No!" Bobby took two steps in the grass and jumped back onto the Oval. "You listen! Stop treating us like kids," he began to skate away, "or you'll never find whatever stupid thing it is you are looking for!"

Twenty Six

"I don't think we should be doing this," Adam stood back and watched his brother Bobby move quickly across the hotel room. It was a standard four star level room. There were two queen beds. Adam and Bobby in the one by the window so they were closer to the air conditioner and Rob alone near the bathroom. Lindsey had her own room. A 48" inch color television was centered on the brown dresser against the wall and a desk with blotter and green office style desk lamp was kitty cornered near the window.

"Aren't you tired of the way they are treating us?" Bobby slid open the mirrored closet door across from the bathroom and bent down towards the pale beige hotel safe bolted to the carpeted floor. He and Adam had been left alone in the hotel for two straight days now while his father and Lindsey had been in the provincial archives. At first it had been kind of cool, being by themselves, and being able to do whatever they wanted to do. Their father usually did not trust them so much and he felt the need to stay with the boys the entire vacation so far. But Rob was beginning to feel guilty about leaving Lindsey by herself as well. This was his crusade, his family, yet Lindsey was doing all the work. It had actually taken a mental push from Bobby and even a little from Adam to convince their father to let them be.

At first, their motives had been genuine. Their father was toting over them like a mother hen and all they wanted to do was just hang out. Being left alone in the hotel room wasn't just what two teenage boys wanted, it was what they needed. The hotel was close enough to be able to walk downtown and check out some shops or go out for a bite to eat. Their dad had left them some more colored Canadian money and even though they still did not fully understand the exchange rate they knew it was plenty to have a good time with. They even had been able to try some of that crazy Canadian poutine!

But now that they were into the third day being left alone, they were starting to get bored and even a little resentful. Fredericton was a small town, even for Canadian standards. They knew they were in trouble when their father had difficulty getting them excited about it in the car ride from Halifax. He had tried to tell them about the parks and the history museum but they had already had enough history and what could they do in a park anyway?

Lindsey had insisted that Fredericton was an essential stop for them. The New Brunswick Provincial Archives were located there and it would have all kinds of information on exactly where the family's land was supposed to be and the

Loyalists who lived there. Maybe Rob could find a cool hotel with a good pool close to downtown that would let the boys have fun, she had suggested.

Unfortunately, the pool was nothing special. And even though the Marriott Rob chose was right on the river and close to downtown, there still was little to do to excite an adolescent and a teenage boy. It also did not help that it had been raining all day. The boys had slept in as long as they could and did not even wake up until after noon time. Indeed Rob had purposely kept the blinds closed and the do not disturb sign on the door in the hopes they would sleep most of the day away and they could do something together later. After all, the archives closed at 4:30 anyway.

"You going to help me or are you just going to stand there?" Bobby punched in four numbers on the safe keypad. They glowed in red on the display screen but the safe did not open. Bobby frowned. He knew his father had placed the envelope in there. Rob thought Bobby was asleep when he opened the safe this morning but Bobby had managed to sneak one eye open under his pillow. Unfortunately, his father's back blocked the view of the combination he entered.

"He probably has it with him." Adam still had not moved. He was really nervous and afraid of his father's terrifying temper. He had already seen Rob almost attack Bobby at the beginning of the vacation; The thought of his father yelling at him with that booming voice and maybe even throwing him across the room, kept Adam completely still.

"You know he doesn't. You and I both overheard Lindsey and he discussing the envelope. I think it was Lindsey who said that it would be safer in the hotel than if they took it with them."

"No that was dad." Adam corrected his brother. He finally took a step forward. His curiosity was starting to take over. Like his brother, Adam too felt that this was all some kind of unfair game. Dad had whisked them away from home, taking him away from his friends, when all Adam wanted to do was hang out and enjoy the summer. Instead, he was stuck in this hotel room with his older, abusive brother, in a foreign country and playing on his phone. Dad was a real jerk to bring them all the way here without even asking them.

"Did you try our birthdays?" Adam crossed the room now and stood over his brother. The safe was in the back of the mirrored closet and Bobby had to crouch down uncomfortably in order to process the keypad. At least this safe did not seem to have some kind of limit to how many times you could try the combination. Bobby was afraid it would lock him out like those computer passwords do.

"Of course I did, and his and mom's." Bobby stared at the safe unsure of what to do next. "Why don't you look through the desk and see if dad wrote the number down somewhere? I know it is a long shot but you know how forgetful he can be."

Adam turned around and walked over to the hotel desk. He started opening the draws and rifling through the brochures that the hotel had left lying around. There were a few pizza coupons, a brochure from the local Fredericton government and a bible. There really wasn't much to do in this town, he sighed. "Nothing in here," he said. "Hey did you try his hockey number?"

"Yeah that was the first thing I tried, "Bobby still was frowning at the keypad. He had not tried any number combination in the past several minutes. "I tried Bobby Orr's number, I tried Gretzky, I even tried the year the Rangers won the cup."

"Did you try Lindsey's number?" A sudden inspiration struck Adam.

"No." Bobby said as he pressed the numbers on the panel. Lindsey had been talking about her college games the other night at the Irish pub they found downtown. Her eyes lit up when she had reminded them that 21 was Cammi Granato's number, the captain of the first American women's Olympic team to win gold. Cammi was why she went out for hockey in the first place.

"It worked! "Bobby whooshed open the safe with a big grin on his face. He reached into the small square dark interior and pulled out the single flat manila folder that Rob had been carrying with him since before they left.

"Figures," Adam replied with a frown. It was like a kick in the gut. For the entire trip he had been defending his father and ignoring the glances and flirts with Lindsey. He may have only been in fifth grade (going into sixth now!), but he could tell when his father was turned on. He had been watching it with disgust between his mother and father for his whole life. To see his father's interest in Lindsey so obvious and bold was a betrayal. It was the first time Adam truly imagined Lindsey replacing his mother. It terrified him.

"Yeah it does, doesn't it?" Bobby scowled as he sat on the edge of his bed and pulled open the clasp on the envelope. He wasn't nearly as upset as his brother was. This was just more evidence proving what Bobby knew already. If anything, it would make it easier between he and his brother now that Adam couldn't defend dad anymore.

Adam watched his brother in silence. This was Bobby's show now. He had been right about dad and right about Lindsey. He was probably right about the envelope too.

Bobby looked around the room as if there were cameras or somebody watching him. Once he opened up this package there was no turning back. He knew he was openly defying his father and breaking any level of trust that the two of them had left. Rob had made it clear in no uncertain terms that this folder was not to be opened by the boys. "It is just too complicated and I don't want to explain it!" He had said firmly. Fear of his father's anger, guilt, bitterness, even shame washed all over him. Maybe he should just put it back.

"Are you going to open it?" Adam stared at his brother. He knew what Bobby was thinking of course and hoping that if Bobby went ahead and opened the envelope that he would be the one to get in trouble if they got caught anyway. He couldn't push his brother too much because that would make him part of the conspiracy. All Adam did was guess the number to open the safe. If Bobby opened this now, Adam was still innocent.

"Yeah, of course," Bobby swallowed his fear and reached into the envelope. He felt the plastic coverings and pulled slightly on it. The articles came out fairly easily.

"That's it?" Bobby put his hand back into the envelope, "Only two things?" He moved his hand around the inside and made a bit of a "whop whop" sound as his hand hit against the edges of the empty envelope. He turned back to the two items sitting on the bed. One was a Ziploc bag with some letters that were bound up tight and the other item looked like an old newspaper.

"Here," Bobby handed his brother the newspaper clipping and carefully opened the Ziploc. "You look at this and I will read the letters."

Adam hesitated just as Bobby had done a moment ago. This was his last chance now too.

"Here!" Bobby thrust the article into Adam's hands. Adam grimaced, took the article and joined his brother in the crime.

Both boys sat on the edge of the bed corner and bent their heads in concentration. Their hands shook a little and they jumped at every noise coming from the hallway. Bobby realized that they could not even hear the elevator "bing" to warn them. Their room was almost at the end of the hall.

"Find anything?" Adam asked his brother after several minutes of silent reading.

"Not really; mostly regular letters. There was a brief mention of owning some land up north and a mention of being related to some famous Americans, but there's no treasure map or lost wills."

"Well it is kind of obvious why they picked this newspaper," Adam held it up and pointed, "because somebody made a big circle around the article in the middle. And I read the articles around it and none of it seems really that important."

"What did they circle?"

"It's a notice about a Loyalist commission being set up."

"Loyalists!" Bobby's head snapped to the paper. "Dad and Lindsey have been talking about Loyalists the entire trip. What kind of a Loyalist commission?"

"It has something to do with compensation."

"Compensation for what?"

"Probably for taking the losing side," Adam speculated. He had just finished learning about the American Revolution in school. They had even read that book about some Sam kid in Connecticut who was a loyalist or a Patriot. He couldn't remember. *My Brother is Dead* or something like that.

"When was the newspaper written?"

Adam looked down again. "1783."

"Was the war over by then?"

"I think so. It started in 1776, so it had to be."

"Do you think they could be asking for land or something?" Bobby was beginning to connect the dots.

"I think that much is obvious." Adam always did have a condescending tone. Even though he was the younger brother, he usually was the first one to pick up on things. Bobby always said it was because Adam was a geek. "Did you finish all the letters?"

"There's one left." Bobby reached back into the Ziploc. This one was in much better condition than the others. It seemed to be double bagged as well as wrapped in something like wax paper. Adam watched as Bobby slowly unwrapped it and began reading.

Bobby whistled.

"What?"

No reply. Bobby kept reading. He whistled again. "Whoa; No way!" Bobby's eyes were fixated on the paper.

"What!" Adam roared.

"The signature," Bobby pointed to the bottom of the letter.

"What about it?"

"It says Franklin."

"Ben Franklin?" *What other Franklin was there*, Adam thought. It had to be him. He felt a surge of excitement travel up his back and to the hair on his neck.

"No," Bobby quickly corrected him. Adam's nerves sank back down. "It's someone named William Franklin."

"Are they related? If it is, it could be worth something. Maybe that is why Dad is keeping it in the safe."

"I think so. He talks about him like that."

"What's that mean?" Adam reached over Bobby's shoulder and pointed to the middle of the page. "He read aloud, 'I have recently gathered in my possession, various documents and letters from my father concerning the most recent Treaty of Paris~'"

"Documents and letters?" Bobby broke in. "That sounds important."

"Do you think that is what dad is looking for?"

The distinct sound of the key being placed in the door brought the boys into full panic mode.

"Fuck!" Bobby grabbed the newspaper clipping from his brother and almost bent it. He started to shove both items back into the folder. Adam leapt off the bed and ran to the back part of the room by the window and A/C unit. He knew it would do no good but it was raw instinct.

The door handle made the large clunk noise all hotel doors make when they open and Bobby managed to get the clasp closed on the folder before their father fully entered the room.

"Hi boys," he smiled as he walked in. "How was your day?"

"Fine, "Bobby flung the envelope behind his back as he sat on the bed facing his father. His big brown eyes shimmered from fear as he tried to casually straighten his messy black hair. He could barely hold himself together, "How about yours?"

"We got a lot done and were able to leave early." Rob reached back for the do not disturb sign which still hung outside and placed it on the inside knob. He let the door close behind him. It slammed with a finality that made Bobby jump again. They were trapped. "Lindsey is downstairs at the front desk asking about checking out. She thinks we can move on now." Rob took a step past the open closet door and noticed that the safe was open. Bobby began to shake.

Rob snapped his head and glared at the boys, his face growing redder with each passing second. "What have you done?" He barked. Bobby jumped back and Adam pushed himself closer against the wall. Neither boy answered. It was obvious what they had done and they knew they had no defense. All they could do was pray that their father would not whack them too hard.

"What have you done!" It was not a question anymore. "You boys went into the safe? After I explicitly told you that the envelope was none of your business?" His voice rose higher with each word. His blood was close to the boiling point. He stood on the edge of his toes and towered over Bobby.

"What did you expect?" Bobby edged himself backwards on the bed with both hands to give himself a little distance from his father. He was still within striking distance though he realized. "After the way you have been treating us?"

"I have been treating you fine!"

"You take us on this trip," Bobby's anger made him bolder. "You don't ask us if we want to go. You don't ask us where we want to go. You bring along this stranger and leave for the entire day. You keep secrets from us. What did you expect?" Bobby was shouting now too.

"I expect you to trust me!"

"Why should we?" He was almost screaming. "Why should we trust anything you say? You say don't worry. You say everything will be fine. Well everything is not fine! You always said," Bobby's voice cracked. Tears began to swell in his eyes. He gasped. He shoved the tears away and started again. "You always said we would be a family and how did that turn out?"

Rob froze. His face lost all color. How many fights had he been in? How many times had he been punched in the face, in the chest, in the gut? This hurt more than anything he had ever felt. The wind left him. His throat dried up and constricted. He took a step back and tried to recover.

Bobby and Adam watched their father struggle. They had never seen him like this and they did not like it. Bobby felt no joy in hurting his father this way. He wanted to reach out. He wanted to say he was sorry, but his ego wouldn't let him. Bobby was not wrong.

"We are still a family." Rob said slowly. His breath was returning and his anger rekindling. "You are still my sons. I expect you to trust me and I expect you to listen."

"You don't always get what you expect," Bobby sneered. That was the wrong thing to say. It was everything bad about teenagers in one nasty sentence. Their disdain, their sarcasm, their desire to inflict pain by saying something mean. It set Rob off all over again.

"No matter how you define them, families are built on trust." His voice was a combination of lecture and rage. He directed it at Bobby but he glared at Adam as well. Both boys were together in this. "Trust and Loyalty; that is what makes all relationships work. We each have a job to do; we each have a role to play. Whether you like it or not, you are my sons and I am your father. You do as I say, and I protect and take care of you. We trust each other, we rely on each other. Without that, we have nothing. You boys just went a long way to destroying that trust and I don't know if we can get it back."

"We didn't start it dad," Adam finally joined in. He could tell by his father's looks and his words that he was in just as much trouble as Bobby. He might as well get a few shots in as well.

"No you didn't," Rob surprisingly agreed. His senses had not completely left him. He could see the boys' point of view and he could see the mistakes he had made and how he helped cause this whole mess in the first place. But he would not let it destroy them. He knew how important trust and loyalty was in a family. It had kept his parents together their entire lives through some pretty tough times and it had done the same for Rob. Whether it was loyalty to your friends, your family or even your teammates, nothing was more important to him. "But I am going to finish it. I am sorry for keeping the secrets I did from you boys but that does not mean I was wrong. You have simply got to trust me and as long as you live under my roof, we are going to trust each other. Is that clear?"

"Maybe we just won't live under your roof anymore!" Bobby stood up. He was sick of his father's blind obsession with loyalty and trust. There was nothing Bobby hated more in life than when his father said "because I said so!" He used it every time he was wrong, every time Bobby made a good point. It was his go to. If he didn't know what to say, he fell back on the fact that he was in charge and therefore correct. How many times had Bobby stormed out of the house mumbling to himself sarcastically "because he said so, because he said so" under his breath? This was the same shit all over again. Where was the loyalty and trust between his father and mother? Who broke the loyalty? Who broke the trust there? What kind of loyalty was he showing being here with Lindsey anyway? What a hypocrite his father was! Bobby couldn't take another second of it. He dodged his father's grab, swung past and headed to the door. "Mom has a perfectly good roof now too!"

"Bobby!" Adam and Rob both shouted as he turned the corner sharply and headed down the hall. He nearly knocked Lindsey down on his way.

“What the hell just happened?” She cried as she entered the room.

“Nothing,” Rob muttered; “Nothing.”

Twenty Seven

"How did you find this?" Bobby looked up from the papers and stared at Lindsey. He still wasn't sure how he felt about all of this Franklin stuff but he was glad his dad was finally starting to trust him. Actually it was all because of Lindsey he had to admit. She had been the one who convinced Rob to open up completely. After the fight in the hotel room, she and Rob had a fight of their own. Adam managed to sneak out in the middle of it and find Bobby while Lindsey and Rob almost screamed at one another.

"You've got to stop treating them like kids," Lindsey had chosen sides immediately. She did not know if it was because she agreed with the boys or she wanted them to accept her more. What better way to get on their good side than by defending them?

"But they are kids!"

It was intense and sometimes heated. Rob could not swing at Lindsey of course and only once did he even think about it. She had him cornered both mentally and physically. Rob couldn't just force his way past her to the hotel room's door. She was standing right in front of it and strategically placing herself to prevent his escape. Then she hit him logically and practically when his defense was only irrational anger and fear. Rob had no chance.

Lindsey brought up the family angle. She reminded him how fragile the boys were and how much their trust and faith was being shattered at such a critical juncture in their lives. Did Rob realize how much of a hypocrite he sounded like when he told the boys to trust him in the middle of a separation between their mother and father? Did he have any idea how much the boys must be torn, how much they are hurting? Lindsey, thank god, did not have any personal experience with divorce either, but her best friend in high school had. Lindsey saw it tear apart all her faith and all her love. Her bright cheery, supportive friend had become a bitter angry teenager who rebelled against anything and anyone. It had destroyed their friendship. Lindsey could see Rob pushing his own boys down that same path. If he didn't stop soon, it could be too late. By keeping secrets and relying on blind trust, Rob was pushing them away, forcing them to take sides in a fight that shouldn't be there in the first place. If he took a leap of faith and placed all his trust in the boys by telling them the truth, it would be a huge move and was well worth the risk.

She brought up the safety angle, both for the boys and the documents. If there was any danger, if they were being followed or if someone were to break into the room; then the best protection for the boys was in knowing what to look for. They could help keep an eye out for strangers, keep an eye on the documents or even hold onto them if they truly understood their value.

She even brought up the two hands are better than one angle. The boys had already mentioned that they were being followed. What if they were right? What kind of danger would that place them all in? The boys knew what the man looked like. The boys could even look out for other people who could be following them like that creepy pawn shop dealer. Their help could be invaluable.

"Then we have to tell them everything, absolutely everything," Rob realized by the time she was done. He had no choice but to agree and if they were going to do this, they would do it right. He was always one to go in either all the way or not at all. Nothing was ever half done by Rob Callahan.

"I'll start by showing them what we found today, that will really knock their socks off." Lindsey grinned.

Adam had found Bobby down by the river behind the hotel. The Marriott backed right up to the St. John's and you could not only see it clearly from the pool, there was even a dock nearby. Bobby had wandered down there and was pacing along the edge of the bank. Adam told him everything he had overheard and how Lindsey was taking their side. Of course Bobby didn't believe it at first. He wanted to be angry. He wanted to blame everything on his father. The rage would not just go away.

Adam, on the other hand, was filled with hope. He listened intently to Lindsey's arguments. He saw how passionately she defended the boys and placed her trust in them. And when she started talking about all that Ben Franklin stuff? Adam couldn't believe it! Dad really did have a reason to keep all this stuff a secret.

That was the first thing Adam said that made Bobby slow down. He wasn't sure whether it was his curiosity or his realization that Dad really did have a good reason but finally the rage began to dissipate. He even stopped texting mom and begging her to come get him. Adam had to repeat Lindsey's argument again as Bobby threw some rocks in the river and gave a few more grunt filled arguments but he was finally listening. Eventually he agreed enough to talk with dad.

They had chosen another Irish pub: Dolan's, on King Street. (A King Street, a Queen street. This really was loyalist country, Rob had realized.) This one was nothing like the one in Halifax but it had the same hometown feel that Rob had loved so much at Grace O'Malley's back in Fairfield. Dark wood tables, dark wood chairs and bar stools and dimmer than normal lighting; Rob was not sure why all Irish pubs had that dark aura, nor why it made him feel more comfortable, but it worked. Of course a pub offered little for two underage boys, but Rob needed some comfort and some beer if he was going to let the boys in so deep.

"I got lucky," Lindsey admitted. She lifted the black pint glass of Guinness to her lips before continuing. Rob had got her hooked on Guinness and Irish pubs by now. She had never really liked them and Guinness had always been too dark for her, especially after a hockey game. But then again, she never had tried it poured the right way or drunk in the right atmosphere. (It was called a double pour, Rob had said. The bartender fills the glass three quarters of the way up, lets the foam settle for a few minutes, then tops it off.) She licked the brown foam off her upper lip and continued. "When we were back in Halifax, I was doing a search on the internet and I typed in William Franklin."

The waitress arrived with the boys drinks. No surprises there: coke.

"Well you know how google finishes what you type and adds suggestions?"

"Of course," Adam and Bobby said in unison.

"Well I was trying all kinds of ideas and was thinking, 'I wonder if there is an obituary out there for William Franklin.' Maybe that could tell us something about what happened to his stuff."

"I didn't hear this." Rob interrupted.

"I didn't tell you?"

"You just told me about the Odell guy."

"Oh sorry," Lindsey turned back to the boys. Bobby had begun to play impatiently with the menu. There were all kinds of weird stuff on it. "Well when I typed in the 'O' for obituary, google suggested William Franklin Odell."

"Who's that?" Adam said. Bobby wasn't sure if he cared. *Did the menu have anything decent on it?*

"I didn't know at first." Lindsey sat up a little and a gleam shown in her eye. This was so cool! "But I wondered if they were related; maybe he was a son or something."

"Were they?"

"No. Better!"

"What's better?"

"He was named after William Franklin by one of Franklin's oldest friends!"

Lindsey almost shouted. This was too good to be true. A nearby couple turned their heads. The bar was relatively empty; too early for the evening crowd and too late for the lunch crowd. Lindsey leaned into the middle of the square table so she could lower her voice. "Franklin was even named his godfather."

"I don't get it." Adam admitted. He was fascinated by all of this, much more so than his brother. Of course he felt intensely proud and honored that his father had decided to trust him. It meant more to Adam than he could realize. But he was also really interested. This was like detective stuff!

"A godfather is,"

"I know what a godfather is," Adam snapped. Bobby smirked. Adam gave his brother a frown, leaned back on his chair a little and took a sip of the coke.

"If William Franklin was the godfather of this man's son," Lindsey tried not to sound condescending. She had finally begun to get on the boys' good side and she wasn't going to blow it. "Then they must have gone through some pretty difficult stuff together."

"Like the revolution." Bobby had found what he wanted and placed the menu down on the table. "Can I get a burger?"

"Sure," Rob was amazed at his son's ability to multi-task.

"Exactly," Lindsey pointed at Bobby then looked back at Adam. "So I did some reading on the father, Jonathan Odell and sure enough, he and William were good friends."

"And?"

"And Odell was a loyalist, just like Franklin."

"So, if these guys were good friends," Adam turned his head in thought. Lindsey let him sort it out, "such good friends that Odell named his kid after him-"

"Franklin sponsored Odell for his first job working for the government of New Jersey," Lindsey interrupted, she couldn't stop herself. This was an incredible find, "saved his life during the Revolution and even got him a job as the Loyalist poet of the British!"

"Then that means," Adam acknowledged Lindsey with a nod and kept going, "that they probably wrote to each other after the war and maybe-"

"Maybe Odell said something about the packet!" Lindsey smiled ear to ear and sat back in the chair in triumph. She raised her half full glass of Guinness and toasted, "To Jonathan Odell!"

No one raised their glass. Lindsey felt a little awkward but she was in too good of a mood to let the boys bother her. "So these two letters you found," Bobby waved politely at the waitress across the pub as he spoke then touched the edges of the papers in front of him, "were written by one of William Franklin's good friends and you found them at UNB?"

"It wasn't easy," Lindsey quickly replied. She knew she had been lucky at first, but this next part was hard. She and Rob spent days looking through microfilm and indexes and scouring all kinds of useless documents before they found these. It had been even harder to keep all this away from the librarian who was a great help but mystified by all the partial questions they were asking him. The best luck they had was that he had been busy with other people when they found the letters. Just to be on the safe side, they also photocopied a bunch of other letters to throw him off the track. "UNB Fredericton has a special Loyalist library on the third floor and basement. They have tons of documents, letters, newspapers and I found an entire collection of Odell letters."

"Why hasn't anyone found this before?" Adam looked down at the menu as the waitress approached. He had been so captivated he had not even looked at it yet.

"Most of it is not on-line," Lindsey looked at her menu as well. "And there are still thousands of documents that have not yet been digitized or even read."

"We're hoping," Rob added. He had plenty of time to look at the menu while Lindsey had explained things. He was going to get the famous fish and chips. At least that is what Dolan's called them. He would be the judge if they deserved to be called famous. "That no one else will think to look there either."

"You would have to know about the land deal," Lindsey had settled on the Chicken Club, "know about William Franklin, know about Odell and not get distracted by all the other information out there."

"And get lucky like you did." Bobby had to add.

"You all know what you want?" The waitress arrived. She had short black hair and a young face. *"Probably a college student,"* Rob thought. He wouldn't even have known she was the waitress except for the small pad in her hand and drink she was carrying. She was dressed in a plain green t-shirt and dark blue jeans. Bobby couldn't help but notice that the t-shirt was perfectly tight in all the right places. He stole a glance at her chest as she leaned away and placed the gold colored whiskey glass on the table next to them. Rob noticed the glance, Adam didn't. The waitress turned back towards them and took out a pen from behind her ear.

After everyone gave their order, Rob turned to the boys and said, "Have you boys tried Poutine yet? It's a famous Canadian dish." Rob looked over at the waitress for approval and back at the boys for a reaction. Adam was smiling and Bobby was harder to read; Of course.

"It's yummy!" Adam said.

"It's ok." Bobby was still distracted by the waitress' chest.

"Well I haven't tried it yet," Rob looked at the waitress with a smile. She smiled back and added, "Then you've got to try our Classic Poutine. There is a reason we call it classic."

"Done," Rob smiled again as he handed her the menu, "one appetizer of Classic Poutine please."

"So let me get this straight," Bobby watched the waitress return to the bar. Her ass was nice too. Adam gave him a look. He hated when his brother took over. He could go from mood to mood, pretend he didn't care, give Adam all this time and space to do his thing and be the one everyone listened to, then Bobby would suddenly jump in, be all "big brother," and make Adam feel like a kid again. "We have one letter in which this Odell guy," Bobby held up the first letter Lindsey had photocopied. "What did he do after the war again?"

"He became the Secretary of the new, New Brunswick Province, helped the British choose settlements and assign land."

"One letter in which this Odell guy," Bobby held the letter up again, "asks William Franklin to meet with some representative of our family-"

"Which proves that your family," Lindsey interrupted yet again and pointed at Rob and the boys; "Was directly petitioning with William Franklin for land from the King."

"But why use Odell and why a representative?" Adam asked. He was not going to let Bobby take over.

"We don't know," his father replied. "We are guessing they were having trouble getting the land they wanted."

"A lot of families in New Brunswick were." Lindsey looked over at the book sitting on the edge of the table that she had bought before they even left Canada. She brought it to the pub in case the boys had any questions. It had lots of stories of Loyalist families desperate to get land grants from the King. "And a few of them formed associations with their neighbors like it looks like your family did."

"And someone in our family or one of their friends," Bobby took over again, "must have met Odell and asked for a favor."

"Odell was instrumental in starting this town of Fredericton right here and a lot of communities on the border. He knew a lot people, and a lot of people knew him."

"Because he was a loyalist?"

"Because he was the most well-known Loyalist poet/propagandist during the war. And, because he became the second most powerful man in New Brunswick."

"Which Fredericton is the Capital of-"

"Which is why we are here."

"And this second letter," Bobby held that one up now, "Is written by William Franklin to Jonathan Odell and it talks about how he and his dad got along?"

"Jonathan knew Ben Franklin too," Lindsey leaned forward. She finally realized that they were being way to out in the open about all this. She looked around the pub for prying eyes. "He had been a member of Ben's philosophical society."

"And this part here," Bobby pointed to the photocopy, "is where William is talking about their relationship?"

"The letter was written after the Revolution was over," Lindsey whispered now. "You can see where William talks about how he hoped they could find some common ground. He tells Jonathan about how much he loved his father and how he still held out hope they could come to an agreement, even though his father had not spoken to him for years."

There was an uncomfortable pause. Everyone realized Lindsey's comment hit too close to home. Father and son not talking, loving each other but having a terrible fight; Bobby quickly moved on. "So you are thinking," Bobby's stomach growled. When would the waitress bring the poutine? He hadn't eaten since before the fight with his dad, "that if Ben and William met after this all was over, and that William was hoping for some kind of reconciliation, that maybe Ben might have given his son something real important to make amends or something?"

"Like his notes on the Treaty," Lindsey had to say.

"But they seemed pretty mad at each other." Adam added.

"Wouldn't you be?" Rob could not stop himself. The parallels to him and his own sons were just too scary. "Father takes one side, son takes the other. Both of them were seen as heroes for their respective sides."

"It wasn't just that," Lindsey could see the parallels as well. Their power only drew her into the story that much more.

"Here you go!" The waitress suddenly appeared with the poutine. Lindsey snapped back in her chair. They all had been so engrossed in the conversation that they did not even see the waitress approach with the food. She reached into the middle of the table and placed their order in the center. It was on a huge black dish overflowing with French fries covered in some brown gravy and what looked like cheese curds. Lindsey realized immediately that it would either be delicious or disgusting. The waitress placed some small multi-colored plates on the table and turned away. Bobby watched her go. Lindsey noticed and smiled. It was refreshing to see some things not changing. She turned back to the conversation. "Ben Franklin and his son William were incredibly close. They worked together for years. They surveyed land together, Ben got him his job as governor, and they even worked on the famous kite experiment together."

"They did?" Adam reached for the poutine before his brother could get a hand in. Despite what he said, Bobby really did love the stuff and Adam knew it. "I never learned that in school. All the pictures show Ben alone."

"Me neither." Bobby quickly followed his brother to the poutine.

"And that's a whole 'nother problem we have to deal with," his father added as he waited patiently for his chance at the appetizer. "It's yet another reason I didn't want to get you two involved in the first place."

"Huh?" Adam mumbled from a face full of cheese and fries.

Rob could barely stifle a laugh. The brown gravy was all over his son's face. "If this blows out of the water like I am afraid it might, it will cause all kinds of political and historical problems in our country and in our schools. It's a fucking Pandora's box of history."

"Well said," Lindsey knew exactly what Rob meant. Just like the famous Greek myth, once this story got out there would be no turning back. She sat back for a moment in thought and watched Bobby grab another huge bite of the poutine. It was disappearing rapidly as the boys tried to counter each other. If Lindsey wanted a taste, she better get in quick.

"But it's the truth," Adam's adolescent mind still had trouble seeing the gray in life. It seemed pretty simple to him.

"The truth is what you make of it," Bobby tried to sound smart. He had heard that quote many times before. He didn't understand what it meant, but it seemed appropriate at this time.

"Listen boys," Rob tried to get the waitresses' attention again. He was going to need another beer. "I don't want to get all into this right now. Lindsey and I have been talking about this shit for months. You boys know all the facts now, and you know all the dangers. You just have to be prepared for the fact that if we keep going like this, we all might find ourselves in the middle of a firestorm."

"We get it dad," Adam picked at the poutine plate and ran his fingers along the edges for any stray pieces of cheese.

"Yeah," Bobby smiled and looked at his brother. "Remember that scout from UMASS who watched our hockey game?"

"Yeah."

"Remember the name of the UMASS team?" Bobby couldn't help but get a sinister smile on the corner of his lips.

"The Minute Men!" Adam smiled as well.

Rob laughed out loud as he waved his hand rapidly at the waitress, "I definitely need another beer!"

Twenty Eight

Agent Foster stood on the porch and admired the beautiful view in front of him. The Bay of Passamaquoddy, a part of the enormous Bay of Fundy, dominated the landscape in front of him. From his vantage point at the top of a wide, grass covered hill, he could see the entire dark blue bay, the many tree covered islands within its waters and maybe even the mainland beyond. He still had trouble figuring out which islands were Canadian and which were American. The bay was so large, both countries lay claim to parts of it. Its waters appeared calm and almost flat in the distance, like something out of a Monet painting. The wind was not strong enough to make any large waves but it was constant and comforting. Coming right off the water, it cooled him down without disturbing his hair or his finely edged, true blue Calvin Klein business suit. Several flocks of birds rode the wind currents calmly over-head and a deer had run out of the woods to his right, crossed the lawn about 50 feet below him and disappeared below. No wonder President Franklin Roosevelt had chosen this island as his vacation spot.

Foster had arrived at Campobello, F.D.R.'s "beloved island," just after sunrise and had been immediately ushered to the Hubbard Cottage where he could wait for the Canadian agents to arrive. Campobello had ceased being a private residence for the Roosevelt family decades ago and now was a tourist site for Canadians and Americans alike but, as Agent Saltman first told him, at extremely unique times like this one, it could be quickly used for meetings between American and Canadian officials. While tourists frequented the main Roosevelt house and the surrounding park, the cottages off to the side were set aside for private rentals, or in Foster's case, secret meetings.

This however was not the only reason Saltman chose Campobello for the meeting. Its symbolism and its connection to this case could not be ignored. As the only park in the world to be jointly owned by two countries at the same time, the United States and Canada, it was the ultimate symbol of friendship and cooperation between nations. Even the budget was split right down the middle and the administration as well. Created in 1964 by President Lyndon Johnson and Prime Minister Lester Pearson, the Roosevelt Campobello International Park was more than just a memorial to President Franklin Delano Roosevelt. It was meant to be a tangible symbol of the enduring friendship between Canada and the United States. Foster was reminded of this immediately when he arrived and saw both the Maple Leaf and Stars and Stripes hanging side by side.

Even its location was perfect. Although the island was on Canadian soil and sat right on the edge of the Bay of Fundy, the largest tidal bay in North America, the United States was just a few miles west across the FDR Memorial Bridge.

FDR had come here for summer vacations long before he became President and even after his polio attack, he managed to return for three visits. Foster could easily see why. The island was a naturalist's dream; bold cliffs and the occasional pebbly beach, forests of spruce, balsam pine, and some hardwood. The abundant wildlife in the bay and on the island was unaffected by the small numbers of residents. Hours from any major city, either Canadian or American, it was quiet, almost eerily so, with just the right amount of human presence to give it the air of a past century. And best of all the weather in the summer was balanced wonderfully by the long days and a constant natural air-conditioning provided by the sea breeze from the bay.

Saltman had arranged to have the meeting here at the Hubbard house, a white two story cottage near the main house, where Foster could meet with the Canadian agents in complete solitude. The house had originally been one of Roosevelt's neighbors, but today it was owned by the park and rented out for both public and private meetings. Although it had just recently been used for tourists to meet and discuss the life of Eleanor Roosevelt, the park had decided a few years ago to move that program to another cottage. No one would disturb them today.

Foster heard voices to his left and turned to see two men in charcoal gray business suits walking from the magnificent red wooden multistory American colonial house that had been Roosevelt's 34-room summer home. Both of the men were well built, clearly athletic and a little older than him. The one leading the way walked with purpose and determination. His forehead and jaw were set tight and he was clearly frowning in what looked to be a permanent scowl. The agent to his left was the polar opposite. He had lightness in his step as his head turned back and forth admiring the beautiful view. His bright blue eyes were opened wide and he appeared to take a deep breath, enjoying the fresh sea air around him. Foster resisted the urge to call out to them and took one last look at the Bay and its many islands. He did not want to seem too eager.

"Agent Foster?" the scowling agent called out once he was close enough to avoid shouting.

"Bonjour," Foster smiled and held out his hand, "Ca va?"

"Bien," he replied, still scowling and grasping Foster's hand in a firm handshake, "Je' mapelle Agent Beauvais."

"Je' mapelle Agent Matt Foster," Matt still had not become accustomed to the lack of first name use in the agency. He had always been an overly open, friendly guy and he saw no reason to change, especially here in this case that was all about friendship and trust.

"You're French Canadian." Agent Beauvais looked surprised. The accent was clearly native to Quebec, not France. The dialects had separated centuries ago and any native Canadian, from Quebec to Vancouver could tell the difference.

"Je suis né à l›extérieur de Québec." Matt explained.

"I was born outside of Quebec City myself," Beauvais smiled. He was pleased they had something in common. And his ability to switch languages back and forth, common to all French Canadians, comforted Foster more than perhaps it should have. "And now you work for the American CIA?"

"Oui," Matt grinned.

"And I am agent Patrick Macleod," the second man stuck out his hand as well. He was clearly the friendlier of the two, not just because the piercing blue of his eyes had a welcoming gleam to them that instantly put Matt at ease, "Nice to meet you."

"You too," Matt took his hand. "Parlez vous Français?"

"Oui," Patrick smiled, "But I prefer English."

Matt frowned. He was looking forward to speaking in his native tongue. Of course almost all French Canadians, or Quebecois as they preferred to be called, were bi-lingual and Matt was no exception. Even though his father had moved the family to North Carolina when he was twelve, Matt had mastered both languages. It had been years since he had been able to speak French with anyone for any length of time, other than with his parents of course.

"Macleod is from Toronto," Agent Beauvais explained, as if that was all he needed to say.

"Hey!" Patrick laughed.

"No offense," Beauvais continued in English. He smiled for the first time to make sure his new partner knew he was only teasing. After all, they had been partners for less than 48 hours. Beauvais, nominally the one in charge due to his local connections, usually worked the drug traffic cases. Canada and the United States shared the longest and friendliest border in the entire world and unfortunately that made protecting it a monumental task, especially in such low density population areas like here in New Brunswick and Maine.

Patrick had the same problem but from a different angle. He was part of

Toronto's anti-terrorism task force guarding the human smuggling that crossed the border. He was considered one of the leading agents in the field and lucky for Beauvais, he had just finished wrapping up a case. The two of them were therefore able to pool their knowledge from two different sides of the same issue: the Canadian-American border.

"Should we go inside?" Matt invited them with an outstretched arm. "The place is as beautiful inside as it is outside."

"After you," Beauvais held out his right hand.

Matt opened the plain wooden door into another century. Inside, everything had been painstakingly restored to resemble the home as it had been during the President's lifetime. Sets of four simple wooden chairs with yellow fabric cushions surrounded three dark what looked like Oak oval tables, each one holding an ornate crystal at its center. The reflection of the tables and of the men almost bounced off the perfectly waxed solid oak hardwood floors. Most of all, it was the wall paper that gave the room its air of the early 20th century. Its bold yellow color and its diamond-like design reminded Matt of the many rooms he had once visited as a tourist in the Newport Mansions. The entire room was dominated by the gigantic oval window facing the bay that somehow gave a better view than the one from the porch itself. It brought the bay directly into the room and almost functioned like a portal of incoming sunlight with its two inch thick solid oak frame. The simple six imitation candle light chandelier in the center was almost unnecessary.

"Whew!" Patrick whistled as he entered the room. "And I thought the view from the hill was outstanding." He stood directly in front of the window and stared into the bay. It was as if he could walk through the portal and step right onto one of the islands.

"Take a seat," Beauvais instructed to his partner. He really was no fun.

"So," Patrick reluctantly turned and placed his right hand on the top of the chair Beauvais had indicated. He looked towards Matt, "dual citizenship or all American now?"

"I'll always be Canadian," Matt remained a little mysterious, he didn't want to get into all the soul searching his family and he had done in order to choose his career path. "But I needed to become an American Citizen to join the service."

"Well I am just glad they sent you and not some ignorant yank that thinks were just a bunch of hockey playing, moose chasing Mounties."

"*Mounties*," Matt smiled. He had to admit, at least to himself, that he had thought of the Mounties the minute he first heard of the case. He actually was looking forward to working with them. Ever since he was a kid, he admired their dedication to service and their respect for tradition. They still dressed in the standard red jacket, black pants and tan cowboy style hat uniform that they been wearing for almost a hundred years. Unfortunately, Matt quickly learned, the Mounties only covered internal cases, not international. He would have to deal with the business suits of the CSIA in front of him.

"I mean look at the three of us sitting here," Patrick waved his hand at Matt and Beauvais. "You a Canadian of African Ancestry, not, I repeat, not an African Canadian or some other hyphen like they use down there."

Matt frowned. That was certainly part of the move to the United States that had upset him. Sure they had racism in Canada, a lot of it. There was perhaps even more racism against the Indians and Eskimos than there was against Africans. But neither he nor his father ever called themselves "African Canadians" or some other hyphen. They just called themselves Canadians.

"And Beauvais over here," Patrick went on, "is even more a mutt."

Beauvais frowned more than the usual. In the short time since he had been working with Macleod, he had already learned that he could not stop the man from talking once he was on a roll. And Patrick was definitely on a roll now.

"I mean look at the guy. What do you think his family is?"

Matt took an uncomfortable look at Beauvais. Jet black hair, tan complexion, hard nose and perfectly shaved sideburns; neither the man's jaw, nor his forehead had lost any of its tension since he had arrived. The only blemish was a slight green tinge in the brown eyes that looked right through Matt as if he wasn't even there. *Guy could melt snow with a stare,* Matt thought to himself.

"Definitely Indian," Matt said. Beauvais' left eyebrow rose. Good guess.

"And with the thick accent, I would have to say from somewhere near Montreal." Both eyes opened a little wider on Beauvais. Matt was good. "So that would probably mean some kind of Iroquois."

"Mohawk," Beauvais said before Matt could guess. He did not like being so transparent.

"But not completely," Matt continued. "You've got some European in you two."

"My grandmother was French," Beauvais stopped the guessing game. He had no interest in playing.

"And mine was Scottish," Patrick smiled and smacked Beauvais lightly on the back. "See what I mean? We got a Quebec raised, African descended emigrant to the USA, a Mohawk/French Quebecois and a Scottish/German," he pointed to himself, "Toronto born and raised westerner all in one room."

Patrick paused for effect. "Now that's Canada!"

"Your boys play hockey," Beauvais' monotone voice was a clear jab. It turned out he did have a sense of humor.

"That's not the point."

"Your girl plays hockey."

Patrick just frowned.

"You play hockey." Beauvais finally smiled.

"But you don't," Patrick struck back. He thought he had him.

"Lacrosse. My boys do too."

"See! A Canadian sport!"

"Invented by the Iroquois," Beauvais was monotone again.

"Exactly my point."

"Can we get down to business please?" Beauvais had enough. He recognized Macleod's need for friendly chit chat. He knew that the man was generally just a nice guy but the cynic in him also realized the Agents' need to form a bond with anyone they worked with. It made getting information much easier. But now it was time to get to the matter at hand.

"Sure," Macleod smiled. He appreciated Beauvais indulging him. He knew exactly how much it bothered him despite their short time together. It was a testament to Patrick's natural skills that he was able to read people so quickly.

Agent Foster filled both of them in. Throughout the conversation, both Agents Macleod and Beauvais simply nodded their heads or even corrected Foster on occasion. They had heard all of this before. Except for the personal part where Foster broke his cover and the time in the Citadel, they knew everything already. The Canadian Security Intelligence Service had been informed at the state level and was already way ahead of the game. It wasn't just that this was their home turf. They had an office in both Fredericton and Halifax. They took this very seriously. The border between the two countries; the Loyalists, even the American Revolution; were all sore spots in Canadian history. From the Atlantic to the Pacific, you had to look far and wide to find a single Canadian who preferred America's story over their own. Unfortunately, Agent Foster had left Canada too early in his childhood to learn it the way Macleod and Beauvais had. Of course he knew all the current information needed for his job. He knew of Canada's role in NATO, about NAFTA, their roles in Iraq and Syria and even one of Canada's proudest moments when they helped free some of the American Hostages during the Iranian Hostage Crisis back in 1979. But his earlier historical knowledge was sorely lacking. He had no idea that the United States had invaded Canada not only once but twice. He barely even knew the details behind Canada getting her own independence from Great Britain. Thank god he was able to hide most of that ignorance from the Agents.

"What's your level of knowledge?" Beauvais asked when Foster was done. For a moment Foster panicked. Did they know? Had they seen it in his eyes? It wasn't his fault he loved his new country and dove deep into its history. What other choice did he have growing up in North Carolina?

"Who knows about this on your side?" Beauvais specified after Foster's awkward silence. He hadn't noticed the lack of knowledge of Canadian history. This was about the case.

"Almost no one," Foster breathed a sigh of relief, "Just my partner, the director and the President himself. We are under the strictest orders to keep this secret."

"That's a relief," Macleod sat back in his chair. He was worried the Americans would blow this. He knew from experience that the Yankees had trouble understanding their northern neighbor. Sure the people he usually dealt with across the border, agents and other law enforcement, were generally well informed and showed a lot of respect for Canada, but he had seen too many instances of complete ignorance by the average every day American to have much faith in them.

"If this gets out," Beauvais warned.

"I know, I know,"

"Do you?" Beauvais dark eyes suddenly bore straight into Foster. It felt like he was drilling a hole right into his skull. "Do you have any idea what will happen if the press gets a hold of this?"

"It will be more than a nightmare," Macleod answered before Foster could. "The locals here are already upset at the land disputes, at big oil, at lumber and just corporations overall. Many of them have been screwed over more times than I care to count."

"They take advantage of the border and the different laws to exploit as much as they can." Beauvais added.

"What do you mean?" This was all news to Foster. He knew about the international and the political angle. He had no idea about the local politics.

"I'll give you an example," Beauvais sat back a little. His intensity turned more informative and maybe a little relaxed. Here was another chance for him to inform people of the shit he had seen over the years. "Almost ten years ago, we had a case where the local lobster was dying because a company had crossed the border and used pesticides that polluted the bay."

"Why would they do that?"

"The environmental laws in the states are not as tough as they are here."

"Companies exploit the laws whenever they can and this crazy border with our islands and the bay make it that much easier."

"And it's not just corporations," Beauvais continued. "Lawyers, land speculators and all kinds of shady businessmen are taking advantage of the local fisherman on the islands and the mainland. It's disgusting."

"Shit," Foster shook his head. He had seen plenty of scumbags and lowlifes taking advantage of border laws to smuggle drugs during his days in the Coast Guard and of course he was no stranger to corporate greed. He had just hoped that up here, in this less urban environment so close to nature and so reminiscent of a day gone by, that they might escape that kind of world.

"We need to control this," Beauvais pressed.

"Of course."

"I mean control the story," he leaned forward again, "the narrative. Our government wants to make sure that if this gets out, it gets out right."

"What do you mean?"

"If the press gets a hold of this first, independently, especially the American press, they will exploit this in ugly, disgusting ways."

"They will divide Americans and Canadians; they will cause debate and extremes." Macleod leaned forward too. He had thought about this a lot and it scared him. The Canadian media was pretty bad but the American media, with its FOX news and MSNBC and CNN, were the poster children for sensationalism.

"They'll put flag wavers up against liberals," Foster was seeing it as well, "just for the entertainment value."

"The politicians will be forced to take sides, they will play to their bases, they will hit the talking points, make the speeches, rally the troops."

"On both sides of the border," Beauvais reminded them.

"Any chance we might have to work this out sanely, like two friends calmly discussing a disagreement will be totally lost."

"And heaven help us when the lawyers get involved." Beauvais finished the conversation. It was clear to all three of them even more than it had been before, how important it was to finish this case and above all keep it quiet. "What do you have on the wife?" he suddenly changed tone and returned to the more formal briefing.

"Whose wife?"

"Callahan's."

"Not much," Foster was thrown off guard by the sudden change in Beauvais' demeanor. He sensed they had missed something. "We know that Callahan visited her shortly before we left but that's it."

Macleod looked at Beauvais with a look of surprise. He expected more. Then he turned to Foster. "She's here."

"Here?"

"We got notice when she crossed the border."

Foster winced. They should have been notified as well. Was this his mistake? Saltman's? Or was it because the agency was trying so hard to keep this a secret that border patrol had not been notified? He figured it was the latter.

"And she's met up with a realtor sleaze we've been tailing."

"A realtor?"

"We've known about this guy for some time," Beauvais explained. New Brunswick and Nova Scotia was not only his district, they were his home. He had spent his entire life in the area. "He turns up whenever there is something shady in the area."

"Oil deals, buying land from locals at reduced prices," Macleod continued. He had been well briefed on this Jim Watts guy. As soon as the Canadians knew there were land issues in the area, they put a tail on him. "If land is involved, this guy will be. And he will exploit and lie every step of the way just to enrich himself. I wouldn't even put blackmail out of his range."

"He met with the wife a few days ago in Halifax." Beauvais added.

"Shit," Foster swore again. This was bad. "How did she find him so quickly?"

"That we are not sure about." Macleod said. "But the guy has so many contacts; one of them could have easily set the two of them up if she had started asking questions."

"Where are they now?" Foster was glad to hear that the Canadians did not know everything. He was already frustrated at his own lack of information.

"They took the ferry from Nova Scotia across to St. John's and are headed south."

"We think they are headed to St. Andrews."

"What's there?"

"Lots of local records of this area; they have an archive downtown."

"This area?" Foster had thought the meeting in Campobello was only about the international park. He did not realize the case headed in this direction as well.

"It's where Callahan's family probably settled."

"How did you find that out so quickly?"

"His mother's maiden name was Appleby right?"

"Yeah,"

"Well the Appleby family is all over this island and the islands nearby," Beauvais gave a nod out the window. "The original settler actually settled here in the beginning."

"Campobello?"

"Not far from this cottage."

"If Callahan is trying to find anything out about his family he will head to St. Andrews."

"And so will Watts."

"And so will we," Macleod smiled.

Twenty Nine

Deborah fiddled with her phone again, waiting for her son to reply. She still wasn't sure she was doing the right thing. Jim had said that they needed to do some investigating in the archives if they wanted to lay any claim for some land but their trip to Saint John had been a bust; at least that is what Jim said. She still did not completely trust him, and now they were headed even further south to some town called Saint Andrews to look in their archive as well.

Watts was a fascinating man, she had to admit. His knowledge of the people, the area and especially the law was crazy. He rattled off dates and statutes and family names as if he had instant download Bluetooth directly to his brain. Yet every time he told Deborah something, she could tell, he wasn't telling her everything. There was a look in his eye, or maybe it was an emotionless stare, that just didn't feel right.

This trip didn't feel right either. She still hadn't told Rob and, if her son was telling her the truth; of course he was. Bobby was her baby. Then Rob had no idea she was investigating his family or that she was even in Canada. It was a huge risk, she realized. Their entire separation was due to a lack of trust between the two of them and here she was breaking that trust in a new and different way. If Rob did not understand why she had to do this; or worse if nothing came of it and she came up empty handed, their marriage would have no chance of surviving.

Of course, Deborah was not even sure she wanted the marriage to survive. She was the one who had left Rob in the first place. Yes it was his nagging, his lack of trust, his accusations that drove her away, but she was the one who took the actual step. Was it a mistake or did she do the right thing?

The sound of a phone ringing startled Deborah. She had been lost in thought watching the scenery go by on Highway NB1. Jim's brand new black BMW had such a smooth ride, the highway was so empty and the dark green oak tree line out the window was so soothing that she had fallen into an almost meditative state. Her eyes shot over to the futuristic dashboard in front of Jim. Computer displays, audio notifications, running GPS displays and of course an interactive blue tooth phone system that allowed Jim to talk while he drove. It made the BMW seem more like a rocket ship than a car.

It was an essential part of his job Jim had told her when they first left Halifax. He spent most of his day driving all over the two provinces, usually several hours at a time. Texting and driving was illegal in New Brunswick and he had so many contacts anyway that he was bound to get in an accident or have to pull over every five minutes just to have a conversation. He had specifically chosen this BMW model because while it drove like a dream, impressed his clients, and was more comfortable than his living room sofa, it had the best computer system he could find for the money.

He proved it to her too. Before they had even left sight of Halifax, Jim's phone had rung with a client call. At first, Jim had tried to cut his conversations down. He didn't want to be rude to Deborah. But after call after call, Deborah gave him permission to talk as long as he liked. She wanted to just enjoy the ride anyway.

So Deborah's first reaction when the phone rang again was surprise. Not surprise that the phone had rung, but more that it had not. They had been driving for almost 20 minutes without a call. Perhaps that's why Deborah had gotten lost in her thoughts so quickly. Finally some silence.

Her second reaction was one of curiosity. Every time the phone had rung, the display gave details on who the caller was. This call's display simply said "black gold." In addition, Jim barely spoke to whoever was on the other line. He brushed them off with a quick, "let me call you back," and that was it. Deborah couldn't let that sit.

"Black gold?" she said. She knew she was prying but she couldn't help herself.

"Heh," Jim chuckled. His eyes remained on the road. "Sometimes I give my callers a nickname. It helps me remember what they do, or what they want or sometimes it's just a joke."

"Black gold," Deborah thought out loud for a moment. She turned and looked at Jim. He still remained focused on the empty highway. "Oil?"

Jim nodded.

"There's oil up here?"

"No not really."

"What do you mean not really?"

"There's a refinery," Jim finally looked at her. Was he relieved that she did not ask about the caller or was he just being friendly? "It's the biggest refinery in North America."

"Really!"

"And," Jim quickly continued. His voice raised a pitch. "They were even going to build a pipeline here from Western Canada to Saint John."

"Like Keystone?" Deborah of course had heard of the Keystone pipeline. Everyone in the states had. It was the most controversial construction project in at least the last twenty years. President Obama had been against it. He did not want a pipeline from Western Canada crossing through the heartland of America all the way down to Texas. He felt the environmental costs were too great, while his opponents claimed that it would bring jobs to Americans. At first Deborah had been interested in the issue, but over time she had lost interest in it. Like all Americans, she became distracted with other news and just in life in general. She knew Trump was for it but for the life of her she couldn't even remember if it had been built or cancelled.

"Precisely," Jim made a scowl. "It was a great idea and would have made this entire area the most valuable port on the Eastern Seaboard. Can you imagine; Millions of barrels of oil taken from hundreds of miles away and transported to the edge of the Atlantic Ocean?"

"Wow; that sounds impressive."

"It was."

"Was?"

"The project was cancelled," Jim grew bitter. "Environmentalist bullshit; I can't tell you how much time I wasted on it. It almost ruined me."

"Sorry to hear that," Deborah was sincere. She may not trust Jim and she still questioned his motives, but the man had been nothing but sweet and kind to her. Without his help, she would be lost. Still, something seemed off. "So if the project was cancelled, why get a call from someone you nicknamed black gold?"

"Just an old friend I made when it all was going down," Jim's eyes returned to the road. This was none of her business and a little rude of her to be prying into his business. "We still stay in touch."

###

"So you're saying the Oil companies could ruin all of this?" Agent Foster shouted over the wind and roar of the boat engine. The two of them, Foster and Macleod were taking the water taxi directly from Campobello to Saint Andrews. Before Beauvais had split off to do his own research on nearby Deer Island, he had arranged to charter the taxi for his partner. They had the boat to themselves, except of course for the driver steering in the back.

The small 33 foot boat only had 12 seats. Normally it was used for whale watching or tours but at times it could also be used as a taxi. Its high speed jet drive could get tourists out to the whales and back in record time with speeds of up to 40 MPH. It had to be doing close to that Foster realized as he watched the aluminum hull almost rise completely out the water. It immediately reminded him of his Coast Guard days with the wind whipping through his hair and the salt spray of the bay on his face. He loved these small fast boats much more than the larger vessels or even the helicopters he had ridden on. There was something about speed that fueled his adrenaline and out on the open water was the best place to feel that freedom. It made him angry to think that this beautiful bay was in danger.

"I didn't say that at all," Macleod corrected him. He pointed and waved at the islands to their left, right and center. "The people on these islands are dealing with all kinds of change and oil may actually be the least of their worries."

"Why is that?" Foster gazed out at the islands Macleod had indicated. All of them showed signs of human life, but none of them seemed overly populated or built up. To his right was Deer Island where Beauvais had headed, to his left and across the unseen international border was Moose Island, better known as Eastport, Maine. It was easily the most built up of the islands. And behind him of course, was Campobello. Saint Andrews, their destination, was ahead and beyond his sight.

Lighthouses were in his view on the big islands while the countless smaller ones were covered mainly in trees with a few having a house or a small dock on its edge. The wildlife was even more prominent out here in the water than it had been back on Campobello. He had already seen an eagle, some deer and an inordinate amount of seals both in the water and basking on the rocks in the heat of the noon day sun. Even with all the places he had seen in the Coast Guard, this still was one of the most unique and beautiful he had ever witnessed.

"The pipeline was cancelled," Macleod answered.

"For good?"

"Never believe that," the pilot interrupted. He had abruptly cut the engine down to an idle and had approached Foster and Macleod. "They still own a lot of land up here and they'll figure out how to use it someday."

Foster and Macleod exchanged glances. It was the first time the pilot had spoken since they left Campobello. The main reason they had chartered the boat in the first place was to keep a low profile. Now not only would they be forced to interact with this guy, they were puzzled as to why he had slowed the boat in the first place. Foster scanned the waters suspiciously.

"Name's Gary," the pilot offered his hand with a smile. He had a down to earth welcoming look about him that instantly put the men at ease. His wind-blown, brown hair had a mix of gray in it and his dark black glasses looked like something right out of a 1950s sears catalogue. The calluses all over his hand showed his blue collar, fisherman's roots and the scar near his thumb Matt immediately identified as the result of a fishing hook.

"Matt."

"Patrick," they all shook hands. "Why did you stop the boat Gary?"

"Wanted to show you something," Gary took a step around them and made his way to the bow. "I show everybody I take through here."

Foster and Macleod followed him to the edge of the boat and scanned the water in the direction Gary was pointing. The water seemed different somehow.

"Notice anything?" Gary looked out at the water then back at the Agents.

"Water's not flowing normally," Macleod offered.

Gary remained silent.

"Whirlpool?" Matt guessed slowly. He hadn't ever seen one before, despite all his years in the Guard. They were pretty rare in the world and often irregular. You had to be pretty lucky to catch one.

"Old Sows' her name," Gary nodded. "I'm impressed you spotted her this early. It'll be a few more hours before she fully forms."

"I've spent a lot of time on the water," was all Foster cared to share. This time he would maintain a low profile.

"Even so you don't want to go near her."

Foster's eyebrow raised but he said nothing. Instead he focused on the water and tried to discern the whirlpool's edge.

"It's the largest tidal whirlpool in the Western Hemisphere and the second largest in the world."

"How big does it get?"

"Seventy six meters wide; at full strength it reaches speeds of up to 27.6 km/h."

Macleod stared at the water some more. He had seen the whirlpool at Niagara Falls but he could not see this one. That seemed to make it all the more threatening.

"You won't see it till the tide is in more," Gary told Foster. "And by then, it would be too late."

"Anyone ever get sucked in?"

"Not recently. It's pretty well known nowadays. I stop every time I have passengers and point it out. We all do."

"What about in the past?"

"Oh it has taken its share of lives," Gary started to back away, "Even a few ships; especially the smugglers."

"Smugglers?" Foster and Macleod said in unison. That was their line of work.

"This place was a haven for smugglers after the revolution and especially during the War of 1812." Gary reached the stern and cranked up the engine. "You know back when our two countries weren't such good friends."

He smiled and revved the engine loud. Foster and Macleod braced themselves as the boat kicked into high gear. "But that kind of stuff is long gone now," he shouted over the engine's roar.

Foster smiled. Macleod smiled. He strolled over Gary's last words about the old days and frowned. A sudden darker thought had occurred to him. He turned to his new partner and said, "You think Callahan has any idea what he has gotten himself into?"

###

"Rob do you have any idea what we have gotten ourselves into?" Lindsey turned around again and looked down the highway. She still could not see the car the boys had spotted a few hours ago.

"I'm sure it's nothing," he tried to assure both Lindsey and the boys.

"I'm telling you dad we're being followed," Bobby insisted. "We're the only ones on the road."

That much was at least true, Rob had to agree. He had decided to take the scenic route to Saint Andrews today. It was only about 15 minutes longer according to google and it went through what looked like a beautiful area called Lake Utopia. With a name like that, how could it not be?

The boys were excited to go there as well. There was a beach and even a legend about some kind of sea monster. Why not? Rob was going to do his damn best to make this into a vacation even with the revelation of the Franklin letter. They would stop for a swim, take a leisurely drive and once they got to Saint

Andrews they would go on a whale watching tour! It seemed like the perfect plan.

Then the boys noticed the dark blue sedan following them and everything changed. Rob could not stop looking in the rearview mirror and neither could Lindsey. How would they ever have a vacation now?

"Who do think it is?" Adam voiced what they all were thinking.

"Nobody," their father insisted. He would continue to deny reality for as long as he could; If not for his own sake, then for the boys.

"It's somebody dad."

"The guy from the ferry and the citadel?" Adam offered.

"The pawn shop dealer?" Lindsey suggested to Rob. She tried to keep it quiet but she was too afraid; that guy really creeped her out.

"No way," Rob was more certain this time. "How would he know to look up here?"

"Well he deals with antiques found in this area. He must have a lot of contacts around."

"He still wouldn't know where we are though."

"Holy shit!" Bobby suddenly swore.

"What?" Rob almost slammed on the brakes.

"Nothing," he looked up from his phone and glared at his brother, "Nothing dad. Just something I saw on Facebook," he lied.

"Don't frigging do that," Rob scolded him. "I almost went off the road."

"Sorry," Bobby turned his phone so his brother could see the text.

"You're still talking to mom?" Adam whispered. He couldn't believe it.

Bobby just scowled and shook the phone at Adam. The command was obvious. "Read it."

Adam looked at the phone, looked back up at his brother with eyes wide open, and back at the phone again.

"I'm on my way to Saint Andrews," it said.

"Fuck," Adam mouthed to his brother.

"I know," Bobby mouthed back.

"Hey dad," Adam quickly spit out, "what town did you say we were headed for again?"

"Saint Andrews."

Adam put his hand over his mouth for a moment to stifle a shout. He looked down over Bobby's fingers and watched him type. "WE ARE HEADED THERE TOO!"

###

Francois looked at his speedometer. He could probably push the old dark blue sedan a little faster and not get pulled over. He had to make it to Saint Andrews before nightfall. He could care less about what it did to the car. After all, it wasn't his. Switching cars with his brother had been an obvious option even if he had to throw a couple hundred his way. His brother knew Francois was in a difficult position and it was just like the old fuck to take advantage of his younger sibling. He knew Francois had a soft spot for the small gray, slightly damaged old station wagon. The two of them had many adventures together and Francois had logged thousands of miles on these same roads looking for antiques to fill his shop. But he couldn't risk the Callahan women spotting him again. There was too much at stake and Jim would never forgive him a second time. "Thanks bro," was all his brother had managed to say through a broken smile.

Francois had been delayed at the border longer than expected. It was unbelievable how much more security there was every day. He could still remember, before 9/11, traveling back and forth to Canada and barely stopping. There were times he felt like he could have smuggled a moose across and no one would know.

He couldn't deny his luck this time though. He had been at a dead end. Following the girl in Fairfield had led to nothing and even breaking into the house had given him practically no clues. When the wife disappeared as well, he had lost hope. Then, a desperate text to his contact in New Brunswick and not only does the guy have information which can help, he is actually working with the wife he had been looking for!

Jim Watts had been a long-time associate of Francois. The two of them had met on one of Francois' many trips to the Saint John's area. It was practically a pilgrimage site to Francois after all. The area was a treasure trove of early French colonial antiques: Francois' specialty. So many people were craftsmen and appreciative of the past that they were always preserving this or selling that. Being a purveyor of estate sales and auctions, it was only natural that he and Watts would eventually meet and later become partners. He just hoped he could truly trust Jim on such an incredible find.

They would have to be careful. Being spotted was of course a danger, but there was no law against him being in Canada. If however, the wife or someone else in the family put two and two together, and realized he and Jim were working together, then it could ruin everything. Francois wondered just how far he or Jim would go in this. Francois himself had already broken the law. *Who cares*, he shrugged his shoulders. *This was the biggest find of their lives*!

Thirty

It was like something out of a Marx Brothers movie or an early Pink Panther. Everyone had somehow congregated in the tiny little seaside town of Saint Andrews and yet somehow, no one had seen each other. When Rob went in, Deborah was just going out. When Francois turned left, Lindsey turned right. They all went to the same places, at roughly the same times, yet they never once crossed paths. Bobby and Adam kept an eye out for whenever their mother and father might connect and would quickly usher Dad and Lindsey out or text mom to warn her. You could almost hear the circus music in the background.

Agents Foster and Macleod rejoined Saltman and the three of them watched it all with amazement. They put a tail on Rob. They put a tail on the boys. They put a tail on Deborah, on Jim and eventually even Francois. Unfortunately there was only the three of them and when the boys or Deborah split off from their respective groups, there were much more than three groups to follow. They couldn't be everywhere.

Fortunately for the agents, the boys and Rob had disappeared for most of the day on a whale watching excursion. Rob had promised it to the boys come hell or high water and the next day was perfectly sunny, and crisp. There was almost a guarantee they would see at least a Finback or a Minke whale and if they were really lucky, possibly a humpback. With the abundance of seals, the chance of seeing a porpoise or a bald eagle, it was certain they would be gone for hours. The agents could safely let the boys go and focus on the others.

Saint Andrews or the name the locals preferred, Saint Andrews by the Sea, was the quintessential small Canadian fishing village. It had been settled (of course) by a group of Loyalists known as the United Empire Loyalists and was named after the town in Scotland. Despite its small size, (the main part of the town was laid out in a grid that was no bigger than about 7 blocks by 13 and the only way in or out of the peninsula was the single Route 127) it had an abundance of things to do. There were historical buildings like the jail and archives (which even had a ghost tour!), a garden and an aquarium and best of all the whale watching tours. It would be child's play to put a tail on them; especially since they had a pretty good idea where everyone was going.

The archives was a tiny building located just a block from King Street (again, of course!) and was easy to keep an eye on. Still, they almost missed Francois' entry at 10 am when it opened, Saltman not expecting any of the group to be up that early. Lindsey was next around 11:30 and finally Deborah and Jim after lunch. The agents were amazed that again, none of them crossed paths. What they didn't know of course was that Bobby had texted his mother to let her know when Lindsey was headed over and Francois had texted Jim as well. At one point Foster had suggested they go in and do some research themselves, but that could endanger their cover both Saltman and Macleod warned. Plus, none of the groups came out of the archives too excited. They were smiling, that was clear, but no one rushed out of the archives with any great vigor like they would have if they had found something astounding. It would be better to let them do the research while the Agents simply followed and waited.

By the time the boys returned from the whale watching expedition, all three of the agents had started to relax. Nothing too spectacular was going to happen in Saint Andrews and it was too late in the day for any of them to go anywhere or do anything. They could safely take turns keeping an eye out. Agent Foster took the first shift. Macleod and Saltman wanted a break, to go grab some dinner and compare notes. Foster was the young guy. He still had some energy left and watching the Callahan's in the hotel was something he couldn't screw up.

The family stayed in one of the Inns by the sea. Lindsey and Rob had really wanted to stay in one of the many B&B's in town and experience some local hospitality but they would need two rooms and the boys would complain if there was no Wi-Fi or a lobby they could hang out in to get away from the adults. Ironically it was the adults, Lindsey and Rob, who went for an evening stroll to get away from the kids.

"How did it go?" Rob crossed his arms and leaned on the iron railing in front of him. The Inn he had chosen sat right on the edge of the water overlooking the south estern part of the bay. There was a gorgeous view of the open water, the islands, and the many flocks of birds flying overhead. Although there was no beach or access to the water itself from where they were, there was a short gravel path running alongside the rocky cliff. Rob found a small spot in the back where they could talk and maybe even catch a sunset. Unfortunately, that was unlikely he realized when he saw how high the sun was still in the sky. He had forgotten how late sunset was this far north and east in the summer.

"Fine," Lindsey seemed nervous as if something was on her mind. She shifted her weight on the railing trying to get comfortable. "It was almost too easy."

"You found the petition right?" Rob knew the answer. Lindsey had already confirmed it with a simple smile and a wave of the paper when they first hooked up. They had been expecting success. They already knew the families had formed an organization to petition the king. They knew roughly when the petition would have been written and they knew it had to be somewhere in Charlotte County, where the families eventually settled. Rob had even suggested skipping the archives completely but Lindsey reminded him they might find other clues there as well. You never knew what might be on the next page or in a footnote nearby.

"I've got it right here if you want to look at it," Lindsey reached into the left pocket of the blue and white athletic shorts she was wearing. It was a little surprising that she was still in shorts this late in the day. The temperature had dropped into the teens. (60s for Americans; Rob was still having trouble with the conversion from Celsius to Fahrenheit. Thank god he had his phone.) So it was a little chilly to be wearing shorts and a t-shirt. Rob decided he didn't care. He liked how she looked in shorts and a t-shirt.

Rob looked the paper over while Lindsey swayed back and forth impatiently. Something was definitely wrong. The last time Rob saw her this jittery was in the Starbucks back home. He scanned over the letter quickly but had trouble focusing. He saw the names at the bottom: Appleby, Adams, Garrison and the others. He saw the date: 1788. He saw the description of the land and a reference to Deer Island: no surprises so far.

"What's wrong?" He snapped at Lindsey. He hated seeing her this way. He was used to her confidence and even leadership. It was powerful and sexy. This nervous, almost agitated state was just not Lindsey at all.

Lindsey snapped her head to the left and the right scanning the area to see if they were alone. There was one other couple sitting outside on their second floor balcony at the opposite end of the Inn and a kayaker in the water taking pictures of local wildlife but other than that, they were alone. "Rob," she said finally, "I wasn't the only one looking for this letter," she gently touched the paper still in Rob's hands.

"What do you mean?"

"The archivist told me I was the second person today to ask for these records."

"Second one?" Rob looked around as well. He noticed an empty brown bench just off to their left set back a few feet from the edge of the sea wall and waved her towards it.

"Some guy had been there ahead of me," Lindsey followed Rob to the bench. "They got there first thing this morning."

"Did they see you?" Rob sat down. Lindsey sat next to him. Both of them looked around again for any signs of human life.

"No."

"Did you see them?"

"No," Lindsey snapped. "But I asked her what the person looked like."

"And?"

"It was the pawn shop guy, Rob!"

"What! Are you sure?"

"Positive. As soon as she said how strange he looked I mentioned the eye twitch and the gold trimmed wire glasses. It was him Rob!"

"Fuck!" Rob looked around again. "Fuck!"

"I'm really scared Rob," Lindsey was shaking a little. "It took all I had not to blurt it out in front of the boys."

"I'm glad you didn't."

"They probably would have thought it was cool," Lindsey smiled uncomfortably.

"Yeah," Rob returned with his own awkward smile. He was as scared as Lindsey was. The guy was creepy enough as it was but to learn he was up here, probably following them. Rob looked behind him. Was he following them now? It felt like it, but he couldn't see anyone. Maybe he was following the boys? Rob started to get up.

"Where you going?" Lindsey put her hand on Rob's leg and held it there. The touch gave him that same tingle he kept getting every time Lindsey was this close. Man, his hormones didn't quit; even at times like this.

"To check on the boys," Rob sat back down. Lindsey's hand stayed where it was. Did she know it was still there?

"They aren't in any immediate danger," Lindsey reminded him. "I need you right now."

"Ok," Rob said. What did she mean by that?

"I really am scared Rob," Lindsey admitted both to herself and to Rob. It wasn't something she felt comfortable admitting, especially to Rob. She was supposed to be his teammate, just one of the boys, and she had prided herself on fitting in. It hadn't always been easy, that was for sure. On the ice, drinking beer outside and eventually even in the locker room, Lindsey really did feel like one of the boys. But there were times every once in a while, and fortunately less and less often, when she just wanted to be herself and not worry what the boys thought of her. She sometimes grew tired of hiding her feelings, of faking a laugh when she didn't get a crude joke or pretending one of their sexist comments didn't bother her. It had been hard sometimes.

Now, she was beginning to realize in a wave of conflicting emotions, it was all boiling over. This time she was having with Rob, pretending she had no feelings for him; seeing how he was with the boys and even wondering what it would be like if she truly was the woman in his life. She realized she even was feeling jealous at times of the relations he had with his sons. Lindsey someday wanted a family, and girls to teach to skate. But she had no boyfriend, no prospects and no time to find anyone. The only men she knew, the only men she liked, were the guys on her team; especially Rob.

"I know I am supposed to be the tough girl, the hockey player with the skills and the drive, but I really am scared. How did he find us? What if he tries something? What if he has friends? They've said this packet is priceless. Who knows what people would do to us or even to the kids? I mean, God, do you even have a gun?"

"Hey," Rob commanded. Lindsey was losing control. "Hey," he repeated a little softer. "I'm scared too."

"Really?" Lindsey looked up at Rob for the first time. Their eyes met and held. "Don't fuck with me."

"Really," Rob gently held Lindsey's hand. He knew it was risky. His body was aching all over and his head was a mess, but Lindsey needed this. She needed his reassurance. She had been so great the entire trip, always thinking of how she could help, what she could do for the boys. She hadn't once done something for herself, or yelled or even complained. She'd been a saint. "I wouldn't ever fuck with you, at least not that way."

It came out before he could stop it. It was too easy; almost like a joke he would make in the locker room and probably already had. He regretted it instantly. Part of him though was relieved.

"Heh," Lindsey laughed, trying her best to brush off the comment as a joke. She looked away for a moment but her eyes returned to his. The silence was deafening. Neither of them wanted to make a move; in either direction. If ever they were to get physical, this was the moment and that was exactly the problem. It was now or never.

They could read each other's internal struggle. There was no need for words at this point. They both knew how the other felt. There had been too many signs, too many jokes, too many sideways glances and too many innuendos. Who would be the braver one? And what did that bravery mean? Was it braver to make a move or to not make a move? Was the courageous move to take a chance on their feelings, to forge a whole new path no matter the cost? Or, was the courageous move to submerge how they felt, to save Rob's family, to save the team, to save their friendship? The answer was unclear to both of them and with the rational answer being in doubt; their emotions began to take over.

"Rob," Lindsey said softly as their faces began to drift closer. It wasn't clear if that was a warning to Rob or an invitation.

"Lindsey, I," Rob struggled to say.

Their lips met. It was glorious. All the weeks of tension melted away in an instant and morphed into passion. Rob could feel himself getting more and more turned on by the moment. The bulge in his pants was pushing against the seams and Lindsey's hand was only inches away. Soon, he wouldn't be able to control himself.

"I can't watch this anymore," Agent Foster put down the high resolution camera and placed it on the red Kayak in front of him. This had nothing to do with the case and if Saltman wanted them tailed all the time, he could take a shift. He looked at his black water proof watch. It was about time for Salty to take over anyway. Foster gave Rob and Lindsey one last curious glance and began to paddle away. There had to be some decency left in the world, he thought with a grin.

Rob placed his hand on Lindsey's thigh. He could feel the powerful muscle under her soft skin. Slowly, his fingers moved up, approaching the edge of her shorts. If this was going to happen, he could barely think now, the moment could not be more perfect. They were alone; the boys were nowhere to be seen and would never see. The bench, the waves crashing gently on the shore, the setting sun-"

"Shit!" Rob jumped up. He pulled his shirt down over his crotch to hide his feelings and staggered backward. Lindsey almost fell off the bench.

"What?" Lindsey shook it off as well. She was as hot as Rob was. She rubbed her sweaty hand on the side of her shorts.

"The boys," Rob suddenly remembered. He was both relieved and horribly disappointed at the exact same time, "The ghost tour! Sunset! I promised the boys I would take them on the ghost tour!"

"You don't want to let them down," Lindsey struggled to say.

"I could tell them I forgot," Rob took a step back towards Lindsey. His body ached for her.

"No," Lindsey held up her hand. "You're just starting to make progress with them."

"It starts in 30 minutes," Rob's eyes pleaded for forgiveness. He could see the longing in Lindsey's face. He recognized the passion in her trembling frame as well. He had seen it countless times with Deborah. How easy it would be right now to just forget the boys and lose himself in Lindsey. He couldn't let her down. He couldn't let his boys down. Rob was frozen in conflict.

"Well then get going," Lindsey laughed and waved. She couldn't take Rob knowing it would cost him the boys. A surge of relief and disappointment overwhelmed her. If the two of them were ever to be more than friends, it would have to wait for another time. Her face fell into the palm of her hands as Rob rushed away.

Thirty One

"You didn't delete it did you?" Agent Saltman looked worried. This could be the leverage they might need.

"I was about to," Agent Foster admitted, placing the camera down gently on the perfectly made bed in front of him. He hated this part of the job. It was one thing to take pictures of criminals or dirty politicians or fellow spies, but this Callahan family was just a group of innocent civilians thrown into a mess they didn't understand. He even kind of liked them.

"Well don't," Saltman looked at his watch. He needed to get on with his shift. He didn't like leaving the target alone like this. He would have been there already but at this hour there really was nothing they could do of any concern. "We can use that to control Callahan if we need to."

"I know," Foster nodded. He sat on the corner of the queen bed next to his camera. The room was impeccably comfortable. The crisp sheets, the fluffy pillows, the paintings of wildlife on the wall and even the scented candle on the mahogany desk; it was a testament to how much care the owner of the B&B put into making her guests comfortable. He couldn't decide if he wanted to throw off his shoes and catch a quick nap in this welcoming homey environment or go back out for a quick bite. The B&B they had chosen was right in the heart of downtown and he still had not had a chance to check out the local scene. "I just hate using it on people like this."

"We won't," Saltman meant it. He liked the Callahans as well, but he also knew how important this case was. He had learned many times over, that in this business the end sometimes had to justify the means. "But if Callahan finds something and won't release it, that picture of he and the girl is the only thing we have that could stop him."

###

Rob stood on the edge of the gravel parking lot, lost in thought. Why had he come here again? Thoughts of Lindsey, the boys, Deborah; they all were swirling around in his head. He had barely slept at all last night and the dreams he had provided no comfort. How was he going to handle all of this? What direction should he take? What was best for his boys? What was best for him? Could he really do this to his team? He remembered his hand on Lindsey's thigh and the heat from her lips and began to get aroused again. "Shit!" he swore, shaking his head in an effort to force himself out of this funk. He looked ahead and tried to remember the reason he had come here this morning in the first place.

This was the second time in less than 24 hours that Rob had stood in this spot. Last night however, it had been too dark to admire the beauty of the building. He and the boys had run right past it on the way to the Archive next door. The Ghost tour had started there and he had sprinted with the boys almost the entire way just to make it on time. It almost took his mind off of Lindsey. The boys were laughing a lot, teasing each other playfully and taking it all in. Hopefully they had no idea of the internal struggle going on within their father.

He had come here again, first thing in the morning, for two reasons. He had to keep moving if he wasn't going to go crazy thinking about Lindsey. The kiss at first had seemed to melt away all of his fears and concerns but the way it was interrupted had only made matters worse. As soon as they saw each other again, things were a hundred times more awkward. They didn't speak about it and they barely even looked at each other. Rob had to get out of there.

He shook his head a second time and took a few steps towards the courthouse trying to focus on his mission. In front of him, standing alone in the grass, was an auburn and gold plaque attached to the face of a three foot high concrete block. It said that the 19th century Charlotte County Courthouse was the oldest courthouse still in continuous use in Canada. Rob held onto that history and pushed the other thoughts to the side. He walked backwards and to his right to take the time to admire the building's beauty. White with green trim, four cylindrical white Pillars holding up the triangular portico; he couldn't help but admire the preservation of it. The most impressive part of the building was its façade complete with a brightly colored Royal Coat of Arms and a British style Lion and Unicorn adorning its top. Rob could see why the County took such great care to preserve it.

The second reason he had come to the Archives was much more practical. He had to find out more about Francois. Lindsey had been too freaked out at first to do anything, but they both realized that they needed to know more. Did Francois know they were there or was he just following the same trail? Where was he going next? Had he given any indication that he was alone or with friends? Rob hoped the same archivist who had helped Lindsey was there again today. He took one last look around the well-manicured, grassy hill that the Courthouse and Archives sat upon and sighed. There was no sign of Francois or anyone else. It was safe to return to the archives.

The Charlotte County Archives was located in the old jail right next to the courthouse. It looked much older and much less impressive with its two story stone block frame, simple orange entry door and a lack of anything ornate. Only the oval blue and gold sign gave any indication there was anything important inside. It was both a strange place to house an archive and a perfect place, Rob realized as he walked towards the main entrance. Unimpressive and plain on the one hand, and ancient and well preserved on the other; it was just like the documents it held in its vault.

Rob got lucky. The same woman was there again today. Her name, Lindsey had said, was Veronique and she was the friendliest older woman Lindsey had ever met. Her dark black hair and slightly worn face hid a fire for learning that burned whenever she came across something new in her archive. Veronique had taken the job (Rob quickly learned, she was certainly one to offer information freely.), a little over ten years ago. After her husband died and she retired, she took this volunteer job at the archive to help pass the time and serve her community. But over the years she had become fascinated with the local history and the families that had settled there. She felt, she had told Rob with a smile, like a little old lady detective.

At first, she offered Rob little information on Francois. Despite her friendliness and ease of offering information, she did not like discussing other researchers. It took a little prodding and some back handed questions, but eventually Rob was able to find out that Francois was not alone. Someone else had come after Lindsey and asked for the documents as well!

"That's what got me so interested," Veronique went on. "What are the chances that three different researchers would all be asking for the same document on the same day?" She started to walk down the hall.

"Yeah pretty strange," Rob followed her. The archives were dark inside and it seemed that more time was spent in the jail part of it than the archives themselves. The color of the dark red wooden floors reminded Rob a little too much of blood and he wondered if that was on purpose. The paint on the inner jail doors was chipped in a Rorschach's test mix of red and white. Some small benches and tables lined the halls and Rob almost stopped to look at one of the many framed pictures of life in the jail long ago. Veronique mumbled something about one of the jail cells as she hurried past and turned into what seemed to be the office. Rob hustled to keep up.

"I hope you don't mind," she reached for a manila folder sitting on the left corner of an impeccably neat wooden desk, "I know it is your family history, but I took the liberty of digging a little further."

"No of course not," Rob took the folder gently from her. His heart began to race.

"You sparked my interest," Veronique did not feel completely proud of her research. Volunteers were free of course to look the archives over themselves and often did research for patrons when contacted by them, but this was still a little beyond the normal. No one had asked her to do more. "After the third person left, I had some extra time." She pointed to some dark older photos that were starting to yellow around the edge on a table nearby. "But most of our time is spent scanning old photos into the database and I needed a break."

Rob opened up the folder but continued to listen as he scanned the document over.

"So I took the liberty of just bouncing around the general area of where we found your letter," Rob's eyes began to widen as Veronique went on. He saw the words, "Franklin" and "packet". "And I found this not too far away."

Rob almost completely ignored what Veronique was saying now and went back up to read the letter in its entirety.

"It was folded over, almost hidden, and it seems to be a second petition written by a man named Oliver Rockwell."

"Rockwell?" That was not a name Rob recognized.

"He is listed on the other letter as a member of your association and he seems to be representing them."

The letter was addressed directly to the King. It was dated 1792, about five years after the first petition. The tone however, was much more hostile, almost brazen. The purposeful, polite sense of humility and respect, so often seen in every letter written to a King, was almost completely missing.

"And I am not sure exactly what it means,"

They were not just asking for land grants, they were demanding them. Maybe they were even threatening the King himself.

"The only reason we have the letter at all is that it was never sent."

"Never sent?" Rob stopped reading and stared at Veronique. "What do you mean?"

"I mean that for whatever reason, this man Rockwell or his associates decided to hold onto it instead."

"Why would they do that?"

"I do not know. But I found it fascinating that Franklin himself was mentioned."

Ben Franklin or William Franklin? Rob jumped to the middle part of the letter again. It was unclear. They just said Franklin.

"And what do you think they mean about a packet?"

"We have in our hands a packet," Rob's heart skipped a beat. He read it again. "We have in our hands a packet," It exists! Or at least it existed! He had found proof! It wasn't some elaborate hoax or National Treasure adventure movie. This was real! "That we have obtained from Franklin," Rob read on, "that could jeopardize your entire relationship with the new United States."

"I don't know," Rob lied to Veronique. How much did she know? Should he steal the letter? How could he keep others from finding this? Should he? "Can I have a copy of this?" Rob knew he could not have the original. He had been with Lindsey enough to learn that much about archives. But how did he keep it away from others?

"Of course," Veronique turned back to her desk to look for the necessary paperwork. "You will just need to fill out this form and pay the fee."

"Same as yesterday?" Rob reached into his wallet. He could barely think straight. What should he do next? Could he get Veronique to keep this a secret? What about Francois?

"You didn't show this to anyone else?"

"No. I just found it yesterday afternoon and you are the first one to come back."

Rob had to get Francois and any others who might be with him out of town before they could think to come back here. He had to do it now.

"I could leave it out for them if you like. I am off the next several days."

"No, no, that won't be necessary," Rob rushed to say. If they were following him, and he left town, they would too.

"Where should I go next if I want to learn more?" Rob quickly changed the subject.

"Your family settled on Deer Island correct?"

"That's right."

"Well I know the name of the local historian there," Veronique reached for a small pad of paper on her desk. "His name is William Luisi and he knows just about everything about that island that anyone could know."

Rob watched Veronique write the name down. He had to consciously prevent himself from running out the door and screaming. It was incredible how it was all working out! The packet was real! Their research was paying off! He was planning on going to go to Deer Island eventually anyway. He wanted to see the land where his family first settled and Lindsey had suggested they could look up some of the families who still lived there. Maybe they had keepsakes like Nana had.

Rob was about to burst by the time Veronique finished writing the name down. He did his best to gently take the paper and read the name aloud. "William Luisi, on Deer Island, got it." He swung around and headed to the exit. "Thank you so much!" he called back to her. "You have no idea what a help you have been!"

L8

July 1790

London

"Not exactly like old times is it?" Governor Franklin extended his hand with the full glass of golden Jamaican Rum. He drank Rum quite often, especially in the company of a fellow Loyalist. Brandy may have been more the drink of the upper classes and of his father, but Rum, especially the sweet Caribbean kind, had a special meaning to him. As with all products crossing the Atlantic, Rum was controlled by the British Navy. The moment the war began, it was one of the first things the Rebels were deprived of. And now that the war was over, Franklin could enjoy its pleasures while the backwards, coffee drinking Americans were all switching to whiskey. Just one more reason to love the Empire, he grinned as Oliver gently took the glass from his hands.

Franklin had not seen Oliver Rockwell in over seven years, not since he had left New York and finally sailed for England in August 1782. Oliver's request for a meeting had taken him by surprise and at first, Franklin was not even sure he wanted to see him. The two, after all had very little in common. Franklin, dressed in his hand sewn beige wool suit with its narrow silver braid, was every bit the fashionable Gentlemen. The fine wool was the standard dress for visiting friends for tea, walking in a park or shopping. And despite all of his hardships and all of his bitterness, Franklin was still the Aristocratic London Gentlemen. His critics, and even his father had often accused the Governor of "putting on airs" and of loving the finer things too much. But the Governor knew that the only way to make it in London Society was to be perceived with a certain respectability. This was, after all, still the land of Kings and Nobles.

When first arriving in London eight years ago, Franklin felt uncomfortable with London Society. Oh to be sure, he loved the city. He and his father had spent many years in London together when he was younger and he had even been called to the bar here. This second trip, more of an exile, left him feeling awkward at first, even unwelcome. He found himself spending more time hobnobbing in the countryside visiting old friends, than in polite London Society; but his work had to be done. And for that he needed to be in London. He even had to remarry. Two years ago, he had met Mary Develyn, a respectable Irish gentlewoman. While she was nothing like his dear departed Elizabeth, she was a fine companion and a good woman. Franklin would not spend his final years alone.

Oliver Rockwell, on the other hand, looked more like an American rebel than the Gentleman Loyalist Franklin had expected when Jonathan Odell forwarded him the request for a meeting. Dressed in standard gray colonial gear complete with wrinkles and stains earned in his long voyage from Deer Island, Oliver had made no attempt to impress expecting, Franklin assumed, that their service together during the war was all that was needed to bring this meeting together.

"What do I know of this man?" Franklin frowned as he poured his own glass of rum. It was only sheer curiosity combined with his personal mission to help any Loyalist he could that opened Franklin's door in the first place. Even after their years together, Franklin knew little about the man other than he was a loyalist like himself. The two had met in New York City while Franklin was recruiting for his Board of Associated Loyalists. Oliver had been referred by a friend as one of the most passionate, driven loyalists in the city. At the time of the war, nothing else mattered; not background, not social class and barely even character. Franklin was looking for bodies to fight the rebels with and Oliver had been more than willing to do anything and go to any measure to win the war for the King. What more could Franklin ask for?

"There cannot be good living where there is not good drinking." Oliver held up his glass in a toast. He did not realize his mistake.

"The Antediluvians were all very sober," the Governor frowned and looked away.

"What?" Oliver still held the glass in toast but did not drink.

"A song my father wrote," Franklin explained without turning back. "Your toast, common in all circles I might add, comes from that song."

"Oh," Oliver realized his mistake instantly and tried to backtrack. Benjamin Franklin was one of the most prolific writers ever. His *"Poor Richard's Almanac"* had been one of the most popular readings in both England and America long before the war had ever begun. Oliver didn't realize Franklin had also written songs. "S-sorry Governor, I didn't mean to."

"No apology necessary," the Governor quickly shook off the faux pas and returned his glance with a smile. "My father's sayings are all over America and England. If I let them bother me every time I heard them, I would have been in an early grave."

"Still," Oliver was angry at himself. How could he ever get a favor from the Governor if he kept making mistakes like that? He needed to be more careful. "I could have been more sensitive."

"Perhaps," Franklin agreed as he returned his glass to the toast position. "Nothing more like a fool than a drunken man," he smiled and took a large gulp. The burn in his throat caused a momentary grimace but when he looked at Oliver again, the confusion on the man's face almost made Franklin laugh out loud. "Another one of my Father's quotes in that damnable almanac," Franklin explained. "He never was much of a drinker."

"Really?" Oliver had still not taken a sip.

"Oh he drank," Franklin smiled again; "But never to excess and never quite to my taste."

Oliver realized the Governor was staring at the full glass of rum still in his hands and waiting. Immediately he swallowed down a similar size gulp and let the burn warm his throat.

"He had a milk punch he was famous for though," the Governor continued as he finally took a seat in the red cushioned chair in the center of the room. It was clearly a well-made chair, with brass buttons and hand carved arms, but it seemed out of place in the mostly barren room. "But I found it much too bland."

"Milk?" Oliver knew that milk punch was a popular drink; he had tasted it himself on occasion. Hearing that Benjamin Franklin also had his own recipe was just getting to be too much for him though. What hadn't the man done?

He reached for the second chair to pull next to the Governor and looked around the room for perhaps the first time. This Suffolk street home Governor Franklin had in London was much more Spartan than he expected. Of course he did not know the Governor before the war, but during their service together the Governor often talked longingly of his beautiful mansion in New Jersey and the wonderful furniture and decorations that his wife had painstakingly put together. Perth Amboy, the home of the New Jersey Colonial Governor was one of the greatest homes in America: four full levels furnished from top to bottom! In the basement there was a kitchen, a wine cellar, servants' hall, butler's quarters, and housekeeper's room. On the main floor was a spectacular eighteen foot wide marble hallway entrance, a drawing room, a Governor's study with a library, a dining room, a marble mantled ballroom, breakfast parlor, and housekeeper's quarters. Upstairs was the master bedroom, dressing room, and guest bedroom. It had sixteen fireplaces to warm it in winter and it even boasted such advanced architectural features as lead gutters and the protection of a lightning rod!

During the revolution of course, the Governor was forced to abandon the house. Most of his belongings were moved to a warehouse, where just a short time later, they were destroyed by a fire including almost all of his personal books and papers. The Governor literally had nothing left except the shirt on his back when he finally left for England.

So his new house was nothing like the old one. It was in every way a modest house with only random pieces of furniture and a mahogany desk on the other side of the room indicating any of the splendor the Governor once lived in. There were no mementos, no antiques, not even any knickknacks. The only signs of anything personal were the painting he had of he and his wife and surprisingly a painting of his father.

"Is that Elizabeth?" Oliver nodded towards the painting of the Governor and his first wife. He was a little surprised to find it there. After all, the Governor had remarried.

Franklin winced. This was yet another sore subject. June 19, 1776, was the last day he ever saw his wife or his Perth Amboy mansion. After his arrest that day, Elizabeth had continued to weaken and despair. When she died alone during the war it crushed him and with his exile shortly afterward he was forced to abandon her in death as well. Her body, buried in a church in New York, was lost to him. All he could do was have a bitter plaque made for her which still adorned her gravesite:

"Compelled by the adverse Circumstances of the Times, to part from the Husband she loved, and at length deprived of the hope of his speedy return, she sunk under accumulated distress, and departed this life on the 28th Day of July 1778, in the 49th Year of her Age."

Franklin of course blamed the rebels. "Damn them all," the Governor spat.

"Hey," Oliver tried to establish a connection with the Governor. This was not going well at all. Everything he said only seemed to upset the Governor more. It was time to reminisce, "Do you remember that time when we intercepted the rebel convoy carrying all those beer kegs?"

"That was a nice surprise wasn't it?" The Governor smiled. He did not have many good memories of his years during the revolution. It was comforting somehow that not all of it was horrible. "Those men were never going to use it that's for sure."

"I'm relieved we didn't have to kill them."

"We were in no condition to kill anyone after a few hours with that rebel swill."

"It really was dreadful!" Oliver laughed. The Governor joined him.

"I never expected that whole Lippincott affair to go as badly as it did." Franklin suddenly changed the subject. It caught Oliver off balance. He couldn't see the connection, but somewhere the Governor could. Perhaps it was the mention of killing men during the revolution. Perhaps it was merely the mention of the revolution itself. Besides the loss of his wife and home, Lippincott was Franklin's worst memory of those years. The whole affair had been a stain on the Governor's honor the moment it occurred. Of course being a loyalist in America was a stain all on its own but at the time he was so filled with anger he never realized how much hatred the hanging would cause.

"We were in the right," Oliver said firmly. Unlike Franklin he had no misgivings about Lippincott. After all the rebels had hanged a British officer first and throughout the war both sides had bent the rules and in some cases outright broken them in order to win. No one's hands were clean.

"I suppose," Franklin conceded. He knew it had been necessary, that it had been logical. It didn't help him sleep any better though. "Unfortunately very few people agree with us, even here. And believe it or not it has become a sticking point in my negotiations with the crown."

"How are those progressing?" Oliver was eager to turn the conversation to his purpose for being here.

"They are not progressing at all," Franklin snapped. He had no desire to discuss his failures or to disappoint yet another Loyalist friend. "But you knew that of course."

"I did."

"And you know that I have been frustrated at every turn."

"I do."

"Did you know that I had to prove my own loyalty?" Franklin held the rum to his lips again. The glass partially hid his face, but Oliver could still see the anger burning in his eyes.

"What?"

"The commission actually claimed I was colluding with my father the entire time." Franklin downed the remainder of his rum in a massive gulp then slammed the glass down on the liquor cabinet next to the glass decanter of rum. "They actually tried to argue that my father and I took opposite sides to guarantee that one of us came out ahead."

"What?" Oliver had to stifle a laugh. It was all just so unbelievable.

"After everything I have suffered. After everything I have lost and all that I have done in the name of the crown,"

"I thought they gave you a pension?"

"They did," Franklin scoffed, "800 pounds and a further 1800 for my losses. But that is not much more than I received as a colonial Governor ten years ago and it doesn't come anywhere near to covering my losses."

"I-I," Oliver stuttered. He had no idea how difficult it had been for the Governor. People had always just assumed as the most well-known Loyalist from America, that Franklin would be welcomed in London like a hero. Maybe no parades would be held in his honor, but how could the English Government not want to shed the man with praise and fortune in recognition for all he had sacrificed for the King. Oliver knew of course that Benedict Arnold was having it difficult living in Canada amongst fellow Loyalists. No one trusted him there either. But Arnold was a traitor, a man who chose one side then sold them out to choose another. Franklin had always been Loyal and had never wavered. It was perhaps the quality Oliver respected the most of the Governor. And he had received only scorn for it. If things were so bad for Governor Franklin, what chance did any of them have?

"I still live in the shadow of my father," Franklin continued. His voice grew melancholy and he quickly turned away from Oliver. Benjamin had died just a few months ago. "My political enemies, unscrupulous men or even members of the press accuse me of using him, of using his name to gain my role as Governor years ago."

"I had no idea."

"Of course you didn't," Franklin returned to the glass decanter of rum and poured himself another generous drink. He was already feeling the effects of the first one but he didn't care. All this talk of his father and his failures was putting him in a foul mood.

"I am still not sure what you expect me to be able to do for you." It was time to get to the point; enough of the pleasantries.

Oliver held the half full glass of Rum up to his lips. Perhaps he could stall. He could not afford to get as drunk as the Governor, at least not so quickly. He had not expected to have to jump right into his request. He had hoped for more discussion, more reminiscing of old times and hopefully a little more laughter to break Franklin in. He took a slow full sip of the rum and looked around the room again.

"I have heard that Lord North believes Parliament must still help the loyalists." He needed some hope that his cause was not lost.

"That is true," Franklin conceded. "He believes, as I do, that the honor of the King and the Empire demands it."

"Well then maybe,"

"You know the commission has ended its work," Franklin interrupted.

"But this new one,"

"Is much more difficult to deal with," Franklin interrupted again.

"Our story is somewhat unique," Oliver quickly began. He had to get his story out before Franklin sent him away. "Unlike some of your other clients, we have an extra issue to deal with."

"Extra?" Franklin raised an eyebrow.

"We are the victims of a most unscrupulous man," Oliver began his rehearsed explanation. "For years, he has been buying up the land around our island,"

"Your island?"

"We live on Deer Island in the midst of Passamaquoddy Bay."

Franklin nodded his head in understanding. He knew the area of Passamaquoddy, New Brunswick and Nova Scotia very well. After all, not only had his father left him some worthless land in Canada (it was the only thing Ben had left him at all. A last jab at his son was all the Governor could think.) But Governor Franklin had even been considered by some for the position of new Governor of New Brunswick. He was quite familiar with the area, even Deer Island itself.

And of course, the Governor was intimately familiar with the story of unscrupulous men taking advantage of the Loyalist refugees. It had become his entire reason for existence. While he had not heard of this Thomas Farrell that Oliver was talking about, he knew of many men like him who had descended on the new lands like a plague. They were powerful and clever and Franklin had little success stopping them.

"Oh what I would give to see the look on at least one of these men's faces as I tore up their deeds," Franklin shook his head slowly as Oliver finished his explanation. This depressing story of the Deer Island Loyalists, his own frustrations over years of failures and the recent death of his father were dragging him down. The alcohol was only heightening his melancholy mood. "To be able to serve the cause of justice and righteousness in the name of the King once more..." his voice drifted off as he turned away from Oliver and stared at the picture of his father. His last years were supposed to be the justification for his lifetime of service to

King and country. The loss of his home, his wife, his father and even his son were at least supposed to be offset by his accomplishments as the champion of the hundreds, nay thousands of Loyalists who owed him their thanks.

"We both believed in the Empire you know," the Governor's eyes drifted across the portrait of his father as he recalled their years together. William's own service to the King had been born in the admiration and even adoration the young boy held for his famous father, "My father and I."

"Oh?" Oliver had hoped for a better reaction than this to his tale. The Governor almost seemed to be ignoring it.

"Long before he became a revolutionary patriot," Franklin took another sip of rum, placed the glass gently on the small end table next to his chair then continued. "My father was as loyal as anyone, probably more so. 'A fervent supporter of the Anglo-American connection', was how many have spoken of him," the Governor's voice turned sour, " His political activities and voluminous writings in support of the British empire were well recognized in his own day and have been hailed for their soaring vision of the Anglo-American partnership." He held his glass high in the air as if he was about to make a toast. Oliver did not respond.

"He taught me to view authority positively, to look to my superiors for guidance, support, and approval. As a servant of the empire himself in so many ways before the revolution, he instilled in me the belief that loyalty to the crown and service to the colonies were not mutually exclusive, and that the crown was the best guarantor of colonial rights."

The Governor stood up. His face had turned dark and menacing. Oliver was unsure of what to do next or how to respond. He never anticipated this. He never expected his visit to turn into some kind of personal expulsion of the Governor's demons. This had grown far beyond anything he knew how to handle.

"It was my father who paved the way for my decision to remain loyal." He shouted. Oliver took a step back. "It was he who taught me about service and the benefits of a benevolent government. It was he who turned me into a servant of King and country. And it was he who turned away from our values, not me!"

Oliver stood his ground. He suddenly realized he had to allow Franklin to let it all out. Perhaps, when he was done, the release of emotion might make him more willing to help.

"I did not abandon my father," the Governor puffed out his chest and stood taller than before. It was the first time Oliver realized just how physically intimidating the man could be. He was quite well built and powerful for his age and status. "My father abandoned me!"

Franklin's voice echoed off the walls of the small room. It seemed as if all of London had heard his protest. These were words that had been burning inside Franklin for years, words that he had screamed to himself at night, or in despair. They sounded rehearsed, as if Franklin were on trial, which of course he was. It was a not a trial by jury but a trial in the public eye. Everywhere Franklin went, he felt as if all eyes were on him. As if all of London and especially the nobles he worked with, were judging him and finding him wanting. He had never imagined that even in London he would find his loyalty and his character questioned.

"You must have loved him very much," Oliver waited several seconds for the Governor's breathing to settle down. He was beginning to get a sense of the man now. What must it have been like to grow up as the son of the most famous man in America, if not the world? An author, a diplomat, an inventor, a printer, a postmaster, a scientist, the list went on and on. It was staggering how many things Benjamin Franklin had his hands on. Most people only thought of the lightning experiment. They didn't even know that William had been the one holding the kite! Oliver could not even begin to imagine the pain the Governor must be feeling. Benedict Arnold had been vilified and scorned. William Franklin was being forgotten and erased. Which was worse?

The room was quiet for a moment. Franklin was clearly having difficulty with this level of intimacy. He began to pace back and forth. "I saw him you know," he blurted out.

"Your father?"

"Shortly before he died."

"How did it go?" this was shocking! Oliver had no idea. What a moment that must have been! The two most famous men of the revolution, on opposite sides yet bonded forever as father and son. Neither of them had seen each other in over a decade. What was it like? Did they hug? Did they cry? Did they yell at each other? Were the last words father spoke to son words of forgiveness or of anger? Oliver took a step towards the Governor and resisted the urge to place a comforting hand on his shoulder.

"Not very well at all," Franklin frowned. Oliver's face fell. If there had been hope for William, there was hope for them all. "We talked business only."

"Business?"

"I wrote to him six years ago, asking to renew our relationship. " Franklin reached into his jacket pocket and unfolded a piece of paper. Oliver found it strange that the Governor kept such a personal letter folded in his pocket. Had he planned on discussing this with him? Did he always carry the letter around with him? Had he been reading it because of his father's recent passing? "This was his reply."

The Governor scanned the letter in his hands and found the spot he was looking for. "I am glad to find you desire to revive the affectionate intercourse that formerly existed between us." The Governor's voice cracked. Oliver's ears perked up. This sounded promising! "Indeed nothing has ever hurt me so much and affected me with such keen sensibilities," Franklin's voice grew angry, "as to find myself deserted in my old age by my only son!" Franklin glanced up at Oliver for a moment. His eyes were burning but Oliver could not tell if it was from rage or despair, "and not only deserted but to find him taking up arms against me in a cause wherein my good fame, fortune and life were all at stake!"

"My Lord," Oliver stepped back. He was afraid to look the Governor in the eyes. This was unbelievable! All of the hopes for some kind of peace between father and son were dashed in a single sentence. It must have devastated the Governor. How could he even speak about it now?

"He goes on to explain away my reasons and in his sarcastic, annoying way places all the blame on me."

Franklin looked at Oliver waiting for a reaction. There was none. How could he respond properly to such startling news?

"I never asked him for forgiveness!" The Governor turned away. Whatever reaction he was hoping for from Oliver was clearly not forthcoming. "I did not even wish to speak of the Revolution!" He turned back again. He was almost out of control. "My father just hurls these accusations at me then quickly ends with, 'this is a disagreeable subject; I drop it."

Franklin almost balled the paper up in his rage but somehow he found the fortitude to resist. The man's inner strength was astounding. Oliver could not help but admire him even more. "That was it?" Oliver said. "No chance for you to respond or react?"

"None!"

"You had no more discourse after that?"

"How could I?" Franklin swung around again and shouted into the air. "My father had made up his mind. There was no room for discussion, no time to speak my piece. He made sure to get in the last word."

"But you met with him?"

"Five years ago. And as I said before, it was all business. He knew we would never see each other again and he needed to get his affairs in order before returning to America."

"There was no discussion of the past by either of you?"

"When my father has his say, he has his say. There was nothing more I could do."

"But," was all Oliver could manage. This was all so new to him and all so sudden. The last time he had seen the Governor was during the war and he had been a completely different man. He never talked about his father or his family at all other than to curse the rebels about his wife's death. Now, for whatever reason, whether it was his age, his treatment at the hands of the British government, his failure to be the champion of the loyalists he so hoped to be or the sudden death of his father, Governor Franklin was suddenly an open book.

His story was captivating, compelling and tragic of course. Both men, father and son, loyal to their causes born into a relationship based on loyalty to each other, were torn apart viciously by this war. Oliver's own losses in the war seemed almost trivial by comparison. He wasn't even sure he wanted to continue.

"Do you know he left me nothing in his will except some worthless land in Nova Scotia?"

"To be honest," Oliver took a step back and returned to his chair. He picked up his glass of rum and raised it to his lips. He was still uncomfortable with all of this and decided to try some sarcasm of his own. "I am surprised he left you anything at all."

Both men laughed at that, Franklin the loudest. It was the only thing he could do. He finished his own glass of rum and returned to his chair as well. "I suppose you are right!" he let out one more chuckle. "Maybe I should be glad I got even that."

"Do you regret meeting with him?"

"No, no," Franklin surprised himself with his quick reaction to that. He was indeed upset after meeting with his father. The loss and hurt he felt were palpable. He did not even tell Oliver that his father had added a codicil to his will disinheriting him and made him pay for every expense Benjamin had ever spent on him, including back to his school days. Nor did he tell Oliver that his own son had left him and chosen Grandfather Benjamin over father William and that worst of all, Benjamin left without even saying goodbye. All of that was too personal, too hurtful. William could barely think on it, never mind voice it; but talking to Oliver about this so openly, and without any safeguards or political concerns he surprised himself when realizing that he did indeed value that last meeting.

"He gave me something," Franklin blurted out. Again he was surprised at his own reaction. He still wanted to help Oliver and the sudden realization that he might be able to, launched him into action. For some reason Oliver's story had touched him. Perhaps it was because the two of them shared the bond of war. Perhaps it was because Oliver was the first one Franklin had seen in a long time that reminded him of what he had been fighting for. Perhaps he was just tired of the secrecy. Or perhaps it was the liquor. Whatever the reason it was a weight off of his shoulders. Oliver raised an eyebrow waiting for the Governor to continue.

"I was not sure what to do with it, and I am not sure what to do with it now either." The Governor's large frame quickly crossed the room to the mahogany desk on the other side. It was inordinately kept and polished with golden original swan neck handles and a golden feather fountain pen sitting alone on its top. "But perhaps it can help us negotiate for some compensation for your association." Oliver watched as Franklin opened the desk face, reached into one of the draws, lifted up some blackened paper coverings, pulled out a large envelope and waved it at Oliver.

"Here it is," the Governor returned to his chair and placed the envelope on the end table next to his empty glass of rum.

"What is that?"

"As you may know," the Governor refilled his glass and offered another to Oliver. Oliver waved it aside. How many glasses was that now for him? "My father had left me with many of his papers many years ago. He was a man of impeccable research and sense of history. He knew what he was doing would be looked at for years after his passing. Unfortunately he had grown quite suspicious in his later years of how he would be viewed once he was gone."

"What do you mean?"

"These recent negotiations for the Treaty of Paris did not go well for my father." The Governor sat back in his chair and got comfortable. This might take a while. "He was frustrated at every turn by both the London government and his own government back in the colonies. Eventually the Congress felt the need to send both Adams and Jay to finish the treaty. "

"Yes I know," Oliver replied. It was important he remain engaged and show his knowledge. Whatever the Governor had in that envelope, Oliver could tell it was important. "From what I understand Adams could not stand Franklin and there was even talk of replacing him."

"Correct," the Governor was relieved he did not have to explain that part. "My father was quite concerned with how the press would treat him and what future generations might think of his final role as an American statesman. He knew that Adams was saying many negative things about him and that the Congress was not happy with him. But still he was a man of high integrity." Franklin paused. The silence grew a little awkward. It was clear that he was rethinking his decision to tell Oliver of what he had found. He stood up abruptly and crossed the room again. Oliver waited patiently, not daring to say a word as Franklin looked out the window then finally returned back down to his chair. He looked up at Oliver and continued.

"I do not know if you are aware of this part," the Governor felt a deep need to explain his father's actions. Even though the two of them had become so estranged, and his father had refused to speak to him for so many years, Franklin still wanted everyone to respect his father like he did. Of course the two men had split, of course they had been hurt beyond the bounds of perhaps any hurt father and son could feel, but Franklin still loved his father and respected him immensely. He had no desire to see his father's legacy hurt in any way. Benjamin had done what he felt was right and William had done what he felt was right. Both men were stubborn with their loyalty to the end. William wanted to make sure that Oliver understood this before he went on.

"My father was extremely unhealthy during the time he was in Paris. He was more than 73 years old and his body was falling apart. There were days he could not even get out of bed. He was tired, he was angry and he was frustrated at his government."

Oliver wanted to add in a jab at the colonial government but he chose not to do so. Franklin was deep in his story and Oliver could tell how sensitive he was to anything he could say.

"My father had bouts of anger and frustration. There were times when he felt like the whole world was against him and he was alone. He was angry at Adams especially. So in these times of anger he would record his thoughts and mention information about negotiations that he kept from everyone."

"What do you mean?" Oliver began to sense that William was telling him something much more important than just an old man's musings or some heartbreak story between father and son.

"My father knew how to play politics," the Governor smiled wryly. "At times he leaked information or even made things up to hide his embarrassment."

"Really?"

"This packet contains information that is essential to the Treaty of Paris." Franklin held the packet up again and waved it in the air. "He gave it to me at our last meeting to add to other papers I already had. He never had any intention of making any of it public, but he wanted it kept in case other information was released which tarnished the truth or was used to further a cause he would not support. There are some notes in which my father defends himself, in which he discusses the decisions that he made and the discussions he had with several dignitaries during the entire negotiations."

"What kind of negotiations?" Oliver was still unclear how this could help his cause.

"Border issues, Loyalist issues, financial issues, anything they talked about that my father wanted left out of the official record."

"Did you say border issues?"

"Yes."

"I thought he kept an official journal."

"This is the unofficial one."

"Are you saying," Oliver could not believe what he was hearing. He leaned so far forward he almost fell out of his chair. "That you have information that could change the entire ending of the war? Maybe even the border?" Oliver's voice cracked. He was trying desperately to control his emotions. But it was near impossible. This was a gold mine that could change everything. The power one could wield with such information was incalculable. How could the Governor keep it a secret?

The Governor stood up abruptly. The look in Oliver's eyes, the opening of this Pandora's Box, was too much for him. He realized what a mistake he had made. "Maybe this was not such a good idea." The Governor made his way to his desk.

"What was not a good idea?" Oliver tried to not sound desperate. He still wasn't quite clear how he could use the packet, but now that the Governor was changing his mind, Oliver began to get angry.

"I was thinking that maybe I could pressure Lord North or some of the other members with this knowledge." The Governor reached into his pocket and took out a small silver key.

"You mean blackmail?"

"Nothing so barbaric," the Governor opened a different drawer in his desk and placed the envelope inside. Oliver's last comment cemented his decision to keep the packet to himself, blackmail indeed! "Just some friendly gentlemanly pressure."

"But now you've changed your mind," Oliver's voice turned harsh. He couldn't stop himself. The Governor had taken him on this emotional personal journey, made this outlandish announcement, raised his hopes and then dashed them before he fully understood their implication. Oliver resented being toyed with like this, "Just like that."

"I am sorry if I led you to believe I could be of service," Franklin's tone became as harsh as Oliver's. It was shocking the way both men seemed to turn on switches in their demeanor. Yet another thing they had in common, perhaps from their years in the war.

"I understand," Oliver watched carefully as Franklin placed the silver key in his suit pocket and walked away from the desk. There was no use trying to change the Governor's mind; that was clear. He would have to try something else. His voice suddenly was strangely friendly again. "You had a moment of weakness."

"Perhaps," Franklin replied. He was uncomfortable with the tone in Oliver's voice and the glare in his eyes. Franklin could almost see the wheels turning in Oliver's head. Had he made a terrible mistake?

<h1 align="center">Thirty Two</h1>

"Are we being followed?" Adam still could not get the excitement out of his voice. He had tried, especially after his dad yelled at him and explained how serious this was. He couldn't help it though. The adolescent in him could not relate to the real dangers everyone was in.

"No Adam," Rob made no attempt to hide his frustration but still could not stop himself from looking at the side and rearview mirrors again. He didn't know what to do. The whole plan to get Francois and whoever else was tailing them away from the archives was predicated on being followed. Of course a part of him was relieved that they seemed to be alone. Route 172 was a non-descript country road that led directly to the ferry and anyone going to Deer Island would have to go that way. The only other ways to get to the island was by boat or the other ferry which was on the American side and almost an hour longer drive. It wasn't the most popular of islands in the first place and with the traffic in most of New Brunswick being relatively light, the road was almost deserted. Rob would be able to see any car that was within several hundred yards of them.

So if they weren't being followed, what was going on? Had Francois returned to the Archive? Had he or someone else learned of the second petition as well? Rob didn't know if he should keep going or turn around and Adam's nagging only made it that much harder to figure things out. "Just sit back and play on your phone will you?" Rob snapped. He couldn't believe he was actually saying that. He hated how much the boys' faces were in their phones, but this was just one of those times. At least Bobby seemed to be preoccupied. "Your brother hasn't said a word since we left."

Bobby looked over at his brother with a nervous grin. He did have his head in his phone, but that was because he had been texting his mother all morning and Adam knew it. They knew exactly where mom was and they knew why she wasn't following, but they couldn't tell their father that. And if mom knew, Bobby reasoned, that realtor guy knew; and if that realtor guy knew, then what? It might explain why no one was following them. The entire situation put Bobby's head in a spin. He didn't care about all this Franklin/Loyalist land stuff in the first place. He tried to care, he really did. It was just so irrelevant compared to what was going on in his life right now. With mom and dad split up, everything he knew was falling apart and now, ironically, it seemed like he was the only one trying to put it back together. He hadn't at first. Indeed, when the separation first occurred he had been the last one to care. After all, he was a teenager. He was supposed to rebel and leave the family and hang out with friends and stay out late. And back home, he had been doing all those things but now that Dad had whisked him away, he couldn't even do that. He was stuck here, on this stupid trip; God how he wanted to go home.

"So what do we got so far?" Rob ignored the boys and engaged Lindsey. She had been uncharacteristically quiet all afternoon and it was making him nervous. Things had seemed a little better when he returned to the Inn with the news of the unsent letter. Her eyes lit up, she shouted and she had even given him a hug! That of course became another awkward moment of tension but after a second or two of sideways glances, the excitement returned and she talked non-stop about what the discovery meant and where they should go and what they should do.

Lindsey agreed with Rob that they should go to Deer Island and not just to get Francois away from the Archives. She knew that they needed to find out more about the land in Rob's family. So far, they knew nothing. There had been no deeds, no land grants, and no evidence at all that anyone in Rob's family owned any land today or even back then. There was plenty of evidence of them asking for land, but none that they actually received it. The only thing they could be sure of was that many of the descendants of the original petition were still living on the island. They should know something about the land grants and maybe they even had keepsakes boxes like Nana. Deer Island had to have the answers they were looking for.

"OK here goes," Lindsey took a breath and looked down at her notes. She had been updating them and editing them since they left for Canada. The manila folder had grown almost as thick as a text book by now and her yellow legal pad had so many cross-outs, underlines and stars written on it that it looked more like a secret codebook than a notepad. "Patricia Appleby, your mother, was born in New Brunswick but moved to the United States shortly after that. Her family, the Appleby's, still have descendants living in the area, especially Deer Island. In her keepsakes we found an article about Loyalists wanting land in this area as well as a letter from William Franklin to someone supposedly in her family, about a packet containing notes from his father Benjamin. We know that the Appleby family were well known Loyalists and therefore could possibly have met William Franklin. We know that your family petitioned the King for land and even contacted William Franklin, the main man advocating to help Loyalist with their problems. And now we know that the packet containing notes on the Treaty was real and that someone close to your family may have got their hands on it. What we don't know is what happened to the packet and why it was with William Franklin in the first place."

"And of course all the shit about how this could affect the border today."

"I'm still kind of fuzzy on that dad," Adam leaned forward towards the front seat.

"I thought I told you to play on your phone,"

"We're fuzzy on that too Adam," Lindsey interrupted. Despite Rob agreeing to let the kids in on the secret, he still had problems opening up. His default position was to protect the kids or to leave them out of it so they could have fun. Lindsey respected that and even admired it but she knew Adam was really interested in this. "We know that the border between Canada and the United States was a big sticking point and it took years to settle it. So what this packet might contain could confuse the issue all over again."

"Would there be a war?"

"I doubt it."

"No," Rob said firmly. "They would work it out."

"So what's the big deal?"

"It's about money dummy," Bobby spoke up. There he was again, suddenly getting involved when everyone thought he was zoning out.

"Bobby what have I told you!"

"Sorry dad," Bobby sat back and picked up his phone again. For once, he didn't argue.

"You too Adam," Rob commanded. "Let Lindsey and I talk."

Lindsey watched Adam frown and sit back again. She felt a little sorry for him but continued. "What has been clawing at me lately is why Benjamin Franklin would create the packet in the first place."

"That's been bugging me too."

"It just didn't make any sense," Lindsey's voice was starting to rise. Rob could tell she had found something. "Founding Father, inventor, rebel, and diplomat: Why would he hold onto things that could hurt the peace treaty and why would he give it to his son the traitor?"

Rob didn't answer; *Side mirror, rear view; still no cars.*

"So I found this Professor Schiff's e-book on line and downloaded it." Lindsey pressed a few buttons on her phone and held the screen up so Rob could see it. *A Great Improvisation: Franklin, France, and the Birth of America.* Rob was impressed. When did she have the time to find a book like that, let alone read it? "It's is all about Benjamin Franklin's time in Paris when he wrote the treaty."

"Did it say anything about a packet?"

"C'mon Rob," Lindsey scolded, "it's not going to be that easy."

Rob frowned.

"It's just like that National Park lady told you. He was an old, lonely man who had lost his son to war, had been questioned by men he thought were his friends and had been away from home far too long. The Congress didn't even trust him. That's why they sent John Adams and John Jay there in the first place. One of the Congressmen even called him an old corrupt serpent."

"Really?"

"Franklin began to leak information to hide his name."

"You've got to be kidding me."

"It was a twisted scene of lies and counter lies; ambassadors coming and going, no one willing to take a stand or say what they really wanted."

"Sounds just like politics today."

"Exactly!" Lindsey whacked the dashboard in front of her. "That's why this makes so much sense. They were all politicians, making promises and vying for position. I mean they had to know they were making history."

"So everyone wanted the credit and no one wanted the blame."

"Yeah," Lindsey chuckled. "Then I read that on May 9th, he started keeping a journal to protect himself."

"You think that's in the packet?"

"No. I found it on-line."

"Oh."

"And it didn't say anything too spectacular or give away the location of the packet or anything like that."

"What did it say?"

"Again, not much; But I found something that could lead us to understand why he might have kept things secret."

"What?"

"He uses the phrase 'hidden round about ways of communicating'. He says how difficult it is to get people to say what they mean. Then about half way through, he says that he wrote a letter to John Adams but that he omitted some notes and just kind of summarized them."

"So?"

"He then goes on to say that he was not happy with himself for omitting them."

"Again. So?"

"It means," Lindsey was struggling to say. She knew as well as Rob did that this was certainly not proof of anything, but it at least showed the possibilities, "that at least once Franklin left information out during his correspondence with John Adams and kept notes to himself."

"Which you think establishes a pattern."

"No, not a pattern; but an environment. If you truly understand what it was like for Franklin in Paris, how lonely he was, how bitter, how many enemies he had and how everyone around him was acting,"

"Then it is perfectly believable," Rob finished, "that he could have kept certain notes to himself either for his protection or because he was afraid of what others would say."

"Exactly!"

"But why give them to his son?"

"I have no idea."

Thirty Three

"This is it," Jim Watts gently placed the black BMW in park and shut off the engine. "Not much is it?" He turned to Deborah and smiled.

Deborah looked around the empty parking lot, if it could even be called that. Driveway was a better term. It was a wide flat swath of asphalt in the middle of an overgrown grassy field with no painted yellow lines or curb blockers. There were no signs anywhere or even any windows so she could see inside. The building they parked in front of was just a big white single story box lying in the grass with a few flat gray stones forming a path from it to the parking lot. It looked more like it belonged in a trailer park.

"There's the bay right there," Jim got out of the car and pointed across the street and down the hill. Despite the fact that Deer Island was the largest island in the West Isles Parish it still was only about 17 square miles which of course meant that no matter where you were, there was a decent chance you could see Passamaquoddy Bay in front of you. Jim looked down at the blue and white quartz watch on his wrist. It was a bit bulky and a little ostentatious but it fit Jim's personality perfectly, like everything else he owned. "He should be here any minute," he said as Deborah stepped out of the car.

They had arrived at Deer Island first thing in the morning. Jim knew that there was nothing else to be gained at the Charlotte County Archives and that they would need all day at Deer Island if they were going to get anything done. The people here all woke up before dawn and were out of their homes and off to work or out on the water before most city folk had finished their first cup of coffee. They were a hard-working people, he had told Deborah.

Jim had been to the island many times. Although it was small, with only one major road and no real downtown, the island was important to his work. It sat just across the border from Eastport Maine and had therefore seen its share of land disputes. Indeed he had already bought some of the land himself and would have had even more if he had won that lawsuit. It frustrated him to discuss it even now and Deborah could easily tell it was a sore spot for him.

Jim's contact (or at least the one they were meeting today) was the local historian on the island. Deer Island did not have any museum or archive like the other towns they had visited. What they did have, what they always had, like most small towns did, was someone who knew the story; someone who kept track of all the issues, all the gossip, all the relationships, good and bad, past and present; someone who could only be known as the local historian. That was why, Deborah realized, there were no signs on the doors or around the building. This was either a home or a business or perhaps, Deborah laughed to herself, just some old guy's shack.

The man they were expecting however was not some old guy. He was the newest keeper of the torch, so to speak and was, at least in the way one thinks of a town historian, relatively young. Jim had only met him once before. Most of his dealings had been with his predecessor. But from what Jim could see, William Luisi was an honest man and well versed in the history of Deer Island. Unfortunately, he wasn't always prompt.

Deborah walked away from the car and randomly kicked some of the loose gravel on the driveway. It could use a good pressure washing, she noted to herself. Although from what she saw already, this didn't seem like the kind of place where people worried about pressure washing their driveways. They had other concerns on their minds. She walked to the edge of the driveway to get a better view. The thick trees on both sides and the bend in the road prevented her from seeing any car approaching and nothing had gone by in the last five minutes. There was some activity out on the water beyond the trees she noticed; a fishing boat or two and maybe a kayak, but no one headed in their direction. After all, maybe he was arriving by boat. It was an island.

Finally she heard the distinct sound of loose asphalt being kicked up and air being pushed forward by a vehicle. She looked to her right and saw a dirty brown, older Ford pickup truck rounding the corner and coming towards them. She stood up a little straighter and tried to see into the window. Then her shoulders slumped as the truck drove past.

"You sure he is coming?"

"Absolutely," Jim was annoyed too. He prided himself on keeping a tight schedule and being prompt.

"You sure he can help us?"

"If he can't, no one on the island can," Jim turned back towards Deborah and reminded her of why they came. "We still don't have deed records or a copy of a land grant. And that petition we found in St. Andrews makes it clear that the family formed some kind of association and my guess would be they contacted William Franklin somehow."

Deborah winced at that. She had never told Jim about the original letter or the packet. Between Jim's knowledge of the history of the land and their finding of that petition however, he had put much of it together. It was just uncanny how much he knew and how much he was able to piece together. Deborah wondered what other contacts he had that she didn't know about. By now she was certain that she could not trust the man. He was too mysterious with his information and too often on his phone. He would answer Deborah's questions but never elaborate. He would sometimes talk in code or end a conversation abruptly when she entered the room. If he ever found out about the packet though, she was in deep trouble. What he would do with any knowledge of a secret packet could be disastrous and she shuddered to even think about it.

"Your husband's family owned land up here, of that much I am certain. But whether they actually legally owned it or were squatters, remains to be seen."

Another car began to approach, this time from the other direction. Deborah hoped it wasn't the same truck she had just seen somehow doubling back. This sound fortunately was a little different. The ride sounded smoother and the wind disturbance was quieter. It was definitely a different vehicle, probably newer and more aerodynamic.

A blue Ford Taurus rounded the corner. Deborah sighed. It already had its blinker on. She stepped back a little from the edge of the road and gave it room to park. Thank goodness!

"William," Jim smiled and reached out his hand as soon as the car's occupant emerged. Jim's charm was undeniable, Deborah realized. Dressed in that impeccable brown pin stripe suit, with his always perfectly folded white handkerchief in the lapel pocket, one immediately saw class and even suave. The man really did have talent.

"Jim," the smile from the historian was not as welcoming but seemed more real. He took Jim's hand, "Nice to see you again."

"Deborah," Jim immediately turned to her. He was also a man of well-rehearsed manners. "I'd like you to meet William Luisi, Deer Island's resident historian and all around sage."

"Oh I wouldn't say that," William reached out to Deborah with a laugh and shook her hand. "I haven't really been at this very long."

"You don't look old enough anyway," Deborah smiled. She instantly liked the man. He was down to earth, dressed in a simple checkered plaid shirt and blue jeans. His brown hair was parted perfectly a little off to the left and his thin sideburns ran just to the base of his eardrum. He had a firm, but not too eager handshake and his matching brown eyes reflected warmth as he held her stare. Wrinkles around his eyes and on his forehead had only begun to form.

"I'm 37," William offered. "And I've only been doing this for a few years."

"But that's enough to help us," Jim quickly reassured Deborah. He placed a hand in between the two of them and gently nudged William on the shoulder. "Why don't we go inside?"

The inside of the building was barely more impressive than the outside. In the immediate foyer were several small square tables covered in red and white checkered tablecloths like something out of the 1970s. Deborah almost giggled when she saw them. She didn't even think they made those anymore. Each table was also surrounded by four plain, tan wooden chairs. On the white walls were several framed old photographs of people on the island and along the side wall was a large 2'x5' freezer or fridge about three feet high running horizontally along the back. To the left and right were ante rooms separated only by half walls. There were no doors other than the one they entered through. The ante-room to Deborah's right looked dark and messy and the other, facing the road, had some cabinets and even a window facing the opposite side of the building.

"I come here only about twice a week," William quickly explained. He could sense Deborah's confusion. There still was no clear indication what the building was used for. "It's my archive/restaurant multi-purpose shack that I just call the big shack," he grinned. "Sometimes I serve a lunch or early supper to locals, usually Lobster or salmon, but most of the time I just do some research."

"Did you find anything?" Jim got right to business; No time for small talk.

"You didn't give me much time," William pulled out one of the tan wooden chairs from the nearest table for Deborah and walked briskly into the other room. Jim sat down next to her. "But fortunately, I had already been investigating this anyway." Deborah could still see him in the other room and watched as he reached into one of the cabinets. The paper was right on top.

"This document has resisted any categorization," William returned and pulled out another chair, sitting across from Jim and next to Deborah.

"What does that mean?" Even Jim didn't know. Guess he wasn't an expert in everything.

"It means that it sits alone," William placed the document in the middle of the table. It was well preserved, even laminated, but it still had the expected yellowing around the edges and faded black ink they all had gotten used to. "There is no other letter like it, no family that lays claim to it, or any other way to connect it to something else."

"That's strange," Jim admitted.

"Especially around here," William stood up again and headed to the cooler against the back wall. "Deer Island is one of the few places left on earth where everybody knows everybody. Almost all of us can trace our lineage back to the original settlement." He lifted up the top of the cooler and turned back towards them. "Would either of you like something to drink, a water or a soda?"

"Water please," Deborah smiled.

"Make it two," Jim had already picked up the letter and begun to read it.

"The man in this letter, an Oliver Rockwell, has no family ties to anyone on the island," William returned with two bottles of water and placed them on the table in front them. "He has no descendants, no relatives of any kind. I can't even find his surname anywhere in Charlotte County."

"That's strange," Deborah reached for the water bottle and twisted the cap.

"Right? It's one of the major reasons we have it here. No one knows what to do with it. It's been a mystery for years. So when you contacted me Jim and asked for anything I had on William Franklin," Jim's eyes looked up for a moment at the mention of Franklin's name, "I thought of this immediately."

"Did Franklin write it?" Deborah's voice rose.

"He did," William smiled, "to Rockwell. However I cannot find any other mention of Rockwell anywhere and have no idea why he has a relation with Franklin in the first place. I thought about contacting the people in Philadelphia or Jersey or even London but the name of Franklin comes with so much baggage, I didn't want all the attention."

Jim and Deborah exchanged nervous glances.

"It is all very strange." William's smile turned to a frown. He was pretty happy the two of them were there. This letter had been nagging at him for a long time, but he had never had the time or the resources to do anything with it. Maybe, they could help. "The only reason we had it at all was because Rockwell once lived on Deer Island."

"Where did you find it?" Jim had still not touched the water bottle or taken his eyes off the document.

"To be honest I am not sure. It was donated years ago, maybe decades ago, by one of the families here. It had been part of someone's collection and they no longer wanted it or forgot why they had it. That kind of thing happens all the time." He turned towards Deborah who was nodding her head in understanding. After all, the reason she was here in the first place was because of a mysterious letter found in the family keepsakes.

"It's really a shame," William's voice lowered and grew melancholy. "So much history, so many stories are lost over time. Children, grandchildren lose connection with their parents and their families and never get a chance or worse, aren't even interested in where they came from or-"

"This is incredible," Jim interrupted. "It's beyond belief."

"What?" the other two immediately responded.

"Something was stolen from Franklin, something important!"

"Yes, I know. It says that over and over again. But he doesn't say what it is, just the item in question. Why do you think it's important?"

"Don't you see the desperation in Franklin's voice? He is practically begging this man, this Rockwell gentleman to return it."

"Of course I did. I assumed it was of something of personal nature perhaps a family memento or an engraved watch or something. What do you think it is?"

"Oh," Jim's demeanor suddenly changed as he realized his mistake. That wasn't like him. He was usually so calm and collected. He just couldn't help himself this time. He took a moment to slow his heart down and control his breathing. After all, he couldn't tell William what he already knew, what he learned from Francois, why he was here in the first place. He couldn't tell him that information on the entire Treaty of Paris, a Treaty that ended the American Revolution and decided the border between two great nations, might be hidden out there somewhere and could even change the border today! He couldn't tell him of the incredible amount of money he could make on the land disputes resulting from such a find. He couldn't tell him anything! "I really have no idea. I was hoping you would know."

Deborah frowned. She wasn't sure what to do. She was relieved Jim had not told William anything but she was uncomfortable with the obvious lie. William was a friendly, helpful, honest man. She squirmed in her chair and avoided eye contact with both of them.

"Can I have this?" Jim was still holding the letter.

"Oh I can't part with that."

"I can pay you for it."

"It's not for sale."

"Well at least let me take a picture."

William sat back for a moment and placed his hand on his chin. Jim had already taken out his phone. "I guess it can't hurt. Just take it over by the window under the natural light and don't use your flash."

"Thanks!" Jim pushed his chair back so quickly it almost fell over. Deborah remained seated.

"I'm still not sure what you are going to do with it," William was disappointed. He was no closer to understanding that letter than he had been before.

"Neither am I," Jim lied, "I've just got a feeling this could lead to something big."

Thirty Four

"I'm still not sure what this is all about," William admitted as he opened the door of the big shack for Deborah. He kept it opened wide for an extra moment or two. The air grew pretty stale in there with only the one window. Fortunately, the cool breeze coming off the water and blowing through the pine trees on the shore quickly reinvigorated the air. "What does William Franklin have to do with land on Deer Island?"

"Hold on a minute," Jim stopped and turned back into the shack. He stood next to the checkered table they had just got up from, but he did not sit down. He held his phone to his ear. "I have to take this."

"William Franklin himself doesn't have anything to do with it," Deborah stepped onto one of the gray stones forming the path to the driveway. She tried to put some distance between herself and William. If he saw the distorted grimace she was making, he might realize she wasn't telling him the truth. "At least that we know of so far," she added to make herself feel a little better.

"Well then why are you here?"

"To find land for my husband," Deborah stopped at the BMW and turned back to face William. That was the truth. She didn't need to tell him it was only a half truth.

"Who is your husband?" William crossed his arms and maintained a comfortable distance from Deborah. He was a little disappointed to hear she had a husband. Deborah, after all, was beautiful and he was single. There were not many opportunities for courtship here on Deer Island. That much was certain.

"Robert Callahan."

"Callahan," William thought for a moment. He turned and noticed Jim close the door behind them so he could continue his phone call in private. "I don't know of any Callahan's up here."

"His mother's maiden name was Appleby."

"Oh well that explains it," William laughed. "Appleby is a well-known name up here."

"I've heard."

"Did you hear they even have an island?"

"An island?"

"Apple Island," William smiled and raised an eyebrow.

"I saw that on the map just to the north of here," Deborah took a small step closer to William. This was news to her. Why hadn't Jim told her that? "I thought it was just where they grew apples."

"They don't grow apples around here," William chuckled. "The weather is too crazy. Just up North and further inland."

"Who owns the island?" Deborah snapped on the information. Maybe this was what she had been looking for.

"A descendant of John Appleby."

"The original?" Deborah had done her reading too. It was all there on the internet. All she had to do was type in "Appleby and Loyalist" and John's name came up immediately. He hadn't just been a refugee; he had volunteered to fight for a New Jersey company, had been taken prisoner by the Patriots and later moved here to New Brunswick. What Deborah didn't know, and neither did her husband, was what kind of land he received from the King and how exactly Nana was related to him.

"Yes but it wasn't easy for him to keep it."

"What do you mean?"

"There have been lawsuits for decades over who owned the island," William lowered his voice and nodded back towards the shack. "Your buddy Jim was even involved in some of them."

"Jim?" Deborah's eyes went wide as she glared at the plain white shack. She could almost see through the walls at Jim standing there, probably making more secret deals on his cell phone, "How?"

"I don't know all the details," William took another step back and leaned against his own car. He had been captivated by Deborah and given away more than he should just because she was pretty. That was information Jim did not want public and William knew it. It wasn't secret information or anything. Everyone on the island knew it. Even so, William was afraid of how Jim would react once he realized that William spilled the beans. Jim was not known for his forgiveness. "And it's all old news now," he tried to recover from his mistake, "but Jim had tried to buy the island at one point."

"Thanks guys," Jim closed the door behind him and smiled. He took care to walk only on the stones and not get grass stains on his brightly shined Dockers. "I just had to wrap up a few things." He stomped his shoes once or twice to dislodge the pebbles underneath and joined the pair on the driveway.

"No problem," William took out his car keys. He preferred to open his car on his own and not have the car do it for him. It had been difficult to find a car that still needed keys, although probably not as difficult as it was in the States. The dealer found it a little strange that he didn't want the convenience of the push button starter and keyless entry, but whatever. The customer was always right. William put the key in the door and turned. Maybe he could get away before all hell broke loose.

"Yeah," Deborah's voice trailed off. She was still trying to sort out everything she had just learned. Why hadn't Jim said anything about the island immediately? What were these lawsuits? What else was he keeping from her? She reached for the car door but did not pull on the handle.

"You okay?" The BMW gave two loud beeps as it sensed Jim's presence. Jim opened the door partially, looked across the hood and noticed Deborah's face. It was starting to turn flush.

"Why didn't you tell me about Apple Island?" Deborah blurted out.

"What?" Jim looked over at William who was already getting in his car. He looked back at Deborah who was glaring and back at William. Jim scowled. William started the engine.

"Why didn't you tell me about Apple Island?" Deborah repeated with a growl.

Jim took a step towards William's car but he was already pulling away. He turned back towards Deborah.

"What would you like to know?" The cat was out of the bag. Jim knew how to play it though. It was not the first time one of his secrets was discovered. His control was amazing.

"Why you didn't tell me to start with?"

"I didn't think it was important," Jim walked back slowly towards the car.

"You didn't think it was important to tell me that there was an island in my husband's name?" Deborah shouted.

"It's not in his name," Jim's calmness was infuriating. "It's in the family name."

"That's not-"

Jim cut her off. "The Appleby family is huge. There are literally hundreds of descendants. Your husband has no more claim to the island than you or I."

"But," Deborah was caught off guard, "What about?"

"Deborah, Deborah," Jim's voice remained calm, but this time it had the desired effect. "Trust me. I know all about Apple Island. "Did William tell you about the lawsuits?" Jim took a risk offering that but he needed to know what she knew.

"A little bit."

"Then you know I have been very involved with the island and the Appleby family. You have to if you are going to deal with land in this area. The name is huge. So trust me when I tell you that we will need to find something else out there if we are going to find your husband's land."

"I still don't-"

"Deborah, come on," Jim opened the car door again. "Let's get in the car. We still have to deal with this letter we found on William Franklin." He held up the original laminated letter and smiled.

"You stole it?" Deborah gasped and opened her door as well. Jim was already sitting in the driver's seat.

"Borrowed it," Jim corrected her. He pressed the small black button in front of him to start the engine. "I will return it shortly," he reached down to his charging cord and plugged his phone in. Then he set it down on the armrest in between them. "I promise."

"That's what you were doing in there?" Deborah realized. "You weren't making a call."

"Oh I was making a call," Jim shifted the car into reverse, "It just wasn't all I was doing."

Deborah immediately thought, "You son a bitch," but she didn't say it. She wasn't sure what to say out loud. Everything she suspected about Jim was coming true and she wasn't sure how to react. He was clever, aggressive, conniving and dishonest. But he also got the job done. With the letter in their hands, no one else could follow the path they were on. The secret was safe; for now. What else was he hiding though?

"Damn," Jim threw the car back into park. "I gotta take a leak before we go. It's a good thing no one locks anything around here." He smiled and opened the car door. "Be right back," he closed the door behind him and headed back quickly into the shack.

Deborah leaned her head against the headrest and sighed. What should she do? Jim no doubt was a son of a bitch, but he was her son of a bitch. He had already led her to information she would never have found on her own, and as long as she was with him, she would find out more. There was clearly nothing she could do at this point to stop him. He knew almost everything she knew. If she just blew up at him, he would continue on without her. Better to tag along and keep an eye on him than not.

Jim's text alert buzzed. He had left the phone plugged in and on the armrest. The oil rig sign appeared on the screen. Deborah glanced at it then looked away.

It buzzed again, another text. Deborah looked at the building. Jim was still inside.

It buzzed a third time. It had to be something urgent. Deborah picked it up. She had been waiting for the right moment. Another glance around the car and she tapped in the numbers. He may be brilliant, conniving and secretive, but he wasn't very good at hiding his password. With the massive number of times he used his phone it was child's play for Deborah to figure it out.

The text conversation came up. "Did you find anything?" was repeated over and over again. That was ominous. Deborah scrolled back in time and scanned the conversation. It dated back to her first day in Canada. She saw words like border and lawsuits. She saw references to the refinery and the pipeline. Even Trans Canada was directly mentioned. There were phrases like "don't worry," "I got this," "are you sure," and "don't screw this up." The most obvious words, repeated over and over again, were "millions of dollars." She rapidly scrolled up and down, over and over again. No sign of the word "Franklin."

"What are you doing?" Jim opened the door. Deborah jumped and almost dropped the phone.

"You son of a bitch!" She said it out loud this time. The phone was still in her hand.

"Give it back Deborah," Jim commanded as he stretched his arm across the car. He did not sit down. The door remained opened and the look on Jim's face was dark. It was the first time Deborah was truly scared of him.

"You've been talking with the oil companies!" Deborah snapped. Her anger kept her terror in check.

"No," he said calmly, which only infuriated Deborah more, "A lawyer representing oil. He has no actual connection to them."

"Give it back Deborah," he waved his hand in a "give it to me" motion. A small drop of perspiration appeared on his forehead. It was the first time Deborah had ever seen him sweat.

"Did you tell him about Franklin?" Deborah shot back. "What did you hope to gain?"

"Give it back Deborah."

"You asshole," Deborah flung the phone at him. It hit him in the chest and fell in between the seats. "You've been using me all along."

Jim did not respond. His hands were reaching down in between the seats as he tried desperately to pull his phone out.

"All you care about is the money," Deborah opened the door and jumped out. "You're going to use the threat of a border dispute to make yourself rich."

Jim's hand found the phone. He stood up and stared at her from across the top of the BMW. His lack of a response only made Deborah that much more angry.

"It doesn't even matter if you find the packet," Deborah began to realize. His plan was so simple and so disgusting in every way. "All you need is a dispute, a theory, a possibility that land will change in value or ownership for you to win."

A slight smile appeared on the edge of Jim's lips. It drove Deborah crazy.

"Don't you care? Even a little bit? Don't you have any second thoughts about all the lives you're ruining?"

Jim methodically took out the perfectly folded handkerchief from his lapel pocket and wiped his forehead. He said nothing as Deborah's chest heaved up and down breathlessly waiting for a response.

"I suppose our relationship is at an end," Jim said simply as he reached for the car door handle.

"Hey! Hey!" Deborah banged on the top of the car. He had locked the doors and shifted into reverse.

"Hey!" she banged on the front hood as Jim swung the car around and shifted into drive. "God-damn you!" Deborah pulled some loose gravel from the driveway and vainly threw it at the car. "God-damn you!" she screamed again as the car screeched away and turned down the road. What was she to do now?

Thirty Five

They knew it was a gamble, every one of them: Foster, Saltman, Beauvais and Macleod. The Agents' chances of being spotted were extremely high on an island as small as Deer Island. There was only one motel which was also the most popular of the two island restaurants, one major road (New Brunswick Route 772) and no real town center. The year round population itself was only around 1,000 people with so few children that the teenagers had to attend high school on the mainland. At least, there was a primary school for the little ones.

The island might never have been settled at all if it weren't for the Loyalists. Before the Revolution, the local Passamaquoddy tribe of the Abnaki nation was the main visitors. They came from the mainland to hunt and fish and repair their boats in its secluded and sheltered harbors but they did not settle year round. Then the first colonist, John Fountain, settled in 1770 but he was practically alone on the island until the Loyalists came 13 years later.

They came from abandoned land grants in New Brunswick or were refugees from the new United States. The King's promises to protect them and aid them largely went unfulfilled however, so the original settlers were forced to squat on land and fight to survive for long into the 19th century. If not perhaps for the lucrative smuggling trade across the border or the abundance of salmon and lobster, the island may have been abandoned all together.

Fortunately for the agents, the island's fishing and aquaculture economy also received a small boost from tourism. People from Canada and the States visit in the summer for bird watching, cycling, hiking, whale watching and kayaking. Its unique location, exactly half-way between the Equator and North Pole, (hence the name of the island's most well-known restaurant, the 45th parallel) also draws tourists if for no other reason than to say they were there. Add to that the first Lobster pound in North America, the first Atlantic Salmon Sea farm in Atlantic Canada and of course the largest Tidal Whirlpool in the Western Hemisphere, "Old Sow" and there is plenty to do. It would not be too much of a stretch for all four of them to pose as tourists.

At first Beauvais thought sports fishing would be a good cover but with photography also being a big draw on the island, he felt that amateur photojournalism would be better. They already had all the necessary camera equipment as part of their regular issue gear and the tourist clothes they had packed in the first place would fit the bill. They only needed some groceries and perhaps a folding chair or two to perfect the disguise. Beauvais could get those things on the island if he had too. His decision to head there right after the Campobello meeting the other day, turned out to be the perfect call otherwise he would have never had enough time to get their cover established. Thank goodness he was familiar with the area.

Foster, Saltman and Macleod had left St. Andrews dressed as photojournalists as soon as they observed Callahan's rapid departure. It was the second of their two gambles that day but they all felt pretty confident that Callahan was on his way to Deer Island. They knew that the ferry to the island was too small for them to go unnoticed. There were only four total ferries operating at all and none of them carried more than a handful of cars. If they followed Callahan, they would either be spotted on the only road to the ferry or on the ferry itself. Taking the water taxi again from St. Andrews to Deer Island was their best option, especially since they were able to contact the same pilot as before.

"Where you gentlemen want to be dropped off?" Gary cut the engine down so he could be heard. He was dressed exactly like he was the first time he met them; His down to earth, welcoming look, his wind- blown, brown hair with the mix of gray in it and his dark black glasses complete with the orange life vest was the quintessential blue collar fisherman.

"Wherever is closest," Macleod called back to him. All three of the agents were sitting at the bow. It was where Matt felt the most comfortable. He even had his camera out and was snapping a few pictures of a bald eagle overhead. "We've got someone on the island waiting for us."

"Want a look at Old Sow again?" Gary pointed away from Deer Island and into the waters between the island and Eastport Maine where the whirlpool always appeared. "It's getting close to a full moon and high tide is only about an hour away; should be a good one."

"No thanks," Macleod responded before Matt could get his opinion heard. He would love to see the whirlpool at high tide. "We're kind of in a hurry."

"Well with the tides being so high today," Gary reached back down to the motor, preparing to start her up again. "I can get you right up to the shore no problem," the boat's bow leapt into the air as Gary gunned the engine. Spray hit all three men, but only Matt smiled with delight.

It wouldn't take long to reach Deer Island. Although the Bay was populated with so many other islands, large and small, populated and deserted, rocky and tree lined, that Matt had lost count, there was no island in their direct path. It was a straight shot from St. Andrews to the southern edge of the island where Gary had decided to let the men off. For the time being, the agents could enjoy the ride and the scenery while Gary did all the work.

"You've got to be kidding me," Macleod broke the silence a few minutes later. The men had fallen into an almost meditative state with the constant humming of the engine, the sunny blue sky above and the spray of the water. Foster and Saltman jumped at the sound of Macleod's voice. He looked up from his phone and shouted at his partners over the engine noise, taking care to still keep the conversation out of Gary's attention.

"What?" Saltman turned. He was annoyed by the disruption. The last time he had been in the field was years ago and he was taking it all in. A part of him of course missed the excitement, the adventure, the wind in your hair and the thrill of the chase. But he also experienced enough near misses and close calls that he was content leaving the danger behind for his office job. At least this assignment seemed relatively benign; so far.

"Beauvais' got the wife."

"Callahan?" Saltman's voice raised an octave. What the hell happened?

"He picked her up about an hour ago; said she flagged him down from the road."

"Is his cover blown?" Matt looked away from the water and at Macleod's phone. Had Beauvais screwed up like he had done with the kids?

"No," Macleod put the phone back in his pocket. Beauvais couldn't text anymore. "Turns out Watts abandoned her and Beauvais just happened to be driving by."

###

Deborah still couldn't believe it. How did it get this bad? She was stuck alone, on some remote island with no car and no idea where to go or how to get there. What was she going to do? She kicked the gravel on the driveway and she reached down to pick up the red sport duffel bag. Fortunately it had landed safely in the grass. At least Watts had thrown it out the window when he pulled away. She didn't know what she would do without it.

Deborah had always been one to see the best in people and in any situation that came her way. She was the classic "glass is half full" person. It was what had kept her marriage going for so long and allowed her to rise so high in the male dominated world of medicine and engineering. So as she stood on the edge of the driveway, alone and abandoned, her natural tendencies took over.

She had her money, she had her clothes, she had her phone and she even had her research. It was all in the duffel bag. Thank goodness she had packed light to avoid the baggage fees and fit everything into the one carry-on. She would have looked ridiculous dragging a suitcase along the side of the road. Most importantly, she was finally in control. Jim had been exposed. He couldn't lead her around like a fish on a hook anymore. He didn't even know much more than she did at this point. In fact, she realized, she had used Jim just as much as he had used her. She knew the answers had to be on the island somewhere. All she had to do was figure out a way to get them.

She couldn't text the boys. As soon as they found out she was alone, they would try to help her or worse, tell Robert. She was in no way ready to do that yet. She needed more information. She looked across the road again and down to the water. There was a small wooden dock but no one was near it. The boats she had seen earlier were further out in the bay, probably fishing or something. She looked left. She looked right and shrugged her shoulders. She didn't even know which direction to go. Did they even have taxis or, she smiled for a moment, hell even an Uber on the island?

The sound of a vehicle approaching from the left startled her. Was it Jim? William? The sound was clearly a larger, slower vehicle than either Jim's BMW or William's Taurus. Deborah took a step back from the edge of the road and waited. Should she ask for a ride?

It was the dirty brown, older Ford pickup truck again! And this time she was close enough to the road to see the driver. His jet black hair, tan complexion, and perfectly shaved sideburns gave nothing away. He didn't look crazy or anything, but he didn't look friendly either. He just looked determined. Deborah was about to let him go by then realized she had not seen any other cars in the last 10 minutes. This could be her only chance.

"Hey!" she waved her arms and called out. "Hey, please!"

The truck passed Deborah then came to a hard stop without managing to screech or skid. The red break lights glared in full illuminating the black letters FORD painted across the rear bed of the truck. Then the passenger side window came down. Deborah thought for one more second, realized that on an island like this the chances of the driver being some mass murderer or rapist were practically nil, and jogged towards the open window.

"Thanks!" she peered into the truck's cabin. The man was definitely alone. Some gear was in the bed of the truck and a grocery bag or two sat on the double seats behind the driver. This was one of those double cab four or five seat trucks. Maybe the guy had kids.

"What can I do for you?" his voice was friendly enough.

"I've lost my ride," that was true enough, "and I was hoping I could get a lift."

"No problem," Beauvais answered. He didn't have much choice. If he said no, word might get back around the town somehow. He didn't need that kind of a rep if he was going to keep his cover. Besides, he realized, this was a perfect opportunity to evaluate the wife, find out what she knew. Maybe they could even find the packet for themselves. Then they wouldn't need Callahan at all. "Hop in."

"Thanks so much," Deborah opened the door and threw her duffle bag on the seat behind her. "I don't know what I would have done if you hadn't shown up."

Thirty Six

Francois placed his bony index finger at the center of his gold trimmed wire glasses and pushed them up his nose. It was an action that he performed hundreds of times every day and he barely noticed it anymore. He should have bought bifocals years ago when his optometrist suggested it. But it wasn't the image Francois wanted to portray. Somehow it felt more authentic for an antiques dealer to have old glasses on the edge of his nose whenever he wanted to read something. It gave an aura of a time gone by and a sense of old fashioned that he needed to project to his customers.

His customers, he almost snorted. *What customers?* The regulars had vanished years ago and the odd straggler or tourist who wandered into his shop barely paid the bills anymore. That's why this whole "adventure" of his had to pan out. It was all he had left.

St. Andrews had been pretty much a bust and if Jim Watts had not convinced Francois to remain behind for a while just to make sure, he would have left for the ferry to Deer Island hours ago. Fortunately, the road, as always, had been practically empty so he didn't have speed too much along Route 172. It was a good thing too. He still didn't trust his brother's old dark blue sedan. It was a piece of crap compared to his lovely blessed station wagon. It infuriated Francois that he probably was stuck with the Sedan forever. There was no way his brother would give him the station wagon back. That just wasn't Brad's style. What's his was always his whether you were family or not.

Family, Francois scoffed. That was a generous word for what he had left. His father was dead, his mother was in a home and the only member of the family Francois truly cared about, his little sister, had died of cancer over a decade ago. And ironically, it was her death, or more specifically, her funeral that even got him talking to his older brother again after almost twenty years.

Francois' brother was the typical older brother success story. He was good looking, athletic, popular in high school and at least passably smart. In other words he was everything Francois was not. Growing up sick for most of his childhood, almost dying on the hospital bed, Francois' body never developed the way it should. Somehow, his older brother blamed that on Francois and because all of the attention in the family was focused on little sickly Francois, his older brother grew up almost alone and resented Francois for every moment of it. It was an unhealthy, complex, pathetic relationship but it was all Francois had left. This final attempt to show his mother (before she died too) that he really was as much of a success as Brad; was the most desperate thing he had ever done.

Francois squinted harder trying to forget about his brother and focus on the beauty of the bay in front of him. The small blue ferry wasn't much more than a floating rectangular metal sheet but its engines were pretty powerful and it was moving relatively fast through the choppy waters. At that speed, the late day salty breeze playfully whisked through his thin graying hair while the summer sun warmed his face. He loved being out on the open waters and he wished he could do it more often.

He had seen Passamaquoddy many times in his travels to New Brunswick but never from this particular vantage point. The islands, the sea life, the eagles, and of course the dark blue rough water all looked the same to him. Only the yellowing orange sunlight, reflecting off the water this late in the evening was something new. He might have thought it was beautiful if he could have focused his eyes more. Even his long distance sight was having trouble in these old glasses.

"Is that a whale?" A young boy standing at the railing dressed in shorts and a t-shirt screamed. He pointed out into the water as his mother grabbed him by the scruff of the neck and pulled him back to her side.

"Stay away from the railing!" she scolded.

There were only four other cars on the small ferry, with one of the occupants staying inside. On deck, in the open crisp evening air were only Francois, the mother and child by the railing and two groups of fisherman talking by the bow and watching the sea. With this being almost the last ferry of the day it was no surprise that Francois was pretty much alone and he preferred it that way. This wasn't a vacation after all.

Ironically, Francois had never vacationed here. He chuckled a little with that realization. It was always about business. What had he made; ten or fifteen trips to Passamaquoddy itself over the years? He had been south to Campobello, north to St. John's and had even spent several nights in St. Andrews before but he had never been to Deer Island. Why bother? No one there ever seemed interested in what he was looking for; until now.

Watts watched the ferry making its way slowly towards his position at the northernmost point of Deer Island and sighed. He turned his wrist and checked his blue and white quartz watch again. He couldn't believe Francois had cut it so close. The sun was already sinking in the sky towards the water line and many of the sea birds were making their way home to their nests. Things were starting to close up all over the island. The ferry was still a good ten minutes from shore and they would really have to hustle.

"Son of a bitch," he swore under his breath as he turned away from the water and kicked some loose gravel off the side of the road. Another man dressed in jeans and a flannel, most likely a Deer Island resident and the only other person waiting for the ferry, turned his head momentarily. Watts moved a little further down the road to give himself some space. He hated dealing with bystanders as he called them and he hated putting his plans in anyone's hands but his own.

Ever since Watts was a teenager, he had worked alone. It was a skill or a behavior that he learned from his mostly absent father. Men were no good, his dad had said. The only one you could trust was yourself, people are weak, make the most of what you got, you only get one shot at this and all the other stock phrases that a pessimistic, always traveling father would say when he never had time to spend with his son.

Watts' mother wasn't much better. Oh she loved him and cherished him, of that there was no doubt. And Watts returned that love, at least most of the time; when he wasn't obsessed with himself. But she also doted on him and spoiled him. She never disciplined him or scolded him in any way. As Watts grew older he even realized that she was using him to fill the void left from her husband. That only caused him to resent his father even more and to do whatever he could to be better than him. Indeed, he grew up feeling more like the provider than his old man. His father made enough money; that was never really the problem. But he never did more than supply the necessities. Watts wanted much more than that; for himself and for his mother.

But while his attitude and mannerisms came from his father, his brains came from his mother. And she was brilliant! The typical public education bored Watts beyond belief and he probably would have dropped out of school if his mother didn't demand otherwise. Fortunately for him, he found a calling in manipulating the hundreds of gullible children and teenagers surrounding him. By the time he was in middle school he had his hands in all kinds of schemes and even an illegal activity or two. A few businesses he invented on his own like forging signatures and arranging deals between rival gangs. Once he was a junior in high school, his attitude had changed and he was actually happy staying in school. It was the best place to make good money without any real consequences he cared about.

College was a different story. There was no need for that. Within weeks of high school graduation, he had his realtor's license and shortly after that he was able to close a deal between a naïve married couple and a new widow. It was the easiest money he ever made and he never looked back.

But none of his exploits, deals, even adventures if you wanted to call them that ever had the potential like this one did. It was the only reason he even considered working so closely with Francois.

The ferry's metal gangway slammed down on the asphalt road. The loud bang reverberated through the cool evening air and burst Watts from his thoughts. He turned and saw Francois' bony hand sticking out of the blue sedan and waving from the boat. Watts turned away in disgust.

"Idiot," he mumbled.

Watts watched as the cars began driving off the ferry and onto Deer Island. The two blue pick-up trucks with the fishermen inside sped right past him while the small red Honda with the mother and boy pulled off to the side and parked in front of the man dressed in jeans and a flannel who had been waiting nearby. Francois' car was the last one off.

"Bout time," Watts ignored the pleasantries as Francois stopped the blue sedan next to him and rolled down the passenger side window.

"You told me to stay behind," Francois defended himself. He couldn't stand Watts' control obsession. The condescending ass always assumed he was in charge no matter the situation. And yes, New Brunswick was his neck of the woods. But Francois knew his way around too. And this time, Watts would have nothing at all if Francois hadn't decided to call him in the first place. He was beginning to regret that decision more and more. He placed the car in park, pressed the door unlock button on the console to his left and waved Watts in. He wasn't going to let Watts stand over him any more than he had to.

"We need to make this fast," Watts said even before he had finished sitting down next to Francois. He slammed the door shut a little too fast and winced at the loud slam.

"What's the rush?"

"The girl found out," Watts kept his eyes forward and away from Francois. He didn't need his judgment or his whining.

"Found out what?" Francois looked around nervously, unsure of what Watts had let slip. Should he be on the lookout for the police? There was no one around except that family from the ferry. Otherwise the road was deserted.

"Just about everything," Watts remained vague. It was how he kept control and Francois hated it.

"Everything?" Francois almost shouted. He knew better than to lose his temper with Watts. The man had the shortest fuse on earth and his anger was terrifying. Francois only had to experience it once to never want to see it again. It was downright murderous.

"She doesn't know about you," Watts read his mind. Francois had always been the paranoid one; the one who needed to be pushed and prodded and reminded what they were after. If Watts hadn't threatened to go it alone when this all began, Francois would have never broke into the Callahan house in the first place. "But she knows I am working with Kossman and has realized our goal."

"Which goal is that?" Francois pressed. He and Watts had never really spelled out their entire plans with each other. All Francois knew was that they both wanted to get their hands on the packet. What they would do with it afterwards was still up for debate.

Watts shook his head, "We don't have time for this. You need to check in to the hotel and I need to get ready for tomorrow."

"Tomorrow?"

"The girl is ahead of us now," Watts finally turned and looked at Francois. Now that the bad news was out, he could take charge again. He had already worked everything through and as long as Francois played his part, they could make up for their mistakes. "And we can't let that continue."

"What do you plan to do?" A tinge of fear escaped from Francois. He had already committed one crime and did not want to be implicated in another. Yes, this was worth the risk and he was willing to break some rules and even some laws to find one of the greatest secrets in history, but he knew he would never be as willing as Watts was nor as eager. Francois wasn't sure if there was any line Watts wouldn't cross.

"Whatever is necessary," Watts almost smiled.

"Don't," Francois tried to protest. Watts stopped him in his tracks.

"I already told you she could ruin everything," Watt's grew angry. This was why he preferred to work alone. "And I don't need to remind you that she has been lying to us all along."

Francois nodded slowly in agreement. That much was certainly true.

"Maybe if she had come forward right away and been honest with us," Watts reached for the door handle and gently pulled. "We could be a little more understanding, even forgiving." He turned his torso and stepped completely out of the car.

"But where do you think she's going?" Francois raised his voice over the car door being shut.

"I know exactly where she's going," Watts replied as he headed for his own car. "The only place she can go."

Thirty Seven

A day later everyone was settled on the island. Lindsey used Airbnb to find the family a beautiful three bedroom house along the water, complete with full kitchen and outdoor grill. Rob was thrilled that he would actually get to cook for a change. Barbecuing was one of his greatest joys in life. He could sit back, smell the meat on the grill, listen to it sizzle, have a beer and let all the complicated shit of life fade away. It would have been a perfect setting if Lindsey had remembered to tell him the island had no liquor store! He might have lost his temper if the boys weren't so excited about the Kayaks they found in the back yard. Or was it the front yard? Beach houses could be so confusing.

Deborah was also pleased with her choice of accommodation. She found a beautiful 19th century style B&B run by a wonderful young woman who had emigrated from Germany. She didn't even mind driving Deborah around the island when she needed it. Somehow this had suddenly turned into a vacation.

The Agents: Beauvais, Macleod, Foster and Saltman found double rooms at the 45th Parallel motel and restaurant. It was the only choice of either hotel or motel on the entire island, not to mention it had the most popular restaurant. Everyone on the island, at one point in time or another, swung in for a quick bite or just to say hi to the owners. It was that kind of place. Perfect for getting information, Beauvais had told them. Even Francois was staying there unaware that Saltman had pegged him the moment he got involved back in St. Andrews.

Jim Watts had disappeared.

It was a real problem. No one knew where he was, not even Beauvais. The moment he had found Deborah alone on the side of the road, he remembered again what a danger the man could be. Watts was someone they had been watching for years. His hands had been in every controversy, every shady deal, and every questionable case. It was a testament to his cunning that he had avoided jail for so long. With him on the loose and nowhere to be found, Beauvais was afraid the entire mission could fail.

Deborah realized the danger as well, not nearly as much as Beauvais did of course, but she didn't need any more evidence to prove to her that Watts was dangerous. She had to get ahead of him somehow. The only clue she had left was the existence of Apple Island. It might not have anything to do with Franklin, but it should have something to do with Rob's land; if he had any. Maybe whoever owned the island could put her back on track.

Deborah's lovely hostess, a Mrs. Hegel, had been more than willing to arrange a boat ride to the island for her. While Deborah indulged herself over Mrs. Hegel's delicious German breakfast of poached eggs, ham and various cheeses, freshly baked breads, marmalade, honey, and wonderfully strong coffee, the hostess was able to make a few calls to some local fishermen she knew. By the time Deborah was wiping the yoke off the plate with the last bit of rye, she had a name and a time slot. Mrs. Hegel would even give her a ride!

Apple Island was not far off the northwestern coast of Deer Island. It was sandwiched right in between about six other small islands, only one of which was occupied; a salmon fisherman who was looking to start another fish farm there. The boat captain, a man by the name of Jimmy, was also a salmon fisherman and was dressed every inch the part. From his sun bleached hat with the fish hooks clipped around, to the knee high black rubber boots with the red soles, Jimmy was ready for the water. Fortunately for Deborah, he was able to spare the time to give Deborah a quick ride. It would only take about ten minutes at full throttle for the small single engine boat to make it there.

Along the way, Jimmy pointed out the wildlife and the various homes and businesses along the shore. He had been living on Deer Island all of his life and knew just about everyone and everything. He told Deborah about the troubles they all were having with competition from the big Salmon companies, with the fish farms and their worries about a pipeline being built. Deer Island was always on the verge of economic collapse but somehow, through sheer force of will and a lot of luck, they managed to keep their heads above water; pun intended.

Deborah giggled at the pun and then felt a tinge of guilt for lying to Jimmy. She had told him she had an appointment with the owner and that she was expected. She brushed the feeling away quickly though. She knew she certainly couldn't tell him the truth. She wasn't even sure what the truth was. Why was she going to some tiny island in the middle of a bay she had never heard of before yesterday? This should be Rob's journey, not hers. What would he say when he found out she went there without him? Would he be furious? Would he forgive her? Why was she doing this? Her desperation to get Rob back was the only thing she could think of and it startled her to realize it. Wait! Did she want Rob back? She was the one who left him in the first place? No of course she didn't want him back, at least not the way he was now. She wanted the Rob back that she had fallen in love with, her best friend, the father of her children. All of this crazy shit was just getting in the way. What did she expect anyway? The only thing this stupid little trip could lead to was another fight with Rob. Deborah turned her head suddenly and looked back at the fading shoreline of Deer Island. Was it too late to ask Jimmy to turn around?

"Here it is!"

Apple Island was nothing like what she expected. Despite what William had said back at the shack yesterday, she still envisioned Apples somewhere on the island or some kind of Apple theme. All she saw at first were rocks and dirt. There was no beach. There was no three story beach house with windows and a view like she half expected. After all, this might even be Rob's land someday and she couldn't help but daydream of some tropical view with Pina Coladas and sunsets. She knew her expectations were totally unrealistic and ridiculous. This was Canada, not Bermuda. The only trees here were the large pine trees all along the shoreline and even larger boulders that blocked any view and warned all visitors to stay away. The waves were not calm and soothing but angry and violent as they smashed onto the rocky shore with enough force that Jimmy needed to keep the engine going at all times. The tide was coming in he told her, and the bay tides here were so powerful he could easily get trapped in a swell or an unseen rock beneath the surface. Even his vast knowledge of the waters was not immune to the shifting tidal forces of Fundy and Passamaquoddy. It was like a living creature itself, Jimmy had warned her.

They made a complete circle around the island before approaching and if Jimmy hadn't pointed out the house up on the hill or the dock at the shore, Deborah might not have thought anyone lived there at all. Whoever lived there, Deborah thought as she stepped onto the dock, must lead a pretty lonely life. She hoped he wouldn't be too upset that she arrived unannounced.

"I'll be back in a couple of hours," Jimmy waved while the boat slowly drifted away. "Say hi to Lawrence for me!"

"Will do," Deborah waved back. At least now she knew the owner's name.

As the small boat pulled away, Deborah immediately started second guessing herself. She really was in the middle of nowhere. There were no roads, no buildings, no signs of any human life. She took out her cell phone from her pocket and looked at the display; no signal either. What the hell was she doing here?

She turned around and looked up the grassy hill to the house beyond. It was a fine house; two stories, solid gray wooden frame and a sturdy, shingled roof. It looked like any typical colonial home you might find back in Fairfield. She wondered if it had electricity or running water.

No one came out to greet her. It didn't even look like anyone was home. There was no movement, no sounds other than the waves crashing on the surf. What if the owner was in town?

Deborah decided to look around. She still did not have the nerve to walk up to the front door and she realized that maybe if she walked around the island, she might find something that could provide clues about who lived there now or what the island was being used for. She took off her sneakers, stuffed her socks inside them and rolled up her jeans to her knees. She could have dressed better for an island adventure.

The rocks were slippery. With the tide coming in and the algae on the surface, she had to be careful not to fall. Fortunately they were all pretty large, flat, smooth and sturdy. Centuries of tides washing over them had wedged them in pretty tight. The rocks weren't going anywhere. Once she got a rhythm going, she could walk from rock to rock with every step. It was almost like that childhood game she used to play, hopscotch.

About ten minutes later, she had rounded the corner and was completely out of sight of the house. Stopping for a minute to catch her breath, she noticed how quickly the trees took over the landscape and how their shade had darkened the rocks all around her. It was getting harder to see the crevices and algae spots she needed to avoid. A few more steps and it began to get buggy. She waved her arms in front of her face again and again but it only grew worse.

"What the fuck am I doing?" she stopped and looked up. The trees had only grown thicker and darker. There was nothing to look at here. She couldn't even see the island's interior. Deborah shook her head and decided to turn around.

"Shit!" A large bug or fly bit her on the cheek. Deborah swung wildly in the air trying to swat it away. A wave crashed at the base of her feet at the exact same moment causing her to tumble uncontrollably.

"Oh!" she cried as her elbow was the first to land hard on a nearby rock. It had taken all of her weight and immediately began to bleed. Thankfully she had kept her balance enough to prevent herself from hitting her head but that didn't prevent the nausea from forming in her throat. She closed her eyes and gritted her teeth, willing the pain to go away. Her chest heaved up and down as she tried to control her breathing. At least the cold sea water numbed the pain somewhat.

After almost a minute, the pain began to subside and she opened her eyes to examine her elbow. Blood was still streaming from the wound even with the tide washing the rock clean every few seconds. She would need a good amount of stitches.

"Fuck!" she swore again. She lifted her foot to steady herself but nothing happened. She tried again. Was it broken or something? Shit that was all she needed.

It wasn't broken. It was stuck. Somehow when she fell, her foot had twisted in between two sharp edges and become wedged in between. If she pulled too hard she might slash her Achilles tendon wide open. This was not good.

Deborah tried to hold back tears. Her elbow was pulsing and her foot was beginning to throb. The salty spray from the icy water had started to hit her in the face as well. Jimmy wasn't kidding about how fast the tide moved in. She looked all around her. Nothing but rocks and trees; not even a nearby boat she could wave at. What the hell was she going to do?

Deborah did her best to avoid panic. That would only make things worse. She tried moving her foot again. It only slipped in deeper. She held her hand over the elbow wound, trying to stop the bleeding; waste of time. Her heart began to race. Maybe she could move the rocks with her free leg.

She pushed. She screamed. She swore. The rocks were solid. They had to weigh hundreds of pounds each. She couldn't even get any leverage. The algae and water gave the rocks an almost ice like surface. With a gasp, she lay down again. The water continued to rise. She started to breathe faster and faster as her eyes darted back and forth. What could she do? What could she do?

"You know," a voice broke the silence! Deborah snapped her head towards the sound. "Jim!"

"They say the tides in this area are between 10 and 20 feet high," Jim made no move towards Deborah. He had emerged from the tree line and was standing on the small amount of dirt between rocks and tree. "And I would have to assume that with the moon being almost full; it would be closer to 20 feet today."

"Jim, help me please!"

"Have you ever been to Hopewell Rocks Park on the Northwestern edge of the Bay of Fundy?" Jim still made no movement whatsoever. He just stood there in yet another pin stripe suit, calmly watching Deborah struggle. He couldn't believe his luck. Despite his bravado and claims to Francois, he did not have any idea what to do about the girl. He had broken many laws in his life and crossed many lines, but he had never murdered anyone. It was something that he had never really considered. There was always some other way to get what he wanted.

But this situation could not have been more perfect. The girl had left him little choice. He had to stop her. And this wasn't really murder. Indeed, it really was nothing. That's all he would do; nothing. No one would ever know he was here. And even if they did, what could they do about it?

"Hopewell Park?" Deborah shook her head. "No! Why would I go there?" What was he talking about? Why wasn't he helping her? His inaction terrified her.

"It is the best place on the east coast to appreciate the power of the tides."

Deborah turned away and grabbed at her ankle again. It was no use. She would never get it free on her own.

"You can literally walk on the bottom of the ocean floor at low tide," Jim continued calmly. "Then the rangers warn you when the tide is coming in and if you don't retreat quickly, you will find yourself at the bottom of more than 30 feet of water covering where you were standing mere hours ago. It's amazing."

"Jim, please! My foot is stuck. I can't move."

"They say if you are not careful, the tide can wash over you before you know it."

"Jim!" Deborah was beginning to sob. The water had completely covered her foot now and was approaching her knees.

"Why didn't you tell me about the packet?" Jim's tone turned dark.

"Packet; what packet?" Deborah wasn't even sure what he was talking about in her distress. Was this about Franklin? How did he even know?

"You still feign ignorance, even now."

"Jim, you've got to help! I'll die here if I can't get my foot out."

"What else haven't you told me?"

"Nothing! I swear! If you know about the packet, you know everything I do!"

"I knew you would come here," his voice became calm again. He hadn't made up his mind what to do with Deborah until she said yet another lie. "It was the only clue you had. I never realized how stupid you would be though once you got here."

"Jim!" Tears were streaming down Deborah's face. She would never see her boys again. She would never have a chance to fix things with Rob. My god, Rob may never even know what happened to her. The terrifying thought of her body rotting alone on the rocks was unbearable. "Please!"

"Well then," Jim started to turn. "Either you are lying or I have no further need of you anyway." He took a step away from her then turned back. He wondered what he would tell Francois. The old fool would never understand and most certainly disapprove. Better to not tell him at all. "I wonder when they will find you. It really is a shame, such a beautiful woman."

"Wham!" A large two by four piece of wood hit Jim in the back of the head. His body fell forward and crashed onto the smaller rocks on the shoreline.

"That guy's a fucking asshole," a red faced man dressed in blue jean overalls and a simple red t-shirt suddenly appeared. The two by four he had used to fell Jim was still in his hands. "You need some help miss?" he said as he tossed the wood to the side and made his way down to Deborah.

Thirty Eight

"How's that feel?" Deborah's savior finished wrapping up her elbow. After he had carried her away from the rocks and to the house, he had gently placed her comfortably in his living room and begun to treat her wounds. Another half hour later, he had cleaned the wound, stopped the bleeding and bandaged it up enough until she could get it looked at in town or even at home. Lawrence, that was his name she slowly remembered, had a top notch first aid kit in his home that would rival any walk-in clinic. He had to, living alone and so far removed from the "civilized world."

Lawrence Whittaker was a fascinating man. Deborah had expected some kind of Grizzly Adams or Unabomber wacko to be living all alone in the middle of the bay. She could not have been more wrong. Not only was his face perfectly clean shaven with no sign of beard or even sideburns, his curly brown hair was well kept, his manners were gentlemanly bordering on old fashioned and he even wore a cologne that reminded her of Rob. The only "odd" thing about him was the two or three small moles on the left side of his face, probably a result of all the sun he got out here.

Whittaker had known from the moment Deborah arrived that she was on the island. He had noted Jim's arrival as well. Nothing escaped him here on his own little kingdom. After watching both of them for a while, it was easy to decide who to help. Once he had freed Deborah, he left Jim lying unconscious in the dirt to fend for himself. If Deborah had not suggested they move Jim behind the tree line, he may have washed out with the tide.

Watts wasn't dead of course, although both Lawrence and Deborah felt like he deserved it. He would probably wake up hours later with a huge headache and slink off to wherever he came from. They couldn't press charges against him other than perhaps trespassing and Deborah knew if she tried, then everyone would find out about her little escapade. For his part, Whittaker was happy to leave the man lying in the dirt. Jim Watts had crossed paths with Lawrence Whittaker far too many times to count. Almost all of them were in court. Who knows how much more Whittaker could have done with the house and the island if he hadn't spent so much of his time and money trying to keep what was already his.

Apple Island was indeed named for the Appleby family and Lawrence was a member of it. He was not an immediate descendant, but at least the connection was through blood and not just marriage. The reason he held the island in the first place was exactly because of that shaky connection. The original settler, John

Appleby, did indeed own land on Deer Island, in a place called Chocolate Cove. (There was no connection to the candy at all, Deborah was disappointed to learn.) The Whittaker branch however, did not receive any of that land and it took them decades to fight with the King to receive any at all. By then it was too little, too late. In the meantime, Lawrence's great, great, great, great, great grandmother moved the family to this unsettled island and named it after their family while they awaited the land grant that never came.

Jim Watts was just the kind of man who tried to exploit situations like that. Whittaker wasn't even sure why Watts wanted the land in the first place. There was nothing there. If Whittaker himself had not built this house with his own two hands, there would be only trees and rocks. The original house of his ancestors was long gone. Only a hole remained where it had once been.

It had taken Whittaker years to build his house on Apple Island and it was still not complete. It wasn't just the court battles with Watts that slowed him up, everything he needed; the tools, the raw materials, the food, even the nails had to be brought over from the mainland. It had reminded Whittaker of the stories he heard of as a kid about frontiersman who would burn down their own homes before they moved on just to sift through the dust for the precious nails needed for the next house.

He had wanted to give Deborah a tour of course. The simple living room they were in was one of the few rooms left in the house that he still hadn't finished. The old recliner she sat in, the large white square table in the middle of the room, were all going to be replaced on his next few trips. The rest of the house, Lawrence stood a little taller and smiled broadly as he told her, was a wonderful combination of matched colors and schemes with an appreciation for his own personal history and that of the community. Indeed he had an entire room reserved for his French Colonial antique collection. But unfortunately, Deborah was in no condition to walk around so Whittaker contented himself with giving her the history of the place. He told her how he first excavated a foundation, why he chose this spot overlooking the mouth of the bay, what items he had to bring first, and the storms that set him back every few months or few years.

Deborah listened politely at first, then intently as he continued. She could not believe how much she took for granted back home. Not just the basics like electricity and indoor plumbing, but 7-eleven trips for the quick milk run, the supermarket trips, even her morning coffee ritual; they all made her feel like royalty as Whittaker explained every mundane task needed to build an island house from scratch. She could not believe he had done it all by himself.

Whittaker's family had moved away years ago, generations ago. During prohibition, they had done fine smuggling alcohol across the border but once the Great Depression hit, Deer Island suffered like the rest of the world and the family slowly made their way to Eastport and later other parts of the United States. Whittaker's grandmother was the only one who stayed and once she passed away, Lawrence's hold on Apple Island fell into just enough uncertainty that Watts was able to challenge it in court.

So when Deborah let it slip that she too had come here searching for land, Lawrence was immediately suspicious. He had faced too many lawsuits to trust anyone looking at his island. He might have even thrown her out until Deborah mentioned Rob and Nana. Suddenly, Lawrence became all smiles again. He actually had been in contact with Rob's mother for years when Nana began looking into an island that seemed to bear her maiden name. She had even done some research which helped him win his court cases. By the time Nana realized Apple Island was not in her family's branch, she and Lawrence had become friends. "A friend of Patricia's is a friend of mine," Lawrence had called back to Deborah on his way to fetch her some water and something to eat.

"So I know you came here seeking answers," he returned a few moments later with a bottle of water, a loaf of bread and a small marble cutting board with various slices of cheese and salami, "but I feel as if you need more."

"Thank you," Deborah took the water gently and eyed the cutting board. The ordeal had left her famished. She took a huge gulp of water, almost half the bottle, lay it down on the table next to her and reached for a slice of salami and cheese. Her movements were slow and painful as she tried to keep her elbow from moving or rubbing against the bandage Lawrence had made. "I do feel the need to find out a little more. Are you saying that Rob definitely has no land up here?"

"Nothing dealing with land is ever definite here," Whittaker gave a wry smile. He knew that first hand. "There could be another island somewhere or even something on the mainland you haven't found. Patricia was looking at that possibility shortly before she died."

"Really?" Deborah leaned back a little in the dark brown recliner Lawrence first settled her in. It was a little old but that just made the cushions that much softer. "Do you have any idea where?"

"Let me show you something," Lawrence pushed back on the small wooden stool he had been sitting on to dress her bandage. He smiled like a little boy with a secret and left the room.

Deborah nibbled some more on the meat and cheese while she waited for him to return. She stopped for a second in mid chew as the day's events flashed in her mind's eye again. She had almost died; died! It was terrifying. It was humiliating. She felt her elbow throb as if she had fallen again and wondered if she would even be able to walk. The swelling on her ankle was growing even with the ice pack Lawrence had put there.

"I've gathered all this during my time in court," Lawrence rushed back into the room carrying the largest yellow envelope Deborah had ever seen. It reminded her of the x-ray packets they put the films in. He placed the entire envelope gently on the large table in the middle of the room and reached inside.

"These are maps of Deer Island, New Brunswick and our borders with the United States."

"Borders?" Deborah noticed the use of the plural form of the word. "What do you mean borders?"

"One of the reasons I have had so much trouble with my land is because the border of Canada and the United States is still fuzzy." Lawrence reached over and gently helped Deborah stand up and hobble to the table. Her ankle shot a needle like pain into her head and she flinched. Leaning on the table itself, seemed to take away most of the pain.

"Really?" Deborah feigned ignorance although her surprise at her luck was just as shocking. Did he have any idea about the Franklin packet?

"There is still an island on the edge of the bay which both sides dispute." Deborah looked down at the map Lawrence had spread out in front of her. It looked like a current map. She could see Eastport, Deer Island and even Campobello easily. A red circle was drawn around Apple Island itself but his finger was covering a different tiny island at the mouth of the bay. "It's called Machias Seal Island."

"And both sides claim it?"

"They have for years. Fortunately no one lives on it but that doesn't mean it's not important."

"I don't understand."

"Remember that land borders define water borders as well." Lawrence sounded like he had said this before, maybe many times. "So even though there is no one on the island, it's unclear who owns the water around it."

"And the fish in that water."

"Actually the lobster," Lawrence was pleased to see how quickly Deborah caught on. "And there is a lot of it. Maine lobstermen and New Brunswick lobstermen both get a large amount of their lobster from around that island.

They call it a gray area."

"But what does that have to do with you?"

"It gets worse," Lawrence frowned. He pulled out some more maps. "I've had to go all the way back to before the American Revolution," Deborah's ears perked up, "in order to fight my claim to this island."

"Really!"

"No matter where the border between the United States and Canada is, it goes somewhere through Passamaquoddy Bay. The original line was said to be a river called the St. Croix but once they started work on the Treaty, they disagreed over which river was the original St. Croix. Was it the Schoodic or Digdeguash or one of these others?"

"I thought the border cut right in between Eastport, Maine and Deer Island," Deborah tried to wrap her head around all of this. She had no idea it was so confusing.

"It is today," Lawrence replied, "but that was not always the case. Look," he pointed at the next map, "this map is from 1842, right after they signed the Ashburton Treaty which ended a war."

"A war? Between who?"

"The United States and Canada."

"I never heard of it."

"No one in the States has. But we all know it up here. Guess what it was over."

"The border?"

"Bingo!" he pointed at her chest. "And that was more than 50 years after the American Revolution."

"I had no idea."

"Now look at this map," he pulled another one out. This was even harder to read, with a few yellow spots and what looked like a coffee stain in the middle of Maine, "It was made shortly after the Revolution. Notice the border looks different?"

Deborah looked at the two maps. The border had changed! It was easy to see on this blow up of the area.

"Did you ever hear of the Jay Treaty?" Lawrence reached across for one of the few remaining pieces of Salami on the cutting board. Deborah had become too interested to eat anymore and he was hungry too.

"No," Deborah said softly. She was embarrassed by her lack of history knowledge, even with a college degree.

"It was written a decade after the Revolution because, in part, the border was so confusing."

"Confusing?"

"I have a copy of the treaty right here," Lawrence took a regular piece of paper and handed it to Deborah. It looked like a computer print-out copy of Article five and the top sentence had been underlined. "Read that sentence."

"Whereas doubts have arisen," Deborah read aloud as a chill ran up her spine. What kind of doubts? About land? About the border? "What River was truly intended under the name of the River St. Croix mentioned in the said Treaty of Peace-"

"They messed up!" His voice was edged with anger and frustration. Deborah leaned away from him as far as she could. Her ankle reminded her not to move to fast.

"Franklin, Jay, and Adams; they made it so vague that the border has been in dispute for over 200 years!" Lawrence leapt out of his seat and waved his arms. This was the first time in a long time that he had been able to express his frustration to someone. He couldn't bounce around and wave his arms in court, but he could do it in his own home. "Can you believe it?" he continued, "so many lives have been affected by that little line."

"What line?"

"Look here," he stopped abruptly and returned to the yellow envelope. There was one last map. It had to have been drawn even before the Revolution, maybe even when Indians still lived there. "Do you see the St. Croix river?"

Deborah stared down at the map. It was hard to read; not because of the reproduction. The map lines were fairly clear and distinguishable. Lawrence had a fine copy. The problem swas in the map itself. There were few labels and the labels that there were did not always match an exact spot. She couldn't find the river.

"It's right there," Lawrence reached over her shoulder and pointed. "But you wouldn't know that from the map in front of you."

Deborah looked up. She did not understand what he was getting at.

"The original Treaty of 1783 that Franklin, Adams and Jay negotiated between the United States and England said that the border between the two countries, the border running right outside my home," he pointed out the double framed windows to the sunny blue sky beyond, "starts at the mouth of the river St. Croix and runs northwest."

Deborah looked down at the map and then back up at Lawrence. "But-"

"But the mouth of the river is unclear!" He slammed his palm on the table. "It's unclear! Get it! Get it! If Franklin or Adams or Jay had been more clear with the border, if it had not been so vague, then there would be no need for the Jay treaty saying 'Whereas doubts have arisen what River', there would be no need for the war of 1842, and there would probably be no dispute between our two countries today! My god! If only!"

Deborah was stunned. She couldn't believe how simple it was. Everything depended on everything else and it all went back to Franklin. It had all seemed so vague before, like a joke or a footnote in history. But if the packet were indeed real, if there was something in it that made the border clear and removed any doubts, then that would affect everything else written as a result of it. The consequences were staggering.

"Deborah?" Lawrence suddenly stopped pacing and turned towards her. She did not look well. "Are you okay?"

"It's all so unbelievable," Deborah wiped her forehead. She had no idea how pale she had become. Perhaps it was the blood loss, or the shock of the revelation or a mixture of the two. She reached for the bottle of water and weakly brought it to her mouth.

"Let's get you back," Lawrence realized.

Thirty Nine

It was their first time alone since the kiss and the silence was deafening. Lindsey and Rob sat awkwardly in the car neither one of them knowing what to say or how to begin and they hated it. Both wanted a return to the playful jabs and light hearted friendship of before. This stupid tension, the classic "kind you can cut with a knife" was absolutely the worst!

They had left the boys alone by request. Bobby and Adam wanted to just hang out, enjoy the beach house and maybe do some kayaking. Both of them had used Kayak's before in camp and just wanted to do something without their father standing over them like a nervous mother hen. Besides, Rob was desperate to find some beer he could barbeque with and Lindsey felt like if they went to the restaurant, they might sell them a few bottles. It would also be a good place to find out more about the island and where they could go next.

Problem was, the drive to the restaurant was longer than either of them expected. There were no signs to read or any real scenery to distract them. New Brunswick Route 772 was just a plain dark asphalt road with the single painted yellow line running down the center and tall pine trees on both sides. Only once in a while could they get a glimpse of the bay beyond. With little traffic and no traffic lights, there was not even any sound other than the hum of the engine and the tires on the road. At one point, Rob thought he could even hear Lindsey breathing.

"It was just a stupid kiss," Rob finally blurted out. He couldn't take it anymore.

"It could have been more." Did that mean that Lindsey wanted more or was it a warning of its danger?

"I wanted more." He was going to have to be honest, completely brutally honest if there was any chance of recovery from this. "At least I did at the time."

Did that mean he didn't want it anymore?

"I wanted more too," Lindsey kept her eyes forward, staring at the road. She couldn't look at Rob yet.

"You were so fuckin' hot," Rob was starting to get aroused again. *Dammit*, he swore to himself. He thought of a cold shower and his classroom.

"You've got to settle things with your wife," Lindsey took control and threw the last bit of emotional water in Rob's face. It worked. "I'm not going to be some kind of marriage wrecking bimbo."

"Do you want me to?"

"Yes. No. Shit." Lindsey shook her head and started again. "I don't want you to do anything on my account." She finally looked at Rob. "I want it to go back to the way it was. I want to be your friend again. I want to laugh with you in the locker room again. I don't want to wreck your marriage, destroy our friendship and our team."

"Me neither," Rob quickly agreed. He was sure of that.

"But I can't deny how I feel either." And back to square one. Lindsey looked away from him again.

"How do you feel?"

"I like you Rob," She looked at him again. It was like a tennis match. "I like you a lot. You're a great friend, honest, reliable and even a little funny."

"A little?" he laughed.

"A little." A smile; finally!

"But I don't know if I like you in that other way at least not yet, and I don't know if ever."

Rob did not respond. That hurt; At least a little bit, even if the feelings were probably reciprocated. He felt the same away about Lindsey. The sex appeal was obvious, but the feelings that made a relationship work, the connection or the spark so to speak, to be blunt, the love, he wasn't so sure if that was there either. It had definitely been there with Deborah and maybe it still was.

"I mean sex, God-damn," she continued to think out loud, "it's been a while, a fucking long while. And you and I could do some real damage." She was starting to get hot as well. She needed to move on, fast. "But do we really want to destroy everything we have, everything you have with your family for some fun in the sheets?"

"No," Rob looked directly at Lindsey. It was the first time he had the entire ride. He may still be turned on but he wasn't lying, to Lindsey or to himself. He didn't want to ruin it all. They had come to the edge of the proverbial cliff and looked down. Certainly, a part of the attraction was the danger of a relationship. The tension, the flirting, the excitement of something new, played a role for sure. Once that was taken away however, once they both could see where the sex could take them, they realized it was not somewhere either of them wanted to go; At least for now.

"Me neither," Lindsey held his stare. She placed her hand gently on Rob's arm. It was a bold move and it worked. In one simple gesture Lindsey had said to both of them that she could still be friends with Rob; that she could touch him and smile and it would not lead to sex. It was almost as if they had each taken a blood oath in that little moment. Rob breathed a sigh of relief and smiled back at her for the first time since the kiss.

"Let's get some beer!" he grinned. Their errand was more important now than ever.

Rob slowed the car as it rounded the corner. The 49th Parallel Restaurant and Motel was just ahead. He could already see the big lobster painted on the sign as his mouth began to water. They had been in Canada for almost a week now and he hadn't eaten any lobster yet. How could that be? He would have to get some soon.

Set back a little more from the road was a large gravel parking lot for the motel with two or three cars and a dirty brown pick-up truck parked in front. The motel was just one long rectangular building with a big red metal roof. It couldn't have had more than 10 rooms, each one with a double window and plain white door. Surrounded by tall trees on all sides, it seemed out of place and alone as if it wasn't sure it belonged. It wasn't run down or dangerous or anything, not like the kind that you found in a city where prostitutes and drug dealers hang out. It was just a simple motel, non-descript and functional, like everything else on the island. The restaurant just beyond was a little brighter and welcoming, with white paint, a small balcony and even some flower beds at the entrance. It was not directly attached but was an easy walk from the rooms. You didn't even need to cross the road. In fact, it looked like someone was leaving their room and heading to it right then.

"Rob; slow down!" Lindsey commanded. He almost hit the brakes and skidded it was so abrupt.

"What?"

"Look at that guy," Lindsey bent down in her seat as if she was afraid of being seen and pointed at the man headed towards the restaurant. He was scrawny and strange looking. "Recognize him?"

"Holy shit!"

"It's Francois!"

"What the fuck is he doing here?"

"He couldn't have followed us."

Rob sped up past the restaurant, hoping Francois didn't notice. He pulled the car deep off to the side of the road using the tall trees as a shield and threw it into park. "You think he saw us?"

"Didn't seem to; his head was down and he was reading the signs in the window."

"What'll we do?"

"Did you see which room he came from?" Lindsey had. She was already forming a plan.

"Yeah."

"Let's check it out."

"You serious?" Rob was surprised at Lindsey's boldness and a little nervous as well.

"Absolutely," Lindsey turned and looked back toward the Restaurant. She could still see the sign but not the building. "It's about fucking time we put the puck in his zone."

Rob chuckled at the hockey analogy and looked back at the motel. He noticed the trees were not as thick there as they were on other parts of the island. "We can cut through behind the Restaurant and swing right to the motel."

Lindsey nodded, opened the car door and quietly shut it behind her. Rob did the same. Within in a few minutes they were safely in front of the motel room. No one had seen them and no one was in the parking lot. The other rooms all had their blinds closed. Rob looked around again and then back at Lindsey. He reached for the door handle. It was just a regular brass knob like you would find in anyone's home, not one of those fancy hotel key doors.

"You just going to open it?"

"Maybe we will get lucky." Either the old joke about Canadians never locking their doors was right or Francois had forgotten to lock it.

"Don't touch anything yet," Lindsey whispered as they both stepped in and she quietly closed the door. "We don't want him to know we were in here."

The room was impeccably neat. Both double beds were still made with sheets and a cover that came from the last century. The wallpaper was slightly faded and two framed pictures of sea life hung on the walls. The only sign that the room was occupied at all was the small black suitcase lying on the bed and some paper and a pen lying on top of a folder on the small desk. Lindsey headed right for it.

"What is it?" Rob whispered. He thought about turning on a light but enough sunlight streamed through the white plastic window blinds that they could see what they needed to see.

"A picture of the back of your car," Lindsey had opened the folder and was already beginning to get angry. "A picture of your house, a half picture of the Franklin letter which he managed to take before you ripped it away."

"Son of a bitch," Rob swore.

"The letter we found in St. Andrews."

Of course; Rob knew that was coming.

"And something I don't recognize." Lindsey's voice trailed off as she investigated the paper. It was definitely a copy of something much older. Francois must have got it from an archive or a library. It looked like a list of some sort.

"What is it?" Rob took a step closer and looked over her shoulder. He failed to notice the shadow in front of the window.

"The names," Lindsey looked up at Rob. Her shoulders tensed, "many of them match the names on Nana's list."

"From the index?"

Lindsey didn't reply. She looked down at the paper again. "And below the names is another list with things like letter to Adams or received from Shelburne."

"Who's Shelburne?"

"I don't know. But I think we should take it."

"Take it?" Rob was nervous. Now it had become theft as well as breaking and entering. Another shadow passed by the front window. He noticed that time.

"If we have it, Francois doesn't."

"We better go," Rob insisted. The shadow had gone past but his nerves were shot. They had what they needed and Francois could come back at any minute.

Lindsey carefully put the rest of the folder back the way she had found it.

Hopefully Francois would not notice right away that anything was missing, especially since the paper had been at the bottom of the pile anyway. She turned and quietly followed Rob out the door.

"You folks mind telling me what you're doing?" A man dressed in a t-shirt and blue jeans stepped into their path. He had appeared out of nowhere.

Rob froze. His right arm flung out instinctively stopping Lindsey in her tracks. The man looked like a tourist and his accent was definitely from the States. It even sounded like a Boston accent.

"Were you breaking into that room?" Another man appeared as well. He was also dressed like a tourist but his accent was harder to place. He was obviously an African –American, if nothing else the U.S. coast guard t-shirt gave the American part away. With his perfectly formed buzz cut hair top and goatee, he looked like he could be a cover boy for GQ. His partner on the other hand looked almost uncomfortable in his pink Floyd t-shirt and new balance sneakers. He must have been at least a decade or two older. His jet black, stringy hair showed spots of gray and behind his glasses his face showed signs of wrinkles. They made an odd pair.

Agents Saltman and Foster seized upon this opportunity. They of course did not have any jurisdiction to arrest Callahan here in Canada, but they had already alerted the Canadian agents and they would be there at any minute. They didn't care about the crime, but they knew they could at least question Callahan legitimately and go from there.

"We just got the rooms mixed up," Rob thought that might work. "We're two doors down. C'mon honey," he motioned to Lindsey.

"You stole something from that man's room," Saltman and Foster shuffled to their left and blocked the space between the motel and the old dark blue sedan parked in front. Saltman nodded to the paper in Lindsey's hand. She snapped it behind her back but it was too late.

"We had that when we came in," Rob sounded silly now. He knew that he had been found out. He looked around the parking lot considering his options. These guys were just tourists, not cops. He wasn't even sure if there were cops on the island at all. There were no cameras around and no one else in sight. He could even see his car parked through the trees.

"Lindsey go!" Rob shoved Saltman square in the chest with the full force of both of his hands. Saltman tumbled back a few feet and slammed into the passenger door of Francois' parked car. Lindsey did the same to Foster and leapt in between the two men. She sprinted towards the woods.

"Hey," Foster reached for her but grabbed only thin air. He had not stumbled far and with a second swing was able to get a hand on Rob's shoulder. Rob turned and slugged Foster right in the jaw. It was his classic hockey brawl reflex. Foster staggered but did not fall.

Saltman recovered, grabbed Rob's free arm and twisted it up behind his back. Rob cried out in pain then slugged Saltman in the jaw with the other fist. The blood started to flow out of Saltman's nose. Foster then caught Rob in the gut. It was right on his diaphragm. Rob's breath left him completely and he bent over.

Foster's head snapped forward and he fell into Rob. Lindsey had run back and punched Foster in the back of the head. Saltman tackled her. Rob took a huge breath of air to re-inflate his lungs then raised his fist to strike Foster again.

Suddenly Rob felt a sharp pain on his free hand and heard a loud click. "Alright that's enough," a voice from behind him said. Rob turned just as the stranger grabbed his other hand and snapped the cuffs on them as well. "You're under arrest buddy."

Forty

It was a tight fit in Beauvais' and Macleod's motel room. The two Canadian agents stood side by side in between the beds, arms crossed staring down at their captives while Foster stood over by the door; just in case. Rob sat on the edge of the bed, hands cuffed behind his back. Lindsey sat next to him, un-cuffed. She had immediately surrendered when Macleod flashed his I.D. and none of the agents felt the need to cuff her as well. They would have even let Rob off if Saltman wasn't still pissed about his nose. He stood in the back part of the room by the sink, rinsing the white washcloth whenever it filled up with his blood.

"So, Mr. Callahan, Ms. Craig," Beauvais began. Lindsey and Rob both looked at each other, wondering how he knew their names already. They hadn't said a word since they were quickly ushered into the nearby motel room and no one had looked in their pockets. "What are we going to do with you?"

"How do you know our names?" Rob looked at all four men, trying to size them up. Were they all cops? *Shit had he slugged a cop?* All of them were dressed as tourists, how was he to know?

"We've been following you for quite some time," Beauvais glanced at his partners for approval. Macleod and Foster both nodded, Saltman just shrugged his shoulders. It wasn't normal procedure and he still wasn't sure it was a good idea. But the plan Beauvais came up with seemed to be a good one and they had a way to control Callahan regardless, "since before you arrived in our country."

"Who the fuck are you guys?" Lindsey started to stand up but quickly thought better of it. She didn't want to be cuffed like Rob.

"I'm Agent Beauvais, this is Agent Macleod," he pointed at his partner. Macleod was dressed as a tourist like Foster and Saltman. He looked the most comfortable in that role. With a Toronto Maple Leafs t-shirt, Levis jeans and black Nike sneakers, the outfit seemed like a second skin to him. Beauvais, on the other hand, looked even more uncomfortable and awkward than Saltman. He had a button down short sleeve dress shirt and light blue slacks that made him look more prepared for an afternoon of golf or a casual business meeting. "We represent the Canadian Intelligence Service."

Rob and Lindsey's eyes both widened and their jaws dropped simultaneously in shock. They were screwed!

"Representing your own country's CIA are the two men you have already met," a wry smile appeared on Beauvais' face, "Agent Foster," Matt nodded from his position by the door, "and Agent Saltman doing repairs by the sink." Saltman glared.

"Seems like overkill for a breaking and entering," Lindsey said sarcastically. She desperately hoped this wasn't about the Franklin letter even though all the evidence appeared otherwise. Why else would the CIA and CSIS be involved?

"Let's just get everything out in the open," Beauvais ignored Lindsey's comment, pulled the black chair from the desk, swung it around backwards and sat directly in front of she and Rob. Their faces were only a few feet apart. "We know about the Franklin letter, we know about the packet, we know about the kids and we know what you found in St. Andrews."

Lindsey did some quick calculations. They didn't know about the letter in Fredericton. Did they know about Francois?

"We also know you are being followed by a pawn shop dealer," Beauvais seemed to read her mind, "as well as his partner."

"He has a partner?"

"They've worked together for years." Beauvais did not tell them about Deborah.

"How do you know all this?" Rob said. He couldn't believe he had been so naïve.

"We have our methods Mr. Callahan. What we don't have is your cooperation."

"Cooperation? What do you want from us?"

"We want you to tell us everything you know," Saltman took a step forward and tossed the bloody washcloth in the sink. The blood had stopped flowing finally and he wanted to get this going forward. "And we want you to continue to tell us everything as you uncover it."

"Why should we?"

"Well Mr. Callahan," Saltman took another step closer. He placed his left hand on the edge of Beauvais' chair. "I could appeal to your patriotism and tell you this is a matter of national security. Or I can appeal to your sense of justice and remind you that this could become an ugly international incident." Saltman interrupted himself for a moment and gestured toward Foster. "But I sense that would not be enough."

Foster grabbed an 8 and a ½ by 11 inch manila folder from the desk and walked towards the bed. "You seem to be the stubborn, independent type Mr. Callahan," Saltman continued as Foster's fingers waited along the edge of the folder, "the kind of man who thinks he knows better than everyone else."

Rob didn't like Saltman's tone. It was like something out of a supervillain movie. He almost expected a maniacal laugh.

"You also seem to be a decent family man Mr. Callahan," Saltman motioned again to Foster who slowly opened the folder in front of them. The picture of Rob and Lindsey kissing had been blown up to full size and lay right in front of them. Their lips could not be locked any tighter. Rob's heart sank.

"We don't want to use this Mr. Callahan," Rob was barely listening. Just after they had worked everything out in the car, he thought it was going to be alright. What was he going to do now? What were they going to do with the picture? Would they show the boys? Deborah? What if the team saw it? He was fucked; fucked, fucked, fucked, fucked, fucked! His head dropped to his chin and his eyes closed.

"And we won't use this," Saltman quickly continued. Despite the bloody nose, he had no desire to hurt Rob; none of the agents did. Callahan was a good guy. He was a decent father, a teacher and a good citizen. He was exactly the kind of man whose lives they had sworn to protect, "as long as you cooperate."

"Cooperate?" Rob slowly lifted his head up. It felt like a 50 pound dead weight and it took all his strength just to keep it there, "How?"

"First of all," Beauvais took over, "no one is to know we are government agents. We need to keep our cover. We are simply here to enjoy the island and snap some pictures."

"Ok," Rob mumbled. Lindsey nodded her head as well. She felt as defeated as he did.

"We need you to share any information you find with us and if you are about to uncover the packet, you need to contact us before you obtain it."

Rob and Lindsey looked at each other again. That was a much bigger request. It truly meant they had lost. The packet would not be theirs. They would have no say in what happened with it, whether they wanted to sell it, donate it to a museum or keep it for themselves, the choice would be out of their hands. It was like they were just pawns, working for the government.

"Mr. Callahan," Beauvais prompted. Rob looked at the picture again. Foster was still holding it open.

"OK, OK" Rob said. He looked at Lindsey. She just nodded; she couldn't even lift her head. She felt as bad as Rob did, maybe even worse. In many ways this was her mission as much as if not more than Rob's. She had taken the lead in the entire adventure. It had been her idea to come to Canada. It had been her idea to go to the archives, to go to Deer Island, to buy the books, to do the research. It was the first time in years she had felt so alive. Sure, she loved her work, she loved the idea of it and the fact she was making a difference in people's lives. But it had also become routine, almost monotonous. She had been trapped in the hectic professional world with no end in sight and no way out. She was finally feeling alive again, excited again, like she had back when she had been in college. And now, it was all coming crashing down. Everything she had done, all the energy and the time she had put into this and it had all been for nothing; nothing!

"Excellent," Saltman waved his hand at Foster who closed the folder and placed it back on the desk. Lindsey's heart lifted for a moment wondering if she could somehow steal it. That would be useless though, she realized immediately, her dejection driving even deeper. They must have a digital copy somewhere too.

"Agent Foster is typing our contact info into your phone," Saltman pointed again in Foster's direction. Rob glared at Foster. How did he get Rob's phone? During the fight? Rob never felt a thing. "Whenever you find anything or need to get a hold of us, you will contact this number; Understood?"

Rob nodded and watched Foster tapping on his phone. His mind was still trying to take it all in. They had lost; completely and totally lost. All of it was a waste of time. He wasn't even sure he wanted to go on. What would his boys say? Deborah? The team? Maybe they could just let him go home and he could leave the information with them.

Rob's phone buzzed in Foster's hand. He had received a text. It could only be the boys. He had told them to text whenever they decided to do something. "Are those my boys?"

"Says Adam," Foster replied.

"Can I see it?"

"He says they are going kayaking," Foster made no motion to return the phone.

"Ask them where," Rob racked his brain trying to figure out some way he could clue the boys in on what was happening.

Foster tapped on the phone. The entire room was quiet awaiting a response.

The phone buzzed. "Into the bay," Foster said. "The shore is boring."

"Tell them-" Rob stopped. Foster was already typing rapidly on his phone. "Hey!" Rob shouted.

"Aren't you staying near the southern part of the island, not too far from the park?" Foster ignored Rob's protest. Something was clearly on his mind. His jaw was set and he sounded worried. He tapped some more on the phone.

"Hey!" Rob shouted again. "What are you doing?"

"When is high tide?" Foster ignored Rob again and asked Macleod. *What the hell was going on?*

"In an hour or so," Macleod leaned over and read the message on the phone in Foster's hand. His face fell.

"Did your boys read up on the waters around here before they left?" Macleod asked Rob.

"I- I don't know," Rob looked at Lindsey then back at Macleod. "There was something laminated on the kitchen counter, but I don't know if they read it. What the fuck is going on!"

"Doesn't sound like they did," Foster answered. He held the phone up. "Listen; we are heading out towards the border. Bobby thinks it would be cool if we paddled to the United States and back."

"So?"

"Fuck!" Beauvais stood up abruptly almost knocking over the chair. He knew what that meant as well.

"What the fuck is going on God dammit!" Rob jumped off the bed and glared. Cuffs or no cuffs, government agents or no, he was going to find out what was happening to his boys.

"Old Sow," Foster said slowly. He was hoping Rob knew what he was talking about.

"Old Sow?" Rob didn't know.

"The whirlpool."

"There's a fucking Whirlpool! What the hell!"

Macleod already had his keys out and was moving towards Rob. "We will explain in the car," Macleod swiftly plugged the key into the cuffs and unbuckled them. Rob instinctively waved his hands in freedom. "Your boys are in terrible danger. Let's go!"

Deborah kept looking at her phone. When would she finally get a signal?

She turned around and watched Apple Island recede in the distance. She wondered if she would ever go back.

"Shouldn't take too long to get to shore," Lawrence shouted over the motor. He was still standing in the back of the little gray boat, probably looking for sea life to point out. Normally he sat on the back seat, which really was a bench, and comfortably held the throttle of the single engine craft. It was closer to a row boat with an engine than anything else. Still, it was enough though to get Lawrence back and forth to the mainland and not much else. He didn't need to go sightseeing or fishing with it. He had a much larger boat docked on the main island for that.

"Maybe we will get lucky and see a whale," he scanned the horizon for Deborah. Lawrence didn't care that much. He had seen so many whales, dolphin and seals in his life that they were as natural to him as litter was to a city dweller. Difference was he could take pride in what there was to see, and he almost always did.

"That would be nice," Deborah kept her eyes on the phone. She had no idea how many messages she had missed and needed to get in touch with her hostess back at the B&B. She didn't want to ask Lawrence for anything else.

"You know Mrs. Callahan..." Deborah let Lawrence's voice trail off into background noise. The signal finally came on and the text's poured in. Most of them were from Bobby.

"Hey mom, mom you there, mom? Mom? Yo!" there must have been at least 20 messages just asking her where she was. Finally she scrolled down to the most recent ones and read. The time stamp was about 15 minutes ago. The messages said something about kayaking to Maine. They must have already left.

Deborah stopped reading. Something Lawrence was saying nagged at her. "What were you saying about the tides around here?" she looked up from her phone and called back to him.

"I said that we have some of the strongest tides in the world up here and boaters have to be very careful, especially at times like this when the moon is full and the tide is so high."

Deborah knew exactly what he meant. She had felt it first-hand. "Is it safe for small boats like kayaks?"

"As long as you stay close to shore and know what you are doing!"

Deborah felt a sudden sense of dread. Her boys had only been on kayaks a few times in their life. She scrolled back down on Bobby's texts and read it again; "We're going to head out into the bay towards Maine!"

"What if you don't?"

"Don't what?"

"Don't stay close to shore in a kayak?"

"Well usually it's no big deal," Lawrence could hear the fear in Deborah's voice. He wasn't sure of the source but did not want to fuel it, "Especially on this side of the island, with all these smaller islands around." He waved his hand at the many islands, including Apple Island, dotting the seascape around them. "But it can be a little rough on the other side, especially near the whirlpool."

"Whirlpool!" Deborah's eyes went wide. "There's a whirlpool?"

"Old Sow," Lawrence remained calm, "One of the biggest in the world."

"Is it on the southern end?" That is where the boys were staying with Rob.

"Yeah."

"Near the border with Maine?" Deborah was close to panic now.

"Yeah."

"Oh my god!" her hand covered her mouth, "Oh my god! We've got to warn them!"

Forty One

"I didn't even think whirlpools were real," Lindsey said from the back seat of the double cabin truck. She was sitting next to Foster with Macleod in front of him and Beauvais at the wheel. Rob was driving his own car with Saltman in the passenger seat. They weren't ready to trust them yet.

"They sure are," Foster replied. He glanced forward over Beauvais shoulder and looked at the speedometer. The truck could handle high speed no problem but Foster wasn't so sure it could handle the curves.

"Do they swallow up boats and stuff like in the movies?"

"They can. But they don't really anymore. Between motorized power and the navigation of the seas, we know where just about every tidal phenomenon is."

"You sound like you are talking from experience."

"10 years in the coast guard," Foster smiled.

"So the kids will see warning signs then right?"

"There are no signs in the water."

"There's one by the lighthouse," Beauvais offered. Most of his focus was on keeping the truck on the road. "But it's an information sign, not a warning and you can only see it from the park."

###

"Please hurry," Deborah pleaded. Her right foot was on the edge of the bow and she leaned forward almost into the water as if that would somehow make them go faster. The strong wind whipped her long black hair like a whirling dervish and the spray kicked up from Lawrence's boat soaked her shirt but none of that mattered. She had to get to the boys.

"I'm at full throttle," Lawrence assured her.

Deborah looked at her phone. No response from the boys. She tried calling again; "Score!" Bobby's voicemail screamed. They must have put their phones away.

"How dangerous is it?" She didn't want to ask, but she couldn't stop herself.

"It's not to be fooled with," Lawrence had a healthy respect for the power of the Bay. He had seen too many storms, too many wrecks and too many fools. It had been a while though since he heard of anyone getting caught in Old Sow, "especially without a motor."

"Won't they see it ahead of time?"

"They might."

"Might?"

"It's not always that easy to see and sometimes by the time you do, it's too late."

###

"Can't he go any faster?" Rob was practically on the old brown truck's bumper.

"Take it easy," Saltman kept a level voice. Rob was close to bursting and Saltman was worried this could put him over the edge.

"Easy for you to say, your kids' lives aren't in danger."

"They'll be ok," Saltman was unconvincing to say the least.

"There's gotta be other boats out there," Rob hoped. "Someone is bound to warn them."

"Maybe the ferry, it lands at the southernmost point."

"Maybe?"

"It only runs once an hour."

"Well there's got to be other boats," Rob knew how desperate that sounded. He had already seen what little boat traffic there was in the area. It was nothing like the waters back in the states. That was part of the appeal of the bay. Almost everyone was too busy fishing or working to be out on the water. There were no pleasure crafts or sail boats that he had seen at all. The jet-ski, windsurfing crowd was non-existent. Saltman did not even bother to reply.

"God dammit," Rob gunned the engine and swerved his Camry over the double yellow line and into the other lane. Fortunately there were no oncoming cars in his way. His speedometer quickly swung past 90 as he raced past the truck. He couldn't wait anymore.

###

"Will they be able to get out of it if they get stuck?" Deborah continued looking for something to hope for. Her boys were strong. They were young. They were hockey players. Maybe they could paddle through it.

"If they don't panic, they might. The old girl has been known to just spit boats out once she's had her fun."

"Fun?" Deborah snapped.

"Sorry. But seriously," Lawrence tried to reassure her. "Plenty of people have been caught in the whirlpool and survived. There even are a few idiots who started an Old Sow survivors club."

"Were any of them in Kayaks?"

"I'm not sure."

###

Bobby placed the paddle gently on his lap. This was easy. With the tide coming in, he barely had to paddle at all, especially since he had to keep stopping to wait for his brother.

"C'mon slow poke," he turned back to Adam and called. He was about 30 feet back in the yellow Kayak. Bobby had taken the red one.

"I saw an eagle," Adam made a few strong paddles to catch up to his brother. Once you got caught in an eddy, it was easy to rush forward.

"Where?"

"Over there," Adam pointed to the trees on shore. There was a pretty large cliff on their right, it had to be about 50 feet high or more. It's brown, yellowish dirt held thousands of little pebbles that every once in a while fell into the water and made a tiny splash. The boys had made sure to paddle far enough away from the shore to not get hit accidently. It was also where the stronger currents were so the paddling was that much easier.

"I don't see it."

"On that lone pine tree over there," Adam pointed again. There was a part of the cliff that jutted out more than the rest and a single pine tree rose up from the very edge. Erosion had exposed much of its roots but it still hung on desperately to the soil. At the very top, where the pine needles had receded, was a majestic bald eagle complete with dark brown feathers and a bright white head. Bobby had never seen one before, and neither had Adam.

"Cool!"

"This is too easy," Adam also put his paddle on his lap as he coasted next to Bobby.

"You complaining?"

"Just wondering what it is going to be like on the way back."

"Tide should be going the other way by then."

"You think?"

"Sure," Bobby picked up the paddle again and placed it in the water, before his brother could ask any more questions. He pulled the right arm towards him and the kayak lunged forward. He wasn't as sure as he could be.

The boys paddled in silence for a little while. It was easy to get lost in thought as the "Swoosh, swoosh," sounds of the paddles lifting water created a rhythmic meditative beat. The small waves landing on the nearby rocky shore added to the tranquility while the lack of any human activity on the water made them feel totally alone. It was comforting to Bobby, not so much so to Adam. He was still closer to a child than a teenager. He didn't get lost in thought nearly as easily.

"What's that?" Adam stopped paddling for a moment and pointed to his left. There was a big flat white and blue boat heading away from them.

"Looks like the ferry," Bobby stopped paddling for a moment as well. The ferry was the only moving thing in sight, except for a few birds of course. He couldn't see the cars very well, but it only looked about half full.

"Is it headed to America?"

"I don't think so," Bobby was still trying to get a grasp on the geography. All of these islands looked alike and he wasn't even sure if the land in the distance was another island or the mainland. There were so many green trees and so few houses and certainly no big buildings. To his immediate right, there was the rocky shore and trees of Deer Island. In the water to his immediate left were some gigantic round net like things that probably were for fish. In front of the boys, on the other side of the bay was a big island or maybe mainland with a lot of houses on it, at least compared to everything else. And to the left of that, was yet another big island. That was where the ferry seemed to be heading. "It's going more east than south."

"Well where is America?"

"That way!" Bobby pointed directly in front of him towards the most populated land mass.

"Are you sure?"

"Of course dummy," he pointed up to the bright afternoon sun still hanging high in the sky. "Sun is on the west, Deer Island is on our direct right which is east, and we are pointed due south."

"When will we know we have crossed?"

"Uh," Bobby hadn't thought too much about that, "when we are just over halfway there."

"You sure?"

"Stop saying that," Bobby picked up the paddle again. He was starting to drift. "Once we get out there we will know."

Adam shrugged and followed his brother. Bobby was wrong about a lot of things and he could be wrong about this as well. It didn't really matter. He was having fun and if he told all his friends that he paddled from Canada to the United States, how would they know the difference anyway?

###

Rob swung the steering wheel right, taking the Camry onto the campground dirt road and sped through the campsites towards the southernmost point on the island. The car tires kicked up dirt and dust and made a tremendous clattering noise. He almost ran over two young kids bike riding near their camper. Then he whipped the car into the half gravel, half grass parking lot and rammed the gears into park. He leapt out of the car. The truck rushed in behind him and swerved on the dirt, barely missing Rob's car. Lindsey was the first one out. "Rob!" she sprinted behind him.

Rob ran through the bare, weed covered field past the faded "Old Sow" sign and frowned in anger. There was no warning on the sign, just a boast about it being the biggest whirlpool in North America. He jumped on top of a large stone next to a 20 foot tall, plain white lighthouse and peered out into the bay. Lindsey stopped next to him, followed by all four of the agents. No one said a word.

The bay was almost empty. To the direct south, they could see the homes of Eastport Maine. To the left of that, they could see the Ferry in the distance heading towards Campobello. The rest of their view was all water and it was definitely moving.

"Can you see the whirlpool?" Rob turned to Saltman for some assurance.

"Not yet."

"We may not be able to see it from here," Beauvais informed them. He had actually seen the whirlpool several times on his various trips to the area. He thought it was an amazing demonstration of the awesome power of nature and he loved being reminded of how small man was in comparison. He had even brought his wife here once to see it.

"Do you see the boys?" Lindsey asked Rob.

"Not yet," Rob prayed they had changed their minds or that Foster was wrong.

"They would be coming from over there," Beauvais pointed to his direct left. There was a line of trees running alongside the western edge of the island that blocked much of their view of the water. Everyone focused on the area where the tree line ended. "See those swirls," Beauvais pointed to the strange currents to the left and right of where they were standing.

"Is that the whirlpool forming?" Lindsey asked.

"Not really," Beauvais explained. "Those appear all the time. Sometimes that's all you see. The whirlpool is much bigger. You'll know it if you see it."

The moment was surreal; the blue sky, the strong fresh sea breeze blowing through their clothes and messing up their hair, the birds flying overhead and the silence of the bay. It was in complete contrast to Rob's sense of dread. He wanted to see the boys and he was terrified to see them all at the same time. What would he do if they did head out into the bay? He couldn't swim out and there were no boats that he could see in the area, not even a damn canoe.

"There they are!" Lindsey pointed at the red and yellow kayaks that suddenly appeared in their view. It was definitely Bobby and Adam; she could see Bobby's New York Rangers hat turned backwards like he always wore it.

"Bobby! Adam!" she and Rob began to scream and wave their arms. They ran through the grass, bounded over the rocks and hustled towards the little beach nearest the boys. But the boys were moving too fast and were already beyond the island and into the open waters. "Bobby! Adam!" They screamed desperately.

Bobby and Adam were paddling hard now. They could easily see the homes of Eastport, Maine on the other side and both of them wanted to be the first one to the states. They barely paid any attention to the people screaming and waving at them from the shore, nor did they notice how much they were drifting west.

"Hey," Adam turned and pointed as he finally recognized his name being called. He looked back at Deer Island. "Is that dad?"

"I think so," Bobby glided for a moment and squinted in the direction Adam was pointing. The position of the sun and the shadows from the trees cast the group in a dark aura but he could make out his father's strong build and especially Lindsey. "And Lindsey is with him too."

"Who are those other guys?" The agents had joined Rob and Lindsey and were waving as well.

"Who knows?"

"Are they waving us in?"

"Nah, he just probably came to watch." Bobby grinned and started paddling again. "He wants to see me kick your ass."

"You sure?" Adam started to get a little nervous. "He is waving pretty wildly."

"There's a whirlpool!" Rob shouted as the top of his lungs. He leaned forward to project his voice more and even jumped into the water as far as he could.

"Rob!" Lindsey grabbed the back of his shirt between the shoulders. "You'll get swept up too!"

"Did he say there is a whirlpool?" Adam stopped paddling and his face was pale. He looked over at his brother.

"Don't worry about it," Bobby lifted the paddle off of his lap and made several hard strokes, "we're almost there." He wasn't going to get stopped by his father now.

"Bobby! Adam!" Rob screamed again and again and again. It was hopeless. The boys were too far away to realize the urgency in his voice and were too focused on racing each other. Rob splashed in the water uselessly, searching the coastline for any boat or raft or anything that could get him to his boys.

Adam remained motionless in his kayak, trying to decide what to do. His brother had already started racing forward again and for the moment, Adam drifted aimlessly watching him take the lead. If he didn't move soon he would have no chance of catching him. But dad was screaming that there was a whirlpool and he looked pretty upset. The water did seem different somehow. Adam stared at the surface of the dark blue bay searching for anything odd while his Kayak continued to drift west. The current was definitely getting much stronger here. He could even see small swirls in the water, spinning like little tops. That must what be what his father meant. They were nothing to worry about.

"Hey Bobby," he called ahead to his brother. Bobby was a good 30 feet ahead and still paddling strong. "Wait up!"

"Paddle idiot," Bobby did not even look back. He needed to be the first to America!

Rob could barely watch as his younger son started paddling away again. He had hoped he would listen. It looked like he was going to. Then he had to follow his stupid brother. God, Rob could kill him if the whirlpool didn't do it first.

Adam's kayak drifted more. He was almost going sideways at this point. "No seriously Bobby!" he cried to his brother. "Wait up! I can't stop drifting!"

Bobby finally turned and looked at his brother. He had already drifted a good 50 feet to the west. It would have been even more of a gap between the two boys if Bobby had not been drifting as well. He stopped paddling for just a moment and felt the kayak moving on its own. The current was really strong!

"Turn away from it!" he yelled to his brother as he turned his own kayak to the left ninety degrees. "It's just the mouth of the bay!"

Bobby started paddling hard but made no forward progress at all. It was as if he was paddling upstream against a raging river. Adam was doing even worse. He was actually going backwards. Beyond him, Bobby could see some debris in the water, logs or something. He scanned the water to see where the current was going but there was nothing there.

"I can't get out!" Adam shouted. He was paddling desperately to no effect at all. He turned his neck to see where he was going. A few small logs rushed past him.

"Hold on," Bobby commanded. *"Damn it,"* he thought, they would never make it to the states at this rate. In one smooth move, Bobby leaned his body to the left, stuck his paddle deep into the water and did a complete one hundred and eighty degree turn. In seconds he was heading towards his brother.

"I'm stuck!" Adam cried as Bobby pulled up alongside him. He stuck out his paddle for his brother to bring him in and the Kayaks collided loudly.

"Turn into it," Bobby suggested. The water was starting to swirl so much that he had to raise his voice to be heard. "Maybe we can ride it through."

Adam made the same move Bobby had done, just not as smooth. He dropped the paddle on his lap in relief and let the kayak go forward.

"What are they doing?" Rob cried from his spot on the edge of the island. He was still standing in the water waist deep, watching helplessly. "What good is that going to do?"

"They are riding right into it," Lindsey had jumped into the water as well and was only slightly behind Rob.

"Not necessarily," Beauvais pointed out. He had poised himself close enough to grab either Rob or Lindsey if they decided to do something stupid like swim out there. "They may be able to ride along the edges until they get thrown out."

"How?" Rob snapped. His heart was racing and every nerve was on fire. He had never in his life felt so helpless. He wanted to dive into the water or clap his hands and make it all go away. Anything would be better than this total helplessness he was experiencing now.

"Many of the people who have been caught in it," Beauvais tried his best to sound calm. Rob was about to explode, "report that they let the Old Sow ride them along until it threw them out."

"Survivors?"

"They actually have certificates," Macleod smirked, trying to lighten the mood.

"As long as they don't fight it," Beauvais continued, "they have a chance."

"Don't fight it!" Bobby yelled to his brother. They had begun to separate again. "It's like skidding in a car," Bobby remembered his Driver's Ed class and what his dad had taught him about skidding in the snow, "you just gotta ride it through until you get control back!"

"Ok," Adam tried, but he was too nervous or too tired to do much good. His muscles were burning and felt like they had been lifting weights for hours. They were beginning to get that spaghetti like feel to them. Soon, they would be completely useless. "Oh my god!" he suddenly screamed. "There's the whirlpool!"

A large gaping hole of blackness appeared in the center of the currents. Everything was swirling around it at incredible speeds. It reminded Adam of the water going down his bathtub drain but with power and suction hundreds of times greater. The logs and other debris that had floated past him were already in its maw and being sucked down to heaven knows where.

"Ride it out, Ride it out!" Bobby cried desperately. It was taking everything he had to stay on the edge of the whirlpool but he knew he would not last long, and his brother wouldn't last at all.

"Bobby!" Adam screamed. He had lost complete control and was in full panic mode. He paddled in every direction, he moved his body, he tried bouncing in the water but nothing seemed to work. All Bobby could do was watch.

"Adam!" Rob jumped hysterically. He could see everything that was going on. "Adam!"

"Look!" Lindsey cried out as she pointed to the left of the island. A boat had just screamed into view.

"Bobby!" His mother cried out from the front of the boat. She was standing at the very front with a long rope in her hand. "Bobby!" she screamed again.

Bobby looked up. He couldn't hear his mother screaming over the noise of the boat engine but he could see her standing there like some angel from heaven. She had a rope in her hand and was waving it desperately.

"Who is that?" Rob turned to Lindsey. He couldn't see the figure on the boat through the water spray it was kicking up.

"I don't know," Lindsey replied.

"Mom!" Bobby called to her. He was slowly losing ground to the whirlpool as exhaustion began to take over, "Help!"

The boat's engine was able to maneuver through the whirlpool but only along the edges. Lawrence knew enough stories of even motor boats stalling out fighting against Old Sow's awesome pull. He came around the worst part of the pull and cut the engine to an idle.

"Throw him the rope!" he yelled to Deborah.

"You're going to have to paddle this to your brother," Deborah instructed her son as her boat's momentum brought her close to Bobby. "We can't take our boat that close or it could get stuck too."

"What about me?" Bobby's eyes grew wide at the prospect of paddling into the whirlpool.

"We've got more than enough power to pull you both out," Lawrence revved the engine just to impress Bobby. "But you better hurry!"

"Save your brother!" Deborah commanded.

Bobby turned and looked back towards his brother. Terror ripped through him in a wave. Adam's kayak was wrapping around the edges like a ball on a roulette wheel. In a few more minutes, he would be swept up completely.

"Adam hold on!" Bobby wrapped the rope around his waist and started to paddle, while Lawrence pulled the boat back to the edge. "I'm coming!"

Adam looked up to see his brother steaming towards him, almost too fast. He had a rope in his hands and Adam could see his mother in the boat beyond. His heart lifted and he smiled from ear to ear. "Mom!" he cried out in utter delight.

"Just hold on Adam!" she cried out, "your brother is almost there."

Rob and Lindsey watched the action from the shore. Their eyes, focused on Adam as Bobby's kayak sped so fast into the center that it almost knocked both the boys over when they collided. Then suddenly, as abruptly as the whirlpool had appeared, the drama dissipated. The motor boat gunned the engine and had no trouble pulling the boys out of the current and back to safety.

Rob turned to Lindsey and hugged her so tight that all the air went out of her chest. "Thank god!" he looked up to the sky in prayer. Lindsey pushed back against him, refilled her lungs with air and smiled back. "Thank that boater!" she added.

Rob and Lindsey both turned back towards the water desperate to learn the identity of the mysterious boater who had saved the boys and was now pulling them safely towards their island. They could see a man steering in the back and an athletic looking, black haired woman holding the rope and sitting in the front. She looked incredibly familiar.

"Is that?" Rob stared at Lindsey in disbelief and back at the boat. He rubbed his eyes and looked again.

"Is that Deborah?"

Forty Two

The secret was out! In all the emotion of the moment and the excitement of the boy's rescue, no one paid much attention to what they were saying or who they were saying it too. As soon as Rob ran down to the shore and cried, "what in god's name are you doing here?" to Deborah, she told him everything about her journey, Jim Watts and the house being broken into back in Connecticut.

Beauvais, Saltman, Macleod and Foster all tried to somehow stop the conversation but they couldn't say much without blowing what was left of their own cover. Maybe this would even be a good thing, they realized. If the group could finally work together now, they could get a lot more done; as long as no one else found out.

Rob did not even scold the boys. He was too relieved to see them alive and too distracted by Deborah's sudden appearance. Lindsey, on the other hand, wasn't sure what to think. Of course she was thrilled the boys were ok, but if things were complicated between her and Rob before, how would it look now? She stood a little off to the side of the family, awkwardly unsure of how to react. Maybe Rob and Deborah would get back together, she hoped. Or did she? Damn, she still wasn't sure.

They certainly seemed happy to see one another. As soon as Deborah had reached the shore, Rob gave her a hug that would have broken a less athletic woman's back. He didn't frown or yell or complain at all that she was suddenly there. Nothing else seemed more important to him than that his family was still alive and breathing and, at least for the moment, together.

Lawrence watched it all with deep concern. He was glad to have been a help; obviously. But as soon as they all started talking about borders and letters and William Franklin, he knew something important was going on. Fortunately, his suspicion did not last. With everyone bending over backwards to thank him and with Deborah bringing him up to speed on all of it, including the missing packet, he felt he could trust these people. They seemed like good folk, even if they were ignorant Yankees, he chuckled to himself.

Deborah truly thought Lawrence could help. With all the knowledge he had shown about the border and the research he had done to win his lawsuits, he would be an invaluable asset to them. Besides, his heart seemed pure and they all had a common enemy in Jim Watts.

People had started to gather around them. The ferry was due to be back soon and the people waiting had left their cars to see what all the fuss was about. Beauvais suggested they throw the kayaks in the back of his truck and head back to the motel.

"Great!" Rob quickly agreed. I could use a beer!"

"Or two!" Lindsey grinned.

"Or three!" Deborah laughed.

The 45th Parallel Restaurant could not have been more hospitable. They set everyone up with lobster, fish and chips, crabs and even burgers for the boys. They brought out beer and wine, plates, forks, ketchup, mustard, malt vinegar packets, the works! They even handed out the cute little lobster bibs with the plastic ties. It was everything the group might need to have a picnic around the fire-pit. With the sun still high in the sky, they would have plenty of light to see the food. There were just enough multi-colored plastic lawn chairs sitting around the pit that everyone could sit in a perfect circle and they would not have to worry about bothering other patrons or someone listening in. They could light the fire to keep any bugs away because even though it was the middle of the summer, it was still Canada and still the Bay. And best of all, the fire would provide some welcome warmth after their adventure around Old Sow.

Macleod knew that if they sat outside the motel, around the fire-pit that they would be in full view of Francois' room. No one had seen him since the break in and now that they were surrounded by CIA and CSIS agents, Rob and Lindsey were no longer afraid of him. Of course they couldn't tell Deborah or the kids that. They had to make up a lie to protect the agents cover. There was still that photo to worry about.

It ate at Rob of course. He had hoped to start everything off again on a clean slate and one of the first things he had to do was lie again to his wife. He knew it was for the best but it didn't stop him from thinking about it constantly.

"So what now?" Deborah broke off a lobster claw and pulled at the meat. She was a lobster-aholic if there ever was one. It was easy enough getting lobster in New England and she tried to have it at least once a month. But there was something almost sinful of practically getting it off the boat right here in the bay. She held the small paper basket on her lap and made sure not a single bit of meat dropped on the ground. And even if some did, there was the five second rule of course. With Lobster it might even be 10 seconds!

"Let's start with that paper you got from Francois' room," Rob turned to Lindsey who had strategically placed herself a few chairs away from him. She was not going to give any more ammunition to Deborah, who, at least so far, had avoided any uncomfortable stares. Rob sat next to Deborah and his boys without even giving it a second thought and was now enjoying his lobster with the same zeal that his wife was. He had never worshipped the red claw as much as she did, but he appreciated it almost as much. Deborah teased him all the time that while he needed to dip his meat in butter, she sucked it right out of the claw. Rob ignored her. It was no different than adding cream to your coffee he would say. Now, after everything that had happened and the craziness of his life, losing himself in the barbarity of eating lobster seemed like paradise. He viscously ripped the claw off and smiled. Juice flew everywhere. "You still have it Lindsey?"

"It's in the car," Lindsey stood up and placed the paper plate covered with food on her yellow plastic chair. The fish and chips were half eaten and the malt vinegar packets sat on the edge of the plate. She took a swig of her bottled beer and placed the empty gently on the ground next to her chair. "Anyone else need a refill while I am gone?" She offered.

For Lindsey, the meal was more about the beer than the fish. She never had been much of a lobster girl anyway and she needed beer a lot more now than Rob did. He was not nearly as conflicted as she was. Rob could smile and enjoy Deborah's company while all Lindsey could do was avoid it. So far, Deborah had not paid her much attention but she knew it wouldn't take long for the angry glares to start up again. Maybe the beer would help her ignore it, she hoped.

"I could use one," Beauvais said.

"Me too," Saltman added. Both of them were trying to keep up the façade of being tourists. They smiled a lot, talked about the photos they had taken already, discussed their wives and kids and tried to act as natural as possible. Joining the group in this meal may have been a risk, but it would also add to that façade. They could not completely count on Rob and Lindsey to keep their secret, either one of them could let it slip; by accident or on purpose.

"Let me help you," Macleod got up quickly and jogged to join Lindsey.

"Sorry about this," he said once they were beyond the group. "I know it can't be easy."

"What can't be easy?" Lindsey kept walking but slowed her pace a little. She was in no hurry to get back.

"All this subterfuge," Macleod kept pace with her. He truly did feel sorry for Lindsey. She seemed like a real nice woman, with a sincere heart and a fun personality. He especially admired her athletic, smooth legs. If he hadn't been married for 15 years, he might have even made a move on her. Instead he hoped to be some kind of friend to her. He could already sense how awkward she felt around Rob now.

"It is what it is," Lindsey stayed non-committal. She didn't know this guy at all. To her, Macleod was a stranger, a spy, a man of deceit and lies. Just because he was Canadian with a friendly smile and a love for hockey didn't mean she was going to let her guard down.

"Well I just want you to know," he placed his hand on her arm for a moment. The move was sincere but it still made Lindsey uncomfortable. "That we are here to help and protect you, not just find the packet."

"Really?" Lindsey stopped. She looked at Macleod, trying to size him up. His bright blue eyes were opened wide and there was lightness about him that she couldn't shake. He seemed sincere and even a little cute but she couldn't forget what he and his partners were doing to them. It made her seethe with bitterness and even rage. She hadn't felt like this since she was a girl trying to break into a boy's sport. She didn't let the coaches stop her then and she wasn't going to let these guys do it now, "seems like you are just using us to get the job done."

"We are," he admitted. His honesty caught Lindsey off guard, "but that doesn't mean we can't protect you at the same time."

"You willing to give me that picture?" Lindsey wasn't buying it.

"I'll get the beer," Macleod ignored the comment and turned towards the restaurant. He had done all he could at this point. Lindsey watched him walk up the small red wooden staircase into the 45th, "Hypocrite," she said to herself as she turned back towards the car.

"Here it is," she returned a few minutes later with the paper in hand. She picked up her plate again with one hand, sat back down and placed it on her lap. The fries slid along the plate but did not fall off. She threw the largest one in her mouth before she continued.

"Here's your beer," Macleod returned with two Molsons in each hand and handed one to Lindsey with another smile. She couldn't tell if that was Macleod the tourist or Macleod the Agent and that pissed her off. She took a quick swig of the beer and watched as he handed the other bottles to Beauvais and Saltman, then sat back in his own seat. "Thanks," she finally said.

"Rob, can I speak to you for a minute in private?" Deborah suddenly interrupted. She placed the basket of lobster carcass on the ground, licked her fingers and wiped them on a wet nap.

"Sure," Rob frowned and did the same. He looked over at Lindsey and shrugged his shoulders. Deborah noticed the look but didn't say anything. It might have upset her, but her mind was on something else. Lindsey on the other hand, felt encouraged. At least Rob had not thrown her under the bus with Deborah's return. "Be right back," Rob said to the rest of the group as he stood up and followed his wife.

"What's up?" Rob stopped and stared at Deborah once they were about 40 feet away. She was as beautiful as the day he met her, especially in the light of the sun. Her black hair glistened in the contrast and her piercing green eyes held the passion that swept him up every time he stared into them. God it was great to see her, he realized yet again. He looked back at the group nervously wondering if anyone else noticed how he was staring at his wife. They were all sitting quietly, eating their food or drinking their beer and doing their best not to look at Rob and Deborah. At least they were polite about it, Rob thought.

"Are you sure we should be talking about this in front of those strangers," Deborah nodded back towards them. She of course recognized the longing in Rob's eyes and did her best to ignore it. Despite everything that had happened in the past few days, she still did not know what she wanted next. She loved Rob and the boys, of that she had no doubt. But unlike her husband, she could not just ignore all the issues plaguing them over the years. Her feelings were all over the place and her mind was in conflict; Best to focus on what she could control.

"The photo guys?" Rob feigned surprise. He knew exactly how weird this was. Ever since he had found the Franklin letter, he had been all hush, hush. He hadn't even told the boys until he had too. Now all of sudden he was discussing it in front of total strangers. How could he seem so casual about it without telling Deborah about the photo?

"We don't have any choice," Rob decided to use logic. His wife was a scientist and he always found the best way to get her to do anything was to appeal to that side of her. If he used passion and emotion, appealed to her trust in human nature or something like that, she might find something to argue about. "We already let things slip too much."

"But they don't know everything."

"Think about what they will do if we don't tell them," Rob was using the CIA's own argument but applying it to himself this time. "They could go off on their own, maybe tell someone else or heaven help us, find it on their own."

Deborah thought about that for a moment.

"This way we can keep an eye on them and control what they do and what they find out."

"Still," Deborah wasn't going to give in that easily. She knew how big this was.

"Besides, they're good guys," Rob lied. He didn't trust any of them for a second. "They were the ones who figured out that Bobby and Adam were in danger. They rushed us out to Old Sow. We kind of owe them." That much was true, Rob realized as he said it. Guess they weren't all bad.

"Well," Deborah still resisted. "Ok," she started back towards the fire-pit. "But just remember this was your idea."

"Sorry guys," Rob lead the way back. "Just some husband wife shit," he lied. Deborah frowned. She would have preferred a different excuse. She didn't need to be reminded in any way that she and Rob had issues no matter what the circumstances were. "Want to go ahead Lindsey?"

"Well like I said when we first saw this," Lindsey had finished her fish and chips while Rob had been talking. The plate lay on the ground in front of her with the used malt vinegar packets on top and another empty bottle of Molson beside it. She held the paper on her lap and read some of the names. "Lawless, Brawn, Coley, the names match the ones on Nana's index."

"I recognize all of those names," Lawrence finally spoke. It startled everyone. Rob, Deborah, even Lindsey had kept their eyes on the agents. They glanced over at the hotel every once in a while searching for any signs of Francois. Sitting on the edge of the circle, dressed in his blue jean overalls and simple red t-shirt, Whittaker almost blended in with the local scenery. He had said practically nothing the entire meal or in the car ride to the motel. Deborah had started to wonder if she had made a mistake trusting him but how could she question the man who had saved her son's life? "They are all families here on the island."

"And this list beneath their names describes items that sound like they were written by Ben or William Franklin," Lindsey took more time to read it now. In Francois' room she only had a second, but now she could take her time with it. As she read each item off the list, her voice grew louder and more excited with every item. "Listen to some of these things," she almost screamed, "Letter from Congress, notes on meeting with Shelburne,"

"That's the official who worked with Franklin on the Treaty!" Lawrence shouted.

"What Treaty?" Beauvais said. He knew they had to feign some level of ignorance.

"The Treaty of Paris," Lawrence was still shouting, "the one that set the border here."

"Here?" Adam looked around the area. He was still sitting with a green towel wrapped over his shoulders. The water had chilled him to the bone and his voice almost cracked with excitement when he finally spoke. Neither boy had said a word since the rescue; everyone had almost forgotten the boys were even there. Perhaps it was the shock of it all or the embarrassment that they had not listened to their father or the hunger exploding from their ordeal or just because they were teenagers. By now, some of that discomfort had faded away or Adam's curiosity had returned. Or maybe it was a mixture of both.

"Not here dummy," at least Bobby was acting normal again. His towel had fallen to the ground and he made no attempt to pick it up. He still saw this entire screw up as his fault despite how his mother had tried to comfort him. Adam almost died because of him and he was not sure he would ever be able to forget that. Still, that was no reason to let his brother think anything had changed, "Out there!" He snapped and pointed somewhat south. "Remember?"

Adam quickly hung his head. The last thing he wanted was a reminder of the border and the whirlpool nearby. He felt like an idiot.

"It also mentions a letter from Franklin and a letter from Adams," Lindsey tried to bring attention back to the paper in her hands, "Even something from the King."

"It sounds like an inventory of some kind," Deborah had seen enough of those.

"Yes!" Rob agreed. "That must be the items that are in the packet."

"And the names of these families..." Lindsey realized.

"Are the families who have the packet!" Deborah finished for her, "But which one?"

"Lawrence," Rob left Deborah's question unanswered and turned to Whittaker abruptly. "You say you know all these families?"

"I was the town historian for 29 years," he offered, "until I handed the job over to William."

A light went off in Deborah's head and she nodded quietly. That's what William meant the other day at the shack when he said he was new to the historian's job. Now it was all starting to make sense. She knew Lawrence would be a great help.

"So can you put us in touch with these families?" Lindsey's eyes lit up.

"Certainly," Lawrence grinned like the Cheshire cat as he lifted his dark brown bottle of beer to his lips.

Forty Three

They had decided to split up and would start first thing tomorrow. It was too late in the day already and the Kayaks had to be brought back to the house, Lawrence had to get back to his boat and Lindsey had finished off too much beer. After a little bit of arguing the teams were set. The boys insisted on "cool code names" so "Team Callahan" would be Rob, Deborah and Adam. They would return to the historian's shack (that wasn't the name of it, but they had no other name for the shack William worked out of) and recruit William Luisi. Lawrence and Deborah said that they would need his knowledge of the island's history and insisted he could be trusted. With Lawrence on the other team, they would need someone who knew Deer Island History.

Lawrence would be going with Lindsey and Bobby on "Team Cool". (That name took a little longer. Bobby couldn't find much in common with his teammates except for the fact that Lawrence and Lindsey both started with "L," which made him think of LL Cool, which made him think of ice and hockey and what the heck.) Lawrence didn't care what the name was. This was much too important to him to be worried about silly names. He had enough trouble with a teenager on his team in the first place.

Everyone agreed that the boys were not to be left alone. And in the beginning, both boys naturally started to protest. It was not nearly as strong of a teenage protest as it could have been however. They were still frazzled by the whirlpool and once Bobby made sure to get himself on Lindsey's team he stopped complaining completely. He didn't want to admit it but he was starting to develop a crush on her.

Adam was more than happy to be put with mom and dad. He had forgotten all the anger he was holding towards his mother the moment she rescued him. He would never forget how she appeared like an angel out of nowhere and saved both of their lives. Maybe, if he could forget everything, dad could too. Perhaps he could even nudge them together again.

As soon as the opportunity presented itself, Adam pulled his mother aside and gave her another hug. He thanked her again and told her how much he loved her. Then he brought up dad. He made sure Deborah knew that he had never touched Lindsey. That as far as Adam could see, Lindsey was just his friend. Bobby stared at Lindsey more than dad did, Adam said. They both got a good laugh out of that.

Foster, Saltman, Macleod and Beauvais decided to bow out. The group would be too large with them in it and their cover was hanging on by a thread. Bobby and Adam already thought it was weird of course for a group of four men to be on a photo trip together and Deborah still gave them enough sideways glances to unnerve them. Fortunately there was a kayak adventure company that ran out of Deer Island and the pristine condition of the bay was a photographers dream. The men claimed that they had already planned a long day of picture taking and promised that they would meet up with everyone later. Once they got Rob and Lindsey off to the side however, they made it clear to the two of them that they were to text them updates on a regular basis and send pictures of anything they found. To be on the safe side, the agents also decided to plant themselves at every ferry entrance. Rob and Lindsey would not be able to get off the island without them knowing.

The real reason for splitting up of course was the threat of Watts and Francois. By now, they had realized the two men were working together and they couldn't take the chance of them getting to the families before they did. Sure Lindsey had stolen the paper from Francois' room but that didn't mean he didn't make a second copy or send a picture of it to Jim. They had to be sure.

Lawrence offered to organize the search. He knew all the families on the island and he knew what they had in their family keepsakes. He had been the historian for almost three decades and every family had either offered to have him look through their stuff or he had visited them in an attempt to piece together as much as he could about the island's story. He had even been toying with the idea of writing a book someday. Unfortunately, not all of the families had organized their heirlooms and many of them did not even know where any of the keepsakes were. It had been over eight generations since the island was first settled after all. Some families kept their stuff in shoe boxes, some of them had donated items to his collection and only a select few had actually itemized and kept track of what they had. They would start with those families first.

The first thing Team Callahan learned was that they had already been beaten. Francois had been there yesterday and the owner had shown him the clue. After all, Sturgis Adams was proud of his family's history. He had spent decades researching it, had made a family tree which he put on-line and had traced everyone back to either England, Scotland or Ireland. The only mystery he had was this one letter which Francois specifically knew to ask for. It was strange that he knew about it, but Sturgis was too excited to let that bother him. He easily found the letter from its secure place in the family safe and showed it to Francois. Thank goodness Sturgis wasn't stupid enough to let him have it. A picture is all he would let Francois have.

"Don't worry about it Sturgis," William tried to comfort him. "You couldn't have known. Heck I just found out yesterday myself."

"Found out what?" Sturgis said from the comfort of his red cushioned lazy chair. He was an eccentric old man with the classic Santa style gray beard and even the pot belly to match. His eyes were as black as coal and his nose a little bent as if he had broken it on several occasion. Adam thought the man smelled a little funny and his mother had to push him into the house once Sturgis allowed them in.

The house itself was as eccentric as Sturgis was. Everywhere they looked a memento or antique lay on a stand, hung on the wall or sat on a bureau. No wonder Francois had been let in so quickly. It must have been a paradise for the strange antique dealer. Even the wallpaper seemed to be from another time period. Its ornate decoration and faded green and yellow background reminded Rob and Deborah of Nana's living room.

Once they sat in the parlor however, Sturgis became friendly enough. He knew William well. After all, he had been the first one on the island introduced to William once he began taking over the historian's job. Sturgis himself might have taken the job after Lawrence quit if William had not been so much younger. They needed the next generation to pass on Deer Island's story now.

They all took seats around Sturgis. Deborah and Rob sat on the old faded flower fabric sofa with Adam in the middle. William sat uncomfortably on the love seat placed neatly next to Sturgis' chair. He had no idea what to tell the old man. He didn't want to tell Sturgis everything and wasn't sure if he should tell him anything. What was Lawrence thinking throwing him into the middle of all this? He was just a part time historian, trying to make ends meet like everyone else on Deer Island. He didn't have time for detective work and 200 year old stories. Sure, he loved the history of the island. It was why he moved to Passamaquoddy in the first place. He had been looking for a life that had more meaning after living in the urban sprawl of Toronto for so long. The bay, with its quiet, empty roads, hard-working down to earth people and family stories that went back to the Revolution put his life more in perspective and allowed him to appreciate every day more. It even helped him forget his ex-fiancé who abandoned him for another man.

But he still was nothing like Lawrence. He didn't eat breathe and live for Deer Island. He could have been just as happy in St. Andrews or Campobello or even in Nova Scotia. In fact, now that he thought about it, he couldn't even remember why he had chosen this island in the first place.

"Found out what?" Sturgis repeated to William's blank stare.

"That you had something so valuable," Deborah interjected. She had sensed William's confusion and realized the critical mistake they all had made. They should have discussed more what they would tell all these families. How could the team ask questions about documents that seemed old and irrelevant? How did they know about them in the first place? The families probably had no idea what the items meant if they even had them at all. Without the Franklin letter, none of this would make any sense. At best, each Deer Island family would feel just like Rob and Lindsey when they first found out.

"Valuable?" Sturgis frowned. He would know by now if any of the items in his safe were of value. Who were these people?

"Valuable in the sense that other people would find it interesting," William recovered. "After all, you've been doing this research for what 30 years?"

"Closer to 50," Sturgis beamed. It was the first time he had smiled much and it made everyone feel better, even Adam. The old guy was kind of cute.

"Fifty years," Rob took a turn. He would play on the man's pride. "You must know so much more than anyone on the island about your family."

"Except Lawrence," Sturgis waved his hand. "He has been at this even longer than I have. And he has an even better reason."

"That's part of what we came to tell you," William saw his angle. "That man you saw yesterday is working with Jim Watts."

"Watts!" Sturgis almost rose from his chair, "That lying snake."

"We're not sure what he is after this time," William felt a little awkward about the small lie. He hoped it would be his only one, "but we know he is up to no good."

"That's all he is ever up to."

"So we need you to show us what you showed him."

Rob and Deborah were on the edge of their seats when Sturgis brought out the letter. Despite their many successes and failures, they still felt that chill up their spine every time they found a document. William, being a historian was in awe and Adam thought it was cool. He had never seen anything written by someone important before. Just the way Sturgis handled it made it seem so old and powerful. It was double vacuum packed, sealed and protected with acid free cardboard and held in a plastic sheath. It still was yellow around the edges and faded but that just added to its power.

The letter was indeed written by Ben Franklin. So at least Rob and Deborah knew that they were on the right path. That matched what it said in the inventory and it was the first thing any of them had found written by Ben himself. Yet while it confirmed they were on the right path, it did not help them go further along it. The letter, written while Franklin was in Paris, was a defense of himself and an attack on John Adams. It justified many of the things Franklin had done while in Paris and criticized Adams for his lack of faith. But it didn't offer any new or helpful information. There was no discussion of the border or lines and barely even of the treaty. There certainly was no mention of a packet or the location of other items. It was disjointed and confusing, probably written in the middle of the night and obviously during a fit of anger or pain or both. No wonder Franklin had hidden it away. It was not complementary for either he or John Adams. The only thing it did was help confirm their entire theory; that Ben Franklin really was upset while in Paris and did write at least one thing about his time there that was never found. Until now, that is.

The team hid their disappointment well. Despite everything they had told Sturgis, the old man still beamed with pride upon showing them his collection. He had insisted on showing the Callahan's other items from his safe, including the family tree which indeed went all the way back to the revolution. Rob would have tried to come up with some excuse to get out of there sooner if Adam was not enjoying it so much. He had no idea his boy loved genealogy and history. Perhaps the other team would do better. At least it wouldn't help Francois or Jim any more than them.

Forty Four

They were beaten again! Things were not looking good at this point. Yes they had found a few items first; a survey map, some letters to local lawyers and even another letter to Odell, but none of it was much help. If Francois and Watts kept this up, they would have no chance.

This time the person they needed to find wasn't old or innocent. He was a much younger, vibrant, politically active family man who was known all over the island and beyond.

John McTaggart was the most loved and hated man in the province of New Brunswick; loved by everyone who knew him, and hated by businessmen, lawyers and realtors. Standing nearly six and a half feet tall with the build of a lumberjack and the face of a teddy bear, he was as intimidating physically as he was emotionally. There was no gray area for John McTaggart, who his friends called Moose and his enemies called Mr. McTaggart. Life was black and white. You either were a friend of the earth and its thousands of species, including humans, or its enemy. You worked hard to help others, contributed to the positive energy around us all, or you were a drain on it. It was almost a simple Star Wars like view of the world; you either were on the side of good, or you were part of the dark side.

No one laughed at Moose however. His cut and dried view of the world was fueled by an almost irresistible drive to see his side come out on top. It was kind of odd that he lived on Deer Island of course. Being secluded from much of the modern world, in a rural, almost time gone by surrounding did not seem like the best place for such a political activist to be setting up camp. But Deer Island was also one of the last battlefields left in Canada that still had a chance, at least in John's eyes. According to Moose, Deer Island had to be saved. The fishing companies, the oil companies and even to some degree the tourists, had to be kept away. Not a single spot of earth could be contaminated or bought by these "bloodsuckers". That's why it was so strange that he would even talk to Jim Watts or anyone who associated with him.

"Oh I didn't help him," Moose laughed at the look on Lawrence's face. Lawrence was the only man, maybe in the world, who hated Jim Watts more than Moose did. That's why Moose couldn't resist teasing him a little when "Team Cool" first arrived. (Of course they did not introduce themselves like that. Lawrence was careful to introduce Lindsey and Bobby as friends of his; friends that were on the right side of the battle, he made sure to add.) "But I did give him what he was looking for," Moose teased even more as he led the three of them into his house.

John McTaggart's home was nothing like Sturgis Adams'. It was modern in every sense of the word with not a single kilowatt of wasted energy. The light bulbs were energy reducing and long lasting, the oven and heat were natural gas, the furniture he carved himself from local trees and the floors were a beautiful natural stone granite that had to have come from a nearby quarry. It was the perfect use of modern science and the understanding of human impact combined with an artists' appreciation for nature and the physical world. Lindsey felt like she had stepped into the next century. Bobby could care less.

"What the hell are you talking about Moose?" Lawrence raised his voice even before they could sit down in the open air kitchen. He was in no mood for being teased and was not impressed with the incredible view in front of him of the bay. He lived on an island after all. Lindsey and Bobby on the other hand, stood in front of the large sliding glass doors with mouths wide open as they stared into the heart of Passamaquoddy Bay. "Why did you give Watts anything at all?"

"Hold on, hold on," Moose smiled one last time while he handed each of them a tall glass of cold water taken from a pitcher in his refrigerator. "Let me explain." He pointed at the individually carved bar stools positioned around the marble island in the middle of the kitchen.

"I can't believe you even let them into your house," Lawrence took one of the stools Moose had pointed to and slid it under his butt in one simple motion. He clearly had been in this house many times before.

"What makes you think I did that?" Moose suddenly became serious, his eyes burning with the passion he was so well known for. "What makes you think I would let that son of a bitch anywhere near this sanctuary?" His voice became gruff and fell an entire octave. It was if an entire different person somehow took over.

"But-"

"Watts and some same strange skinny, freaky looking man," his voice rose again and became a little more normal.

"His name's Francois," Lindsey offered.

"Came to my door talking about some letter I was supposed to have."

Lawrence finally took a sip of the water glass in front of him and settled down a little. Finally something was starting to make sense. Lindsey leaned forward in anticipation and Bobby used the opportunity to sneak a peek at her breasts.

"He went on and on about William Franklin and Loyalists," Moose waved his hand back and forth in disdain, "even offered to pay me a bunch of money-"

"And you gave it to him?" Lindsey cried in disbelief. She almost spit out the water onto the marble counter.

"Now what made you say something as stupid as that?" Moose shook his head in disgust. "Lawrence, where did you get this girl?" He turned to his friend and said. "Did you even tell her a word about me or what I do?"

"I didn't really have time," Lawrence said sheepishly.

"No missy," Moose turned back to Lindsey, "I didn't give him any letter, least of all the one he was looking for."

"But you said,"

"I said I gave him what he wanted. I didn't say it was what he was looking for."

"OK Moose," Lawrence lifted his head in frustration. "Now you've got me too. Would you care to explain what the hell you are talking about?"

Moose smiled. He was pretty proud of himself, they could at least tell that much. "Well," he began slowly. "I knew he was after something big. The two of them practically stumbled over each other to get a word in."

"Watts and Francois," Lawrence clarified.

"Yeah. So I could tell it was some kind of treasure hunt or mystery or some shit that Watts was involved in."

That was true enough, everyone realized.

"And of course I wasn't about to give them what they were asking for or help them in any way, but I knew I could throw them an irresistible bone to keep 'em busy for a while."

"You threw them off the track?" Lindsey almost shouted. She liked this guy.

"Better than that honey," his grin was ear to ear by now.

"What did you tell them?" Lawrence finally smiled. Any day you could get under Jim Watt's skin was a good day.

"I acted like I knew exactly what they were talking about. I nodded, I grinned, I even let the son of a bitch throw me a couple of hundred," he reached into his pocket, pulled out the colorful Canadian money and waved it around. "Then I told him I buried it in a secret box up in the cemetery."

Lawrence and Lindsey immediately burst into laughter. Bobby chuckled awkwardly. He wasn't sure what was so funny. He did love how Lindsey threw her hair back and laughed though. Her long blond hair swept up over her shoulders and into the air, like those commercials for perfumes and all the sexy models. Bobby could barely contain himself.

"Which cemetery?" Lawrence was still laughing.

"The one you take care of in Chocolate Cove."

###

"Is this the place?" Francois watched Jim pull the BMW off to the side of the road and gently place the gears in park. He still felt uncomfortable working this closely with Watts but there was no way he was going to take his eye off him. In the past, all their work had been done alongside each other, on text or by email. They were rarely in the same exact place at the same exact time, and when they were, they kept their distance. Now he was a passenger in Watts' car, just along for the ride. Francois had become totally dependent on the man and he didn't like it. He didn't know the people, he didn't know the area and worst of all, he didn't know how much Watts was on the up and up. He couldn't trust him. He had learned that over the many years they had done business together. What kept them together was the money they made. Their profits had been pretty damn great and he had pulled the wool over Watt's eyes himself once or twice. It was a match made in hell.

"Yeah," Watts got out of the car and walked to the back. He pulled open the trunk and reached in for a small wooden shovel. Francois thought it was a little strange that Watts always kept a shovel in the back of his trunk but the bent, rusty metal base was proof that it got some use. Francois did not want to know what for. "C'mon," Watts said as he slammed the trunk closed and turned to the small path heading up the hill to the cemetery.

There was no sign indicating the cemetery. There was no gate, there was no parking lot. Watts had just parked the car on the side of the two-lane road and looked for the gravel path McTaggart had told him about.

Cemeteries were special places on Deer Island and there were several of them. Some were better marked and bigger. Some had signs and places to park. All of them had a unique character. They had to on an island with so much history and so many generations of the same families. They were not fancy or ornate. There were no mausoleums or monuments. There were no statues or gate keepers. The headstones for the most part were simple and direct. Name, dates and a loving message or two were the most seen on any of them.

This particular cemetery was one of the older ones and one of the smallest.

There were only around 20 marked graves and most of the headstones were illegible, the rough Bay weather having worn away the letters decades ago. A few could be made out; names like Appleby and Lloyd and maybe a Fountain or two. But Watts ignored all these and found the small green path between two large pine trees that McTaggart had directed him too. Moose wasn't about to let Watts desecrate the cemetery.

The spot was supposed to be in a little clearing about 100 feet behind the main cemetery. Moose knew of a small boulder in the middle of the clearing that Lawrence had talked about several times. Lawrence, after all, among many of his other odd jobs on the island, was the caretaker of some of the cemeteries. For the most part, that simply meant mowing the lawn on occasion. It only took an hour or so every couple of weeks on the tractor Lawrence used. After he almost broke the blade on that boulder, he mentioned to Moose how he was thinking of removing the rock all together. Fortunately for Moose's prank, Lawrence never got around to doing that.

"It's supposed to be buried by the boulder," Watts pointed to the half oval rock sticking out of the ground. It could not have been more obvious. The clearing was almost a perfect circle of green grass and weeds surrounded by pine trees. It was only about 40 feet in diameter with the boulder almost dead center. The tractor path from Lawrence's mower could even be made out if one knew to look for it. The boulder itself was covered with a small amount of brown mold and its surface had been smoothed over by centuries of erosion. The way it curved into the ground made it clear that most of it was buried under solid dirt and grass growing over its base. It was the perfect spot to bury something valuable.

"Let me try," Francois grabbed the shovel from Watts' hands and ran ahead.

"Hey!" Watts protested and ran behind. He gave up trying to keep his brightly shined Dockers clean. Francois thought he was an idiot for wearing them here in the first place but Watts had an image to uphold, he had claimed.

They dug for hours. Neither man was willing to allow the other any advantage or time alone. If one of them had to take a leak, they would stand a few feet away and go right there in the grass, never taking their eye off of the large hole they could now almost stand in. By dusk the mosquitos arrived in full force. Neither one of them had thought to bring bug spray and both of them were covered in sweat. It was a rare feast that the swarm was not about to pass up no matter how many of them were swatted away.

Watts was more protected in his suit but he was also therefore sweatier. While his arms were protected, his jet-black hair was like an international airport welcoming every mosquito from miles around. Francois tried to cover his arms with mud and dirt but that only made it harder to hold the shovel and it had to be reapplied every time he rubbed or sweat any of it away. By the time the hole was about four feet deep both men were ready to burst.

It was the rectangular rock in the center of the hole that finally broke them. When Francois first hit it with the shovel, they both assumed it was the metal box McTaggart had told them he had buried. With neither of them wanting to lose it to the other and their wits and nerves at the breaking point, it only took one grab of the shovel to start the fight. They pushed and shoved, they screamed and yelled and rolled in the dirt. Watts was the stronger man by far and landed several blows on Francois' chin and ribs but Francois had the shovel. A few good swings at the shoulders and a stab in the gut caused Watts to back off. Then one vicious uncontrolled, furious swing to the head completely knocked Watts out and Francois was free to dig for the prize that never was there. It was the perfect prank, and it was well deserved.

###

"So do you really have the letter?" Lawrence finally asked after they had all finished laughing. It felt great to get a win, even if it was a simple one like this. No one deserved to be pranked more than Jim Watts.

"I have a letter," Moose emphasized the "a" to indicate he had no idea if it was the right one. The grin turned to a slight frown now that they were brought back to the real reason for Lawrence and Lindsey and Bobby's visit. "But I am not sure if it is the one you are looking for."

Forty Five

The letter could not have been more depressing. Lindsey was ready to give up once she read it a third time. It pretty much made it clear that the packet was nowhere to be found and that they had been chasing a wild goose for the last month or more. It had taken them almost three hours just to find it in the mess of McTaggart's keepsakes. He hadn't looked at them in years and almost all of the time he did spend with them was with the pictures he could relate to like his grandparents and the different homes they had built. The stuff from way back was in a disjointed unorganized mess. Thank God someone had been smart enough to put all the old letters in some kind of protective plastic cover.

The four of them were all gathered around the marble island countertop with the letters and keepsakes spread all over it. Moose had two entire boxes of old shit he didn't care about or even know about in some cases. It reminded Bobby too much of going through his grandmother's stuff last month and it put him in a foul mood. Even Lindsey's enthusiasm and giddiness couldn't completely bring him out of it.

After several hours of searching and more than one snack provided by their gracious host, they found themselves near the bottom of the pile of "stuff". Bobby was still off to the side taking yet another break and standing in front of the sliding glass doors looking out at the view when Lindsey screamed she found it. He almost banged his head against the glass she had startled him so much. His anger only lasted for a moment though as the entire group of them hovered over Lindsey's shoulder and read along with her.

It was pretty clear that it was the letter they were looking for. It was written by William Franklin himself shortly after the American Revolution and talked directly of the Loyalists. At first, it started off promising. William Franklin was writing a letter to one of John McTaggart's distant relatives. In it he was discussing the land issues, their need to be compensated for their losses in the revolution and how much he would try to help out everyone in their little association. He even directly mentioned his father.

Lindsey could easily see the connection between father and son in the language William used. He sounded depressed and melancholy. Just as Ben Franklin had been frustrated with his friends in the U.S. Congress and stymied at every turn during the Treaty negotiations, so too had William felt in trying to get compensation for the loyalists. How odd was it that in the last job either Franklin ever had in representing America that they both had similar, painful experiences?

William went on for three pages, sounding depressed and angry, discussing how the Parliament and various ministers made it almost impossible for him to get the Loyalists any true compensation. He was at his wits' end.

Finally, William mentioned the packet; not directly, but through allusion. Lindsey pointed out a specific paragraph in which he said to McTaggart's ancestor:

"Some progress has been made. I hinted to the King's ministers that my father was quite frustrated with how Jay and Adams treated him during the Treaty negotiations and that he had certain information about them that I now am in possession of."

"Bingo!" Lindsey had exclaimed as she pumped her fist. To her that was the last bit of proof they needed. Ben Franklin *had* kept information and notes during the treaty negotiations that somehow made it to his son. They still had no idea how it got to William or what he had done with it but as the letter progressed, instead of progress the letter showed failure. Lindsey's hopes sunk as she read, her voice grew softer and she had to reread it two or three times.

William went on to say, "I am loathe however to use this information. My father trusted my family with this information and I was never to make it public unless certain conditions arose."

What were those conditions? Everyone wondered. And had they been met? Was this information Ben Franklin was holding onto in case anyone ever questioned or attacked his work? Was his son to protect the father's legacy or pass it on through the generations just in case? Worst of all, was it because the packet was worthless? Were the documents inside simply not enough to make any difference? Maybe that is why no one ever did anything with it! The last part of the letter was what destroyed their hopes completely:

"I have decided to not use these letters. It is not yet time, and I am not sure it will ever be. I must respect my father's wishes. You are on your own and there is nothing more I can do for you. Good luck,

Your humble servant

W. Franklin

"We're screwed." Lindsey dropped the letter on the marble countertop and placed her face in her hands.

"Why didn't you ever show me this letter?" Lawrence was on the edge of anger. He was truly looking forward to some closure on what had become a generational battle. For so long he and his father and his father before him had fought for some kind of recognition. The Franklin packet could finally settle the Canada/ USA border once and for all and there would never again be any questions on the St. Croix River, Machias Seal Island or even Apple Island. Of course it could make matters a whole lot worse as well.

"I didn't even know I had it," Moose shrugged his shoulders. "It was in the stuff I never used, and, to be honest, it was clear that my family wanted all this stuff held onto."

"Why would they want to hold onto it all if Franklin gave up?" Bobby couldn't help himself. He had continued to resist any interest in the Franklin letter or the possibility of land in the family. It was his last act of rebellion against his father. But as he listened more and he saw the passion Lindsey had for it, he began to soften and even become hopeful himself. He was almost as frustrated as the rest of them. "It doesn't make any sense."

"That's bugging me too," Lindsey finally took her face out of her hands and thought. "It doesn't add up with the other clues." She turned to Moose, "Can we take a picture of this?"

"I suppose so," Moose pushed the letter across the counter back towards Lindsey.

"Thanks," Lindsey took out her phone and clicked the photo icon. She took several pictures and sent them to Rob. Then a thought occurred to her and her lip curled up several centimeters in an almost imperceptible smile. She clicked on the picture that revealed Franklin giving up, typed in all caps on her phone "IT'S OVER!" and sent it to Beauvais. Maybe that would get them off their backs. "Let's meet with the others," she placed the phone back in her pocket. "Maybe they had more luck."

They didn't have any more luck. None of the families listed in the inventory had any keepsakes organized except for two and neither had anything even remotely resembling what they were looking for. They spent two hours at another house helping old lady Lawless go through her messy shoebox full of papers, but all they got for their trouble was some home-made tea and biscuits. It seemed hopeless. To expect families all over a single island to hold onto letters they did not understand or value for over two hundred years, really did seem ridiculous. Rob was shocked that Nana had held onto the stuff for so long once he really began to think about it. Why would something like this still be around, and how naïve it was of them all to think even if it were, that it would be as easy as visiting a few homes.

Both teams suggested they gather back at the 45th parallel restaurant. It had become their go to place. It wasn't just because it was the only real restaurant on the island or that it also sold beer. It had a homey local feel that all the Callahans and Lindsey adored. The owners were overly friendly, the regulars who came in all knew each other and exchanged small talk and sometimes even a hug. It made the adults long for the days when community meant the people who lived alongside and next to you, not some digital friend half a world away. This time, they all agreed to eat inside. Everyone was exhausted from a depressing, wasted day and they had no energy to eat outside. It was comfort food time and the small, tightly packed dining room had an intimate feel to it that made them feel welcome. Everyone could hear everyone else and the owner was never more than an "excuse me miss," away.

Fortunately the restaurant had room for them. A young couple was sitting at the back table against the far wall and in the opposite corner by the window sat a lone fisherman. Other than that, the restaurant was empty. It only took one quick "over here?" from Lindsey and a nod from Deborah to choose the empty space in the middle of the dining room. There were only four or five tables and each one of them was covered with a red and white checkered plastic tablecloth so it really didn't matter which ones they chose. They all looked the same. It was easy to push two of them together and make one long table that everyone could sit at. It was a little more difficult arranging the chairs however. The waitress, a pleasant looking petite woman with blue eyes and a pencil sticking threw the blonde bun in her hair, had swiftly glided across the small room to direct them. She would point out one chair that needed to stay, another that could be moved, and another that had to be switched. Each one of the wooden, barely cushioned chairs was no more comfortable than any other chair, but apparently each patron had his or her own favorite seat.

Rob watched the women rearranging the chairs and chuckled a little to himself imagining tiny golden plaques on the underside of the chairs with each person's name on it. It comforted him more than he realized thinking of how down to earth everyone was here. They all knew each other. Generations of families going back decades or more all living happily amongst each other while struggling against the elements and modernization every day. Just the idea that this tight knit community could get harassed or destroyed by someone like Jim Watts or a media craze or big business made Rob's blood boil.

He stood off to the side and watched the waitress in action. Apparently she and her husband had owned the place for decades. While her husband manned the kitchen, she greeted the customers and took their orders. Rob was spellbound listening to her friendly voice and watching her genuine smile. She seemed too young to be the owner of a restaurant and had the energy of a cyclone. She placed down menus, handed everyone silverware sets, responded to questions and even called across the room to the couple in the corner to tell them their food was almost ready. Rob marveled at her speed, her wit and her charm. He couldn't even focus on the conversation. It was as if he was caught in some surreal dream, seeing the life of the people on the island unfold before his eyes and unable to warn them of the impending danger. He grabbed a chair by the end of the table and reflexively sat down. He heard his younger son laugh at something the waitress said and he smiled.

By the time everyone had ordered their food, Rob was lost in thought. He had no idea what anyone was saying as he played out the destruction of Deer Island in his mind. The Franklin letter would ruin everyone's lives as the press and lawyers and land speculators swooped down like starving seagulls fighting over the last morsel of bread. He saw families arguing, neighbor set against neighbor and everywhere he looked, Jim Watts taking advantage of and smiling that sinister cat smile at every turn.

He snapped his head up for a moment, jarred out of his daydream by sudden laughter. Everyone else had been listening to the practical joke Moose played on Watts and Francois. Lindsey had been telling the story; Bobby was throwing in anything she forgot and everyone; Deborah, Adam, William and Lawrence were all leaning forward in their chairs and grinning; all except Rob. He was not even paying attention. Sitting at one end of the table plagued by the conflict of his own thoughts and distracted by yet another friendly family coming into the restaurant, smiling and taking their usual seats, he finally burst. "Are we sure we even want to find it?"

"What the hell are you talking about?" Lindsey's voice easily carried across the table even though she sat next to Rob. Despite the last clue from Moose, she had not given up. She took it personally that Rob would even consider it. Was this Deborah's doing?

"It could destroy this community," Rob held up both his hands in a stop to hold Lindsey back. Everyone had snapped their heads in surprise at his words, even the boys.

"Again," Lindsey was angry now. "What the hell are you talking about?"

"Language," Deborah scolded as she nudged her head at the small family of four that had just walked in and sat at the small square table behind her. They had not seen a lot of children on the island and Lindsey's words must have reached their ears.

"Language?" Lindsey glared across the table at Deborah. "Who are you to talk about language? You're the one who's been calling me a bitch since the day we met."

"Lindsey, hey!" Rob placed a hand on her shoulder. "Calm down."

"I won't calm down," Lindsey shook the hand off her shoulder. "Dammit. We've put so much into this. I've put so much into this!" Lindsey could feel the adrenalin surge rising in her and she welcomed it. She had put a bottle on her emotions for far too long. "I took time off of work, spent my own money, spent countless hours on the computer and all this time with you; And for what?"

Everyone had grown silent as Lindsey took over the conversation. The moment was all the more awkward as even the other people in the restaurant had stopped talking and looked over at her. That didn't matter. She was too angry. She gazed at everyone sitting around her but her eyes fixed on Deborah.

"So I could be thrown away like yesterday's garbage?" Lindsey made a wave with her hand but Deborah only returned her comment with a frown of confusion. "You come in here like the cavalry coming over the hill," Lindsey's eyes fixed on Deborah, "save your boys, take charge of the search, go off with Rob and ditch me like a used rag."

"We didn't ditch you," Rob protested. He didn't like where this was going and he realized part of it was his own fault. He had ditched Lindsey, at least somewhat. The moment Deb showed up his entire attitude changed. He was so happy to see her and of course see his kids with her, that he almost stopped talking to Lindsey entirely. Even his demeanor had changed.

"Really Rob?" Lindsey turned to him now, "really? You've barely talked me at all since she arrived and now, less than 48 hours after she gets here, you're talking about giving up? What the fuck man?"

"Miss I am afraid this language is going to have to stop," the owner suddenly interrupted. She still had her lobster apron on and was carrying a glass of water in her hand that was destined for the nearby table. "There are other patrons here."

"Oh," Lindsey's face fell. She was thoroughly embarrassed and ashamed. She had always prided herself on her manners and how she treated people, especially strangers. She said her please and thank yous like her momma and daddy taught her and she never made a scene in public. This was so unlike her, especially in such a wonderfully friendly and down to earth place such as this. Her anger disappeared in a heartbeat. "I am so sorry," she almost begged the woman to forgive her. "I never talk like this, especially in public. It won't happen again. I promise."

"Okay," the woman smiled and started to turn away. "Just see that it doesn't."

"This is exactly what I was talking about," Rob tried to take over the conversation, explain himself, and give Lindsey time to process everything. He really did feel bad for her and angry at himself for causing this. "See what these people are like?" he pointed to the other patrons and the owner who had just placed the glass of water in front of the older boy in the nearby family. "Can you imagine how an international incident would affect them? Can you imagine the press swooping down here and asking questions and digging into everyone's dirt? It would be a nightmare!"

"Of that I have no doubt," Lawrence spoke up again. It was eerie the way he almost drifted outside of the group, let them have their discussions and almost disappear from their view. It was like he magically returned to his island then reappeared at will. "But that doesn't mean it wouldn't be worth it." Lawrence looked across the table at William. He nodded in agreement already knowing what Lawrence was about to say. "We could use a little attention here," Lawrence continued. "Not just with the border issue and the problems I have had with my island."

Deborah also nodded in understanding. In the short time in which she had known Lawrence, she could already see that his passion went beyond his own island. Yes, winning the court battles and defeating Jim Watts was an obsession with the man, but he also showed a true love for Deer Island and the people living on it. He was almost like some caretaker or wise old shaman voluntarily safeguarding his tribe. She also was relieved that the conversation had turned away from her and Lindsey, especially because she knew Lindsey was right. Rob had changed. He was softer, kinder, and more careful with his words around her. The bitterness and anger of their break up must somehow have been forgotten in this strange new environment they all found themselves in. Her job, his job, salesmen, bills to pay, the separation; it all disappeared here. He was like the man she first fell in love with.

That thought warmed Deborah. She began to reminisce on all their wonderful memories together; the boys, their wedding, meeting for the first time, falling in love and wild crazy sex. Her lip curled a little at that last thought and she looked around to see if anyone noticed her smile. Thankfully, all their eyes were still on Lawrence.

"We've suffered quietly for a long time," Lawrence caught William's gaze and again he was nodding in agreement. "Between the huge fishing companies' competition and our land being bought up for next to nothing, this island has been slowly dying. That's why some people have turned to tourists. It's probably the last industry we have left."

"The attention could help us for sure," William now added. He had not lived on Deer Island nearly as long as Lawrence had. He was not even born here. But he knew how much of a daily struggle it was. All they needed was some kind of natural disaster or a final push by a greedy capitalist and the island was done for. "It could bring more government involvement, maybe more settlers or even, what the heck, more tourists. Anything would help."

"But what kind of attention do you want?" Rob wasn't sure what to think at this point. All he had seen was the quaint, friendly part of the island. He had no idea things were so difficult. "You don't need any more Jim Watts."

"That's for sure," William said.

"Don't you see?" Lindsey recovered from her tirade. She was still a quagmire of emotions but her senses had not lost her and she needed to find a reason to continue the search. "The right kind of attention could really help this place," her eyes began to light up as she imagined the possibilities. "If people knew the history of Deer Island, of the Loyalists, of the struggles the people made and are still making to survive..."

"And the beauty of this place," Deborah added. She could see where Lindsey was going with this. Lindsey wasn't sure if she liked it.

"It would stop being some forgotten place no one ever heard about or ever cared."

"We don't want a wave of tourists," Lawrence warned.

"No, no, that's not what I mean," Lindsey held up her hands. "You'll never get over run with tourists; this place is too far away from any major metropolitan areas anyway-"

"That means there are no big airports nearby dummy," Bobby turned away from staring at Lindsey and said to his brother. He wanted to make sure Lindsey knew he was listening. She was so hot when she got excited like this. Adam rolled his eyeballs but did not engage his brother.

"But you would get enough interest that people would begin to know who you are and what your problems are." Lindsey finished.

"At the very least," Rob had to agree with Lindsey. It made sense. "It will make it more difficult for men like Jim Watts to take advantage of you."

"And make Moose's job a little easier," William said. "He knew that despite his bravado, Moose was struggling in his fight against big oil, big real estate, big fishing and everything else big. The conservationist could use a little help.

"But how do we control it?" Deborah, as always, was the practical one. She knew how crazy the media was, even in Canada. And once the American media got a hold of it, who knows what would happen.

"We can't just tell them about the Franklin letter," Lindsey was suddenly terrified at what they were suggesting. This could ruin everything, "especially not now. We have to find it first."

"It's already starting to get too big. Someone will find out soon."

"Watts knows," Lindsey starting counting with her fingers, "Francois, those four photo tourists who helped us save the boys, (no one had yet figured out who they really were), Moose and Sturgis Adams both have a pretty good idea, William," she looked over at him, then turned to his left, "Lawrence. My god I am almost out of fingers. This won't stay a secret for long."

"We have to make sure we stay ahead of everyone else." Rob said to the group. They all nodded their heads in agreement.

"But how?" Adam, the youngest one among them voiced the obvious question.

"I don't know," his father admitted.

Forty Six

The decision was taken from them. Adam was the first to discover it when he woke up the next morning in the Air BnB home they were still renting. Rob's moving about in the kitchen had woken him and he stumbled out of his nearby bedroom and made his way to the small living room, still dressed in his New York Rangers blue and white flannel pajamas. An annoyed, "Dad you woke me up!" complaint was hurled in Rob's general direction as Adam plopped himself down in the brown leather recliner and as always, turned on the T.V. The satellite dish had been set to the local news by the owners. Adam read the red ticker scrolling across the screen and screamed to his father.

"Dad come here! You've got to see this!"

Rob came rushing into the room from the kitchen holding a green dish towel in his hands and wiping them dry. He had been making a simple scrambled egg and toast breakfast for the boys and Lindsey to try to keep things at least a little normal. Lindsey was still staying with them in her own bedroom and Deborah was at the B&B. Things hadn't changed that much.

"Oh shit!" Rob swore as he watched the words go across the screen: "Local realtor reports incredible find that could change the border with the United States-."

"What is it?" Lindsey burst out of the bathroom and down the brown shag carpeted staircase rubbing her hair with a much larger dark green towel. She had just finished showering upstairs and wore another matching towel perfectly wrapped around her waist and chest. Rob couldn't help but notice her naked, muscular legs almost shimmering from the remnants of shower water. Things hadn't changed that much.

"Look," Rob pointed at the ticker on the screen. Adam had muted the T.V. The lady newscaster was talking about some Canadian political issue he didn't understand.

"Watts!" Lindsey smashed her fist on top of the brown leather recliner Adam was still sitting in. She almost hit his head, "That asshole!"

"Why would he do this?" Rob wondered.

"He's desperate," Lindsey thought out loud. "He doesn't know what to do next."

"But why announce it to the press?"

"Remember what Deborah said last night?" Lindsey hated bringing her up. Just the mention of her name changed Rob's complexion. "Watts doesn't need the letter to make money. All he needs is the possibility of a border change to make speculation worthwhile. What better way to send speculation through the roof than to let the press speculate about it on T.V.?"

"How much do you think he told them?"

"I don't know." Lindsey started drying her hair again. She was dripping on the carpet. "Adam, change the channel and see if anyone else is talking about it."

Adam quickly scrolled through the local, national and international news stations. Fortunately, they all were set near each other. Not one of them seemed to have picked up the story.

"It looks like it's only on this station," he looked up at his father. Neither he, nor Lindsey had moved.

"Then we still have some time," Rob said.

"To do what?" Adam looked up at his father.

"Maybe Watts is sending us a message," Lindsey ignored Adam's question. She was trying to sort it all out.

"What do you mean?" Rob glanced back towards the kitchen. He wondered if he should still finish making breakfast.

"He's hit a dead end," Lindsey sat on the matching brown couch next to the recliner and lithely crossed her bare legs. She didn't care so much about Rob but she realized she was making Adam uncomfortable. Then she snapped back to the conversation. "He knows we have all the information and is trying to force our hand."

"It's not the packet he needs," Rob reminded himself, "it's the speculation it will produce."

"And Watts knows if he makes it public, it will force us to speed up."

"That son of a bitch."

"Yeah," Lindsey agreed as she stood up again and headed back upstairs. "But it worked, damn it."

"I better text Deborah," Rob took out his phone. He didn't notice Lindsey flinch at his words.

They decided to meet at William Luisi's archive/restaurant multi-purpose shack where Deborah and Jim Watts had first met him. It was private enough to stay away from the locals and large enough to spread all their information out together. Deborah, Rob, Lindsey, the boys and even Lawrence were all there within the hour. They had not told the agents what they were doing but Lindsey had a feeling they were out there somewhere.

William had been the first to arrive. His home was naturally close to the shack and like the rest of the island's inhabitants he had been awake since dawn. By the time the others arrived, he had already pushed the red and white checkered tables together to form one long table and put on a pot of coffee.

Lawrence was the last to arrive. Deborah's message had caught him in the middle of his chores and it took him almost a half an hour just to put everything away and head to the main island. "It won't be long before the island gets crazy," he warned the moment he opened the door and stood at the entrance wiping his feet. Dressed in his almost knee high black rubber fishing boots and blue jean overalls, he wasn't even sure he wanted to go inside. It was bad enough being in the old shack again. William hadn't changed it a bit; Same chairs, same checkered tables, same white walls still holding the same framed old photographs of people on the island and even the same old three feet high rectangular freezer was still running strong along the back wall. William probably couldn't have moved the old girl if he had tried. It had been several years since Lawrence had given the shack to William and he had hoped to never be in it again. He needed to spend his time working on his island home and fighting Jim Watts, not hold up in a barren box of a building dwelling on the past.

Stepping across the threshold and looking across the long table at the neatly arranged piles of documents and letters, books and notebooks Lindsey had arranged into piles only made Lawrence more uncomfortable. He still didn't trust these strangers, especially Lindsey. She seemed too eager, too driven and he knew her priority was finding the packet and not necessarily protecting Deer Island. He would have to keep an eye on her. Perhaps, he wondered as he finally approached the table, pulled out the last chair and sat down, he should have called Moose. Being the news junkie that he was, Moose had probably already seen the news broadcast and with the passion he felt for Deer Island there was no way he was just sitting idly by. Better to have Moose with you than on the outside looking in.

"So here's what we have," Lindsey began as she pushed back in her chair to give William room to pour her coffee. She watched the bold dark liquid quickly filling up her mug, the bubbles forming at the top and the steam rising gently into the air. The aroma reached her nose and she took a deep breath before she continued. Coffee was proof to her that there was indeed a god. "I've separated our information into what we know for sure, what we don't know and what we need confirmed." William finished pouring her coffee and moved the coffee pot from in front of her. "Thanks," she looked up at him for a moment before he moved on.

"No problem," William smiled broadly. It was the first time Lindsey had noticed his warm brown eyes and down to earth smile. It distracted her for a moment. She had never paid William much attention. After all, Deborah was the one who had found him first and somehow that made him off limits. At least it had.

"I don't understand," Bobby interrupted in that annoying tone that teenagers always seemed to have when they were not the center of attention. "I thought we had given up."

"We only did that to,"

Lindsey interrupted Rob and finished for him. He had almost said *"to fool the agents,"* or something like that. Lindsey gave him a glare as she said to Bobby, "to give us some time." She looked away from Rob's red face and turned to the rest of the group. "This is all happening so fast; we just needed a moment to catch our breath."

"We don't have a moment," Deborah snapped. She tried not to sound too bitchy, especially to Rob and the kids but she felt pretty guilty about the entire situation. She was the one who had brought Jim Watts into their lives in the first place. It was her fault they were in this mess and the fact that she had arrived like some angel in the night to rescue her sons was only hiding that horrific fact. She knew at some point everyone could turn on her; especially Rob. "That news story could ruin everything."

"It's not a story yet," Lindsey naturally argued with Deborah. She couldn't help it. All of sudden Deborah was part of this group again and was muscling her way into the heart of it. If Lindsey did not stand her ground she could be pushed to the side completely or even pushed out. She wouldn't let that happen. "And if we can stay ahead of the press we can keep it that way."

"Deborah's right," Lawrence warned. He liked Deborah; not in any kind of romantic way, although he had noticed how beautiful she was the moment he first set eyes on her back on the island. Maybe it was how vulnerable she was, maybe it was because he felt like her knight in shining armor, or maybe it was just because Deborah had been so open and honest with him. Whatever the reason, Lawrence felt like he could trust Deborah, and through her, the group. "That story will spread all over the island and all over New Brunswick in a few hours and once it does, any families we need to contact or clues left untouched will be impossible to get our hands on."

"I thought we got everything on the list," Deborah smiled back at Lawrence. Somehow the two of them had formed a mutual bond that she was desperately thankful for. Everyone else in that room, she realized as she scanned the table, had a reason to be angry or resentful of Deborah. Despite recent events, she knew that just under the surface, the boys and Rob were still upset with her for the separation, William Luisi still associated her with Jim Watts and Lindsey of course was the enemy. Only Lawrence had no real reason to hate or mistrust her. It comforted her while also filling her with a painful sadness and longing for easier times.

"Let's make sure," Lindsey reached for the list they had stolen from Francois. She cross referenced it with the index from Nana and read the names aloud. "Adams, Appleby, Brawn," she looked at Lawrence and William. Both of them were nodding their heads up and down in acknowledgement. They were intensely familiar with all those names. "Garrison, Lloyd," she went on and on until she reached the end then quietly double checked and returned her gaze to the historians. "The only family we have nothing from is this Rockwell family."

"We have that," Deborah almost shouted. Suddenly she realized she had something to contribute to the search, something substantial. "Or at least we did," she corrected.

"What do you mean?" Lindsey said.

"Watts stole it from William," Deborah looked at William sheepishly. She hadn't purposely kept that from him; she had just forgotten to say anything in all the confusion. Hopefully William would believe that.

"He stole it?" William almost knocked the table over in his anger. Several of the more full mugs of coffee spilled over onto the tablecloths, "That son of a bitch!"

"Which one did he steal?" Lawrence said. He wasn't surprised in the slightest.

"Which one?" William turned from anger to confusion in a heartbeat. "What do you mean which one?"

"There are two Rockwell items."

"Two?"

"The one written to Rockwell and the one written by him."

"Wait," William leaned forward and looked directly at Lawrence. He was upset and embarrassed that there was still some research out there he had not yet finished. It didn't surprise him of course. It would take him years to catch up to Lawrence, but he didn't like it coming out in the open in front of the group. "I thought there was only the one letter. You never mentioned another."

"You never asked."

"Hold on, hold on," Lindsey interrupted. She could tell something important was happening and she needed to be brought up to speed. "What are you two talking about and how is Watts mixed up in this?"

"Watts stole a letter from William's shack," Deborah explained. She felt good being able to contribute, especially adding something that Lindsey was unaware of.

"When?"

"When we first got here," Deborah lowered her eyes. She still had not given much detail on her arrival in Canada and Deer Island and she preferred to keep it that way. "It was a letter William found from Franklin about wanting something returned."

"A letter from Franklin?" Lindsey snapped.

"What kind of a letter?" Rob glared. It was the first time since Deborah's arrival that he was angry at her and he didn't like it.

"Franklin was writing this Rockwell character about needing something returned," William took over. He could easily sense the tension in the room and tried to cut through it. He was always good at working with groups and sorting out feelings and issues but this group was a challenge even for him.

"My god the packet?" Lindsey almost fell out of her chair. "You had a letter about the packet all this time and never told us?"

"It never mentioned a packet," Deborah leaped to the defense. She would not have her moment in the sun ruined. "It never said what was stolen at all."

"But something was stolen," Rob offered.

"Not even that was clear," William again tried to calm everyone down. "Nothing about the letter was clear at all, that was why we held onto it for so long."

"And it's why we never even catalogued it," Lawrence came to William's defense. He was angry at himself for never putting any stock in that Franklin letter, but he too felt that it really was nothing special. It was only after all this other information came out that he realized what a find it was, "or paired it up with the other one."

"Again," William was trying to be patient. He knew Lawrence could easily get sidetracked. "What other letter?"

"It's in the unclaimed associations folder." Lawrence waved in the direction of the darkened archive room behind him.

"Unclaimed associations?" Lindsey repeated.

"That's where we put all the letters and documents that don't clearly belong to any one family and also reference any kind of associations various families put together," Lawrence watched William swiftly rise from the table and head to the other room. He heard the distinct click of the light switch as the yellowish glare filled the old room. "It's the red folder way in the back."

"I know what folder it is," William called from the entrance to the room. His patience was wearing thin.

"You have an entire folder like that?" Lindsey should not have been surprised. After all the documents and letters she had seen in the many archives throughout their trip, this was nothing new. Maybe it was because she didn't expect such a small island and such a ramshackle operation like William was running to be that organized.

"Not every family or person in Deer Island is accounted for," Lawrence explained. He leaned back to peak at William but he had disappeared around the corner. "Whenever we found something that did not match any known family, we put it aside and as the years have gone by, we began to categorize and organize even those items as they grew in number."

"Here it is," William returned quickly holding a red file folder in his hands.

"You brought the whole folder?"

"I left my gloves in here," William shook his head at Lawrence in annoyance. Would he ever stop being an 'I told you so'? "And I didn't want to touch any of the other letters without them on."

"What do you need gloves for?" It was the first time Adam spoke up and his voice almost cracked. He found all this extremely exciting and hadn't said anything so far for fear he might be sent in the other room. It happened almost every time his father or mother was involved in "adult things".

"To protect the documents," William reached into one of the plain white cabinets hanging on the far wall and pulled out a small tissue sized box of surgical gloves. He quickly slipped them on with the classic rubber band snap that broke the brief silence.

Lindsey, Deborah, Rob, Adam and even Bobby all watched William go through the folder in an almost trancelike anticipation. Everyone in the room knew that this was perhaps their last chance. No more clues remained and nothing else held out any more promise. If this last letter did not lead them somewhere else, if it was indeed their last dead end, then the whole adventure would be over and everything would go back to the way it was. It had to be the answer, it had to!

Forty Seven

Oval office

"I've got to go public," President John Custis placed his hands on the mahogany desk and started to stand. He hadn't moved for thirty seconds and for a man like John Custis, that was an eternity. His Chief of Staff Martha even wondered if she should have handled the matter more herself before breaking the news. After all, she knew what he was going to say. "I can't lie to the American people."

"You do it all the time sir," Alex reminded him with a smile. "Or rather I do for you."

"That's different and you know it," the President sat back down and glared at his emotional Press Secretary. If she wasn't such a good friend he might have slugged her. "This isn't about national security-"

"Well actually it is sir," Bill Donovan, head of the CIA interrupted from directly in front of the desk. He was the one who had brought the President the news in the first place. Always abrupt, confrontational and direct, Bill Donovan was never one to mince words. He took the words national security way too seriously but as a career politician he had built up so many habits inside the beltway that he overreacted to any words that could be misused, misconstrued or mistaken. It drove the President crazy.

"Would everybody stop fucking arguing with me!" the President shouted. He was furious that the news had broken about the border dispute and he was in no mood for petty quarrels. "I am the god-damned President of the United States. Stop wasting my fucking time correcting things we both know are true and let's deal with this shit storm in our laps."

"You don't need to go public yet," Martha said calmly. As always, the President's Chief of Staff was dressed perfectly in yet another colorful yet reserved outfit that reflected her position of power and still somehow highlighted her beauty. Custis had lost track of how many outfits she had and was pretty sure he had not seen her in the same one twice even though he was into his second year in office. Yet while her suit dress and her demeanor were calm as always, he could sense her discomfort. He had known Martha too long and he knew she hated it when she was not in control. As the President's chief of staff it was her job to call meetings and not only was this one she didn't call, she was staggered by the sudden revelation that the story had broken. There had been no warning or sign that this was coming and she resented Bill Donovan for not giving her a heads up. It was just like that bastard to keep secrets to himself; she directed her anger at him with a glare.

"There is still time to squash this," Bill reminded them. "Our agents have reported that the news is only on one local channel and that it is no more than a rumor at this point."

"And what are you doing about it?" The President snapped.

"The Canadians are on it sir."

"What the fuck does that mean?"

"They are hoping to discredit the story," Donovan took an involuntary step backwards. He was unprepared for the President's anger, "make it look like some kind of a hoax."

"What are our boys doing?"

"They've put a tail on Callahan."

"Callahan," the President turned to Martha. He had lost patience with Donovan and his cryptic answers. "We're still depending on that hockey player and his girlfriend?"

"It keeps our deniability secure sir," Martha looked up from her iPad. She took notes on everything that was ever said or done in all of her meetings, formal and informal. Donovan and Lewis were of course freaked out at first by her diligence to keep track of their conversations but she had assured them over and over again that her iPad had absolutely no connection to the internet and could never be broken into. Besides, she recorded it all in her own personal short hand that only she could decipher. Martha was no amateur. "And right now, that is our top priority."

"Do they have any idea where the packet is?" The President shifted gears. He hated discussions of deniability and secrecy. It went against everything his mother taught him ever since the day she washed his mouth out with soap for lying about his sister. Honesty was the backbone for everything John Custis did.

"Not yet sir," Martha said.

"Where the fuck is Randolph?" The President turned his head anxiously towards the open door and then behind him out the windows. Even the bright blue sky and sunshine streaming in through the large floor to ceiling bullet proof windows was not enough to brighten his mood.

"He should be here any moment sir," Martha at least had been able to arrange that. While Donovan and Johnson arrived unannounced, Martha knew that the President would want everyone from the first meeting involved. He was not a man who liked anyone kept out of the loop. Secrets among secrets only made for headaches, aggravation, mistrust and inefficiency. Unfortunately, that was how Washington was used to operating and it made Martha's job all the more difficult doing it Custis' way.

As if on cue; Dr. Randolph burst into the Oval Office followed by his boss, Secretary of State Lewis. Two Secret Service men rushed in behind them and almost tackled the pair before the President waved them off. "Sorry sir," Randolph stopped in front of the desk and saluted. He could not prevent his military training and even though Custis was dressed in a pin stripe navy suit, he still was the commander in chief.

"Apology accepted," Custis returned the salute. He was a veteran too of course.

"We would have been here even sooner sir," Secretary Lewis added. He did not salute. "But I had to find Randolph first," Lewis gave Dr. Randolph a glare. He still had not forgiven Randolph for going over his head with this in the first place but there was nothing he could do about it. Since then, Randolph had not broken any more protocols. He had been professional, diligent and loyal. Most importantly he had been discreet, even more than Lewis himself. It had been a monumental task keeping this news a secret, especially in a place like Washington. Lewis found himself slipping up more than once and only his position over Randolph kept him from letting it all out. He had to beat that smug son of a bitch. Smug, but efficient, Lewis was forced to admit. No news had leaked from his department or to anyone other than Lewis and Randolph. Indeed it was secure enough that Lewis even gave in to Randolph's request and allowed him to continue his research.

"I have done some more digging sir," Randolph got right to business and pulled at the snaps on his briefcase. He pulled out an eagle embroidered brown leather pad folio and opened it to the plain white lined notepad with black and blue chicken scratch inside, "And it does not look good."

Custis stood up and moved across the "E Pluribus Unum" carpet in the center of the office with his usual limp. He collapsed onto the dark brown suede couch. Right now he needed some comfort. He was tired and angry and in no mood to sit at his desk or in the formal colonial wooden chairs. "Explain," he commanded.

"I have been reading more letters and documents from Franklin as well as other Congressmen and statesmen on both sides of the Atlantic and both sides of the issue." Randolph remained standing next to the President's recliner, paused and nervously scanned through his notes. He flipped several pages back and forth.

"Just summarize the fucking notes," The President snapped.

"Yes sir," Randolph stood straighter and almost saluted again. His military training snapped back into place and he immediately calmed down. When he first walked in, he was of course nervous. The first time meeting the President had been thrilling and intimidating but it had at least been offset by the excitement of it being the first time. Now that thrill was gone and the President was furious. Dr. Randolph was terrified of being caught in the President's angry wake and did not want to become collateral damage from this crisis. He had worked too hard for his career to be flushed down the toilet like this.

"It is as we said before," Randolph closed the notebook and looked up. He didn't need the notes he realized. The conclusions were inescapable. "Franklin had a lot of enemies and was almost at his wits' end by this point in his career. I found letters to Joseph Priestley," Randolph almost opened up his notebook to quote the letters but thought better of it, "in which Franklin is down on mankind, depressed and disillusioned. James Madison, I think we all know him," Randolph smiled at everyone in the room. They all were standing in their same spots. No one smiled in return. "James Madison said that John Adams shoots venom every time he even talks of Franklin and the Congress themselves were seriously considering firing him, calling Franklin "that old corrupt serpent."

"Jesus Christ," the President shook his head. He was shocked by these political revelations. Of course, he knew better than anyone else in that room how ugly and corrupt politics could get. He had seen the open-faced lies, the playing to the cameras, the vain and petty men (and a few women). But even so, like probably most Americans, he still held almost a god-like fascination of the Founding Fathers, especially Benjamin Franklin, the cute little old man with the glasses and the kite. He couldn't believe the way he was being treated by his friends, especially near the end of his life. Being reminded that the Founding Fathers were men like any other hit his patriotism hard.

"There's more," Randolph pressed. "When you look specifically at the negotiations, something odd occurs."

"Odd, how?"

"As you may remember sir, eventually John Jay and John Adams joined Franklin in Paris. And you know what Adams thought of Franklin."

"Uh-huh," the President nodded. That was already covered in the first meeting. He was starting to grow impatient again.

"Well Jay also wrote letters back to Congress criticizing Franklin. Both men, Franklin and Jay and of course Adams, kept notes to themselves. The mistrust and venom between them all was almost palpable. Then suddenly, in November of 1783, Franklin abruptly agrees with Jay and Adams and shortly after that, they have the Treaty."

"What do you mean suddenly?"

"It just doesn't make sense sir," Randolph frowned. "Franklin bitterly opposed many of the ideas of Adams and Jay and held on to them stubbornly. I wouldn't describe it as a one hundred and eighty degree shift, but it's not far from that."

"And you think,"

"I don't think anything sir," Randolph quickly interrupted. He would not get dragged into speculation. He knew where that could lead.

"What matters sir," Lewis was happy to takeover. He was tired of his subordinate Randolph running the show, "is not what we think, it's what we know."

"Explain," Custis hated poetic melodramatic statements like Lewis was known to make. The man was constantly pumping his chest, trying to be the alpha-male in the room. You would think having the title Secretary of State would be enough for any man's resume, especially an African American like Tom Lewis who had fought for civil rights, graduated Harvard and had a career that would make anyone jealous; man, woman, black or white. Yet somehow he always felt the need to overdramatize every statement and use up time and energy with mysterious and cryptic allusions.

"The border has been controversial for the entire history between the United States and Canada," Lewis began. He knew the President was short on patience, especially right now, but he didn't care. He would have his moment.

"I know that Tom,"

"You know that sir, we know it, and of course the Canadian Government knows it." There he was being cryptic again.

"Tom!" the President barked. It was a tone that Tom dare not ignore and it finally broke the melodrama.

"Sir, before today," Lewis finally got to the point. He talked slowly and methodically, trying to balance the line between sounding condescending and making every point of his precise argument clear. "No one in the world really cared or even knew that the United States and Canada had a border issue. It was the ultimate example of agreeing to disagree."

"Was?"

"Once this story is out in the general public," Tom eyed his adversary Alex Johnson, knowing she could chime in at any moment, "everyone will be aware of the issue whether the Franklin packet exists or not."

"It's part of the backstory sir," Alex reluctantly agreed. She hated it when someone else did her speaking for her, especially when it was Tom Lewis. He was such a melodramatic pain in the ass. "Any news station will do its due research and discover what we already know."

"They'll find out about Franklin's issues with his health and his arguments with Adams," Lewis took control back and Alex would have tried to interject except unlike him, she did not need to be the Alpha in the room. This was way too important of an issue. Let Tom have his space. "They'll find out about the Jay Treaty and the War with Canada."

"The only thing anyone knows about the war of 1812 is the date," Dr. Randolph suddenly spoke up. He had been content to let his boss handle the meeting now but a chord had just been struck. Randolph knew more about the ignorance of the American public better than anyone in that room. It wasn't just because as the State Historian and in his career as a faculty member at Georgetown he had seen first-hand how little his fellow American knew, it was also a passion of his. He had read studies, participated in historical organizations for the preservation of history and even toyed with writing a book on the subject. "Americans have no idea that we went to war twice with the nation of Canada."

"They just think they are a bunch of hockey playing Moose hunters," Alex couldn't resist the jab at Tom, remembering his comment from the first meeting. The President smiled as well. He remembered it too.

"My department will be pressured by both the media and grandstanding Congressmen to settle the border and the issue," Tom smiled at Alex's jab as well. He was not such an ass that he couldn't laugh at himself.

"Alex," the President sighed and turned to his press secretary and good friend. He was glad to be done with Tom, at least for the moment. "What's your take on this?"

"The border issue is only the tip of the iceberg," Alex began. She was glad to put Tom in his place and point out that he had failed to see the bigger picture. "And despite what Tom just said, the pressure on his department will be nothing compared to the pressure on you."

"Me?" Custis pointed at his chest. He knew this was coming, but he still didn't like hearing it.

"As we said in the last meeting," Alex finally sat on the couch near President Custis. She knew she had his permission to be in his personal space. There was no romantic interest between the two friends; they had been through too much together in Afghanistan for that to be the case. They were two veterans, bonded by their love of country and shared experiences. Alex couldn't make the President uncomfortable even if she were sitting next to him totally naked. They were solid. "The press will be all over you to take a side."

"I already told you I won't be pushed into an extreme position," the President said firmly.

"You may not be able to prevent it," Alex stared right into Custis' dark green eyes. She hated making John uncomfortable. She knew what a passionate man he was and what high expectations he had for himself. She knew how deep his convictions were and how much he believed in the idea of America. The thought of people trying to exploit his values for their own personal celebrity filled her with a hatred that she thought was only reserved for the Taliban.

"Now it's your turn to explain," Custis tried to joke, but it fell flat.

"Sir this reminds me of the flag burning issue," Alex said slowly, "Or the NFL players taking a knee during the national anthem a few years back."

"You've got to be kidding me,"

"It's that polarizing sir."

"Polarizing?"

"While you and I both know and lean towards the middle ground," Alex instinctively lowered her voice and leaned forward. She was not trying to keep any secrets. Everyone in the room knew the President's views on flag burning. But Alex and the President shared a bond with the sensitivity of the issue. As veterans, the flag meant everything to them and to many of their comrades. Every single one of their buddies who had come home from the war in a box came home with that flag draped over them. The two of them agonized over the issue and stayed up long nights trying to wrap their head around their feelings. As soldiers however, they knew that they were protecting more than the flag, they were protecting the Constitution and the freedom it represents. If someone wanted to express their freedom of speech by burning a flag, no matter how much that offended them, Alex and John were forced to defend it. Alex herself had once brought up the point that if enough people had burned flags during the war in Vietnam, maybe more soldiers would be alive today. Unfortunately, a complicated view was something most Presidents did not have the luxury of holding, at least not in today's media charged world.

"Your enemies and even your friends will all take the high ground," Alex used the military analogy. "They'll take shots at your from both sides to build up their own positions, play to their bases and force you to either choose a side or lose."

"Yeah, I get it," the President rolled his eyes. He had already seen this coming. Patriots on one side, Loyalists on the other; that story had already played out and everyone knew how it had turned out.

"I'm not sure if you do," Alex didn't often criticize the President and her words stung. "I've already played out the scenario assuming you order me to take the middle ground," she looked at Martha for a moment who hadn't said a word since the beginning of the meeting. Custis noticed the glance and it pissed him off. He knew his Chief of Staff and Press Secretary often talked behind his back and it had nothing to do with the fact that they were both women. They each, in their own way, had a mother like instinct to protect the President and sometimes that included keeping secrets from him. He tolerated it as much as he could; telling himself that they were just doing their jobs. However, in his first month in office he had exploded. He shouted at both of them, claiming that he was not a child that needed to be protected. He told them that there was nothing either of them could handle that he couldn't. He almost ordered them to tell him everything. Almost; He was not stupid enough to do that. He calmed down. He looked in Alex's terrified eyes and the truth hit him like a brick. Clearly, the two of them needed to talk about him when he wasn't around. He understood that. Hell, he got annoyed with himself sometimes. He couldn't imagine what it was like to be in their shoes.

"And I don't see any way around it," Alex played out how she envisioned the news unfolding. "In order to take the middle ground, I will need to defend the Loyalists in some way."

"Why do you have to defend them?"

Alex opened up her notebook, pointed to a line in the middle of a page and read directly from it:

"New York Times: Does this mean the President thinks the Loyalists were treated unfairly?

Alex: Fair or unfair is not the President's job to judge. This was over 200 years ago. He simply doesn't see the Loyalists as villains.

Fox News: Does the President still see George Washington as a hero then?

Alex: Of course he does. The President's devotion to the Founding Fathers has never changed.

Washington Post: Then what of Benjamin Franklin? Certainly the President has an issue with a diplomat for the United States-"

Alex looked up from her notebook. "Here's why I interrupt them and say that The President is not here to evaluate the performance of any Founding Father."

"Why interrupt them?"

"Sir," Alex's voice again softened, "We cannot allow anyone in the press to directly question you on the Founding Fathers like this. If they even utter these words, it becomes headlines they can manipulate."

"Even an innocuous headline like," Martha interjected from her position near the desk. She still had not moved the entire meeting. "'President questioned on Benjamin's Franklin's service to our country', would be a disaster."

The President's face turned white. He couldn't believe how easy it would be to warp his beliefs into an attack.

"We simply cannot allow this to happen John," Alex placed a hand on the President's knee. It was the first time in his life that John Custis had felt so powerless. Even in Afghanistan, surrounded by people he did not know and could not trust, he always had options. He had his buddies, he had his gun; there was always something he could do. In his political life, no matter how bad it had become, he still had his faithful. He had his base; he had his friends and allies. There was always some option to solve any problem. But this time, he could see no way out. He wouldn't lie. He wouldn't deceive. But even if he did, what would be the effect? The best case scenario was that half the country hated him.

"How do we stop it?" he finally said.

"The Canadians have some leverage," Bill Donovan suddenly said something positive. The President was pissed that Bill he hadn't said that at the beginning but at least the color returned to his face. "Their operatives are going after the Watts character to see if they can discredit him."

"Discredit him?"

"He's been under their radar for years," Donovan informed them. Custis wanted to punch the smugness right off his face. "They have several options available to them."

"What about our boys?"

"They're tailing Callahan as we speak."

"I want you in constant communication with them," the President said.

"I already am sir," Donavan held up his phone. "They've got their eyes on him, right now."

"What are we going to do about the border?" the President turned back to his Secretary of State. He could use a distraction from Benjamin Franklin and Loyalists. It was ironic that a border dispute with America's greatest friend could actually be at the level of a distraction. This was crazy!

"We have played out several scenarios," Lewis took a formal tone as if he was suddenly in charge of the meeting. The President didn't like it.

"Scenarios?" he repeated with a bark.

"I-It's standard procedure," Lewis was knocked off guard. He had not expected the President's hostility, "in all diplomatic discussions."

"Just give them the fucking island," Custis swore.

"It's not that simple sir," Martha leapt to the defense of the Secretary of State. It had been her job since day one and she took it very seriously. If the President was going to be able to stay who he was; a passionate man with high standards and morals, then he was going to lose patience in these political meetings that Martha had called and it would be her duty to prevent the meetings from becoming a shouting match between angry dogs with giant egos. It was not an easy job by any stretch of the imagination but she had been doing it for years in the corporate world. That's why Custis chose her in the first place.

"You know we can't just give it away," Alex agreed with Martha and could barely avoid sounding condescending, "It would be yet another media frenzy."

"Why is everything about the god-damned fucking media?" the President said softly this time. He was so tired of this argument every day. Nothing he did ever mattered. The only thing that mattered was how it was painted to the public. He could save the damn world and bring out the resurrection itself but if the press saw a way to spin it to their point of view; he could come across as Satan himself. Why did he ever take this job?

"First amendment," Alex smiled and twirled her finger in the air, attempting to add a little levity to the situation.

"Any amendment, or even law for that matter," Randolph suddenly spoke again. It seemed like he disappeared into the walls anytime political issues were the topic then suddenly re-appeared when a historical button of his was pushed, "is only as good as the people who enforce it. The first amendment doesn't protect us from ourselves."

"I still believe in a free press," Alex was the last one in the room anyone expected to say that. She was in the lion's den every day, dodging accusations and innuendo. It was remarkable that she had lasted as long as she did, "even if they sometimes act like spoiled children."

"Sometimes?" Almost everyone in the room said in unison.

"At the end of the day," Alex laughed along with her colleagues, "the truth eventually comes out." She looked directly at the President. She knew where his priorities lay.

"Why couldn't our glorious Founding Fathers have figured out an easier way to do it though?" The President groaned and turned his head to the famous Gilbert Stuart life size portrait of George Washington hanging on the Oval Office wall. "How did you ever survive George?"

"Sir," Donavan spoke up. His face was white as he stared into his phone.

"What is it?" the President said slowly. He wasn't sure he could handle another revelation.

"It's Callahan sir," Donovan looked up from his phone and at everyone in the room. "They've lost him."

L9

July 11, 1814

Eastport, Massachusetts

Oliver Rockwell couldn't believe this was happening. He had just left Deer Island for Eastport less than two years ago and now the war was coming to him here? All he had wanted to do was take advantage of all the smuggling that was going on across the Canada-U.S. border during the war. It seemed that everyone was doing it and neither government seemed to care about enforcement. They were too busy burning each other's capitals and fighting on Great Lakes, oceans and land to worry about who traded what with who. From Massachusetts to New Brunswick, across Passamaquoddy and the St. John's, everywhere you looked there was smuggling going on in either direction; American flour going to Canada, fine British goods going to the United States. The Swedes were involved, the Spanish were involved, and the Napoleonic Wars threw everything and everyone into chaos. Even before the war of 1812, when the American government started that foolish embargo act, smugglers descended on Eastport like moths drawn to the proverbial flame.

And why shouldn't Oliver add his name to the list of people making boatloads of money off of foolish government policies? He wasn't getting anywhere on Deer Island. Thomas Farrell still held the deeds to his land, the King had never come through, his "friends" had rebuffed his plan to use the Franklin packet and he still was alone after more than twenty years of struggling on that damnable plot of land. Why shouldn't he try something new?

But as he stood in the middle of the small 20 or so crowd of his neighbors gathered by Eastport's sea wall and stared at the approaching British fleet, he couldn't help but reconsider his decisions. The war was coming right to his doorstep now. Decades ago, the sign of the Union Jack flying proudly at the top of the mast filled him with pride and hope; now it filled him with dread. The majestic and deadly British frigate with 74 menacing cannons was accompanied by an occupying force and many other support vessels. This was nothing short of an invasion and Eastport was in no position to prevent it. Its small Fort Sullivan and even smaller American force guarding her was no match for the overwhelming British might. And worse still, the town was in between the two forces.

Major Putnam, the American commander was already discussing plans for resisting the British, which made Oliver's neighbors that much more upset. Why should they be caught in the crossfire? Was it really that important which flag flew over their Fort? This was their livelihood after all.

Oliver had come to like and even respect his neighbors. Like him, many of them were Loyalists or children of them. A few were original settlers and all of them were hard working and determined. Every day had been a struggle to survive and the tiny town of Eastport was just beginning to turn a corner. Profits were being made, luxuries were beginning to become a little more common and it was beginning to look like the town just might rival St. John's or Fredericton for importance. This invasion could put them right back at square one.

"Why are they here?" A little voice said. It was Elly's five year old daughter Josephine of course. Her bright blue curious eyes were always open to the beautiful world around her. Oliver loved the way she questioned everything and saw joy in the simplest of things. This was maybe the first time he ever heard fear in her voice and it angered him more than he realized.

"Will they fire on the town?"

"Should we evacuate?"

"We need to convince Putnam to surrender," Samuel Wheeler said. He was one of the leading citizens of the town and his opinion carried weight. Oliver wondered if it would be enough.

He looked over the seawall again at the approaching fleet. The salt water spray and bright blue sky had a calming effect on him. He had always been comfortable on the water and no matter how nervous everyone else was, he couldn't help but enjoy the warm sun on his face and wind whipping through his hair. A small smile even began to form at the edge of his lips. It was almost amusing listening to the panic in the voices of Oliver's new neighbors. Had they forgotten the Revolution so quickly? Like him, most of them were Loyalists or refugees. Like him, most of them had settled here to get away from the war or remain in the empire or now to take advantage of it all. And like him, they were on the wrong side of the border again.

Oliver shook his head in disbelief and stared across Passamaquoddy's waters, across the unseen border to his old home. He could easily see Deer Island although his old house was beyond his sight further north. How ironic that he would still be safe and sound, living again in the Empire had he never journeyed here in the first place? *"Unbelievable,"* he bent his head down into the palm of his hand, closed his eyes and shook his head slowly. The anger swelled in his chest and threatened to scream out to the heavens. *"Unbelievable,"* he thought again as he barely kept his anger and frustration in check. *"Almost the moment I return to the United States, I am again embroiled in a war and caught on the wrong side."*

"It may be too late," Oliver was ripped out of his thoughts by his neighbor Dr. Mowe. The Dr. was one of the most respected men in the town, especially by Oliver and if he thought the town was in danger then maybe Oliver really should be worried. He turned his head towards him.

"You believe so?" Oliver said.

"The British are in a hurry," the Dr. pointed to the men already on shore and the boats further out. "See how quickly they move?"

Oliver turned to where the Dr. was pointing. He had seen enough actions from British soldiers and sailors to know the Dr. was right. British Redcoats were jogging off the ships and onto the shore, taking offensive positions in preparation for an assault. Officers were yelling and the men were all holding their rifles tight, as if at any moment the order to fire would be given. "They know they have a superior force."

"Will they burn the town?" A woman next to the Dr. asked. Oliver did not remember her name. She was one of the more wealthy women in the town. Her clothes gave that away, especially the fine silk scarf she wore around her neck and the fancy French hat covering her dark red hair; although she could have bought those items for next to nothing. Who knew what prices were like now with all the smuggling going on?

"Unlikely," Dr. Mowe understood her fears. The British had marched into Washington D.C. just last month and burned most of the town, including the White House. Eastport would be an even easier target. The wooden homes and small shops would go up in no time. "Eastport is valuable to them and they have always claimed it was part of the empire."

"Absolutely," Oliver could barely suppress a smile. He knew full well how many disputes there were over the border. Even the contentious Jay Treaty almost 20 years ago did not settle all the issues and he knew it! He knew it better than anyone in the town, and perhaps in the world. He hadn't just stolen the packet from William Franklin, he had read it! He had read every word, countless times. He had scoured the maps, struggled through Ben Franklin's scribbled notes and angry epithets. It was no wonder William wanted to keep it all a secret. Franklin was clearly in pain and in a state of rage, maybe even in a fury when he wrote some of those words.

"Would they occupy the town then?" Oliver snapped his head back towards Dr. Mowe. A sudden realization overtook him. He knew British policy in occupations. Soldiers and officers would quarter themselves in local homes. They would sleep in your beds, dine at your tables and wander through your rooms. *"My god,"* his mind began to race uncontrollably, *"maybe one of them even knows about the packet!"*

Oliver had always assumed that William Franklin would never tell anyone about the packet after he stole it. Franklin's letter begging for its return certainly proved that. And after all these years, it had become clear that neither side was willing to play their card; But what about now? William Franklin was finally dead, just two years ago. Had he told someone on his death bed? Had he instructed someone to find it? His heart began to race faster than his mind. The pounding in his chest and his head made it difficult to even think. He scanned the crowd looking for anyone who could be an enemy. Was there some officer here with specific instructions, on some secret mission, to find the packet and punish the one who stole it? My god, was that why the British started the war in the first place?

Oliver was near panic. He rubbed his sweaty palms on his pants and looked at his neighbors. Were they staring at him? Was Dr. Mowe involved? He was an important man with important connections. Oliver couldn't take any chances. The last part of his rational mind knew that even if all of this was wild speculation, any British officer living in his house was a real danger. Who knows what they could do? Who knows what they could find? He could not watch them every minute of every day. He had to hide the packet now!

Forty Eight

Agents Saltman and Foster were having trouble getting comfortable. The woods around William Luisi's shack were thick, dark and covered with dead leaves and scrub. It was no problem hiding themselves behind these old pine trees and brush but that also meant there were few places to stand without a limb, branch, tree or shrub in your face. There certainly was no place to sit down. With Foster being an open water guy and Saltman being an office jock, the forest was one of the last places either of them wanted to be.

But, they had to. The moment the story broke on the local news they knew that they were in trouble. A quick call to Washington left little doubt that their mission and perhaps even their careers were in deep jeopardy. The Canadian agents Beauvais and Macleod had already flown the coop after their director threatened to throw them out of the country. He screamed that under no uncertain terms were they to return until they had tracked down Watts and put the fear of God and the government in his face. It looked like this shaky Canadian-American international espionage partnership was about to tear apart like the ominous border itself if they couldn't produce something tangible soon.

"When do we move?" Foster said anxiously. He pushed a branch out of his face and snapped a few photos. He felt silly maintaining their cover at this point, especially hiding in the woods. What kind of a tourist hides in the woods and takes pictures of ugly buildings in the middle of a clearing?

"When something happens," Saltman leaned against a pine tree and turned his direction to the road. Not a single car had gone by in fifteen minutes and he found that strange even for Deer Island. "You notice anything odd about the town this morning?" he turned back to look at Foster. "Anything odder than normal," he clarified.

"Motel parking lot was empty and the restaurant was dark," Foster shrugged his shoulders. "And it seemed oddly quiet on the way over here; but other than that, no."

"That news story has gotta break."

Foster just frowned. He knew exactly what Saltman was getting at. There should have been more noise and commotion this morning. They both had been in enough small towns, whether in Canada or the states, to see how a community responded when something exciting or sensational broke. Every Tom, Dick,

Harry, Thelma and Louise came out of the woodwork to spread the gossip. Cars screeched into parking spaces and occupants jumped out, shoppers ran out of and into stores, and sometimes people ran right into the path of a moving car as they sprinted across the street to tell someone else the news. It was chaotic, ugly and intensely human. They both hated it.

That hadn't happened here, at least not yet. Maybe it was because everyone was already up and out working before the news broke. After all, there are no televisions out on the water. Maybe it was because no one believed it. Maybe it was because no one cared. No, that wasn't it. The more the two men tried to come up with some reason for the lack of a town response, the more ridiculous they sounded and the more they realized that something was going to happen soon, if it wasn't happening already.

The sound of a car racing along the road broke the eerie silence. Gravel was being kicked up so loud and the wind was being pushed so fast that it was clear the car was hugging the road at high speeds. Both agents looked out towards the street and within seconds a dark black pick-up truck swept into view and skidded to a halt at the edge of the road and driveway. The driver of the truck, a six and a half foot tall lumberjack like man with the face of a teddy bear jumped out, looked at the several cars already parked in front of the shack and then back down the road. He placed his hands on his hips and gave out a shrug. He seemed to be looking for something or someone.

"You hear that?" Adam was the first to notice the sound of the vehicle outside.

"Don't worry about it," Bobby of course scolded his brother. William Luisi was standing over the group, holding the letter gently with both hands. "Just read the letter," Bobby pleaded.

William turned his head towards the walls. The small amount of wrinkles on his forehead scrunched together into a frown. He knew something was up but he couldn't see outside. He stared for another moment at the blank white walls then turned back to look at the others. No one wanted to pay any attention to anything other than the Oliver Rockwell letter in his hands. He looked down and began to read aloud.

"October 12, 1812

To my dear friends in our association,

"That's how it's addressed?" Lindsey was disappointed. She had hoped for confirmation of the names on her own list. How would she cross reference it? How could she be sure the letter was written to someone in Rob's family?

"That's why it's in our folder," Lawrence quipped. Yet another reason he didn't like Lindsey. She had no patience. "We don't have any idea who he is writing to."

"Then how do you know it's relevant?"

"We don't." Lawrence felt good putting Lindsey in her place. He knew how much work this kind of research was. He had been doing it for decades both as a hobby and to defend his claims from Watts. For Lindsey to think that they would find some kind of treasure map or magic bullet was naïve and annoying. "Keep reading William."

It gives me great pains to write this letter to you now. For although we have disagreed for almost 20 years, I have always maintained hope for a final settlement.

You have never agreed with me on how we should use the packet

"The packet!" Almost all of them cried out. Lindsey, Rob, Bobby and Adam lunged forward in their chairs as their eyes lit up. Deborah let herself finally smile and William paused for a minute to enjoy the excitement in the room. Only Lawrence remained stoic. It was too early.

and of course I understand your reasons. I understand but I still protest. What I did was no worse of a crime than what Farrell has been doing to us for decades or the King or for that matter the Patriots.

"Who's Farrell?" Adam was paying close attention. He didn't want to miss a single clue in this mystery.

"He was a land developer and speculator," William stopped to explain. Everyone on Deer Island knew the name of Thomas Farrell, at least anyone who had lived there longer than a few years. "Right after the war, he held title to large chunks of this island and refused to grant any rights to the families who had settled here and cleared the land."

"Which war?" Bobby asked.

"The revolution dummy," Adam was overjoyed to finally be able to get one in against his brother. Bobby just frowned and ignored the stupid grin on his brother's face.

"Did he control land my family lived on?" Rob said. He had not forgotten his other reason for coming here.

"He controlled the land everyone listed in your index lived on," Lawrence answered this time. No one knew the name Thomas Farrell better than Lawrence. His face contorted when he mentioned the name and his bright red cheeks became even redder. Thomas Farrell was perhaps worse than even Jim Watts, at least in Lawrence's eyes. "And the son of a bitch never worked a day in his life. He just held onto the land, wanting to use it for lumber or some other purpose he knew only to himself. His stubbornness and disrespect for the original settlers is legendary."

"There is no stone to mark his grave, he is hated so much." William added.

The sound of another car outside caught their attention again. Something was going on. "Keep reading," Lindsey urged.

I did agree with you that as long as Franklin was alive that it was dangerous to use the information but now that he is dead, I am reconsidering.

"Franklin!"

"Which one?"

"The letter is dated 1812," Lindsey pointed out. She had done her research. "So he must be talking about William Franklin. Ben died back in the 1790s."

"Why would William Franklin's death matter?"

"Well if Rockwell still has the packet,"

"Keep reading."

"Since I know that you will never agree with me, I take my leave of you. Continue on fighting Farrell. I hope that someday you receive the deeds we so desperately deserve. I am tired of waiting. There are too many opportunities for wealth across this disputed border that I cannot ignore. For now I will hold onto the items. I do not need the few pieces you all have if I decide to go forward. Perhaps someday you will change your mind and we can finally reunite both our association and our items. I bid you good health and happiness.

Your humble servant

Oliver Rockwell

33 Washington St.

Eastport

William gently placed the letter down on the table and looked up.

"That's it?" Adam was the first to voice the disappointment they all were feeling. No one spoke, no one moved, no one responded to Adam's question.

They didn't dare. To respond, to acknowledge what they all were thinking would have put them on that dead end road no one wanted to see. The letter told them nothing. There were no clues, no plans, no hint of intent or purpose. Lindsey shuffled through her own papers, hoping to find something, anything, that would mean it wasn't over.

The sounds outside increased. More cars were pulling into the driveway. Voices could be heard. Car doors opening and closing. It wouldn't be long now.

"No Adam, it's not," Deborah finally spoke. The look on her son's face, mirrored in her husband and older son as well hit Deborah like cold water from a crashing wave. She had never truly been invested in this adventure. It had been Rob's crusade from the start, Rob and Lindsey really. Perhaps at first she had been curious, then later it became a way to get herself back into Rob's good graces, but it was never more than a means to an end. Now, suddenly for the first time, her heart followed her mind. She was determined to press on. Maybe it was because she couldn't bear to see the look of utter disappointment on the faces of everyone she loved more than life itself or maybe it was because Deborah hated losing. She had never lost in her life and she wasn't about to lose now.

"We need to stop letting the chase tell us where to go next and instead figure out for ourselves where to go."

"What do you mean?" Lindsey stopped shuffling the papers. At any other moment she might have taken Deborah's words as poison, as an attack on her methods. After all, it was Lindsey who had truly been directing their course since day one. But now, she was so desperate and depressed that any sign of hope was welcome, even from Deborah.

"We need to put ourselves in the shoes of the people who did this," Deborah resisted the urge to remind them of what they had done wrong and how all they had was puzzle pieces with no box cover to tell them what the puzzle was supposed to look like. It all was starting to come together in her mind's eye now. The turn of the switch, the shift in her heart, released the cynicism and negativity she had been holding onto for the past few weeks and allowed her to see all of this clearly for the first time. The lights in the room had finally been turned on.

"Why would Rockwell have the packet in the first place?" She looked at Rob. "Why would the association break up?" She looked at Adam and Bobby. "Why would Franklin want it back? Why wouldn't they use it?" She looked at Lawrence and William. "Why would he move away? Why were they together in the first place? And why did they split the packet up? We need to start with questions, not with answers." She finally looked at Lindsey.

"Well," Lindsey said slowly. She was disappointed. She thought Deborah saw another clue she did not. But what the hell, she would play along. "We know Rob's family moved to Canada to get away from the Revolution and we know they moved here at some point and we know they petitioned the King for deeds to this land."

"And we know that Rockwell was part of that group that petitioned," Rob added. He was glad for Deborah's help. After all, she had always been the first one in their marriage to sort out solutions to so many of the problems they faced over the years; what schools the kids should go to, what to do about unwelcome neighbors, the bullying incident with Adam, the time Bobby was hospitalized. Deborah always seemed to have an insight that Rob never had. After all, he was the meat and potatoes guy. The only problem she could never solve, he was forced to admit, was that she had never figured out the problems in their marriage. Why?

"Do we know how the King responded to their petition?" Deborah voiced a question no one had ever asked. They had always searched for clues by going from archive to archive and letting each clue determine where they went next. They did not start out looking for any specific clues.

"Do we?" Lindsey turned to Rob. He just shrugged.

"The King would not always respond," Lawrence paused and turned his head towards the wall. He could hear Moose's voice outside and it was angry. Lawrence knew that the news of the border dispute had made it through the town by now and he could imagine the anger and dread spreading through the island like wildfire in a dry forest. The angry voices and shouts outside only confirmed his fears. He turned back to Lindsey, "especially if the news was bad."

"OK then. Let's assume it was bad." Deborah continued. "What would they have done next? Petition again?"

"That's what some people did," William also was enjoying Deborah's line of questioning. She sounded like a real historian, or even a detective.

"But if they were desperate enough, maybe they would look for help," Deborah pressed on.

"From someone like Franklin!" Rob smiled and pointed at Deborah. She really was good at this!

"Well we know that someone in the group knew William Franklin, or at least how to contact him." Lindsey was not as enthusiastic as Rob. She could see Rob's attention turning away from her and back towards his wife. She actually wasn't sure if she wanted Deborah to figure this out and that upset her.

"How do we know that?" Bobby said.

"From the earlier letter," Deborah said softly to her son. The look on his face reminded her of the little boy she loved so much. Bobby was always just a step behind his peers or his family. He wasn't stupid or less intelligent; he just sometimes took a little longer to catch up. More than once, she had rubbed his soft black hair, comforting her little boy on the edge of his bed as he cried out his frustrations. Maybe, the thought came out of left field and almost knocked her over, maybe that was why he was so mean to Adam at times.

"Rockwell took the packet from him!" Adam shouted. Bobby grimaced. Deborah noticed and sighed to herself. "He must have met with Franklin to ask for help and somehow got his hands on the packet."

"That much we figured," Lindsey put a damper on Adam's enthusiasm.

"But what happened next?" Deborah remained confident. They would figure this out.

"They split up the contents," Lindsey realized with a tinge of hope.

"Why didn't they use the packet?" Deborah pressed. One question led to more. "If Franklin had lost it, if it had been stolen by someone with enough desperation to steal it in the first place, why didn't they use it? What was Rockwell thinking?"

"Maybe they were afraid to."

"Afraid of what?"

"The King?"

"Franklin?"

"Maybe they were embarrassed or ashamed."

"It's clear they disagreed," Deborah nodded to the letter William just read. "And that upset Rockwell. Upset him so much that he moved away."

"But why didn't he use it then?" Lindsey was back to square one.

"Hey," Adam suddenly spoke up. His high pitched voice was like a shrill alarm clock that caught everyone's attention. "Didn't you say the date was 1812?"

"Yes," William realized what Adam was getting at but let the boy have his moment.

"We just learned about that war in school," Adam beamed. "Wasn't it between the United States and Canada?"

"Britain," Lawrence corrected him coldly. He had no patience for children. He had never had any and he never would. He was too busy. Sometimes he realized how strange it was that a man obsessed with genealogy would not continue his own family line, but he had plenty of brothers, sisters and cousins who were handling that part of the family history. "Canada was still part of the British Empire in 1812."

"But the war took place right here," William reminded Lawrence with a nod towards Adam. He swung his finger in the air to indicate the immediate area, "and a force occupied Eastport right across the border."

"Maybe the war had something to do with it then!" Adam could not stop himself. He was so proud and excited that he had actually contributed something important. His face was all lit up and his grin was from ear to ear.

"Maybe," Lindsey repeated.

"Something is still bugging me about that letter," Deborah looked at William with a frown, "Can you read it again?"

"Okay," William shrugged his shoulders and picked up the Rockwell letter again. "October 12, 1812," everyone settled down and listened closely to every word William repeated. He read slowly and carefully. A few of them leaned forward as if getting their ears that much closer might help them pick up a clue missed the first time. Outside, the voices grew in volume and intensity. It did not seem like whoever was out there was going away anytime soon. Ignoring them would only last so long.

"I bid you good health and happiness," William got to the end of the letter,

"Your humble servant

Oliver Rockwell

33 Washington St.

Eastport"

"That's it!" Deborah's scream made William and Lindsey jump. They didn't hear anything. "Read that closing again," Deborah commanded.

"I bid you good health and happiness," William read it quickly, his voice containing a mix of sarcasm and confusion, *"Your humble servant, Oliver Rockwell, 33 Washington St., Eastport*

"Yes," Deborah turned to Lawrence, clearly the expert in the room and her biggest ally, "Lawrence, do most letters of this time period end with an address?"

"No," Lawrence said slowly. His eyes started to brighten. "They rarely do."

"So why would he put it?"

"Maybe he's just a weirdo," Bobby blurted out and instantly regretted it. This was his first contribution to the conversation and he realized how immature and disrespectful it sounded, especially to his mother.

"Maybe," Deborah frowned at her son, and then turned back to Lawrence. "Or maybe it is some kind of clue."

"Clue?"

"I'm just spit-balling here," Deborah admitted. This really was a shot in the dark, but what other choice did they have. "But what if he was afraid of losing it, or of someone stealing it during the war?"

"Like who?"

"The British soldiers for one," Lawrence helped out. He was seeing what Deborah was seeing now and perhaps even more. "When the British arrived in Eastport, they stayed for almost four years. The war was already over but the British didn't want to give it back. They lived in local homes, they walked the streets and interacted with the people."

"Why did they stay so long?"

"Were they looking for something?"

"They were looking for the packet!" Adam shouted again.

"That's ridiculous," Lawrence snapped. He was starting to feel some hope as well but the boy was just being stupid at this point. "Eastport was and is a major town on the border. Its strategic location is obvious. And with the confusion of the Treaty of Paris, the British were doing their best to hold onto more land."

"But what if Rockwell thought they were looking for it?" Lindsey almost fell over in her realization. Had she finally seen through Rockwell's eyes? "What if there were even soldiers living in his home? It doesn't matter what the truth is or what you or I think. Rockwell knew he had something incredibly valuable. He was probably paranoid of losing it. If he thought Franklin told anyone on his deathbed, then of course Rockwell would think the British were after it."

"So he leaves this little clue to his friends to tell them where to find it?" Deborah finished for her. It was the first time the two ladies had ever really connected and Deborah was not sure how she felt about it.

"Maybe," Lindsey shrugged her shoulders. She knew how crazy that sounded.

"This is silly," Rob finally spoke up. He was listening to the voices outside that were now becoming shouts. "All the guy did was write his address down."

"But what else do we have?" Lindsey pleaded with Rob. The desperation was almost sad. "Either we check this out, or we give up."

"Look we know that the packet made it to Eastport," Deborah used her logic on her husband. He always responded to that. "So we at least should go there first."

"But where?" Rob shook his head. He was starting to wish he had never discovered Nana's special box. This entire adventure was one silly trip after another: Philly, Halifax, Fredericton, St. Andrews, Deer Island and now Eastport. He wanted to move on and get his life figured out, get his relationships figured out and take control of what he could once more. "We don't know anyone in Eastport or where Washington Street is."

"I do," William volunteered. His curiosity had got the better of him, "and I could-

"William!" A voice called from outside. William's head snapped towards the door. A look of panic flashed across his face.

"Lawrence!" Another voice called out. "We know you're in there."

"That was Moose," Lawrence turned back to the group momentarily. "He must have seen my truck."

"What do they want?" the look of fear in Adam's eyes reflected what they all were starting to feel.

"I don't know," Lawrence admitted. "But it must have something to do with the news story."

"Should we go out there?" Deborah hoped the answer was no.

"I should," Lawrence made clear to emphasize the "I". "You need to sneak out the back and get on to Eastport."

"Why do we need to sneak out?"

"To throw off your buddies," Lawrence pointed with his thumb to the woods outside.

"What buddies?" Lindsey wondered. Had Lawrence seen the agents outside? And how did he know they were agents? Or did he?

"I have lived on this island long enough to be able to tell that those friends of yours are not photo tourists," Lawrence couldn't help but smile. "And the way you two talk around them," he pointed to Lindsey and Rob, "make it clear that you really don't like them."

"I have no idea what you are talking about," Lindsey lied. It wasn't a very good one either.

Deborah frowned at Rob. Her bright green eyes pierced through his soul for any hint of subterfuge. This was news to her, and it was news she definitely didn't like.

"Regardless," Rob felt Deborah's stare and tried to steer the conversation away, "we do need to get out of here, and Lawrence is at least correct that I would rather not deal with that crowd."

"I will go out there," Lawrence volunteered. He turned to William, "and you show them out the back door."

"But," William tried to argue.

"Go," Lawrence repeated. "I can only hold them up for so long."

Forty Nine

"33 Washington Street," Lindsey stood on the edge of the street and stared. "How ironic."

"Huh?" Bobby was already staring at Lindsey. She had become so used to it by now that it was easy to ignore. She didn't even bother to respond to his question. She just stared at the little colonial style home that looked more like a dollhouse than a human house and wondered what to do next.

It was about as down to earth, small town cute as any house could get, even in this tiny little town. The fresh coat of yellow paint and bright white shutters allowed it to stand out amongst the neighbors' homes that were all a little less colorful and a little more blue collar. The people of Eastport did not have a lot of time to make their homes bright and beautiful and new. This was still a frontier town, no matter what century it was.

The square shaped tiny home was surrounded by more grass than the land it occupied and it could not have fit more than a few people or at most a small family. A front door, three small rectangular windows and an American flag adorned the ground level. The second story roof was painted with a forest green and held two square windows on either end that probably housed a bedroom or two. There was no elongated living space or additions like most of the other homes, just a small matching yellow shed in the back where the owner might have stored a small car.

"Should we knock?" Rob finally broke the silence. He looked at his sons and his wife, Lindsey and William and realized how awkward they all looked standing still on the side of the empty street. There was no danger in getting run over. The neighborhood itself was typical small town neighborhood with homes built every half acre or so and cars parked mostly in driveways. There was not even a yellow divider line in the middle of the road. The only thing lacking was any activity. Either everyone was off at work or they were inside. But that was unlikely with such a beautiful summer day and a clear blue sky above them. It was much more likely everyone was out on the water somewhere.

They had parked their cars a little ways down the road, just in case and so their isolation on the street was even more pronounced. Anyone who saw them would probably think they were all salesmen or those religious people who came around to your homes every once in a while.

"That's what we came here for," Deborah started forward, followed quickly by Lindsey. They would compete till the end.

"There's a knocker," Lindsey interrupted Deborah just before she could bang her fist on the door. She reached for the small gold knocker in the center of the dark brown door. On either side of the center handle was engraved the letters "C" and "A". Lindsey lifted the brass handle and knocked three times.

"Coming!" A bright female voiced called from inside. Lindsey and Deborah both took two steps down from the concrete steps and stood with the others at the base. They didn't want to intimidate the owners too much. It was strange enough having this entire group arrive at their door.

"Yes?" the small young woman said as she opened the door wide. She was dressed in a bright purple blouse and comfortable black leggings that looked a little out of place for a hard-working, small town like Eastport. Her black curly hair was well groomed and her make up matched her blouse perfectly. This was a woman who knew how to dress.

"Hi there," Lindsey took the lead. "I'm Lindsey, this is my friend Rob," she swept her hand out towards the group, "and this is his family. We were wondering if we could have a moment of your time."

"Andy!" the woman called back into the house. She did not make any motion to let them in. "There are people at the door!"

Lindsey looked back at Rob and shrugged. They had become used to the friendliness of Deer Island. This was the first time they had been forced to wait outside. Neither of them knew if it was because Eastport was an American town and much bigger, if it was because they were all strangers this time or if it was a quirk in the homeowners themselves. Regardless, it was not a good sign.

"Yes?" the man said, as he pulled the door open wide. Unlike his wife, he was dressed in clothes much more common to Eastport. His red and gray checkered flannel shirt was buttoned almost to the top and his blue jeans had a grass stain or two near the knees. His blonde hair was a mess and a red spot that was maybe ketchup sat awkwardly on his round rosy cheeks. In his left hand he was holding a white cloth napkin that he must have been using during a meal. He reached up and wiped the red spot off his face. He did not look happy to be interrupted. "Can we help you?"

"Uh," Lindsey paused.

"Hi Andy!" William interjected with a smile and a wave. "It's been awhile."

"William," Andy returned the smile but he did not make any move to welcome him in. "What's all this about?"

"Well," William began slowly. He was relieved to see a face he recognized. Andy worked downtown at the hardware store and William had been in there several times over the years. He had always found Andy to be friendly and helpful. This was not a side of Andy that William was used to seeing. Maybe it was because this was his home turf or because they were such a big group. Maybe it was just Andy's city roots taking hold, William guessed.

Andy Wasserman and his wife Cara were not natives to Eastport. William had noticed the accent the first day they had met and Andy was quick to give him the lowdown like he had so many times before. Everyone noticed his thick Bronx accent the moment he spoke and he had become so used to explaining himself to the customers at the store that the story had become almost rehearsed. After all, it was almost stereotypical in its simplicity. He and his wife were both from the city, had tired of the high pressure life and decided to abandon it all and move as far away as they could from that cauldron of humanity and steel. He found the job at the hardware store, worked in his spare time on the movie script while his wife taught at the local high school. It was a simple story but it was what they both wanted.

Still, neither of them could break some of their city habits. They weren't about to let a large group of strangers into their home without first understanding why they were here. And so far, they were not impressed.

"I'm working with these folks," William found his story, "trying to help them with a little family history." The group all started smiling and nodding in agreement. Andy and Cara looked them over. "And our quest has taken us to your house."

"Our house?" Cara said.

"We're looking for something very old that may be here," Rob jumped right to the end. His impatience was palpable. It reminded Lindsey of how he was sometimes in an intense hockey game right before he slugged someone. It was not a pretty sight and Lindsey prayed that Rob would not boil over.

"Like what?" Cara raised an eyebrow, at least she was curious.

"I don't know," Lindsey tried to take over from Rob. "Like a letter or a packet or some kind of keep sake."

"That's a strange request," Cara was blunt. Her voice was still friendly and she smiled when she spoke, but she was not sure how to respond.

"There is nothing like that here," Andy was more firm. He either needed to go back to his meal or he was not happy with the visit. "This is not even the original house."

"Oh!" William shook his head, "Of course!"

"Of course?" Lindsey almost shouted at him. What had he not told them now?

"There was a huge fire in 1882," William explained. He looked up at Andy who was nodding in agreement. "Almost the entire city was destroyed."

"This is not the original house and we are not even the original owners," Andy added. He looked a little more compassionate this time. He couldn't help it. The looks of disappointment and perhaps even despair on everyone's faces cast a dark cloud over them all. "The original one stood about 20 feet to the left and back a bit," he pointed in the direction of his small shed.

"Why didn't you tell us before?" Lindsey hissed at William.

"Did the previous owner leave anything behind?" Deborah stood in between Lindsey and William. She was as upset as Lindsey was but she knew it wasn't William's fault.

"No, I'm sorry," Andy started to close the door and stopped halfway. "Is there anything else?"

"Um, ah…" Lindsey mumbled. Deborah rolled her eyes, trying to think of something to say.

"No thanks," William blurted out. "Sorry we bothered you Andy."

"Why didn't you tell them?" Cara asked her husband the moment the door was closed.

"Tell them what," Andy turned away from his wife and headed back to the kitchen. "That we have some old box in the basement?"

"It's not just any box," Cara followed. "And I thought you always wondered what was inside."

"I did," Andy admitted as he sat down at the small square table and picked up the half eaten hamburger. "But it wasn't like they knew any more than we did."

"They could have helped somehow."

"I doubt it," Andy took a bite of the burger.

"Is it all still downstairs?" Cara walked out of the kitchen and turned toward the unfinished basement door.

"MM-hmmm," Andy mumbled as he chewed. "But I don't think," he called to her once his mouth was clear and she had already made her way half way down the stairs.

"What now?" Adam broke the silence as they all walked slowly down the middle of the empty street back towards the cars. He looked towards his father and mother. Neither one of them spoke.

"Lindsey?" Bobby said to her. He hated seeing her this way and he couldn't decide if she was even sexier when she was upset or if he just was feeling bad too.

"What?" Lindsey snapped, stopping Bobby in his tracks. "What?"

"Uh," Bobby hung his head like a scolded dog. Lindsey just kept walking. Adam walked past his brother and tried his best not to grin. It didn't work. Bobby lifted his middle finger and waved it angrily in his brother's face. His parents were too upset to notice. Adam rushed forward to the car.

"What the fuck did we think would happen?" Lindsey finally broke the silence, waving her arms in the air. "They would just smile and hand the packet over? Man we are a bunch of idiots!"

"Hey don't be so hard on yourself," Rob said as he gently touched Lindsey's arm. "We all thought this would be over by now." The move was meant to be compassionate and comforting, but Lindsey took it as condescending.

"Over! Over? Do you want this to be over?" Lindsey flinched at Rob's touch then swung away from it. "What the fuck? I just don't get you Rob!"

"Is this it?" Cara held up a 1'x 2' rusty, rectangular metal box in her hands. It was dark gray and covered in soot and dents. There were sharp edges to it and she had to be careful to not cut her hands even though it easily fit in her grasp. It looked like it was more than 100 years old.

"Yeah that's it," Andy replied. He was finishing off the French fries with the last bit of ketchup and barely looked up. He knew she was holding the box. He had held it so many times and wondered what was inside he did not need to look at it anymore.

He found it more than a decade ago when he was digging up the ground for a new foundation for his shed. There were many items buried just several feet below the dirt and grime, remnants from the town before the great fire. Most of the items were destroyed or worthless but this one box was built to last. Whatever was inside must have been pretty valuable. In the beginning, he was obsessed with breaking into it. On the shorter edge it looked like there may have once been a keyhole and on the opposite end even something that resembled hinges. But the top of the box seemed to be so damaged from fire and heat that the edges themselves were sealed shut. There was not a single millimeter of space in between and he could not imagine how he could ever open it or if anything remained intact. He had tried a couple of times with the various tools in his workshop and even from the store to open it but he was so afraid of damaging whatever was still left that he eventually gave up and threw it in the cardboard box with other crap in the corner of the basement. That was more than 10 years ago.

"Maybe we should have told them?" Cara looked over the box again. She had tried to open it as well. She had thought that maybe they could use some special chemical or glue remover to loosen things up but Andy was afraid it might leak inside and damage something. Eventually she had given up as well.

"Told them what?" Andy stood up with the empty plate from the table. He crossed the kitchen towards the sink. "That we found some old box in the dirt? We would have sounded like a bunch of crazy fools."

"No more crazy than they sounded."

Rob double clicked the car remote as he watched Lindsey storm ahead. The usual beep beep from the Camry told everyone that he had unlocked all the doors. Lindsey grabbed the handle, swung the car door open violently and jumped inside. Rob and the boys quietly followed.

"Lindsey, I..." Rob began to say then thought better of it. Lindsey's face was dark and angry. He didn't dare say a word. He turned back and looked at the boys who were both staring at him, waiting patiently for him to do something to end the awkward silence.

A rap on his side car window broke the moment. Rob jumped and turned to see Deborah standing outside the car. She had not gone ahead and joined William like he expected. Rob pressed the side button on the panel and the window rolled down.

"Yeah?" He said.

"I need to try something," she said simply, expecting him to trust her.

"What?" Rob was at least curious. He knew better than to doubt Deborah at this point. If anyone could solve this puzzle it was her.

"I've got an idea," Deborah had already turned away and called back to him. That was all she needed to say and she knew it. "And it will only work if I am by myself."

"Hey where is mom going?" Adam leaned forward and almost shouted in his father's ear.

"What the fuck?" Lindsey snapped her head back and watched Deborah heading back towards the house. She opened the car door again and stormed out of the Camry. "What does that bitch think she is doing?"

She hadn't taken two strides before Rob jumped out of his car and jumped into her path. "Hey Lindz, hold up a sec," Rob put up both of his hands in front of Lindsey's face. "Let's see what Deb can do."

"Get out of my way Rob!" Lindsey hissed. It was the harshest tone Lindsey had ever used with Rob. It took him by surprise so much that he let her slip by at first.

"Wait! Wait!" Rob commanded. He could see the crisis about to explode and could not bear the thought of watching some kind of fist fight between his wife and Lindsey in the middle of this quiet neighborhood. Although, a small part of him wondered who would win. He put his hand on Lindsey's shoulder to try to hold her up. Lindsey shrugged it off and pressed on.

"Fuck you Rob!"

"I said wait Lindsey!" Rob grabbed her tight this time. In one swift rehearsed motion he swung his arm underneath her armpit and bent his hand back to hold her neck in a half Nelson. Lindsey turned to her left in reflex, then Rob quickly used his left arm to finish the Nelson. "Wait!" He repeated.

"Dammit Rob!" Lindsey squirmed and pushed against his hold. All of her frustration and rage and passion were boiling over and it was all directed at Deborah. How could she just swoop in here and take over? Deborah was the one who abandoned them; she was the one who was destroying Rob. She couldn't just come back in and take everything from her like this. Rob was hers!

Rob was hers? The thought almost knocked Lindsey over. It was the first time she ever came face to face with how she truly felt and it both terrified and empowered her. She knew she had been lying to herself. She knew that she had been lying to Rob all these times. She simply could not deny how she felt any longer. Accepting that gave her the strength to fight back. She jerked and pushed hard against Rob with the sudden desire to have her way with him but could not break free from the full nelson. Rob was really strong. "She is going to ruin everything!"

"Ruin what?" Rob pressed his large hands firmly on the back of her neck and brought his chest squarely against her back. Her chest heaved back and forth as she pushed against Rob's weight. Standing almost a foot over her, Rob could not help but look down and notice how much her tits pushed out against her tight V-neck t-shirt. With her face only inches away and her ass pushing against his thigh he couldn't stop himself from getting hard. This was like the sex he and Deborah sometimes had.

Lindsey could feel Rob's hard body pushing against her and it thrilled her. Finally it was going to happen! She still wanted him. She wanted him to take her. She wanted him to do all kinds of things to her, things she had been fantasizing about even before she saw his large naked body in the locker room. She imagined Rob swinging her around and forcing his way with her and for a moment, her body softened. If he took her now, there would be no guilt. None of it would be on her. She would be his to take, his to force himself on and that made her want him that much more.

Rob wanted her too. He wanted to press her to the ground and force his way with her. He wanted to explode all of his feelings and passions in one glorious moment. How long had he yearned for this? How long had he fantasized this specific instant with Lindsey in his power to do with as he pleased? He could take it all now and nothing could stop him. But in the corner of his eye was the car. Inside the car were his boys. He knew they were watching. He knew his next moment would be frozen in their eyes and his mind for the rest of their lives. And still, his body yearned for her. A full glance at the car threw the proverbial ice in Rob's face that he needed and with a supreme effort from the most rationale part of his mind, Rob somehow managed to control himself. He took a small step back from her hot body to calm his aching nerves down. "There is nothing left for Deb to ruin." He managed to say.

That was Lindsey's ice. Rob had made his choice. It was over! Nothing was going to happen. "Screw you!" Lindsey screamed in rage and despair. She took advantage of the small space Rob had opened between them to suddenly wrench her arm free and swing an open palm into Rob's face.

"Fuck!" Rob staggered backwards from the blow and held his hands to his face. Blood began to spill from his nose. "God-damn it Lindsey!" Rob shouted as he swung his bloody hands in the air, "God-damn it! You almost broke my goddamn nose!"

"I don't give a fuck about your nose," Lindsey shouted as she looked towards the house. "You've made your choice and I've made mine."

"What the fuck are you talking about?" Rob reached for the base of his t-shirt, pulled it towards his face and began to wipe the blood.

"Deborah!" Lindsey pointed towards the house and turned. "You...," Lindsey paused. She gasped. "Holy fuck," her tone changed dramatically, "Holy fuck!"

"What?" Rob looked up from the blood in his shirt and towards the house to see what Lindsey was staring at. Another person was heading to the house Deborah had just entered. He shook his head and looked again.

"Francois!" he gasped.

Fifty

Jim Watts sat quietly at the small square dining table, touched the white bandage on his head and winced. He would get that son of a bitch Francois.

"Where'd you get that?" the petite waitress with the pencil through her blond hair bun wondered. She was standing on the other side of the small dining room behind the counter, trying to decide if she should approach. She couldn't stand Jim Watts and if she wasn't such a nice person she would be smiling right now at the obvious pain he was in.

"Place is pretty empty," Watts ignored her question. It was none of her fucking business.

"It is," she responded in monotone. Abigail Jones, or "Abby" as she was known by everyone on Deer Island, had to be the friendliest person in existence. As the co-owner of the 45th Parallel Restaurant she was waitress, hostess and community organizer. It was a natural fit for her. Her thoughts were always of others first, to the detriment of herself, and she had found the perfect calling as a restaurant manager on this tiny island community. After over 20 years running the place with her husband John, Abby knew what most customers wanted before they did themselves. If she saw the car pulling into the lot, she already had her husband firing up the grill. For the true regulars, their meal was already on the table before they sat down in their chosen chair. Abby took great pride in not only knowing what her friends wanted to eat, but knowing their moods, their mind and their dreams. If she wasn't so aware of how much it bothered people, she could even finish their sentences.

"Is there something going on around the island?" Watts prompted again. He couldn't seem to get Abby to engage with him, which for Abby was practically never done. She was friendly and charming to everyone, sometimes to a fault! Watts had seen it many times himself. It annoyed him to no end, how much this waitress talked with customers like she was their grandmother or aunt or something. He could sit there for minute after minute after minute and watch her gossip with the customers while ignoring his own needs. Watts would have never come back to the stupid place if there was any other option in town.

"I'm sure you know more about it than I do," Abby's large brown eyes glared through Watts. She met his gaze then purposely turned away and pressed a button to open the cash register. The good old high pitched ding of the register bell inside responded followed by the jiggle of the coins sloshing against the drawer as it whooshed open towards her belly.

"Why would you say that?" Watts tried to play innocent. The game wasn't any fun if no one played.

"I know you Jim Watts," Abby glared again right into his black eyes then took some cash out of the register and began counting to herself.

"Me?" Watts smiled like a five year old boy who had stolen the last cupcake. He was having too much fun to let Abigail Jones best him.

Abby continued counting as if Watts had not said a word. She would not respond to him, no matter how much he pushed. Ever since the sleaze ball first entered her restaurant eight years ago, she knew him for what he was. No amount of style, suave and polish could hide the slime underneath that was Jim Watts. She tolerated him because she had to. She had served him because she would never let any customer leave her restaurant upset. But this time, he had gone too far. She knew Watts was behind the mess going on. She knew all of her friends were gathering to do something about it. What she didn't know was what they could do about it.

"Are you going to take my order?" Watts broke the silence. If the bitch wasn't going to engage him, he would at least get something to eat. He knew she could easily make her way to his table. He had seen her many times moving her petite, lithe body as she balanced massive trays of plates overflowing with food, dodging chair and customer and perfectly arriving at her designated table. Every time, she moved with grace and style, clearly knowing every inch of the restaurant. Watts would be impressed if she didn't annoy him so much.

Of course, Abby knew exactly what she was doing, and by now so too did Watts. The place wasn't practically empty, it was completely empty. Not a single customer sat at any of the red and white checkered tables and not a single other car was in the parking lot. Abby was purposely ignoring him.

Abby just looked up at him and waited. She would not make this easy for him.

"I'll have the usual," Watts smiled again. Abby knew his usual order and he knew she couldn't stop herself from serving him. He was as good at reading people as Abby was, except in Watt's case, he had no conscious to guide him.

"Hold that order," A voice commanded as the double glass paneled front door suddenly opened. It was Beauvais and he wasn't dressed as a tourist this time.

"Excuse me," Abby snapped as she put the cash back in the register and slammed it shut. She wasn't sure if she was angry at being commanded in her own home or relieved that she would not have to serve Watts. Who was this man?

"I'm sorry to interrupt ma'am," Beauvais expertly reached into his navy blue suit jacket inner pocket and flashed his badge. "This is a matter of national security."

"National security?" Abby took an involuntary step back and whipped her head to stare at Watts. Of course he was embroiled in something like this.

Beauvais did not respond. His attention was solely on Watts, every nerve and muscle prepared for the inevitable panic. Nine times out of ten, men freaked the moment they saw the badge and ran. Usually they stumbled and fell, sometimes they got free for a minute or two but it had been almost five years since Beauvais had lost a suspect and he wasn't about to lose a man like Watts now. Not after everything the bastard had done.

Beauvais and Macleod had decided to blow their cover. There was too much at stake now with the news breaking and there was no more time for subtlety. Besides, their new strategy was predicated on intimidating Watts and they couldn't do that dressed as tourists. Unfortunately, the idea wasn't working yet, Beauvais noted as he approached the table. Watts hadn't budged or even blinked since Beauvais walked in, he was completely unreadable.

"What can I do for you officer?" Watts smiled. It would have been a warm pleasing greeting if Beauvais didn't know Watts so well. The man could charm the devil himself.

"Agent Beauvais," he corrected, stressing the word 'Agent'. He hadn't been an officer in decades. "CSIS," he flashed the badge again and felt childish doing it. That wouldn't intimidate a man like Watts. He had seen so many badges in his dark career that nothing fazed the man anymore, not even Canada's Intelligence Service.

"Ahhh, CSIS," Watts smiled even more. "To what do I owe this honor?"

"May I sit down?" Beauvais suddenly became friendly, or at least friendly for him. He placed his hand on the top of the empty chair at Watt's table and waited.

"Of course," Watts did not smile this time. It was a little odd for officers to be so casual with him. Usually they just threw on the cuffs or even roughed him up a little. At least the rookies did. Once they met his lawyer, they learned to treat Watts with a little more respect or even fear.

"I was hoping we could have a conversation," Beauvais waved at Abigail and smiled. She instinctively moved lithely across the dining room to his side.

"Yes?" she said.

"I'm very sorry we have to do this here," Beauvais said sincerely. Despite his gruff manner, Beauvais really did love the 45th parallel as much as everyone else. After all, as a First Nations Canadian himself, he appreciated the history of the way Canada used to be even, if his Canada was that of the Mohawk warriors. He loved this country, more than he ever let on, and he hated what modernization and globalization was doing to its character. Deer Island, and the 45th were doing their best to survive despite those changes and he was going to make damn sure that Watts never got his slimy hands in any of it.

"Here?" Abby repeated slowly. It was the first time in her life she felt uncomfortable in her own restaurant and she hated it.

"I'm going to need you to close up," Beauvais frowned.

"Close up?" Abby snapped back and puffed up her chest like an angry gorilla. No one told her how to run her business.

"To protect your customers," Beauvais quickly responded. He knew the only way to calm this whirlwind of a woman down was to appeal to the mother side in her.

That gave Abby pause. She looked around the dining room. No one was there of course but she imagined what it was like when they were. It was almost noon time and it wouldn't be long before Dale and Gary showed up.

"We won't be that long," Beauvais pushed. He glanced at Watts. The man had been unnaturally silent and he still had that unreadable look on his perfectly shaven face. Not a single hair on those white sideburns was out of place. It infuriated Beauvais. He wondered about the large white bandage across his forehead though. "But I suppose," he said reluctantly looking at his watch. He would have preferred to make Watts starve but Macleod wasn't near yet and Beauvais still needed to kill some time. "You can bring him his meal," Beauvais pointed with his thumb towards Watts.

"And for you?" Abby suddenly smiled. Her reflexes were amazing. Her anger, fear and frustration disappeared in a heartbeat as she became hostess again.

"Just a water thanks," Beauvais watched Abby spin around, head towards the front door and swing the open sign back to closed. "And some privacy," he added.

Beauvais looked at his watch again. The timing was close. He calculated that it would take at least five to ten minutes for Watts' meal to arrive and another ten for him to eat it. Fifteen to twenty if he could keep Watts talking during the meal. Of course, he could just arrest the asshole. He had plenty of reasons, if nothing else from Watt's long rap sheet. No one would question why that M.F. was brought in for questioning. But no matter how much Beauvais would love to do that, it would fuck up the plan and besides, Watts' lawyer would have him out before sunset anyways.

"Going somewhere?" Watts finally spoke. Beauvais had been looking at his watch too long. He would have jumped at the sound of Watt's voice if he hadn't had so much training and experience in the field. Instead, he turned slowly and ominously towards Watts.

"Talk," he commanded.

"About what?" For the first time, Watts was taken off guard. To his credit, he didn't panic, didn't spout off random facts or lies like most perps with less experience did. They were almost always taken aback by Beauvais' glare and his simple command. It was a trick he learned years ago. Most agents and officers asked direct questions, usually the ones the criminal was ready for. Beauvais had found that a simple barked out command gave more information in what the perp said, but also in what they didn't say. It caught Watts by surprise.

"Talk," Beauvais repeated in the exact same tone with the exact same glare. It wasn't often he had to do that.

"What an odd command," Watts smiled and regained his composure. "But I suppose we have nothing else to do, do we?" Watts looked at his own diamond studded gold wrist watch. Was he waiting for something too?

"I so enjoy the meals at this restaurant," Watts reacted to the sound of dishes rattling and metal spatulas clanking on the grill coming from the kitchen in back. "And Abby is such a delightful lady."

Beauvais glanced behind him and caught the image of Abby approaching. She had his glass of water in her hands.

"Here you are," she reached in front of him and placed the red plastic glass of ice water in front of Beauvais and a bottle of Perrier (of course!) in front of Watts. Then she turned and disappeared as quickly as she had arrived.

Beauvais glared at Watts again. He would not command him a third time.

"I suppose you want me to talk about this mess around the island," Watts reached for the blue bottle or Perrier and twisted off the cap. It surprised Beauvais that Watts got right to what he wanted to hear immediately. He thought it would be harder. Maybe the son of a bitch was so pleased with himself and so sure he wouldn't get caught, that he had no fear. "After all," Watts smiled that confident smile again. Beauvais could barely keep himself from slugging the bastard, "what other local realtor is there around this quaint island with information like that?"

"What's your game?" Beauvais might as well get right to it as well.

"Game," Watts raised the Perrier to his lips and took a long sip. The pause was obviously calculated. "My dear, what did you say your name was?" Watts paused again and stared at the agent, clearly enjoying this, "oh yes, Beauvais. My dear Beauvais, I never play games. Everything I do has a purpose and a goal. What you must figure out, before this is all over, is what that goal is."

This time it was Beauvais who was taken by surprise. He had heard that Watts was an overconfident, ego maniac, but he had no idea the man was so brazen. Did he really wish to take on the CSIS in some kind of contest? What did he think this was; a Hollywood movie?

"Listen Watts," Beauvais leaned forward, glanced over his shoulder and lowered his voice. Abby was nowhere to be seen but he still wanted to keep her away from all this. "We already know what your end game is and what you are hoping to find. We've known longer than you've known yourself. Did you think we weren't watching you?"

"Of course you were," Watts leaned forward as well. "And of course you knew that I knew that. Beauvais," Watts leaned back again and comfortably adjusted himself. "You know I am no amateur at this. Why are you wasting my time?"

"Alright then," Beauvais glanced at his watch again and cursed himself. Watts would realize he was waiting for something if he did that again. "Let's put all our cards on the table." Beauvais sat back as well.

"You know I am looking for the Franklin packet," Watts dove right in. Beauvais was again stunned at the man's bravado. Intimidating him was not going to be easy. "And you know that I have not found it yet. If I had, I would not have called the media."

"You'd use it to blackmail someone or sell it to the highest bidder."

"Actually none of the above," Watts smiled again. He so enjoyed playing with the law. It was just so easy. "I would begin by working with investors to buy up any land within the disputed area, then once I had made a considerable profit on that, and purchased much of it for myself, I would sell it to the highest bidder."

"Why are you telling me all this?" Beauvais knew the answer but he just had to hear it to believe it.

"Because my friend," Watts looked past Beauvais towards the kitchen; Still no sign of his food. Bitch was probably letting it get cold on purpose. "There is nothing you can do about it. Everything I am doing or would do is perfectly legal."

"Legal but immoral," Beauvais snapped. God he hated this man.

"Correct," Watts raised the bottle of Perrier in a mock toast.

"And you have no concern for the people on this island or throughout the bay," Beauvais added.

"Again, correct."

"As long as you get your money,"

Watts just smiled. It wasn't a large grin; he had already done that several times. This was the perfectly calculated smile of victory that he reserved precisely for times like this. He knew it would infuriate Beauvais, maybe even enough to slug him. But what better way to get him off balance and off his game?

"Where'd you get the bandage?" Beauvais was not the rookie Watts thought he was. He knew what the man was doing. This wasn't his first rodeo. Time to switch gears and get Watts to talk about something uncomfortable; and by the way he was playing with the edges of the bandage and wincing every once in a while, it was clearly uncomfortable.

"You like it? I did it myself."

"Someone slug you?" It was Beauvais' turn to smile this time, and it was a full face, wide open smile. He didn't have to fake it either.

"More like something,"

"My guess would be a baseball bat or a garden tool," Beauvais was finding it almost too easy to laugh. He didn't let go like this often, but with it all being part of the game, he was enjoying it.

"Glad you are having fun at my expense," Watts did not smile this time. He was having difficulty now controlling himself. He had taken four Motrin and two aspirin and still his head was pounding. This was the second time in as many days that he had been knocked cold and he was having trouble just keeping his thoughts straight. He had to have at least a low level concussion. Between that, his anger at Francois and his annoyance at losing ground in his little tête-à-tête with Beauvais, it was a wonder he did not blow up in return.

"Here you are," Abby approached with uncanny speed and placed the plate of seared salmon and poutine on the table. Steam was rising from the poutine and the salmon jiggled a little as it settled on the plate. It certainly was an odd meal for a man like Watts. The salmon of course, was a local delicacy. And unlike the lobster which was just as local, it was clean and easy to eat. Watts detested the barbaric way everyone ripped apart lobster claws and sucked on its entrails. He was much too classy for anything so pedestrian. However, the poutine sitting next to it was a different story. It was in no way classy. This was a dish for all Canadians; a gastronomic extravaganza of gravy and cheese and carbs. It didn't go at all with the image Watts worked so diligently to maintain. What Beauvais didn't know, and Watts of course would never tell, was that ever since he was a boy, his mother made him the most wonderful poutine he had ever tasted and served it with every meal, including breakfast. With her gone for almost 20 years now, it was a tradition Watts would keep alive as long as he could.

"Listen you slimy piece of shit," Beauvais watched as Watts calmly stuck a fork into the perfectly pink salmon and cut a bite size piece off. It was time to turn up the heat. "If it was up to me, I would have you tied to the back of my pick-up truck out there and dragged along the asphalt until your skin peeled off."

Watts placed the salmon in his mouth and lifted the Perrier to his lips.

"But lucky for you it's not up to me," Beauvais looked away for a minute. When would Macleod arrive?

"I didn't think so," Watts calmly picked up a napkin and dabbed it on his lips. He finished the piece of salmon still in his mouth. "A man like you is obviously not the man in charge."

"You smug son of a bitch!" Beauvais slammed both fists on the table and abruptly stood. Watt's fork and knife danced, the salmon slid across the plate and the chair Beauvais had been sitting in, screeched backward and almost tipped over.

"Beauvais!" A voice behind him called. It was Macleod; finally!

"Thank god," Beauvais swung around. "I was about to kill this asshole."

"I could go back to the car." Macleod smiled and waved his thumb back towards the parking lot. He didn't know Watts like Beauvais did. With his area being mainly Toronto, Macleod didn't get involved with much of the local New Brunswick business. Even so, Watts was enough of a character that he had at least heard of the man; and from the little he had heard, he was not surprised at all that Beauvais was ready to kill him. The two of them were like oil and water.

"Did you bring him?" Beauvais ignored Macleod's joke.

"He's in the car," Macleod stepped into the diner. He was dressed in a similar style business suit as Beauvais; except his was a little brighter blue and he didn't look as sharp in it. A wrinkle or two ran across the right shoulder. "I thought we should have a little alone time first."

"Good idea," Beauvais agreed. "I think Jim would like a little more time to finish his meal." Watts smiled awkwardly at the use of his first name and tried to pretend he was not concerned. He played absently with his poutine but he could not stop himself from keeping one eye on the open door. Who were they talking about?

"Has he seen the light yet?" Macleod nodded towards Watts as he approached. There was an ominous smile on his face that Watts couldn't read. It made him nervous and he didn't like that.

"Not yet," Beauvais indicated the empty chair next to him. Both of them seemed to have an air of confidence about them. Did it have anything to do with the person in the car?

"Did you discuss our new hobby?" Macleod took the empty chair, swung it around and sat backwards on it. His face was that much closer to Watts.

"I was just about to."

"What can I get you?" Abby suddenly appeared with a smile. Both of the veteran, professionally trained CSIS agents jumped. How did she just appear like that?

"Wow!" Macleod was still getting over how she surprised both of them. "Where'd you come from?"

"I've been here the whole time silly," Abby smiled again. This time though there was an edge of mischief on the corner of her bright red lips. "Oh don't worry," she immediately turned to Beauvais. "I've honored your request for privacy. I only came out when the door opened."

"Is it too late for eggs?" Macleod's demeanor changed. He was the friendly Toronto native with the welcoming blue eyes and cheerful smile again. It still impressed Beauvais how quickly he did that.

"Not at all," Abby was pleased. She didn't want to go back and tell her husband that another man showed up with no desire for food. He was grumpy enough already. "Scrambled or fried?"

"Scrambled; and some of that poutine please," Macleod indicated the cold mess left on Watt's plate. He took it as a good sign that Watts had let the poutine grow cold. That meant they were getting to him.

"Coming right up!" Abby swung around and disappeared. Macleod stared at the now empty diner again to see if there was some other entrance she had used to surprise them. What a character she was!

"You haven't met my partner Macleod," Beauvais finally talked to Watts. Macleod just nodded. He did not show his badge. For anyone who knew Macleod, it was a clear sign of how much he despised Watts. "He actually is the one who came up with the idea for our new hobby."

"Hobby?" Watts tried to sound aloof and disinterested. It wasn't working though. Watts was a man who prided himself on always being one step ahead of his opponents. At this rate he was almost feeling behind; far behind.

"You've gotten his attention," Beauvais continued explaining to Watts while Macleod simply stared at him. "And to be blunt, you should be a little proud of yourself."

Watts did not smile.

"Neither one of us really paid much attention to you Watts," Beauvais looked at his partner again. The almost imperceptible nod made it clear he should keep going. "You're too small time, too unimportant. Local law enforcement was all that was needed."

Watts shifted a little in his chair. He considered picking up his fork again, but the poutine was obviously soggy and cold. It not only would taste horrible, it would be a clear sign of his desperation to appear unconcerned.

"My beat is normally drug smuggling, Macleod's," Beauvais swung his thumb in Macleod's direction, "is human trafficking."

"Neither of which is an enterprise I would ever consider," Watts felt good again. Even he would not touch those areas.

"You move around a lot Jim," Beauvais ignored his comment and used the first name again. "And anyone who moves around a lot, especially so close to the border, is cause for our concern."

"It's a free country."

"It is. And we also have the freedom to keep an eye on you."

Watts froze. He knew exactly what that meant. He had heard it many times from officers before and he had always worked around it. But this was the CSIS. They had so much more power. Between their computer resources, their national and international contacts, and their sheer manpower, they would not be so easy to deal with. They could really get in his way.

"You talk to a lot of people," Macleod finally spoke. "Some of whom are also on our radar. That raises concern."

"I assure you gentlemen," it was the most desperate Watts ever sounded and he knew it. He didn't care. "That my activities are of no interest to the CSIS."

"Perhaps," Macleod finally sat back. "But we can never be too sure."

"Here you go," Abby appeared out of nowhere again. This time Watts jumped. She placed the plate of steaming scrambled eggs and hot poutine on the table in front of Macleod. "I took the liberty of bringing you a tomato juice. You looked like a man who would like that."

"I do!" Macleod almost shouted. Who the hell was this woman? *I think I am in love,* he smiled to himself.

"It's time," Beauvais said to Macleod.

"Yeah," he agreed, taking out his cellphone. He texted something on the phone then picked up the fork Abby had brought and dug into his eggs.

Watts wanted to say *'time for what?',* but he still had enough composure to avoid that. Instead he waited in silence as Macleod alternated from eggs to poutine and Beauvais sat stoically. He would not be broken.

"Here you go sir," the double paneled front door opened again and a full uniformed Canadian Mounty stood at the entrance. He looked to be at least six feet tall and with his large tan cowboy style hat, bright red uniform and knee high brown boots, he completely filled the room. Watts could not see more than a hint of who was behind him.

"Thanks Brian," Macleod smiled through a mouthful of eggs. "Let him in."

"Yes sir," Brian saluted and stepped out of the way. He was relieved to be done with this odd assignment. Of course he was glad for any break in the routine and doing a favor for the CSIS was always a pleasure but this was no more than glorified escort service. He couldn't wait to get back to St. John's, see the wife and kids and maybe even catch the game. "Glad to be of service sir."

"Jim!" the much smaller man rushed into the open door once the Mountie had stepped out of the way. He was clearly not any kind of an agent or officer. He was frail, average height, wearing plain, boring brown glasses and wearing a basic white oxford dress shirt with a colorless brown tie. Watts could almost see the words "office clerk" above his head in bright neon lights.

"Uh," was all Watts could say. He had no idea who this man was.

"Michael," the man approached. He was clearly upset that Watts did not know who he was. It didn't matter that Watts had no reason to recognize him. The two may have texted each other regularly and even talked on the phone once or twice, but they had never met face to face.

"Kossman?" Watts guessed correctly.

"Yes!" Kossman said. "Yes!"

"What are you doing here?" Watts was completely off his game now. How did they find him? How did they know who "oil guy" was? Kossman was one of Watts' most important contacts. He didn't tell anyone about his connections deep in the Canadian Oil industry.

"What are you doing here?" Kossman shouted back at Watts. He stood directly across the table from him and flailed his arms in the air. "Are you nuts?"

"Nuts?" Watts barked back angrily. He was beginning to realize just how badly everything was going wrong and he was furious at these agents for ruining everything. He looked at them for an instant and wished he could wipe the smug looks off their faces.

"You were supposed to keep this all a secret," Kossman looked towards the ceiling in frustration.

"I decided not to," Watts' tone suddenly changed back to confidence. He was prepared for this. He knew that Mike would be upset he had let the news out. He just had no idea that the CSIS would bring Mike to his doorstep.

"What do you think this is?" Kossman became angry now too. He had too much riding on this for some grandstanding move like Watts had played, "A Hollywood movie?"

Watts stared blankly which upset Kossman even more.

"We're not some evil villains twirling a mustache and tying the girl to the train tracks," Kossman shook his head in disbelief. He was having enough trouble convincing his family and friends that not every person who worked in the oil industry was some kind of greedy, climate denier. "What the hell were you thinking?"

"I was simply-"

"You weren't thinking at all is what you were doing," Kossman interrupted him. Watts instinctively sat back. He had always taken Kossman for a spineless, sniveling lawyer, hell bent on making a buck any way he could; the perfect man for Watts to work with. He must have struck one hell of a nerve. This side of Kossman took him by surprise. "How is this any help to my company? How is this any help to anyone?"

The utter look of confusion on Watt's face was all Kossman needed to confirm his fears. "You have no idea what I am all about do you?" Kossman slammed his hands on the table suddenly. The tomato juice in Macleod's glass jumped around the edges. It was a good thing he had almost finished it. "You think only in stereotypes, in black and white," Kossman took a breath. "You think that all I want, all the "big bad oil companies" want is to exploit the little guy and grab more power."

"Mr. Kossman," Beauvais interrupted. He was thoroughly enjoying this but he needed to assert some control. "We need you to calm down and get to the reason we brought you here."

"Sorry," Kossman apologized immediately. He was still trying to come to grips with all of this. One day, he's an above average successful real estate lawyer and consultant, working with corporations, oil companies and realtors like Jim Watts and the next he's approached by the CSIS and recruited like some secret agent. Within minutes of the call from Beauvais, a full uniformed six foot tall Canadian Mounty stood at his office door; A few minutes after that and they were speeding towards the ferry. He hadn't even had time to tell his wife!

Kossman pulled a chair from another table and sat down next to Beauvais and across from Watts. "Sorry," he said again. "Jim," he said slowly and calmly, looking directly at Watts, "what you have done is a disaster to my company. All it will do is drive up land prices, bring in politicians and more news cameras and place us under the microscope."

"Of course it will," Watts maintained his composure. Kossman was not the man he hoped and it disappointed him to learn the truth.

"You son of a bitch," Kossman swore as his own suspicions about Watts were confirmed. He had always held out hope that Watts was not this heartless, it was the only reason he stayed in touch with him. Of course Watts had made them money. They had been able to purchase countless acres of land at reduced prices because of his negotiating skills and tactics. It was always legal, always on the up and up. As long as Kossman didn't ask any questions, he could believe that Watts was not the man he was afraid he was. "You have no concern what so ever for your actions do you?"

"Of course I do," Watts said. "Our relationship is of great importance to me."

"Our relationship?" Kossman began to stand up again; then thought better of it. "Our relationship?" he lowered his voice. "You actually think we will have a relationship after this?"

"I..."

"The only way we have a relationship is if you fix this mess," Kossman finally got to the point of his being there. Beauvais and Macleod both let out a sigh only they noticed.

"Fix this mess?" Watts repeated, "How?"

"You've got to tell that reporter this was a scam or a joke," Beauvais broke into the conversation.

"And make her believe it," Macleod added.

"Why would I do that?"

"Because if you don't," Kossman added his own voice. "You can be sure that you will never work with my company again, or any other company for that matter."

Kossman let that last threat hang in the air. He could do it too and Watts knew it. It was the reason Watts had reached out to Kossman in the first place. As a real estate lawyer and consultant for Trans Canada, he had contacts everywhere. A blacklisting from him could ruin Watts. Why hadn't he considered that earlier? How did he box himself into this situation? Was it the blow to the head?

"It's too late," Watts said without conviction. It was almost pathetic.

Fifty One

"They've got him," Saltman looked up from his phone. Foster sighed, let go of the tension in his back and leaned against the tree; finally some good news! Nothing had been going right since this mission began and Foster was tired of all the left turns they were taking. Their "watch party in the woods" was only their most recent crazy outing and that was starting to back fire as well.

"Beauvais and Macleod better get something soon," Foster tensed up again but kept his eyes on the crowd around the shack. No one had done anything since the lumberjack looking fellow had first arrived. The twenty or so men and they all were exclusively men, just stood around mumbling and arguing amongst themselves. And all of them were much too anxious and focused on the news to notice Saltman and Foster still hiding 50 feet away behind the thick foliage and trees. Unfortunately when Lawrence Whittaker opened the door and emerged by himself, they turned angry. Where was Luisi? Why was Whittaker there? No one had seen him near the shack in years. They could tell something was going on and Foster knew it was only a matter of time before something ugly happened.

"I don't think these people are going to back down."

"We're not waiting any longer," Moose shouted as if on cue. His six foot frame and experience as an activist made him their natural leader. No one could tell John "Moose" McTaggart what to do. "Where are they?" He demanded.

"I told you Moose," Whittaker held up his hands in defense. He was standing at the top of the small wooden staircase with the entrance to the shack closed behind him. William, Deborah and the rest of the group would only need a few minutes to sneak around and Whittaker was confident he could keep the crowd busy. They might be angry, afraid and nervous, but the people of Deer Island were his family. They would never lay a hand on him. "They are not the ones you want. It's Jim Watts causing all of this."

Foster stiffened at the sound of Watt's name. "Maybe we should tell them," he looked at Saltman who had tensed as well.

"You mean that we have Watts?" Saltman shook his head and considered. Anything to calm the crowd down couldn't be a bad idea. "What good will that do?"

"Well our cover has already been blown," Foster concluded. It wouldn't take long for that waitress at the 45th to spread the word that Beauvais was CSIS. As soon as they were done with Watts, the truth would come out. "Why not use these people to help?"

Saltman watched the name of Jim Watts filter through the crowd. His name was like a rapid spreading plague, scattering anxiety and anger all over. Maybe his partner was right. This crowd could be used against Watts.

"I don't want to use these people," Saltman realized as much to himself as to Foster. "They've gone through enough."

"Maybe you're right," Foster watch the agitation in the crowd grow. It could easily become a mob.

"But is it true?" One of the younger members of the crowd suddenly shouted over the noise. He was dressed in his fishing gear like so many of the other men and the stubble on his face was barely a shadow. Foster wondered if he even was shaving yet.

"Is what true?" Whittaker replied.

"That something has been found to change the border!"

"Of course not,"

"That's not the whole truth Lawrence," Moose shot back. He remembered the visit a few days ago.

"No it's not, but it's still the truth."

"What's he talking about Moose?"

Moose paused. He wasn't sure what to do at this point. He trusted Lawrence and he knew what that rumor could do. He knew what it was already doing. Why fan the flames of fear? These people were his friends. They were blue collar, hardworking, get-out-every-morning-before-sunrise fishermen. They didn't have time for politics or rumors, for news media crazes and bullshit. Hell he was surprised they had time to be here now! Why turn their lives upside down for some wild goose chase, especially since it wasn't going anywhere in the first place?

"It's just more crazy history people," Moose turned back to his friends and smiled. That much was true and he knew his friends would understand. They had gotten used to the visitors over the years. Whether it was people tracing their family history or local researchers trying to plug a hole in some ivory tower mystery, Deer Island saw its share of amateur detectives.

"Where the hell is Callahan and the others?" Saltman looked through the crowd and at the shack. It had been way too long by now and the crowd was finally calming down. Moose's words had the desired effect.

"You think they gave us the slip?" Foster couldn't believe it. Would anything go right?

"I'd better text Beauvais!"

###

"It's not too late," Beauvais argued. He wouldn't let Watts give up that easy. Neither he nor Kossman had said a word for over a minute and it was getting awkward watching Macleod finish his poutine. "No other news station has picked up the story."

"Especially because there is no story," Macleod wiped the gravy from his lips and finally placed the fork down. That was some of the best poutine he had ever had.

"You have no choice Jim," Kossman added.

"Fuck!" Beauvais looked at his phone.

"What?" Macleod said.

"They've lost Callahan!"

"You've got to be kidding me."

"They disappeared when that crowd showed up."

"Jesus Christ," Macleod swore. "Can't those Yankees do anything right?"

"They are full of surprises," Watts smiled for the first time in a while. He was enjoying their frustrations.

"Shut up Watts," Beauvais glared at him. He noticed the bandage on his head again. "Hey," an idea came to him and he turned to Macleod. "What about Watt's buddy?"

"Francois?" Macleod said.

"He's not my buddy," Watts growled.

"Do you know where he is?" Beauvais said.

"If I knew I wouldn't hesitate to tell you," Watts instinctively rubbed the bandage. "Asshole ditched me in the graveyard and I haven't seen him since."

"He the one that gave you that present?" Macleod pointed at the bandage with a full face smile.

"He just better hope you find him before I do," Watts scowled.

"You think Francois is following Callahan?" Macleod turned to Beauvais.

"Maybe he's got eyes on them."

"Or they on him."

"Your tracker still working?" Beauvais asked. He knew that Macleod had placed the device on Francois' car when they first arrived on the island. It was easy enough with Francois occupying the motel room next door.

"Should be," Macleod looked at his phone and tapped the screen.

"Check it!"

"My god," Macleod's face turned pale.

"What?" Beauvais barked.

"He's left the island!"

Fifty Two

Deborah had no idea she was being watched as she held up the gold brass, "C" and "A" knocker on the front door and tapped gently. She was too busy playing through her head one more time what she would say. It was obvious to her that the Wasserman couple had been overwhelmed by her entire family standing at their front door. It must have taken them by surprise and probably even felt a little intimidating. It was certainly not the friendliest way to approach strangers. This entire adventure her husband had thrown them into had been one poorly planned escapade after another, she realized. Where was the science? Where was the logic? Rob always did have a knack for letting his heart tell him what to do; his heart and his dick. Deborah smiled at her little joke and focused again on her task at hand. Hopefully, without all her family standing around awkwardly in front of the house, she would be able to calmly talk to the Wasserman's and maybe even get invited in. She had already formed a pretty good practical argument in her head during that short walk from the cars to the house.

She would start with logic. That was always her greatest strength. Then she would tell them the truth. After all what could it hurt at this point? If they had the packet or knew anything about it, Rob would need the couple's help and only the truth would get them on their side. If the Wassermans knew nothing about the packet, then they would not know any more than what the whole world was learning from the news release anyway. It seemed to make perfect sense.

"Yes?" Cara Wasserman opened the door again. She was both relieved and surprised to see Deborah returning especially all by herself.

"We got off on the wrong track," Deborah said immediately. "You were probably shocked by having such a large group of people standing at your front door. I know I would be."

"It was a little strange," Cara smiled. That was a good sign.

"I'm sorry for that," Deborah admitted honestly. She would scold Rob later. "Sometimes my husband uses everything but his brain when it comes to thinking." Deborah smiled in the not so hidden message that all women understood.

"I understand," Cara's smile was sincere and she even chuckled a little. That was the ice breaker Deborah needed.

"Would it be OK if I came in?"

"I – I guess so," Cara said slowly as she glanced back into the house. Her husband was still in the kitchen somewhere.

"Thanks," Deborah walked into the open door and stood in the center of the room. The light blue and off white walls were offset perfectly by a tightly woven gray shag carpet. It created an explosion of warm bright light that instantly put Deborah at ease. A small white loveseat and a lazy chair set against the wall and a thin brown rectangular coffee table sat in between. The living room was small enough in this tiny house that Deborah was instantly in the center of it and could appreciate the methodic decorations of glass figurines and matching silk plants. Deborah immediately felt closer to her hostess and smiled realizing that it was just like how she would have decorated a small home like this herself especially if she lived so far away from the city.

"Can I get you anything; a glass of water or perhaps some tea?" Cara pointed towards the kitchen.

"No thank you," Deborah smiled at the offer. She found it interesting that this close to the Canadian border she was offered tea instead of iced coffee; the drink of New Englanders.

"Well please sit down," Cara indicated the open spot on the loveseat.

"I wanted to tell you the truth," Deborah burst out before Cara had even finished placing herself on the opposite end of the loveseat, "before we get off on the wrong track again."

"Truth?" Andy walked into the room wiping his hands with a white kitchen towel. "I kind of felt like you were keeping something from us."

"We weren't really keeping anything from you," Deborah went on the defensive. She didn't need Andy angrily throwing her out of the house and she could see the nervousness in Cara's face the moment her husband walked into the room. "It was more like we did not get the chance to go into more detail. What we said earlier is still true."

"You mean that you are looking for something; something old?" Cara prompted. She was hoping that her husband would see why she let Deborah in the house and not scold her.

"Yes," Deborah smiled as she watched Andy place himself in the middle of the room. He did not sit down. It was a clear sign that he had not decided whether he wanted to let Deborah stay or not. "But we never got a chance to tell you what exactly it was or why we are looking for it." She paused, questioning whether she should open up like this. Rob might never forgive her. "Have you ever heard of William Franklin?" she finally said.

Deborah told them the whole story even the part about the boys getting caught in the whirlpool. She realized that the more human she made the story, the more chance they would open up to her. Cara and Andy both smiled several times and even laughed once or twice. About halfway through, Andy sat down in the recliner next to her. It was clear he appreciated her brutal honesty. She did not leave out a single detail of what she knew, and she admitted to them that she did not know everything. When they asked her questions, she answered. If she didn't know, she told them. It was almost too easy to open up like this. In fact, it was somehow therapeutic. Telling strangers secrets, perhaps even intimate ones, was somehow a release.

"What's François doing?" Rob grabbed Lindsey by the arm (gently) and rushed her back behind the car. This time she did not resist Rob's grasp. She was too freaked out by the presence of François to even notice.

"He's just been looking in the windows," Lindsey placed both hands on the hood of the car and bent down so that only her head was showing. "He must have followed us somehow and is waiting to see whatever he thinks they have."

"But they don't have anything," Rob could not bend down as far as Lindsey but he was still pretty hidden anyway. It didn't matter. Francois was so obsessed with peering into the windows that a bomb would have gone off and he probably wouldn't notice.

"Are you sure?" Lindsey turned to Rob accusingly. She still felt like the couple had turned them away too quickly.

Rob shrugged his shoulders, and then wiped the blood off his nose again with his t-shirt. It was still bleeding.

"You need to take care of that?" Lindsey said without any apology in her voice. She was still fuming at Rob, still devastated by his words and still somehow hot for him. She was a mess and Francois suddenly showing up only made it that much worse. What the hell was he doing now?

"Is that a gun?" Lindsey's eyes pushed at the edges of her face in shock. Her jaw dropped open as she turned back to Rob.

"Looks like one," Rob watched as Francois inspected the small revolver in his hands then reached back to tuck it into the back of his pants. He pulled his plain dark sweater over the gun to hide it and reached up to knock on the door.

"He's going to knock!" Lindsey shouted in horror.

"He'll see Deb if they open the door!"

"And that's why we came to your house," Deborah finished her story, sat back and placed her hands on her lap. Her heart slowed down a little as she finally took a deep breath.

"We did find something," Cara admitted before her husband could protest. She looked over at Andy to see his reaction but there wasn't one. She took that as permission to continue. "But it wasn't here."

"What do you mean?"

"As we told you before," Andy was not as comfortable as his wife in letting the secret out, but he had to admit she was right about one thing. He did want to know what was inside that box and he had failed on his own. "This house is not in the exact place as the original lot."

"So then where,"

"I found it when I broke ground for my shed," Andy stood up and made his way to the kitchen.

"That horrible fire 100 years ago almost wiped out the town," Cara continued the story as Andy disappeared. "Almost every building had to be rebuilt on top of the ashes. When Andy started digging, it didn't take him long to find all kinds of debris."

"What kind of debris?" Deborah asked. She was distracted for a moment by sounds outside and wondered what Rob and the boys were doing. She hadn't been inside that long.

"Nothing of any consequence," Andy returned to the room with the gray rusty box in his hands; "Except this." He held it out for Deborah to see. "I found it a few feet deep in the soil," Andy held the box out for Deborah to see. "Whoever put it there must have been trying to hide it under his original floor boards."

"Is that?" Deborah gasped and leapt to her feet. Had she actually found it? Was the secret to this entire adventure, the secrets of a 200 year old treaty and the notes of an almost god like founding father hidden only a few feet away from her? Her pulse began to race faster than before and she had to consciously take a breath to prevent from screaming.

"I don't know what it is," Andy calmed her down. He took a step forward for her to see how strange the shape was. Still rectangular, its edges were smoothed over haphazardly and almost rounded in some spots. There were dents and marks on all sides and rust was spreading randomly throughout. Deborah gently placed a hand on it as Andy tried to explain its shape. "It's been melted together by intense heat, probably from the fire. I haven't been able to open it."

The knock on the door made all of them jump. Was that Rob? Deborah wondered.

Rob stood up the moment Francois entered the house and raced forward. "Boys stay in the car!" he commanded as he ran.

"Wait Rob," Lindsey leapt up to join him. She grabbed him by the arm like he had done to her only minutes before. "Wait!" She tugged on his hand in desperation. It was like trying to stop a bull.

"What!" Rob threw off her hand and glared. "What?"

"You don't have a gun do you?" Lindsey snapped.

"No," Rob paused. He didn't. Fuck it. That was his wife in there. "Boys I told you to stay in the car!" Rob shouted over Lindsey's head. Both Adam and Bobby had jumped out of the Camry and were making their way towards them. Panic mixed with curiosity was all over their faces. They had never seen their father like this before.

"Lindsey," Rob stared directly into her blue eyes and pleaded. It was a tone Lindsey had never heard from him and it frightened her. It stunned her to hear that level of despair and weakness in such a strong man. "Stop the boys, somehow. I have to go!"

Rob turned and rushed towards the house trusting that his teammate, his line-mate, his friend would have his back. There was nothing that mattered to him more at this moment and there was nothing that was going to stop him.

"Boys," Lindsey held out both arms wide as they approached, "Wait!"

Rob reached the house and glared into one of the three small rectangular windows in the front. There was still enough sense left in him that he did not run right into the house. He snapped his head back towards the boys for a moment and saw that Lindsey had managed to hold them up, at least for now. Shouting from inside brought him back and he looked inside again. What he saw almost knocked him over.

Francois was standing in the middle of the room with his back to Rob. Facing the windows were Deborah and Andy in close proximity. Each them had a single hand on a small rusty box as if they were in the middle of some kind of exchange. Their faces however were not on the box. They were frozen in terror staring at the gun in Francois' hand.

All thoughts left Rob as he rushed towards the steps. It was similar to the way he hurled himself into a hockey fight but with infinitely more energy and desperation. It was the fastest he had ever moved and nothing would stop him, not even a locked door. With the surge of adrenalin and a shoulder hardened by years of contact hockey, he burst the door clear off its hinges and landed inside. "Deborah!" he screamed.

It only took Rob a moment to cross the room but in that moment Francois was able to grab Deborah, spin her around and place the gun to her head. "Hold it right there!" he commanded, making an extra motion with the gun to Deborah's temple.

Rob froze so suddenly he almost fell over. Andy stepped back. Cara was still sitting in the couch, her hands over her mouth in terror. Only Deborah seemed to be calm. It was always one of her greatest strengths. At critical moments, like when the kids were deathly ill, Rob would be prancing around like a maniac, screaming at the top of his lungs, waving his arms and shouting out idea after idea while Deborah would pick up her phone, do some quick research or make a call. Rob both loved it and hated it.

This time was no different. After all, how often was it that a woman got to see her husband burst to the rescue through a solid oak door? At least a part of Deborah had to appreciate that. "Hi honey," she smiled. "What took you so long?"

"Deb," Rob managed to say. He had no idea what to do next. His heart had led him this far, but there was no way his brain would let it lead now. He had to think. He had to come up with some distraction, something; anything, that could give him a chance to save his wife.

"Rob Callahan," Francois' pointed chin snapped forward as he practically spit Rob's name. The twitch over his right eye had somehow taken on a more menacing motion and the gun shook in his bony hand. A bruise had formed recently on his left cheek and his blue jeans were stained from grass and dirt as if he had been in some kind of a fight. Even the odd snake belt buckle was titled awkwardly. He was not a happy man by any measure. "You have given me a lot of grief lately."

"What is it you want Francois?" Rob tried to stall as he scanned the room for a weapon. He thought about jumping this funny looking bastard with the long legs and short torso.

"I think that is obvious," his gray haired head turned to the box that was now in Deborah's hands. In the confusion, Andy had let it slide to Deborah when Francois grabbed her.

"Just take it," Rob said immediately. He meant it.

"No Rob," Deborah protested. "You can't let him have it."

"Shut up Deb," Rob commanded.

"Don't tell me to shut up!" Deborah shot back. "I don't have to take that from you."

Rob immediately saw what his wife was doing. The two of them had been married for over 20 years. "You will take from me whatever I give you!" He shouted.

"Fuck you!" Deborah cursed. She surprised herself with how easy it was. Maybe she still was mad at him.

"Fuck you!" Rob returned.

"Hey!" Francois shouted, "You two-" Deborah spun around. Her right elbow swung straight backwards and punched Francois sharply in the gut. He let out a gasp.

Rob leaped forward and grabbed Deborah's wrist. He pulled with one hand and used the other to punch Francois as hard as he could in the jaw. Teeth went flying in the air as Francois' face folded inwards from Rob's blow.

The gun went off. Francois fell. Cara screamed. Andy shouted. Rob grabbed Deborah and pulled her tight to his chest. Lindsey and the boys ran into the open door.

"Dad!" They screamed, "Mom!"

Rob felt something wet on his hand and looked down at his wife. There was a red hole in her gut and her eyes were closing fast. "Someone call 911!" Rob screamed in utter grief and anguish.

Fifty Three

Rob stood over his wife's hospital bed. Deborah was still pale from blood loss. She looked weak and tired lying asleep with all manner of tubes and needles poked into her. Her hair was still wet from the procedure Rob did not understand and the white machine next to her head beeped regularly. The noise would have driven Rob crazy except that he knew that the yellow, green and red lines going across the screen clearly showed all of Deborah's vital signs. Everything looked okay for now.

How had it come to this? Rob wondered. How did he almost lose her? How could he ever lose her? She looked so beautiful laying asleep there; her flowing black hair and athletic build still obvious through the white bed sheets. Deborah was everything to Rob. She was more than everything. She was why he lived. She was why he did everything he did. His first thought when he woke up every morning was of her, and his last moment when he went to sleep was of her. How would he ever survive without her?

Sixteen years! Sixteen years they had been together! He could still remember that first day like it was yesterday. She was the confident athlete and scientist with a beauty and sex appeal that intimidated any teenage boy she encountered. He was an awkward athlete, just as smart, just as passionate about his own interests; but not nearly as confidant in his own shoes despite his success on the ice. If not for that one party, that one spilled margarita, they might never have met! And now, the thought that he could lose her again, had almost lost her because of his own vanity and insecurity made it hard for him to even stand.

Lindsey stood awkwardly a few feet away next to the boys. Everything was different now. How could she have ever thought of being with Rob? What was she thinking? Was she thinking at all? Rob was a wonderful man, a good husband, a great father and a great friend. She should have been helping him repair his marriage, helping him sort out his feelings, not hoping that he would one day be hers. The thoughts sickened her and the shame at what she almost did made her nauseous. Thank god nothing had happened.

Rob belonged at Deborah's side. He belonged with his boys and the four of them belonged with each other. Everyone in the room knew that, even the nurses who came in regularly to check on Deborah. The family bond was almost visible.

The wound was not fatal. At least not immediately, the Doctor had said. The bullet had gone clean through and would not need to be removed. Deborah was strong, incredibly so, the Doctor commented. He was hopeful that she would recover quickly.

Francois was in prison. Only seconds after Deborah was shot, all four agents; Beauvais, Macleod, Saltman and Foster rushed in to place the cuffs on him. It hadn't taken them long to find Francois' car and only moments more to find the house. The only thing Francois had for his troubles were several gaps in his mouth where his teeth had been.

The box had disappeared. Andy and Cara searched every inch of the house and even the yard to see what had happened to it but in all the confusion with the paramedics, the agents, the police, even the firefighters; no one remembered what happened to it. Neighbors had quickly surrounded the home and a crowd formed on the outside lawn. None of that mattered to Rob. All he could do was hold Deborah's hand and tell her to stay strong as the gurney was placed in the ambulance and he jumped inside with her.

"Dad," Bobby stepped across the hospital room floor and tugged on his father's sleeve. "Can we talk to you?" He gave a slight nod to his brother Adam standing nearby.

"Not now Bobby," his father said harshly not taking his eyes away from Deborah. "This isn't a good time."

"Rob," Lindsey said softly seeing the look in Bobby's eyes. She gently placed her hand on Rob's forearm, being careful to make the motion caring and friendly, not sexual. "I think your boys need you. Deborah's stable. Nothing is going to happen in the next five minutes anyway."

"Well," Rob turned and looked at his son's face. He had not seen Bobby that serious in a long time. Suddenly Rob realized that the boys were worried more than he was. He had been so caught up in losing his wife; he almost forgot they were losing their mother. He felt embarrassed and gave Lindsey a thank you nod as instinct took over. "Of course son," he placed his hand on Bobby's shoulder, "Let's step out into the hallway."

The three of them quickly turned, gently opened the large oak door and stepped into the plain white hospital hallway. Fortunately, they had given Deborah a private room in a largely empty wing so no one was nearby. Rob didn't know if that was just luck or the work of the government agents. "Listen boys," Rob said the moment the door swung closed, "Your mother is going to be fine."

"We know that dad," Bobby stopped Rob before he could go into one of those long boring speeches fathers always make at times like this. "We know mom is a fighter and we heard the doctor say the shot missed all of her vital organs."

"Then what is this about?" Rob frowned. He couldn't decide if he was more angry at them for the deception or curious about why they needed him in the first place. What could be more important than their mother's life? How dare they take him away from her bedside when they didn't need him? This had better be good.

"We have something we need to show you," Bobby said mysteriously.

Rob took a step back and leaned against the plain white wall. He was caught off guard by his sons. He was all set to comfort and console them and give out some good fatherly hugs. He was even looking forward to the moment in some surreal kind of way. He wasn't sure if he was disappointed or relieved that the boys were OK. "What is it?" He finally said.

Bobby looked over at his brother with a nod. Adam took the signal, reached into his blue backpack, looked up and down the hallway to see if anyone was watching and grabbed hold of whatever was inside.

"Holy shit!" Rob grabbed his son by both arms and lifted him straight into the air. It was so sudden that Adam almost dropped the rusty gray box he was holding in between his hands, "Holy shit!"

"You found it!" Rob shouted.

"Hey keep it down," Lindsey's head appeared through the half opened door. She looked at Rob and then at Adam still being held up high in the air by his father. "What the hell is going on with you guys?"

"Look," Rob smiled with the biggest shit eating grin he had ever made in his life. "Look!" He nodded at Adam as he gently lowered the boy down in front of Lindsey. Adam held the rusty gray box in between his hands and smiled wide at Lindsey.

"Holy shit," Lindsey cried as well, "Holy shit!"

Several nurses at the station down the hall looked in their direction and frowned. Lindsey pointed to the family waiting room a couple of doors down in the opposite direction, "Quick, in here," she lead.

The boys all whipped around and followed Lindsey into the small plain, empty waiting room. There was a recliner, a small sofa, a table and a coffee maker inside. Bobby gently closed the door behind them. Rob gave out another yell, "You found it! I can't believe you guys found it!"

"Adam grabbed it in the scuffle," Bobby told them both. He had thought briefly of taking the credit for himself but he was past those kinds of games now. He had to admit his brother was sharper than he and if it wasn't for Adam's quick thinking and nimble feet, who knows what would have happened to the box? Bobby himself had only been a second behind his brother and helped him avoid the agents and the police and the paramedics in all of the chaos. No one paid attention to a couple of teenagers at times like that.

"You guys are awesome!" Lindsey reached out and gave both of them a hug. Bobby did his best to make it last a little longer and could barely contain himself when he felt Lindsey's breasts against his chest. "It was the least we could do," Bobby tried to impress Lindsey a little more. "After everything you and dad have done."

"Well I am just glad you did it," Lindsey smiled again and stepped back. She looked at Rob and back at the box still in Adams hands and back at Rob again, "Now what?" She said.

"We tried to open it," Adam blurted out. "But we couldn't find any opening, or keyhole or anything. The sides and corners are all molded together. It seems like it is sealed shut."

"I am sure," Rob thought out loud, "If it could have been opened then Andy would have opened it by now."

"The government could figure out a way." Lindsey offered.

"What?" Rob was stunned. He could not believe what Lindsey just said. He must have heard her wrong.

"The government could probably open it."

"You don't mean-"

"I don't know what I mean at this point," Lindsey admitted. "This has become so much more than I thought it ever was. I mean what are we going to do with it? What would we do with it even if we could open it up? Would we keep it? Would we give it to the press, would we give it to a museum, would we sell it?"

"I used to think that, remember?" Rob admitted. He was also realizing how much everything had changed since this whole thing began. In the beginning all he wanted to do was get rid of it, to make some money off of it even, but so much had happened with Lindsey, his wife, the boys and all of this craziness, that everything looked different now. What would he do if there actually was information inside that could change the history, the treaty, the border and all the land rights involved? Would he want to even be involved in it? He had seen just what the possibility of a controversy had done and he could not imagine what it would be like once the controversy became real. It was staggering to even think about it. His whole life could get turned upside down. And he was not sure if he wanted that even a little bit. No matter how crazy it was with Deborah and Lindsey and with the boys he still loved the life he was leading. He loved the simple things like hanging out with his sons, playing hockey and drinking beer with his buddies. He did not want to become some kind of celebrity or controversial figure being used by the media or whatever political group wanted to exploit this in some way. And he certainly did not want to deal with all the lawyers and speculators who he knew would descend on this quicker than Jim Watts whisking a deed from under your very nose. When it all boiled down to it, Rob knew in his heart that he truly was the meat and potatoes guy.

"Do you realize what it would mean to both countries?" Lindsey was coming to the same conclusion as Rob. She too liked her life the way it was. Yes she was alone. Yes she worked too hard. But she had great friends like Rob, enjoyed the work that she did and had no desire for it to change. "What would it mean to your family if we just took a leap of faith and put our trust in someone else with this?"

Rob realized what she was getting at. When Deborah finally woke up, there would be no stronger message to her about how much she meant to him than for her to learn that he had given this entire escapade up and handed it off. It had all been a massive distraction in the first place. Coming right in the heart of his grieving for his mother and his separation from Deborah, all this adventure had done was put off the hard choices they both had to make.

"If we presented it to both countries at the same time," Lindsey played out the scenario, "then they would have to work together on this."

"They would have to trust each other."

"But would they still keep it a secret?" Adam tried to find a flaw in their argument. He was crushed that the whole thing was coming to a close. What an adventure this had been! And he had been the hero!

"They might," Rob admitted. He could see the disappointment on Adam's face and he recognized its source. "But that would be their problem. Ours is putting the family back together."

Both boys smiled at that thought as they exchanged glances. Would dad and mom get back together?

"They would have to obviously work it out amongst themselves," Lindsey was concerned with Adam's point. What would the United States and Canada do with this sudden knowledge? They had been friends for two centuries. True, they were not getting along great right now and the friction was almost palpable, but they were still great friends. Heck, we all played in the NHL together, she smiled to herself. "And they would have to trust each other maybe more than they ever have. The most important thing," Lindsey said as much to herself as to Rob and the boys, "is that everything would eventually return to normal."

Rob looked at Lindsey. He looked at his boys. It was almost too simple. How strange was it that this issue of two countries trusting one another reminded him of his own situation with his own wife? They both had started out as friends, went on and lived their life and got so caught up in the mundane issues and everyday distractions that they forgot how much they had in common in the first place. Deborah would never cheat on Rob. He knew that. The only way she would ever even think of doing something like that was if he pushed her away, and that is exactly what he had been doing by not trusting her in the first place. Jealousy was an ugly disgusting thing he admitted to himself and he was ashamed for even feeling it. So, if he ever had a chance to get Deborah back it would have to begin with some trust again. He would have to make that leap of faith that he had resisted for so long. He would have to talk with her, and work out their issues. It would be hard, but it would be worth it.

"I'll text Beauvais," he said, pulling out his phone and watching Lindsey nod in agreement.

Epilogue

August 1785

The coast of England

Benjamin Franklin gripped the splintering wooden handrail of the ship with all the remaining strength he had in his body. His knees were close to buckling, his back was afire with knife like pain from his spine to his shoulder blades and the swaying of the ship threatened to knock him flat; but he would not be moved. He would not see England for the last time while lying on his back. Too much had happened; too much pain had been inflicted and felt for him to end it all lying down. No one, especially not his son, would see him that way.

He could not believe it had come to this. Of course he realized how lucky he was to be nearing his 80th birthday, to still be alive and to have seen so much in his life. The Revolution, the Indian wars before that, the friendships he had made with such great men like Washington and Jefferson. He had literally seen empires tremble and countries be born. But none of that mattered now. He may have been leaving France with a job well done but no one would have known that from the look on his face or the ache in his heart. It almost felt like a failure. He had negotiated a peace between the largest empire in the world and the first true democracy of the modern age and somehow he felt shallow. Maybe it was because of Adams. Maybe it was Jay and the Congress. Maybe it was the press, the public, or the lack of any kind of reception awaiting him. This should have been Franklin's proudest moment; the first true diplomat in American History, returning in triumph after winning his nation's freedom.

He told himself he didn't need recognition. He didn't need parades. But the truth was quite the opposite. He had, like all men, a certain degree of vanity. He enjoyed the spotlight. He enjoyed the challenges. He enjoyed the company and speaking in public. Benjamin Franklin had been a public figure for more than half a century and it was a role he embraced. So why then was his stomach in knots?

He chuckled softly to himself. Was he actually nervous to see his son? Benjamin Franklin, the man who stood up to Kings, who met with the greatest Lords and

468

Ladies of Europe, who had schooled Thomas Jefferson, John Adams and even, at times, George Washington himself, was weak in the knees.

It wasn't his health of course. That had given up long ago. Gout, kidney stones, nearly paralyzed on his left side; was there any malady left that Franklin did not have? If it wasn't for his grandson William Temple Franklin firmly placing his hand on Grandfather's back, the old man would have fallen over in a heartbeat. No, it wasn't his health that filled Benjamin with anxiety, it was meeting his son.

He still had not come to terms with William's betrayal. He put on a good front of course. He had disowned him, repudiated him both publicly and privately and was even planning on making the boy pay for every debt his father ever encumbered for him, all the way back to his school days. Not a single loyalist, starting with his son, would get anything from this war. Franklin had made sure of that. He grimaced for a moment, recognizing the weakness of his own feelings. It all had to be done. How could Benjamin Franklin treat his son with kindness and forgiveness when he himself had argued in Paris that no Loyalist should get any compensation from the Americans? It was logical. It was scientific. And Benjamin Franklin was the most logical, scientific man in America if not the world. Everything he had ever done, every decision he had ever made, was based on rational thought and behavior. He had not been one of the mob. He had never tarred and feathered anyone. He abhorred that! His decisions to leave the Empire had been made slowly, rationally, weighing all the odds and considering all the ramifications. No one could ever accuse Benjamin Franklin of being rash and emotional; although that certainly never stopped Adams.

And then there was his son. How could he be rational here? William had betrayed him in the deepest, darkest recesses of his heart. He had not only chosen a different side, he had actively fought to defeat the Americans and resorted to terror and vengeance to win his cause. If William had won the day, the first man hanged, the first man to lose all his earthly possessions would have been his father Benjamin Franklin. How could he forgive that?

Yet, the rational mind of Benjamin Franklin could understand his son's reasons if not his actions. William had been brought up to respect the Empire. He had served in its army, he had held various positions in its government, including of course the Governor of New Jersey. Benjamin knew that throughout his life, he had taught his son to respect authority, to look for compromise, to ignore the baser instincts and use the rational mind to make decisions that were best for all.

None of that mattered to Benjamin's heart. He had also loved his son. The two of them spent almost every moment together in Williams's youth. As a bastard like his father, William had no mother figure to look up to so Benjamin filled that role in as many ways as he could. They traveled together, they worked together, Benjamin taught him science, mathematics, law and most importantly morality. Someday, Benjamin always felt, his son would take over his legacy and the Franklin name would live forever.

Well the Franklin name would live forever, his thoughts turned bitter, but not because of his son; despite him. Benjamin Franklin knew that his name would live on. He was never the humblest of men and he knew, like all of his peers knew, that his accomplishments would live on. Perhaps this last one, chief negotiator for the Treaty of Paris, was not as glorious. Franklin was still shocked and hurt at his treatment by the American Congress and his friend John Adams. It seemed as if he was not to leave this earth in a blaze of glory but to fade away in sarcasm and disappointment.

He held the packet tightly in his hand; one last test, one last leap of faith. At first he thought of leaving the papers with his beloved daughter Sarah. She was the light of his life, his ardent defender, ally and confidant. Unlike her elder brother, she had never wavered. She had remained loyal to him and to America. Doing relief work, hosting the Ladies Association of Philadelphia to aid the soldiers and even hosting his political meetings after the war; Sarah had been every bit the loyal daughter and hero of the Revolution. Oh how he was yearning to see her and her children! But what if Benjamin did not survive the journey? What if the ship went down or it was taken by pirates? Benjamin could not take the risk. Besides, he had left other papers to his son. He had trusted William with so much of his life before that dreadful war. It was time to trust him one more time, one last task left for the eldest son of Benjamin Franklin. It was a final gesture that could redeem both of them and it warmed Benjamin's heart that he had this opportunity.

As the ship slowly approached the dock and the crew scrambled along the deck, Benjamin Franklin quietly reflected on his legacy. He knew that his own name would live on. For as long as the new United States was in existence, he knew his role in shaping her would not be forgotten. Maybe, he chuckled to himself; they might even name a town or a park after him. But when he looked into the eyes of his son standing patiently on the shore, when he saw the hope, bitterness and despair making it difficult for William to stand still, Benjamin was hit with the most terrible realization and the deepest despair a father could feel for a child. Yes indeed, Benjamin's name would live on but no one, Benjamin shuddered with the idea, no one in the entire world, American or Englishman would ever remember his son, the most infamous Loyalist of them all; William Franklin.

Afterward

What really happened and why is there a bibliography in a fiction book?

One of the most memorable novels I ever read as a young adult was Jurassic Park. Throughout the book and for many months afterward, I wondered if the scientific premise to the story was even a possibility; dinosaur DNA preserved in a fossilized mosquito. I became frustrated that there was no real way to know what parts of Michael Crichton's work was real and what parts were from his imagination. (This of course was before our glorious internet.) When I read more of his novels, the story was the same.

When the movie The Patriot came out, I rushed home to my study and poured through my American Revolution novels to find out if it really happened. It became almost a joke to my wife and me. Whenever we saw any historical fiction movie like Braveheart or Amistad or even Titanic (Yes I know the boat sank!), we would rush home and be the first to go into our book collection.

It upset me as a teacher and more importantly as a lifelong learner that these wonderful stories, both in the past and in the future, provided no information for the reader between what really happened and what was invented by the author. Once I became an author myself, I made sure all my *Young Heroes of History* Novels had a bibliography and I even included lesson plans for the teacher, home educator or student. I felt like stories needed to be entertaining, but also informative.

This amazing story of William and Ben Franklin was a personal journey for me and much of the novel is a self-reflection as well my own story of discovery. It was an adventure that took almost two decades to complete and this novel is the culmination of that journey. Indeed, many of the characters are based on people in my own life and of secrets in my own past that I too discovered. As an AP American History teacher myself, I researched more of the Revolution, read more on Franklin and the Loyalists and came across letters and documents and even lectures. This was too incredible of a story and it had to be told!

Everything in the life of Benjamin Franklin, George Washington, John Adams and Alexander Hamilton happened as described in this book. William Franklin and the loyalists did indeed experience rejection, persecution and exile. The Governor lived in New York and London. He represented the Loyalists, he suffered humiliation from the Crown and he was alienated from his father and America. And in 1785, he did indeed meet his father Benjamin one last time and the exchange did not go well.

There of course was no packet. (That we know of!) But all the pain and alienation Ben suffered in Paris from his "friends" Adams and Jay was all unfortunately very real. The behaviors of these men which convinced Lindsey, Rob and even the President of the possibility of a secret packet also occurred as described. Even the font I chose to use throughout the book for the letters written in the past is a nod to Ben Franklin. I chose to use the "Poor Richard Font" developed circa 1919, believe it or not, by the Keystone Foundry in Philadelphia not far from Ben's own printing press.

The Canadian-United States border is still unsettled. There is a plan to build an East-West trans-Canada pipeline (now on hold) and Machias Seal Island is in a state of limbo. Deer Island and the 45th Parallel Restaurant and even Durty Nellies in Halifax all are real and I have had a drink there myself. They are all well worth the trip. And yes, Old Sow, the biggest whirlpool in North America is right off the coast of Deer Island and there is indeed a survivors club. There are plenty of tiny islands in the Bay of Passamaquoddy (which is even more beautiful than I could describe) however no Apple Island exists. Campobello Island with its International park and home of FDR as well as Eastport, Maine exist exactly as described. Eastport even was occupied in the war of 1812 and did experience a devastating fire in 1886.

Finally, even much of the hockey part of the story is real. There are many rinks in the Fairfield, Connecticut area and beer league hockey is one of my own greatest loves. Women play on a regular basis both on their own teams and on teams with men. And everyone who has ever played it will tell you, that the camaraderie is just as important if not more so, than the game itself.

But don't take my word for it. On the next several pages is a list of all my sources, primary and secondary, both on-line and off. Feel free to explore this amazing story yourself, travel to the Great White North and even go to a hockey game if you get the chance.

Thanks so much for reading. I hope you enjoyed it!

Alan N. Kay

Bibliography

"A Loyalist Crucible: Digby, N.S., 1783-1792." *NS Historical Review.*

Allen, Thomas B. "Who Were the Tories?" *Tories: Fighting for the King in America's First Civil War,* www.toriesfightingfortheking.com/WhoTories.htm.

Allyn, David E. *History of Milford, Connecticut 1639-1939.* Braunworth & Co., 1939.

Bailey, Alfred G. "Dictionary of Canadian Biography- Jonathan Odell." *Dictionary of Canadian Biography,* www.biographi.ca/en/bio/odell_jonathan_5E.html.

Barto, Martha Ford. *Passamaquoddy: Genealogies of West Isles Families.* Lingley Printing Co., 1975.

Brown, Jared. "A Note on British Military Theatre in New York at the End of the American Revolution." *Selected Works of Jared Brown,* 1981, works.bepress.com/jared-brown/18/.

Chernow, Ron. *Alexander Hamilton.* Penguin Books, 2005.

Chopra, Suma. "Loyalists in New York City During the Revolution." 21 Mar. 2013.

Coldham, Peter Wilson, and Sally Lou Mick. Haigh. *American Loyalist Claims*. National Genealogical Society, 1980.

Davis, Harold A. *An International Community on the St. Croix (1604-1930)*. Vol. 64, University of Maine, 1974.

Dictionary of Canadian Biography, University of Toronto, www.biographi.ca/EN/index.html. Accessed 20 Apr. 2019.

Eardley-Wilmot, John. *Historical View of the Commission for Enquiring into the Losses, Services, and Claims of the American Loyalists, at the Close of the War between Great Britain and Her Colonies, in 1783; with an Account of the Compensation Granted to Them by Parliament in 1785 and 88*. J. Nichols, Son, and Bentley, 1815.

Ellis, Joseph J. *His Excellency: George Washington*. Vintage Books, 2005.

Ferling, John E. *Whirlwind: the American Revolution and the War That Won It*. Bloomsbury Press, 2015.

Flick, Alexander Clarence. *History of the State of New York*. Vol. 3, Friedman, 1962.

Franklin, Benjamin. "The Electric Ben Franklin." *Ushistory. org*, Independence Hall Association, www.ushistory.org/franklin/autobiography/page02.htm.

Franklin, Benjamin. *The Papers of Benjamin Franklin*. The American Philosophical Society and Yale University Press, 1962. http://franklinpapers.org/

Freeman, Joanna B. *Who Were the Loyalists?*. Yale Courses YouTube lecture, https://www.youtube.com/watch?v=W5j8TsHAzsA&list=PLDA2BC5E785D495AB&index=10&t=0s.

Forbes, Esther. *Paul Revere & The World He Lived In*. Palladium Press, 2005.

Gallagher, John J. *The Battle of Brooklyn, 1776*. Da Capo Press, 2001.

Gaustad, Edwin S. *Benjamin Franklin*. Oxford University Press, 2006.

George, Mary Dorothy. *London Life in the 18th Century*. Penguin Books, 1965

Hart, Horace. *The Royal Commission on the Losses and Services of American Loyalists: 1783-1785*. Oxford University Press.

Higgins, Margo. "National Genealogical Society." Edited by Sally Lou Haigh and Raphael John Higgins, Sunderland Place, N.W., Washington D.C.

History of Milford Connecticut, 1639-1939. The Milford Tercentenary Committee, Inc. , 1939.

Holmes, Theodore C. *Loyalists to Canada: the 1783 Settlement of Quakers and Others at Passamaquoddy*. Picton Press, 1992.

Holt, John. *The Island City: A History of Eastport, Moose Island, Maine*. Eastport 200 Committee, 1999.

Jasanoff, Maya. *An Imperial Disaster? The Loyalist Diaspora After the American Revolution*. Youtube, 20 Oct. 2010. Accessed 10 July 2010.

Jasanoff, Maya. *Liberty's Exiles: American Loyalists in the Revolutionary World*. Vintage Books, a Division of Random House, 2011.

Jasanoff, Maya. *Liberty's Exiles: The Loss of America and the Remaking of the British Empire*. Harper Press, 2011.

Johnston, Henry Phelps. *The Campaign of 1776 around New York and Brooklyn. Including a New and Circumstantial Account of the Battle of Long Island and the Loss of New York, with a Review of Events to the Close of the Year: Containing Maps, Portraits, and Original Documents*. Kessinger, 1878.

Kay, Alan. *Personal Notes from Trip to Canada*. 2012.

Kay, Alan. Personal Notes from Trip to Philadelphia. 2016.

Kay, Alan. *Personal Notes from Trip to Connecticut and New York*. 2016.

Kilby, William Henry. *Eastport and Passamaquoddy: A Collection of Historical and Biographical Sketches*. Edward E. Shead & Company, 1888.

Mackenzie, Ann. *A Short History of the United Empire Loyalists*. 2008.

Mann, Frank Paul, "The British Occupation of Southern New York during the American Revolution and the Failure to Restore Civilian Government" (2013). History - Dissertations. Paper 100.

McCullough, David. *David McCullough Library: 1776/Brave Companions/ The Great Bridge/John Adams/The Johnstown Flood/Mornings on Horseback/Path Between the Seas/Truman/The Course of Human Events.* Simon & Schuster, 2011.

"News Releases." *Irving Oil and Transcanada Announce Joint Venture to Develop New Saint John Marine Terminal,* Irving Oil, 1 Aug. 2013, irvingoil. com/en/newsroom/news-releases. Accessed 25 June 2018.

Newton, Michael E. *Alexander Hamilton: The Formative Years*. Eleftheria Publishing, 2015.

Norton, Mary Beth. *The British-Americans: the Loyalist Exiles in England, 1774-1789*. Little, Brown and Company, 1972.

Picard, Joseph. *The Loyalist, Or, as George Washington Called Him, "That Villain Moody"*. www.thephoto-news.com. Accessed 24 Sept. 2017.

Randall, Willard Sterne. *A Little Revenge: Benjamin Franklin and His Son*. Little Brown and Co., 1984.

Rozovosky, Lorne Elkin. "Tories in the Revolution." Adult Learning Program . Adult Learning Program , 5 Oct. 2011, Bloomfield, CT, Seabury Heritage Hall.

Ryerson, Egerton. *The Loyalists of America and Their Times, 1620-1816*. Vol. 2, Haskell House Publishers Ltd., 1969.

Sabine, Lorenzo. *Biographical Sketches of Loyalists of the American Revolution: With a Historical Essay*. Vol. 1, University of California Library, 2006.

Sabine, Lorenzo. *Biographical Sketches of Loyalists of the American Revolution: With a Historical Essay*. Vol. 2, University of Michigan Library, 2009.

Schiff, Stacy. *Franklin in Paris*. Holt Paperbacks, 2009.

Schiff, Stacy. *A Great Improvisation: Franklin, France, and the Birth of America*, Holt Paperbacks, 2006.

Skemp, Sheila L. *Benjamin and William Franklin: Father and Son, Patriot and Loyalist*. Bedford Books of St. Martin's Press, 1994.

Skemp, Sheila L. *William Franklin: Son of a Patriot, Servant of a King*. Oxford University Press, 1990.

Smith, Albert Henry. *The Writings of Benjamin Franklin* . IX, The Macmillian Company, 1906.

"The American Revolution Revisited." *The Economist*, The Economist Newspaper, 29 June 2017, www.economist.com/united-states/2017/06/29/the-american-revolution-revisited. Accessed 20 Apr. 2019.

"The Hereditary Order of the Descendants of Loyalists and Patriots of the American Revolution." *Loyalists and Patriots*, Loyalists and Patriots, 2018, loyalistsandpatriots.org/history/.

"The Pennsylvania Journal and the Weekly Advertiser." 13 Sept. 1783.

"The Shelburne Loyalists", *NS Historical Review.*

"The United Empire Loyalists." *United Empire Loyalists' Association of Canada (UELAC),* www.uelac.org/.

"Treaty Of Paris." *Treaty Of Paris*, Evisum Inc., 2000, treatyofparis. com.

United States Congress, Audit Office records in the Public Record Office, and B. F. Stevens. "American Loyalists Collection." *American Loyalists Collection*, 1898.

Wallace, William Stewart. *The United Empire Loyalists : A Chronicle of the Great Migration.* Amazon Digital Services LLC, 2012.

Ward, Christopher. *The War of the Revolution.* Skyhorse Publishing, 2011.

Washington, George. "Special Message to the U.S. Senate." *The American Presidency Project.* www.presidency.ucsb.edu/ws/index. php?pid=65546. Accessed 10 Sept. 2018.

Washington, George. "The Writings of George Washington from the Original Manuscript Sources, 1745-1799; Prepared under the Direction of the United States George Washington Bicentennial Commission and Published by Authority of Congress." *The Writings of George Washington from the Original Manuscript Sources, 1745-1799; Prepared under the Direction of the United States George Washington Bicentennial Commission and Published by Authority of Congress*, edited by John Clement Fitzpatrick, Volume 5, Washington, U.S. Govt. Print. Off., 1931, p. 265.

Whitehead, William A. *A Biographical Sketch of William Franklin, Governor from 1763 to 1776*. New Jersey Historical Society, 1818.

"Who Were the Loyalists?" The American Revolution (HIST 116). New Haven, Connecticut.